Also by Joni Rodgers

Crazy for Trying

a novel by
Joni Rodgers

Spinsters Ink
Duluth, MN
USA

Sugar Land © 1999 by Joni Rodgers
All rights reserved

First edition published May 1999
10-9-8-7-6-5-4-3-2-1

Spinsters Ink
32 E. First St., #330
Duluth, MN 55802-2002, USA

Cover art and design by Sara Sinnard, Sarin Creative
Production: Liz Brissett   Claire Kirch
              Charlene Brown   Kim Riordan
              Helen Dooley   Emily Soltis
              Joan Drury   Amy Strasheim
              Tracy Gilsvik   Liz Tufte
              Marian Hunstiger   Nancy Walker

"Write Me in Care of the Blues" by W.S. Stevenson and Eddie Miller
"Sheik of Araby" by Benjamin W. Green
"Melancholy Baby" by Phillip John Mattson
"Them There Eyes" by Maceo Pinkard, Doris Tauber, and William G. Tracey
"Old Man River" by Oscar Hammerstein II and Jerome Kern
"Minnie the Moocher" by Cab Calloway, Clarence Gaskill, and Irving Mills
"Gloomy Sunday" by Laslo Javor, Samuel M. Lewis, and Rezso Seres
"All the Pretty Little Ponies" Traditional, additional lyrics by Kenny Loggins
and David Pack
"I See the Moon" Traditional, additional lyrics by Joni Rodgers and
Linda Darelius
"All of Me" by Gerald Marks and Seymour B. Simons
"Jolene" by Dolly Parton
"Diamonds Are a Girl's Best Friend" by Eric Bernard Griffin and
Regenia E. Anderson
"If I Only Had a Heart" by Harold Arlen and Yip Harburg
"Beat Me Daddy Eight to the Bar" by Eleanore Sheehy, Hughie Prince, and
Don Raye
Excerpt from *Tao Te Ching* by Lao-tzu translated by Steven Mitchell

Library of Congress Cataloging-in-Publication Data
Rodgers, Joni, 1962 –
Sugar land : a novel / by Joni Rodgers — 1st ed.
    p.   cm.
ISBN 1-883523-32-X (alk. paper)
I. Title.
PS3568.034816S8   1999
813'.54—dc21   99–11176
                                                      CIP

Special thanks to
The Literate Chicks:
Carole Silvoy
Debbie Robertson
Sydney Burgess
Gaylynn Pruitt and
Andrea Schultz
and to Fred Ramey
for reading and sharing insight into
early versions of this manuscript.

Thanks also to
Dr. Wendy Harpham
Dr. Jung-Sil Ro
and Nurse-Midwife Connie Graham
for oncological/obstetrical information
and to Gary Rodgers
for technical information and a steady supply of sushi
and to Malachi Blackstone Rodgers
for his amazing vocabulary of endearments and invectives.

I'm especially grateful to
my editor, Joan Drury,
and the staff of Spinsters Ink
for making this manuscript be a book.

*This book is dedicated
with great love and deep respect to
Gary Rodgers
and to the memory of
Ursula Bird King Rodgers.*

You have ravished my heart
my sister, my bride,
you have ravished my heart
with a glance of your eyes.

Song of Solomon 4:9

Vamp

You know it's nothing good when the phone rings and it's past twelve and your husband isn't home and you're sitting in the bathroom with your jeans around your knees; no, you know your daddy has died or the place where you work is on fire or an old lover of yours is holding ten people hostage in an abandoned warehouse and for some dang reason he gave the cops your name and said you better come with a helicopter and that little faux leopard skin Frederick's-of-Hollywood number or everybody gets it. You know it's not the opportunity you dove for all day, running every time that phone rang, grasping for a friendly voice, a free carpet cleaning, the church quilt raffle, but no, it's the principal's office or a bill collector or the *click!* *hummmm* of somebody too rude to even tell you sorry, wrong number, please excuse the ring, and then after midnight, it grates through the air like a burglar alarm, cutting between claps of B-movie thunder, waking the babies and making your heart jump into your stomach, and this is the moment you know. That's it.

Show's over.

A Memory
Sugar Land, Texas 1969

"Once upon a time," said the mommy, drawing the story out of the ruffled curtains and onto the floor, "there was a woman of uncommon beauty, far beyond what earthly men had ever seen, and her name was Psyche, which is the Greek word for soul, you know."

"Here's Psyche, y'all! Skipper is Psyche," said the littler one. Skipper twirled—lithe, blonde, and leggy in those little-girl hands—as the less littler one propped up stiff-limbed Barbies and Kens to admire her.

"But Psyche was a very lonely girl on account of, while her great beauty inspired an abundance of flattery, she longed for the true love that's awakened when you see into somebody's heart." Then the mommy made Chatty Cathy's voice, regal as Venus, "'What's this? Am I, Aphrodite, scorned while worshippers cast flowers on this little ol' mortal girl?' And she got green-eyed mean jealous when she saw it, and she said she was gonna make Psyche marry a loathsome hideous monster and make her like it!"

Skipper Psyche sighed and begged, but her doll father's painted-on propriety did not waver. She dutifully advanced in her wedding dress to lie on top of the dollhouse, submitting to the will of the gods and all the world who worshipped them.

"Poor Miss Psyche, she laid herself down and cried herself to sleep. And then . . ."

The little girls shrieked with fright and loathing as a cackling Mr. Potato Head swooped in on the power of large ears that were stuck in his armholes to form piggish wings, and their mommy made music like the Wizard of Oz flying monkey theme.

"*Dee-da-deet-dee-deee-deee!* But then! *Ah-aaah-da-da-daaah!*"

The monkey music turned into an aria as Ken soared, naked and magnificent, his bread-bag wings flared and shimmering.

"Eros, the god of love, he was the son of Aphrodite, and she told him to fly on up there, and he did, and he had a bottle of joy in one hand and a bottle of bitterness in the other. And he started to pour the bitterness into Psyche's mouth to make her fall in love with the monster—"

"But if she was in love with him, Mama, she wouldn't think he was a monster, would she?"

"Shut up! I like this part!"

"Say, Bitty Kitty," the mommy reprimanded, "we don't say 'shut up.' It's not ladylike."

"Yes, ma'am."

"He went to open her mouth like this," the mommy smoothed her fingertips across their mouths, "but when he touched her lips, Psyche opened her eyes!"

Skipper bolted upright with a startled cry.

"Now, of course, she couldn't see him on account of he was invisible, but he looked into her eyes and saw how brave and good she was, and he leaned in closer, and '*Augh!*'" she groaned for him as the number two pencil stub grazed his thigh. "He accidentally poked himself with his own magic arrow!"

"He poked himself! He poked himself!"

"Now, *he* has to fall in love!"

"Yes! And instantaneously—"

"Mama, what does—"

"It means right this very second. He instantaneously this very second fell desperately in love, and when he went to kiss his own true love, he spilled that bottle of joy all over her."

This part was more fun in the bathtub when real Mr. Bubble joy could be spilled over Psyche's breast, but for now, the mommy tipped an empty bottle from an old Pretty Me Pink play makeup kit.

"And he called his friend Zephyrus to carry her down to his garden of great delights."

The little girls made the whispering voice of the wind god, mouths like kisses as they wafted her away the way they would do for dandelion feathers. They cupped their hands and floated her down to the rose-colored carpet, sweet Eros at her side. He enfolded her in his plastic embrace, and his wings quivered in their twist-ties as he kissed her.

"'Oh, most beautiful Psyche, you shall be my wife,'" the mommy spoke for him, gentle and low, but raised his inflexible hand above her golden head. "'As long as you obey the rules. You have to stay right here in this house, and you can never see who I really am, 'cause if you ever try to get a look at me, I'll fly away.'"

"And then what happened, Mama?"

"They lived happily in the castle together. And soon Psyche was expecting a baby."

"And then what?"

"Then they all went to sleep because they had to work the next day."

"Mamaaaaa . . . "

"Mama, pleeeeease?"

"You left out the part with the king of the ants!"

"And the rams, Mama! The terrible rams with the golden fleets!"

"And the part where she drinks ambrocious and becomes immoral!"

"Nope nope nope. We leave for San Antonio at seven. I told them you'd be there for a radio thing before the two o'clock show."

The mommy swept the company of gods and goddesses off the bed and lay down, pulling the little girls next to her, each on a side.

"What's 'immoral,' Mama?" asked the littler one.

"Immor-tal, Moon Pie. Big difference. Immortal means a goddess. Immoral means plain ol' human being."

"Did she get wings?"

"I don't know. I suppose she could have."

"Did she have the baby?"

"Yeah, Mama, did she have a boy or a girl?"

"I don't remember, my sweeties. It's time to go to sleep now."

The mommy got up and turned out the light, and the little girls scootched closer together in the ruffled canopy bed, peering into the dark for the focused glow of the Jesus-shaped night-light.

"You know what I want to be when I grow up, Mama?"

"What, Moon Pie?"

"An immoral goddess. *With* wings."

"Well," the mommy kissed her forehead, "good luck with that."

She leaned across to the other side of the bed.

"How 'bout you, Bitty Kitty? What would you like to be?"

"Oh, a goddess, I guess," Kitten yawned. "Or a mommy."

The First Trimester

The butterfly sleeps
well, perched on the temple bell . . .
Until it rings.

Buson

*S*o, you'd think Kit would have known better than to answer that stupid phone again.

She should have known to stay right there in the bathroom, reading "Can This Marriage Be Saved" from a rippled back issue of *Ladies' Home Journal* till she lost the circulation in her legs. She should have let that phone ring until the whole street cried uncle.

She couldn't leave the house, run screaming into the night. That was impossible, because Mitzi and Coo were upstairs sleeping in their footie pajamas, jungle-print sheets all kicked down and tangled up. She was trapped like a wayward skunk in a stainless steel Humane Society trap with that stupid dang phone ringing and ringing and ringing itself half off the kitchen wall and refusing to be slighted. She ran down the stairs, struggling her jeans up, leaping and dodging stuffed animals and Tonka trucks and Mr. Talkity II and Barbie's racy pink Corvette.

"Hello?"

She wouldn't say "Prizer residence" in the middle of the night in case it was some kind of homicidal schizophrenic or salesperson or something.

There was nothing for a moment, so she said again, "Hello?"

"Kit . . ." The voice on the far end of the line was instantly recognizable as her little sister, even though the voice was choked with tears.

"Kiki? Are you okay?"

"Kit, you gotta come pick me up because W-Wayne . . ."

She was in full sob now, and there was no point in trying to understand a word she said, so Kit just hushed her and hummed to her and tried to talk her through it like usual.

"Kalene . . . shhh. Kiki, honey, what's happened?"

"We're really over this time, Kit. He says he loves somebody else." And there was a heartful of sobbing then.

"Oh, Kiki . . . no . . ." Kit pushed her hand against the front of her shirt, as if it were her own life coming undone. She let Kiki cry for another minute or two and then said low and firm, like a mommy who knows best, "Kiki, you listen to me. You put Oscar and Chloe in the car and come over here right now. I don't care what he says, that car is half yours, and he can fight you for it later. No, I can't. I don't have any way to pick you up, sweetie. Mel is working overtime, and his truck was outa gas, and so he took the station wagon. Yes, you can, Kalene, because that's what you have to do. Well, then wait till he has to go to the bathroom or something and then . . . No, you don't need any of that. Just put them in the car in their pj's. They can borrow stuff from my kids in the morning."

After a little more coaxing and hushing and firmness, Kit hung up the phone and went to pull out the couch bed. She had thought of telling Kalene to stop at the Uni-Mart and pick up some chocolate-chip-cookie-dough ice cream, but asking a woman to buy her own comfort food at a time like this would be tantamount to telling a child to kiss her own boo-boo. She checked fridge and freezer, but ten days after the big payday grocery shop, there was little in stock to succor a broken heart. Kit and the kids had eaten macaroni and cheese with sliced up hot dogs for supper the last three nights.

She checked their lunch boxes. Mitzi had a Rice Crispy square that one of the other kindergarten mommies had sent to school as a hand-out birthday treat. That was a possibility. Coo had an *X-Men* comic book, a Fruit Roll-up, and a neon green "Fourth Grade Rules" bookmark, but all three looked like he might have been chewing on them a little.

After double-checking the impoverished cookie jar and even the dusty potty-training reward can, Kit plugged in the air popper and measured a quarter cup of kernels. They could munch on popcorn and split the last can of Diet Coke, she decided, spreading sheets and afghans on the couch bed. Oscar and Chloe could sleep in sleeping bags on the floor upstairs, and in the morning, she'd make pancakes so it would feel like a big camp-out adventure instead of the death throes of a bad marriage.

As the popcorn whirred and snapped, overshooting the mixing bowl, Kit picked up paintbrushes and tubes of acrylic color she'd been using to stencil tulips on the corners of her cupboard doors. She untaped the stencil and pulled it away from the wood, smearing the still-wet paint.

"*Dang.*"

So much for her third try. The door was beginning to look thick from being painted over.

Kit couldn't understand it. This was not a difficult task. She'd been doing far more complicated designs, stencilled and freehand, every Monday, Wednesday, and Friday for the last nine years over at Scandinavian Design and Furnishings. This was something she was supposed to be good at. Under her practiced hand, a plain piece of wood blossomed with gardenias to wilkommen friends to a front door or remind a kitchen that Kaffetåren den bästa är av alla jordiska drycker. Customers would commission a dry sink or chair backs or a nursery ensemble, and Kit could pick up the exact design from a length of wallpaper or scrap of fabric. She could imitate a Gauguin fruit bowl, transfer cartoon characters from a video game box— whatever they wanted—which is what made this cupboard door all the more infuriating.

First, she'd tried to freehand small groups of cherries, but they somehow looked like little red castanets when she was done. She painted over them with daisies, but those inexplicably began to look like the Maguire Sisters, much the same way Ebenezer Scrooge's door knocker transmuted into the face of Jacob Marley. Over those, she was now attempting a pathetically simple *U-Can-Do* stencil from the craft store. She even practiced on the doorjamb first, but the smooth white surface of the door continued to bait and switch on her, warping beneath her touch, resisting any acceptable pattern.

Kit was a believer in signs and omens. This was God telling her to take care of the laundry instead of wasting time on aesthetics. She picked up the drop cloth, pressed lids on the plastic paint containers, put the brushes back in her take-to-work bag, and unplugged the popper.

Upstairs, she pulled sleeping bags from the top shelf of the linen closet, then went to Mitzi's room for extra pillows. Mitzi stirred and whimpered when the closet door slid open, so Kit paused to kiss her and stroke her cheek.

"I love you, my Mitzi," she whispered. "You can be anything you want to be. You are strong and smart and beautiful."

An article Kit had read in a parenting magazine said the mind is very receptive while in the alpha state, so she made it a practice to deliver positive reinforcement to her children while they were sleeping. One of the other mommies at library class swore it was the breakthrough for her un-potty-trainable Kevvy.

"You are Millicent Jane Prizer," Kit said, stroking the key

acupressure points, "Attorney at Law, Doctor of Neurophysics, Majority Leader and Speaker of the House of Representatives."

Next door in Cooper's room, she tucked him back under his blankets and whispered, "I love you, Cooper Theodore Prizer. You are a talented and intelligent individual. You are sensitive to the needs of those around you and value them for who and what they are. Truth, love, and justice are your armaments, and you are gonna pick up after yourself and be very nice to your sister tomorrow."

He rustled and moaned a little, and when he settled back to sleep, he looked so much like Mel, Kit had to press her hand against her shirt again. He was broad-shouldered and beautiful, his legs were already soft with sandy hair, and there were strong indications he'd also inherited Mel's booming baritone, expressive eyebrows, and amazing talent for whistling. Kit knew she couldn't have found a better man for her boy to take after.

Mel was a foreman now, over at the Industrial Aircraft maintenance hangar. Kit used to ask him questions about what that meant, but his answers were full of technical jargon and an airplane mechanic's oblivious confidence. He didn't know that not everyone understands how to fly, that this was an astounding physical secret to which he was privy and Kit was not. To Kit, it seemed like a majikal alchemy of sheet metal and zephyrs, but Mel simply saw a logical progression of paperwork, ball bearing, paycheck, food; the orderly origami whereby Bernoulli became a pound of ground beef.

He spent five nights a week plus overtime, climbing up and down scaffolding, greasing landing gear, checking wing flaps, changing leading edges, and doing a host of other things Kit couldn't even imagine, but which involved expensive tools, smelly lubricants, and a lot of sweat. The hard work used to do good things for his body, but the beer he drank when he got home was winning out, slowly but surely. Kit was just as happy to have him on third shift. They needed the money, and anymore, the evenings he was home were barely discernible from the evenings he wasn't.

Four years earlier—the autumn Cooper went off to kindergarten and Mitzi busied herself and Kit with a toddling reign of terror—Mel had brought home a '62 Ford Falcon from the junkyard and retreated with it into the garage. He became both master and slave to the beast, fattening it up with used auto parts, raising it on a pedestal of cinder blocks, laboring tirelessly on its behalf. Between the carcinomas of rust and abrasion, a patina of royal blue was still discernable; the junk-yard Falcon was a time-battered twin to the hand-me-down, pride-and-joy Falcon Mel had inherited from his big brother when he was discharged from the marines.

It had been Teddy's first car, then Mel's, and Mel had taken immaculate care of it. He'd driven it to Fort Worth, Lubbock, and Louisiana. He'd driven it to New Mexico, old Mexico, El Paso, and Dallas. He'd driven it up to Detroit, Sault Ste. Marie, and even Canada, and a decade later, with no particular destination, he was driving it still.

When Mel finally ran out of gas somewhere south of Houston, he drove Teddy's Falcon to and from a janitorial job at Imperial Sugar. And one day on his lunch break, he met Kit at the café where she waited tables to supplement her singing jobs. Early the next morning, he kissed her goodbye on her mother's front porch, peeled out of the driveway to impress her, and smashed into a telephone pole across the street.

"Couldn't keep my eyes on the road," he used to say with a mischievous grin and nostalgic nod toward her.

That was the end of Mel's first Falcon.

But now, he had this one, and when he wasn't in the garage working on it, he was dozing in his recliner, stirring himself periodically to scratch, swig his tepid beer, and click the remote a few times while Kit paced the kitchen with a lump in her throat.

At first, she tried to talk to him. Then she tried to entice him with food, moody lighting, and Antonio Carlos Jobim music. She bleached her hair, bought a painful push-up bra. Lately, she'd even picked fights with him—anything to elicit some kind of spark—but that just made him trudge around the house with his hands in his pockets, which exacerbated the problem he had keeping his pants from sagging too low on his flabby rear end.

Kit shuddered when she saw him like that. She felt like she was suddenly waking up in someone else's life with someone else's inconvenient galley kitchen and crummy car and saggy-assed husband.

There were moments of panic when she caught sight of Mel's hirsute belly lolling between the bottom of his T-shirt and the top of his sweats. There were long periods of smoldering anger after every carefully planned and consistently failed seduction of him. But most of the time, there was a deep, under-lying ache. She felt it when she saw her favorite old snapshot of him grinning like a rowdy kid in his Semper Fi T-shirt. She felt it when she came across a soft flannel shirt she used to nuzzle or a pair of worn jeans she used to tug at, and she tried not to think about the trim, young, homeless man who would inherit them from the Salvation Army. Mel's rusty fishing gear and dusty bicycle, his half-finished projects, impotent power tools, and well-intentioned building materials lay lethargic in the garage; each symbol of his inertia became another particle of sand, drifting the shelf on which Kit and Mel lived.

Passion was a low priority in their lives now. After a hard night at the hangar, Mel had little energy for coupling or quar-reling. But, Kit guiltily reminded herself, he always came home after those hard nights. He was a good man with no real vices, and as far as he knew or wanted to know, Kit was a good wife with no real complaints.

As cruel as this moment was for Kalene, the quick, choking shock of an unexpected whitecap was kinder, in Kit's mind, than the slow groan of irreversible undertow. She wondered if

Wayne had named the other woman when he was pressed about the car, wondered how it might feel to hear something like that from Mel, how Mel might feel hearing it from her. He probably wouldn't mind, as long as she kept feeding him regularly. There was probably nothing she could do to make him hate her, though Kit thought she might prefer that. Hate being at least an off-brand of passion instead of the cancerous nullifier of love apathy is.

Back in the living room, Kit gathered toys and newspapers from the floor and pitched them under the couch bed. Then she straightened the comforter to hang down and hide the mess and arranged ruffled pillows neatly on top.

❦

Headlights beamed across the living room wall as Kiki pulled the station wagon up to the garage. Kit dashed out the front door to help carry the kids inside, and Kiki kept it together admirably until they were tucked upstairs, snug in the Ninja Turtle sleeping bags, with Raphael, Donatello, and The Shredder duking it out over their heads.

"Would you like some popcorn, Kiki?" Kit offered gently, but her little sister only sobbed.

"Oh, Kit, my life is in ruins!"

"Here, sweetie, have a Diet Coke," Kit struggled.

"I have learned the true meaning of despair."

"Oh, Kiki, honey. What about a Rice Krispies treat?"

"That bastard. That l-lousy bastard."

"Oh, Kiki. I'm so sorry." Kit was crying now, too.

"And you won't believe who he's trying to blame it on!"

Kit's heart froze in her chest. "Who?"

"*George Walker Bush!*"

"What?" Without meaning to, Kit blurted a strangled gasp of laughter.

"That bastard says if George Walker Bush hadn't become governor of Texas, causing Ray Bob Sawyer to have too many beers at the G. W. gubernatorial election celebration, he wouldn't have driven Ray Bob and Darinda home and consequently met Darinda's sister, Cylene, whose husband had been down to Galveston that very morning and got a big ol' redfish, which she had frozen in her chest freezer out in the garage on account of she wanted to get it mounted for him for his fortieth birthday, and then when they brought the thing over, she just happened to be wearing spandex pants and an off-the-shoulder blouse and lolling her cleavage from here to Del Rio and gave Wayne a note that said 'call me tonight' and—that b-bastard!— *he callllllled herrrrr . . ."*

"That bastard," Kit said through gritted teeth. "He is such a bastard."

"He's been with her every Wednesday afternoon all these months and three times while I was at Mom's last week, and I'm such an idiot I never knew. *And!*" Kalene pulled away from Kit indignantly, "Mel knew all about it! The bastard told him!"

"Mel? The bastard told *Mel?*"

"Men are such bastards."

"He told Mel," Kit echoed. "I didn't realize they were that close."

"What am I gonna do, Kit? What'll I tell the kids?"

"I don't know, Kiki. I don't know. What a mess." She put her arms around her baby sister, and they both started crying softly again. "Oh, Kiki, I'm so sorry. I'm so so sorry."

"Oh, don't be sorry for me, Kit. It's my own dang fault. Wayne just keeps getting worse and worse, and I just keep letting him. He's always had a temper on him, and his moods, you know—he's always been like that. But the last three years, ever since Chloe was born, it's like he's a different person. And he always comes back around saying how he's sorry and he didn't mean it and he loves me and I know I'm stupid, but—I love him, Kit. It's getting harder and harder to remember why, but I still love him."

In the morning, Kit made pancakes. Oscar and Coo,

delighted to wake up and find themselves in the same room, came downstairs in their rumpled pj's, bonding in the tree fort's ritual handshake: high five, side five, palm slap, back slap, pinky link, thumb link, Bullwinkle, "*yes!*"

Kit had intended to let Kiki sleep, since they'd only just gone to bed a couple hours earlier, but Kiki showed up at the table with red-rimmed eyes and wan smiles for the kids, giving no indication that she'd learned the true meaning of despair and that her pleasant life in the double-wide surrounded by mature trees and five prime acres in Montgomery County—a life that until last night appeared so shady and clean—was suddenly falling apart on her.

Kit truly never wanted for that to happen. She wanted her and Mel to play cribbage at Kiki and Wayne's every Saturday night and take all the kids on picnics and to baseball games at the Astrodome and on excursions to Splash Town. She wanted the two of them to take the kids to Taco Cabana for lunch, talking and laughing, something of their own childhood coming back to them as they watched their children playing by the fountain. She wanted to sit close to her little sister and let her know how much she loved her, how much she liked belonging with her. She wanted them to share the secrets of their souls and have those secrets be about loving the men to whom they were happily married and about how they had discovered the "Seven Secrets of Renewed Intimacy," as detailed in this month's *Redbook*.

"How's your stomach?" she asked her baby sister.

"Better."

"Do you want some soda crackers or something?"

"No. That never works for me."

"I don't have any 7-Up. How about chamomile tea?"

"You're so lucky you never had morning sickness," Kiki lamented. "It's horrible. Like a hangover without the good time."

Kit made Kiki sit down while she poured thick syrup over the kids' pancakes and used the sides of their forks to cut bite-sized squares.

"That's okay," Oscar said when she came to Chloe's plate. "I'll help her."

"Well, thank you, sir." Kit rumpled his hair. "You're quite a gentleman."

"Mama, Cooper's opening his mouth with chewed-up food in it," Mitzi tattled.

"You're dead, Dog Mouth." Cooper pinched her leg beneath the table, and she screamed.

"You two knock it off," Kit warned, "or there's gonna be some black marks on your star charts."

"Big deal," Cooper said. "I hate that thing, anyway. I'll never fill it up."

"Yes, you will, Cooper." Kit kissed the top of his head. "I know you can."

She was confident, having carefully engineered the chart to ready him for success, not set him up for failure, just as Dr. Brazelton advised in the "Lifestyles" section of the *Houston Chronicle*.

"See? Just three more stars, and you get to rent a video game."

"Hey, Coo," Oscar elbowed him. "Now available at a Blockbuster near you: 'Bubble Man.' My friend Chase showed me a bunch of the secrets on it."

"*Oh, man!*" Cooper groaned.

"I could help you get your stars," Oscar suggested, pushing his glasses up on his freckled nose. "Then we could play it this afternoon."

"Mom?" Cooper was suddenly hopeful.

"That's a great idea," Kit said. "All that's left is pick up sticks and pine cones, pull ten weeds in each flower bed, and bring recycling bins up from curb."

Oscar and Cooper exchanged glances, plugged their

thumbs into their ears and fanned their fingers upward in another Bullwinkle salute.

"*Yes!*"

They chugged the last of their milk and headed upstairs to get dressed.

"Your children are so civilized," Kit wondered at her little sister. "How did you do that?"

"Oscar is a quirk of nature," Kiki reassured her. "Chloe more than makes up for him." She stroked her stomach and added, "Lord knows what this one's gonna be like."

"Mama," Chloe begged, "will you and Aunt Kitty come play Barbies?"

"Play Pandora with us, Mama," Mitzi cried. "Or Persephone!"

"Or Gilligan's Island!" Chloe suggested.

But Kiki had to head for the bathroom again. Kit hushed and urged the little girls toward the living room.

"Today," Ricki Lake was announcing, "*Guess What, Mom! I'm a Girl in Love—With Another Girl!*"

"Let's watch 'Care Bears' instead," Kit said, digging through the sofa cushions for the remote.

She went back to the kitchen and cleaned up the sticky breakfast remains and had just finished mopping beneath the bay window when Kiki came back.

"Gilligan's Island," Kit said. "Is that from *The Odyssey* or *The Iliad*?"

"Oh, Kitty, did it ever occur to you that some Barbies think that stuff is just plain boring?" She dropped a chamomile tea bag into a cup of hot water. "Some Barbies just want to go to the mall without all that pressure on 'em."

"I won't tell Mama you said that," Kit smiled.

"It would only hurt her."

They sat for a while, blowing and sipping at the rims of their teacups.

"*Care Bears, prepare to stare!*" the TV falsettoed as the bears beamed hearts, flowers, and an unstoppable rainbow of righteousness that annihilated everything contrary to their agenda of goodness. They reminded Kit of the Christian Coalition.

"Hey!" Kiki suddenly slapped one palm on the tabletop and snapped her fingers. "You know what we should do?"

Kit didn't know.

"We should get back into the business."

⚜

There's nothing sweatier than gold lamé in the relentless heat of a southeast Texas summer.

That's what Kit remembered most.

The stretchy, sweaty, double knit fabric backing the sequins and beadwork that snapped and sparkled in the sun. The trickling down the small of her back. The prickly inner seam of her half-slip and the tight band of knee-high nylons.

As she and Kiki got older, the high ruffled Loretta Lynn collars dropped to Bobbi Gentry's scooped necklines, and the poofy chiffon sleeves shrank to spaghetti straps, making it slightly more tolerable, but from the first gig they performed as The Sugar Babes when they were six and seven years old, Kit silently swore she'd never put gold lamé on any kid of hers.

But Kiki was always a good little trooper, as their mother was always eager to point out. She never complained one bit that the Elk's Lodge was too smoky or the old folk's home smelled like vomit or that all the other kids were going on carnival rides and popping balloons for a *prize-every-time-you-try!* while they sat beneath the grandstand, waiting to open for Ernest Tubb or Grampa Jones or Tammy Wynette or whomever the wherever-they-were County Fair board had been able to book on its tight budget.

Kiki spent the time practicing her facial expressions in the makeup kit mirror, making small talk with the main act. Mesmerized by their rhinestones and enormous hair, she listened with rapt attention to their tour bus war stories about sold-out crowds and backstage drunks and the glory days of the Grand Ol' Opry. She responded precociously to their questions and compliments while Kit retreated into a corner with paper and crayons, quietly illustrating the world in which she planned to live someday. A world with a dog, a daddy, and quiet trees. A world that had nothing to do with standing up straight and working the mike and smiling even if you twisted your ankle in your high-heeled shoe.

" . . . but right now, we're going to bring up the little bitty girls with the great big voices, all the way from Sugar Land, Texas . . ."

Her heart always turned over when she heard the PA echoing their introduction. She squirmed and straightened her sweaty dress while Kiki applied one of her practiced expressions, the one where her teeth looked whiter than sugar, and her eyes glittered like snow cones.

"Let's give a big El Paso welcome to Kitty and Kiki—*The Sugar Babes!*"

And they would step out, waving, snapping, and sparkling as the backup band kicked into a Patsy Cline number. The crowd reacted with a polite smattering of applause until Kit belted her first line and blew the grandstand back a good three feet on its foundation.

"Now baby if you're missin' me-ee . . . the way that I been missin' you . . ."

"Write me a line," Kiki would take it, strident, innocent, and free, *"sayin' honey you'll be mine . . ."*

Harmony!

"Write me in care of the blues!"

And then the cheering would be there, everyone in the audience astounded that so much sound could bubble up from two tiny dewdrops on a wide and dusty platform at the wide and dusty fairgrounds of a wide and dusty state. They giggled and mugged during the steel guitar solo, reprised the chorus, and ended with their heads back, gold lamé gowns flashing in the sun, mikes held straight up over their bright lipstick mouths.

"*Oh, honey, write me—*"

"Give that postman a letter, honey!"

"*In ca-ya-ya-yare—*"

"First class all the way!"

"*In care of the bloo-oo-ooooooooooooos!*"

Kit and Kiki ended with their heads back, bathrobes falling open over their nightshirts, syrupy forks held high over their mouths, and then they hugged each other and laughed until they started crying again: Kiki for her failed marriage, Kit for her guilty conscience, and both of them for the elusive gold lamé dreams they'd eventually outgrown.

The drone of the garage door opener signalled Mel's home-coming, and Kit and Kiki pulled apart and blew their noses into paper towels from a dispenser over the sink. Kit automatically filled a coffee cup from the cupboard and hastily pulled two towels from the laundry basket, folding them so they'd look clean.

"Morning, honey," she said as he shuffled in the back door, bringing with him the smell of an airplane's underbelly. "How was your night?"

"Morning," he mumbled and bent down a little to meet her reaching up to give him a quick kiss. She offered him the coffee, but he took his towels and headed for the shower.

Kit poured his coffee back into the pot.

"Must have been a rough one."

"I should go," Kiki said.

"Where?" Kit hated to point out the obvious and was relieved when Kiki kept her composure.

"Actually, I was hoping . . ." Her mouth trembled just a little. "Maybe now he's had a chance to sleep it off, and he real-izes—"

"Kiki! You can't be thinking of going back *again*. Not this time. Not after he—"

"Oh, I know, I know, but see—the problem is . . . there's this hanging bougainvillea out on the patio, and these mourning doves made a nest in it. And the babies are only just now hatched. Just day before yesterday, Kit. They're still all tiny and scraggly looking and everything."

"Sweetie, I don't understand what that has to do with—"

"Well, what if Wayne doesn't water the basket and the bougainvillea dies? Or what if he waters it, and he's not careful about the birds? I should be there, Kit. To take care of things. It's my *home*."

"Then go home and throw him out!" Kit exclaimed. "He's the one who's running around. Let him go to a motel or move in with Miss Spandex or something! You've got the kids to think about, Kiki. And the baby."

"You're right," Kiki nodded. "That's right. He should go." She looked up at her big sister. "Will you tell him?"

"Sure," said Kit. "You bet I'll tell him. I'd be glad to tell him. Meanwhile," and she took Kiki's hands in hers to show her she really meant it, "you stay here as long as you need to. We'll take good care of you."

"I know," Kiki said miserably. "You always do. But I hope it doesn't last too long this time."

Mel was upstairs thumping around the bedroom over their heads now, and hearing his dresser drawers banging open and closed, Kit hastily dug some underwear out of the laundry. Folding it didn't really make it look clean, but it was the best she could do at the moment. Mel wouldn't care, anyway. He could wear the same boxers and sweats for a week without a second thought. He'd pick them up off the floor each morning, give them a shake to dislodge the balled-up socks stuck in the ankles, flick off an egg noodle from last night's supper, and figure, hey, good to go. When Kit came in with the folded BVD's, he was foraging through a pile of dirty clothes on the floor, naked and hairy as a caveman rooting for the makings of his first tool.

"Here." She handed him his shorts and sheepishly indicated the pile in the corner. "I'm gonna get to that today. After I get home from work."

"You're working today?" Mel glanced up. "On Saturday?"

"Well, Ander had these window boxes—"

"Whatever." Mel pulled on the boxers and shook the socks out of a pair of jeans. "What's up with the Keekster?"

"She left him."

"Again?" he huffed.

"Yeah, again," Kit said irritably. "And I hope she means it this time."

"Why? What's it about now?"

"I thought your good ol' buddy Wayne told you all about it."

"Ah, for—*geez!* Don't tell me that jackass went and told her about that—that . . . Ah, for—" Mel discovered a clean T-shirt in a far recess of his empty drawer and stretched it over his stomach. "I told that pinhead to keep his mouth shut and leave a good thing alone."

"A good thing?" Kit was more than irritated now. "*A good thing?*"

"I'm talking about Kiki and the kids. Not that—that other thing," Mel struggled. "If he'd just kept his mouth shut, he could have at least kept her—"

"What? Blissfully ignorant? In the dark? Is that how you'd like to be treated?"

"Yes! Yes it is! They have a marriage, Kit. A family." He groped under the bed for one of the sock balls. "You don't just toss that down the dumper."

"No," Kit said. Guilt washed over her like a floodplain, and Mel made it a thousand times worse when he reached over and took her hand.

"But I should have told you, Kit. I'm sorry. I wasn't condoning it or anything. I just figured it would be weird for you sitting there knowing something like that. I know how stuff like that eats on you."

"Whatever," Kit turned away. "C'mon down. I'll get your breakfast."

"Wait." He sat on the edge of their bed and pulled her onto his lap. "You gotta know I'd never do anything like that, Kit. Never."

"I know," Kit said, writhing inside because she did know.

"Never did, never will. Don't even want to."

When he opened the front of her robe and touched her through her nightshirt, Kit wanted to cut her own hands off. When he pressed his nose between her breasts, she wanted to cut them off, too, but she lifted her nightshirt instead, needing every ounce of atonement she could get.

"Mmm. You smell good," Mel told her. "Like pancakes."

🍧

comma   *comma*
     teardrop
comma   *comma*
      slide
comma   *comma*
     teardrop
comma   *comma*
     slide

Down the side of a teal blue hoosier, Kit worked her way, focusing on the exactness of the pattern: two moss-green comma strokes, an azure teardrop, two more commas, then a slightly irregular slide in naphtol crimson #2. She balanced a pallet of color on her palm, alternating different shaped brushes, clenching the spares between her teeth. Her jaw was beginning to ache, and the brush strokes were beginning to blur before her eyes. All these nights of staying up late with Kiki. Tonight, she would tell her they had to get some sleep.

For now, Kit closed her eyes tight, then opened them wide, refocusing on the hoosier.

When the kitchen cupboard first arrived in Ander's workshop, it stood tall and austere as a prairie woman, but over the weeks, Kit had festooned this plain pioneer with florid memories of the old country. On the plain bodice where dishes were shelved behind glass-paned doors, she set apples and pears to ripen at the corners, breaking a delicate border that scrolled like a fine embroidery around the frame. At the slender waist, Kit outlined the dry sink area with a flowing yellow ripple stroke, but used simple white and a straight edge to give a more utilitarian hemline to the cutting board that slid out from under the countertop like an apron that could be taken on and off as needed. The lower cupboard was adorned with her own particular ferns: a hybrid of the stroke Ander had taught her and a vague memory of the fiddleheads that curled upward, bright green among the blue-violet irises behind her grandmother's house in Sugar Land. Irises, she smiled when she remembered that again, and she decided to put irises just outside the wide wooden doors on the hoosier's full, boxy skirt.

Kit crouched now, continuing toward the floor a border pattern she'd begun on tip-toes that morning.

comma   comma
    teardrop
comma slide —

"Shoot," she muttered, dabbing at the mistake with a rag dipped in mineral spirits.

"You look to be some tired, Kit." Ander set a large warm hand on her shoulder. "Are you feel tedious today?"

His finger-paint English always made her smile, even when her shoulders cramped and her neck stiffened. Mitzi and Coo always said he sounded like the Swedish chef on "The Muppet Show." "Hershty bershty gershty."

"Come, you take this break now, Kit." Only he said it like "Ket."

"I'm fine," she said.

"I know this week is many extra hours for you, but we pay to hell we don't deliver this thing Monday in morning. I know is big job for you, but I tell Ruda already, put some bonus paycheck to my girl Kit this week. This week she is very hard work."

Kit didn't mind the overtime. She was proud of the fact that, working three days a week plus extra for special projects, she'd been able to buy a washer and dryer, an upstairs vacuum cleaner, and a five-piece living room set from Gallery Furniture's clearance pavilion. She'd replaced the swing set when it was outgrown, funded several weekend trips to Corpus Christi and San Antonio, and was now saving up for the mother of all family vacations: Disney World.

But more than the money was the peace. As long as she was here, brush in hand, she was able to forgive herself the messy house, the overdue library books, the looming balloon payment on the mortgage. Her mind rested, went with the familiar lines and grapevines that grew right out of her own hand. There was no such thing as ghosts in this perfect world of dapple-cheeked fruit and soft-shouldered flowers and her own special ferns that feathered down the wood, delicate as moss. Kit loved her job. She was good at it, and it was good for her. It gave her something to be. When someone asked, "What do you do?" this job let her say, "Oh, I paint."

Ander was a good friend, and he and his wife, Ruda, were easy employers. They gave Kit two weeks off with pay when Mitzi was born and understood when the kids had ear infections or well-baby checkups and even let her bring them to the store if her babysitter flaked out at the last minute. That was fine with them. There were books, blocks, and a Little Tykes jungle gym in a gated back room where their own preschoolers played while Ruda came in twice a week to do the bookkeeping on a computer that beeped softly and spoke Swedish.

The seven Anderson children ranged from newborn to nine, every one a blunt, blonde clone of their father. They had sweet natures, round cherub faces, flawless rosy skin, cerulean blue eyes, and smooth, straw-colored haircuts: shoulder length bobs on the girls, bicycle helmets on the boys. Mitzi with her fly-away, dishwater pigtails and Cooper with his rowdy red crew cut stood out like a couple of gangsters in this crowd of angels, but Kit kept hoping some of that rosy, blonde sweetness would rub off.

"Shoot!" Kit dabbed in annoyance at another wayward brush stroke and bit the end of her brush.

Ruda came in, smiling and bouncing the latest baby on her hip.

"Ah! G'dagen," Ander lit up, motioned her over, and started speaking enthusiastically in Swedish. Kit caught her name and the word "Monday," but the rest really did sound like the Muppet, and that made her smile again.

Ruda said something in Swedish, and Ander relayed, "Do you want to be done for today, Kit?"

"No, thanks. I better keep at it."

"Don't worry you don't finish today. There still is Wednesday, Friday. You come in Thursday. I tell Ruda is OK. Is no problem for you to come in even on Saturday, too."

"I can't," Kit rolled her head forward and rubbed her neck. "Mel and I are taking the kids to see his parents this weekend. It's their anniversary, so we really can't get out of it." She pulled a footstool over to the bottom of the hoosier and went back to the pattern. She'd confided enough about the Prizer family rodeo of disfunctionality over the years for Ander to know she'd rather be painting.

"Oh, ya, those in-law problem," Ander nodded. "You know how I handle those in-law problem? I leave that country! No more problem!"

They both laughed, and Ander repeated the joke in Swedish for Ruda, and she laughed, too. Even the baby giggled on her hip. Kit turned back to the hoosier.

comma   comma
    teardrop
comma   comma
    slide

She tried to go with the strokes but was dragged back by the feeling this behemoth was going to take the rest of her natural life to complete while the dishes and dirty laundry and yet-to-be-packed suitcase telegraphed her from the utility room at home.

She thought about the serving tray she'd spent a whole day rosemaling for Neeva and Otto's anniversary, knowing full well that Neeva would hate it just like she hated every other gift she'd ever been given. Fuzzy slippers, night-lights, air popper, Mr. Coffee—even The Clapper! Gifts sent by mail were never acknowledged, and those presented in person disappeared into the vortex of her disheveled house. Then Kit would notice a few months later that Neeva had gone out and bought something nearly identical.

It drove her nuts.

She tried giving them cash once, and you would have thought there was a tarantula in the card the way Neeva carried on. Kit kept trying, though, hoping against reason that someday she'd strike on something Neeva liked, and then Mel wouldn't have to listen to the semiannual diatribe, and Kit wouldn't have to put up with his black cloud of silence all the way home.

He always got into a big, dark funk as the obligatory visit drew closer. He was already out of joint earlier that morning because Kit left a *Woman's Own* magazine on the back of the toilet, open to an article on how "You *Can* Teach Your Man (You Deserve an Orgasm Every Time!)," and Mel took it as some kind of veiled insult.

Kit was embarrassed. She *was* secretly hoping he'd read it.

Should have known better, she chided herself. The article on "Take Fifteen (And Put the Passion Back in Your Marriage!)" sat there for a good six weeks without results.

The premise was so simple: every married couple should kiss for fifteen seconds every day. It could be three five-second kisses or five three-second kisses or one long, luxurious fifteen-second kiss, but it had to add up. It hadn't occurred to Kit before how pathetically little she was willing to settle for, what a tiny token, what a Lilliputian effort it would take to make her feel wanted, desired, delicious. Fifteen seconds. But apparently Mel was too large to conceive of such a small gesture. Even when he was coming home, his quick kisses felt like leaving, and their lovemaking had settled into a well-worn groove that circumvented lips and limbs, plotting the most direct course between the useful portions of their torsos, his straight line and her triangle, like safety-railed boardwalks around the organic dangers of a national park.

Sometimes at night, when Mitzi and Coo were breathing softly in the other room, and Mel was somewhere out on his dark tarmac, Kit lay in bed, so hungry for that unnamable feeling, she pressed the back of her own hand to her lips, dwelling on what it used to feel like when they sat for hours out on Galveston Island, car doors open like wings getting ready, windshield full of shining waters, setting sun, and the confused reflection of searching hands, hungry bodies, desperate mouths.

Back then, she was driving the vintage taxicab yellow Mustang she'd bought with the last of the money she'd earned performing with Kiki. "The 69er," Wayne had leered, but Mel always called it "The Golden Chariot" and claimed it was Kit's appreciation for this classic, classic car that left him powerless to resist her.

Back then, he begged her not to turn the key in the ignition, begged her to tell her mother they'd run out of gas, had a flat,

thrown a gasket, had to drive three hitchhiking nuns back to
their convent on the San Jacinto—anything—just to stay, just to
kiss and kiss while the night sky reeled over them, till the stars
set and the sun came up and Kit knew her mother would be
eight shades of livid.

Stay . . . oh, baby, please . . . please stay, he would beg her back
then, pressing her hard against the black vinyl seat, *just one
more hour . . . just a half hour more . . .*

Back then, he never gave up searching until he found the
feeling he knew would keep her there.

> *comma   comma*
> *teardrop*
> *comma   comma*
> *slide*

Now, she couldn't sell him fifteen seconds of that ride.

❧

Kiki pushed into the dishwater, scrubbing at a pool of
syrup that had crystallized to sugar on a Melmac plate. This
was the eleventh consecutive day Kit had served up pancakes
for breakfast, and the first time she'd allowed Kiki to get her
hands wet. But rather than wonder about it, Kiki was trying to
reconstruct that great "River Medley" they used to do. Their
mother had persuaded Pa-Daddy and Mee-Ma to put up
almost six hundred dollars for the arrangement and backup
tapes for it, and it was a real crowd pleaser at the livestock
show and the Petrol-Tech company picnic and the AARP Bicen-
tennial Motor Home Rally the summer of 1976.

"Ol' Man River, that Ol' Man River . . ."

She'd need something to fall back on now, Kiki told herself,
'cause there was no way she'd take Wayne back this time. She
thought a moment about that phrase, *fall back on,* feeling the
foundation shift and dissipate beneath her feet, her body

casting backward in a hellish version of the Nestea plunge, plummeting into an abyss of unknowns.

She'd married Wayne the summer after her graduation from Sugar Land High. She was eighteen plus two months, and she was two months pregnant. He was twenty-three and handsome and funny and already out of vocational school, making good money as a taxidermist. It was a little unnerving, at first, being around all those snarly, glass-eyed dead things, but the clothes and vacations and new station wagon more than made up for it. If she got tired of looking at all those porcelain teeth and high polished horns, she could go out shopping and use a credit card to buy something.

Now she was more frightened at the prospect of having to look at living things like employers and coworkers. She'd have to resist those irresistible clearance sales. She was going to be hard-pressed without the security of those credit cards, but being without Wayne to tell her who she was and what to do with her hair and how her mind ought to be set would more than make up for it.

" . . . that Ol' Man River, he just keeps rollin' and rollin' and roooooollin' . . ."

Key change!

"Rollin'—yeah, honey! Rollin'—ooh, baby! Rollin' on the river..."

Kiki fished a serving spoon out of the dishwater and sang into it.

"Left a good job in the ci-tay—"

"Mama!"

"Dang." Kiki grabbed a towel from the fridge handle and wiped her hands on the way to Kit's front hall. "What is it?" she called up the stairs.

"I can't find my other shoe," Oscar called back.

Kiki went up to Cooper's room, where the floor was so littered with trucks and action figures and comic books, you couldn't have seen a shoe in there if it belonged to Ronald McDonald.

27

"Will you do it, Mama?" Oscar asked.

"Stand back," Kiki told him, taking the known sneaker in her hand and assuming her position beneath the lintel.

When she turned her back to the messy room, Wayne was standing at the top of the stairs in front of her.

"Well," Kiki glared, "the people you meet when you forget to lock your door."

"That never works, you know," Wayne nodded toward the sneaker. "You're teaching them to be superstitious."

"Brother, go find your brother," she chanted like a priestess and threw the shoe over her shoulder into the abyss of little-boy debris. Oscar and Cooper dove for it, and sure enough, with a little digging, they found its mate close by.

"I got it! I got it!" Oscar cried, and he showed it to Wayne. "See, Daddy? I got it. Don't be mad. I got it."

"Yeah, you got it all right, boy!" Wayne swooped him up, tickling him under his arms until he begged for mercy.

"Did you miss me?" he asked when Oscar lay breathless on the floor.

"Yes, sir."

"Well, you boys get on outside now," he said.

Cooper and Oscar bombed down the steps and out the front door. Kiki and Wayne stood silently in the hallway.

"Experts say that tickling can cause a child to stutter," she finally sniffed and started downstairs, too, but Wayne side-saddled the banister and slid down to block her at the newel post.

"Kiki, honey," he said, "I've been so lost without you."

"Well, I guess that explains why it took you ten days to get here."

She sidestepped and spun back toward the kitchen, already fighting tears.

"Kalene! C'mon, Peaches, don't be like this."

Wayne followed her into the kitchen and leaned on the edge of the counter. With his tousled hair and untucked shirt, he looked as young and reckless as he had the first time she saw him leaning over a porch rail at the Wunsche Brothers' Cafe in Old Town Spring. "Full of sparks," her mother had put it, and she was shaking her head for reasons Kiki was only now beginning to understand.

"Baby, please. Talk to me."

"Talk to my lawyer, Wayne," Kiki said, reminding her feet of the solid floor beneath them. "No. Talk to a moving company, then talk to my lawyer after you get your stuff together and get out of my house!"

Something flashed across his face, but when he spoke, his voice was placating and low.

"Baby, I'd give you the house, if that's what you really wanted. But it wouldn't be much of a home without the four of us living there all together, would it? I mean the five of us," he added warmly, laying his hand against her stomach. "Honey, you need to come home now."

"Forget it, Wayne." Kiki got around him as best she could in the narrow kitchen. "I don't like you anymore. And pretty soon, I won't love you either."

"You don't mean that, Peaches. You know I was just being a drunk idiot, and I didn't know what I was saying. You understand—"

"No, Wayne, I don't *understand!* I don't understand how you could go chasing around after another woman and getting drunk and hitting me. I don't understand it, Wayne, and I don't like it! I don't want my kids to be brought up this way."

"I have never once hit you in front of the kids!" Wayne hit the side of the refrigerator just to prove it. "I barely even touched you that night!"

Kiki pulled the sleeve of her T-shirt over her shoulder to expose the lingering mottle of purple, blue, and a sick, greenish yellow.

"Oh, God." Wayne covered his face with his hands. "Oh, baby, I'm so sorry."

He reached out to touch her, but she flinched away.

"Oh, c'mon, Kiki, honey, you know that wasn't my fault. You were acting all hysterical, and I had to take hold of you so you wouldn't go and hurt yourself, but—well, you must have got tangled up and fell."

"You hurt me, Wayne. And it's not the first time. And you know it."

"Oh, what—now we're talking about that old—"

"No, Wayne, we're not talking about any of it. 'Cause it's never your fault, and you never did any of it on purpose. It's not your fault how you won't let me do anything or have any friends or how you probably gave me herpes or AIDS or something, chasing around with that—that—*fish person* who's been Lord knows where!"

"Kiki, men have needs. And when those needs aren't being met at home, well then . . ." He raised his eyebrows and glanced to the inevitable conclusion that waited just off stage. "I'm not saying it's right. I'm just saying sooner or later, every man does it."

"My daddy didn't."

"OK, every man who ain't dead."

"Mel doesn't."

"OK, every man who can."

Wayne sat up on the countertop and lit a cigarette.

"Kit doesn't allow smoking in here," Kiki said.

She took the cigarette from his lips and dropped it into someone's leftover apple juice in the sink. It hissed like a lizard, white paper bleeding yellow. Wayne caught her by the elbow and linked his feet around her waist.

"Kiki, please. I'm sorry, honey. I know I'm just making excuses. I think I just . . . you know—'cause I haven't—I mean, here we are having another baby already and . . . It's a lot of pressure, Kalene. I don't think you appreciate what I have to do to support this family and what that's like for me."

"Well, if I had a job like Kit—"

"Oh, yeah!" Wayne scoffed, gesturing to the small, cluttered kitchen. "Then we could be living in the lap of luxury just like this. Maybe ol' Mel ain't man enough to take care of his family, but—"

"Oh, Wayne! You sound just like your daddy when you say that stuff. 'I never allowed your mama to lift a finger outside the house. She had all she could do caring for the *yak yak yak.*'"

"Okay, maybe I'm being selfish, but I work hard to give you the things you want, and I don't think it's so damn unreasonable for me to expect a few things in return. What am I asking for that's so damn unreasonable? A decent supper? For the kids to be clean and respectful? For you to keep yourself up instead of looking like some old— You used to get dressed up special once in a while, Kalene. You used to like to please me. Baby, we just don't seem to have any *fun* anymore."

"Seems to me, you been having enough fun for the both of us."

"Kiki, I made a mistake." He pulled her close and bowed his head to her shoulder. "I made a terrible mistake, and I'm a terrible person, and I'm sorry. It won't be going on anymore, Kiki. I promise. It won't ever happen again. I swear, Kalene."

She didn't answer, but she didn't pull away.

"I got a surprise for you," he teased like a mosquito in her ear. "And I think you're gonna like it. It's something you been wanting real, real bad."

"I don't want it. Whatever it is," she said. "What is it?"

"Ladies and gentlemen," Wayne took a ladle from the kitchen caddy and held it up in front of his mouth, "it's time tooooo . . . *karaoke!*"

"*Wayneee!*" she jumped up and down. "You did not!"

"I did, Peaches, and it's all hooked up with four speakers and a recording deck so you can tape yourself and everything."

"This is not fair, Wayne. You're not being fair."

"*Don' tell ma hart,*" he sang into the ladle, "*ma achey-breaky hart—*"

"Do you honestly think you can just—"

"Come on, Kiki. Can't you see I'm making an effort here?"

"You think I'm so—that I'm such a—a—"

"No! Honey, of course not! And I know I can't buy you back with some ol'—it's just—it's a gift to—to demonstrate to you how sorry I am. And how much I love you. Please, baby—God . . . I don't know how else to . . . to . . ."

"What?"

He lifted her face between his hands.

"To tell you that what I have with you, Kalene, I will never have with anyone else. We got a history together, you and me. Just think about all we've been through together. Oscar and Chloe and now this baby and the home we've made together. How can I let you walk away from all that? You're my wife. You belong to me." His voice choked, and his eyes pooled with tears. "You're my whole life, Kalene."

He took her in his arms again, and Kiki felt herself swaying with the same familiar dance they always did.

"I love you, baby. I'm so sorry. I miss you so bad," and his voice softened with each sentiment. "You know I can't live without my Peaches." He spanned his hands over the seat of her blue jeans. "I miss my sugar."

She felt herself relax just slightly when he touched his lips to her neck.

"I'm so sorry, baby, I swear I'll never let anything bad happen to you ever again. I swear to God. Just say you forgive me, and we'll forget the whole thing ever happened, okay?"

"I forgive you, Wayne. But I can't forget anymore."

"What do you think you're gonna do?"

"I'm gonna make a life for me and my children without you."

"Yeah," he smiled. "And where have we heard this before? You know it won't work, Kiki. You're gonna be broke. You know how you hate that. And you're gonna be lonesome. You're gonna need some of this," he whispered with his tongue tickling her ear. "You need me," he said, his white, hard teeth on her bottom lip, his flat, hard stomach against the soft swell of her early pregnancy. "You always come crawlin' back sooner or later, so you might as well come on home and fire up your new karaoke machine and sing something pretty for me. C'mon, Peaches. Get the kids in the car and go home now."

"Okay, I will. But where will you go?"

Wayne let go of her and dropped down from the counter.

"I, Miss Smart-ass, will go home with my family to the house I own in the car I paid for."

"I paid for 'em, Wayne. I paid plenty."

"Plenty of what?" he scoffed. "You've never *had* nothin', you've never *done* nothin', you've never *been* nothin'."

"I was a professional singer!" Kalene held up the serving spoon before God and Wayne Liam Daubert, Jr. "And I'm gonna be a professional singer again!"

"Oh, yeah!" He laughed, flat and humorless. "I'll come see you at the Astrodome. Meanwhile, there's no way you're gonna be able to support those children without me."

"You said you needed some freedom. Well, now you got it. You just better be prepared to pay the child support."

"And what if I don't?"

"Then I'll sue your fancy you-know-what, and I'll *make* you pay it!"

"Well," Wayne crossed his arms and smiled, "you see what kind of lawyer you can afford, and I'll see what kind of lawyer I can afford, and then you can kiss my fancy you-know-what on the courthouse steps, Sweet Cakes, 'cause you're not gettin' *diddly shit!*"

"Good!" Kalene crossed her own arms. "'Cause diddly shit is what I've *been* getting from you for ten years, and I don't think much of it!"

Wayne took a step forward, and Kalene automatically covered her face, but Mel's large shadow suddenly loomed between them.

"Hey, Wayne," he said. "Can I give you a ride somewhere?"

※

"Today," Ricki Lake announced, "*I'm a Selfish Bitch Who's Totally Ungrateful for the Great Life I Don't Even Deserve—and I Wish My Little Sister Would Get the Hell Out!*"

The audience booed and hissed righteous condemnation.

"But it's not like that!"

"Well then, what's it like, Kit? Tell us."

"It's—it's just . . . Okay. The thing is—she's been staying with us for almost two weeks now and . . . and of course, she's welcome to stay as long as she needs to, but . . ." Kit squirmed under the studio lights and turned to the clinical psychologist on her left. "See, this isn't the first time this has happened. They fight, and she comes and stays with us for a while and—well, she just doesn't—I mean, she's never been on her own really. Not in her whole life! And he's such a creep! I don't know why she can't just get rid of him, you know. Just get divorced."

"So you could feel superior?"

"No! So she could be happy!"

"Or maybe you're just a teensy bit jealous of the passion Wayne and Kiki share. I mean, isn't a so-called 'stormy relationship' more exciting and rewarding than the dry, droning, day-to-day grind you have with Mel?"

"Mel and I have a very exciting relationship. We're planning a trip to Disney World!"

"Kit has always had difficulty in her relationships with men," said the psychologist. "Her father, who favored her, died when she was young. Her mother plainly preferred her younger sister, who is smaller, prettier, more talented, for all of which Kit would subconsciously like to see Kiki punished, which initiates a cycle of guilt, which generates resentment, more guilt, additional resentment . . ."

"No! That's not . . . I don't resent her! It's just—Mel and I can't afford—"

"I think she's got a lot of nerve," an audience member was telling Ricki, "talking about her sister when her own life is such a piece of crap."

"How 'bout it, Kit?" Ricki nodded wisely. "Maybe you'd better do a little housecleaning of your own before you go peeking under your sister's bed."

"Now, wait just a minute," Kit protested. "My life is fine. Everything is exactly the way it's supposed to be."

"Then why are you so unhappy?" the clinical psychologist pried.

"Because . . . because I'm . . . I don't know."

The audience seemed very far away now. In fact, she seemed to be all alone in the echoing auditorium.

"I think there's something terribly wrong with me."

She looked up just in time to see the falling glass, but before she could shield her face, she woke.

*I*n a little honky-tonky village in Texas, there's a guy . . .
The song in her head.
The rain on the pavement.

Kiki tried to fix her focus on these, rather than the surging of her stomach, but the grillish aroma of bacon-double-cheeseburger traveled over from the stainless steel counter to the booth right behind her. It stopped and sat directly adjacent to where she was sitting, sandwiched between the hard plastic seat and formica tabletop, facing the Whataburger assistant manager across his neon-colored clipboard.

"So, like—you have no other job experience?" he said for the tenth time.

He looked like he was all of about twelve years old, which made her feel all of about a hundred.

"No."

"You never had—you know . . . a job?"

She shook her head, raised her hand to cover her nose as unobtrusively as possible.

When he jams he's a ball . . . he's the daddy of 'em all . . .

"You never like . . . babysat for somebody or worked at like McDonald's or something?"

"No," Kiki swallowed. "Nothing like that. But I was—"

Paper crackled behind her. The limp, white odor of bubbled bacon wafted over her shoulder.

"I was a performing artist."

"What does that mean?"

"Well, I . . ." *when he jams with the bass and guitar* "I worked at Calloway's."

"Y'mean . . . Calloway's? Down by the Galleria?"

"Yes. That Calloway's."

His eyes widened a little and dropped automatically to her breasts.

"And before that, I was a professional singer."

"Wha'd'ya mean?"

"I mean I sang. Professionally."

"Oh."

Picking at his chin uncertainly, he painstakingly printed "PROFSNL SNGER" in a box shaded FOR OFFICE USE ONLY.

. . . when the bass and—no, *when he jams with the bass and guitar . . .*

Salivary glands. Distending tongue. Lips pulling back over cigarette tanned incisors.

"So okay. So you umm . . . I guess . . . Do you mind if I ask, umm, when are you . . . you know—having your baby?"

"Oh, not for a long time," Kiki assured him. "Four months."

A moment in a woman's life, but a venerable career in the fast-food industry. The boy nodded and leafed through his papers. His jaw swiveled, rotating the Doublemint inside his mouth. The motion was beginning to make Kiki a bit dizzy.

. . . when he jams with the bass and guitar . . .

"So okay. So I guess . . ."

He rolled and unrolled her application in his hand. Rain-drops slipped and eddied down the window.

. . . they holler, beat me, daddy, eight to the bar . . .

Kiki took deep slow breaths, but then, in a wave, came the unmistakable fetor of plastic orange cheese congealing with stage-blood ketchup and squirt-yellow mustard over the greasy brown stench of fly-buzzing slaughterhouse cow carcass, and Kiki couldn't even open her mouth to excuse herself as she dashed for the ladies' room.

It took a while before she could come out because she had to take off her shirt and rinse the front under cold water, then hold it in the blowstream of the hand dryer until it looked like something worn by a woman of heartier constitution.

She eventually had to come out, though, and she stood at one end of the counter, waiting while the assistant manager dumped salt over a fresh batch of fries.

"Thanks for coming in," he mumbled. "We'll keep your ap on file."

Kiki nodded, thanked him, and pushed through the glass doors out into the drizzle. In the moist humor of the Houston springtime parking lot, she was better able to breathe, and the rain on her face made her feel less like throwing up.

It wasn't that she wanted the job, anyway, but she and the kids had been staying with Mel and Kit for going on two weeks now, and Kiki wished she could at least kick in a bag of groceries. Her original plan was to get one of those cute little apartments over on 1960 West and invite them all over for a nice dinner, but that grand scheme had dwindled to this pitiful, single-sack aspiration. Pathetic, she knew, but even a scanty contribution to her own upkeep, any meager measure of independence—it would have given her something of her own.

After Wayne finished his bacon-double-cheeseburger and used the men's room, he sauntered out to the sidewalk, settling a wide-brimmed hat that always made him feel especially Texan.

"How'd it go, Peaches?" he asked and softly stroked his thumb across the wetness on her cheek.

"I don't care," Kiki told him. "I got another interview this afternoon."

"Perfume squirt girl or waitress?"

"Squirt girl," she confessed, but did her best to look defiant. "You gonna follow me over there, too?"

"Might make more sense if I give you a ride, as long as I'm here."

"No thanks."

"Then you wouldn't have to take the Metro."

Kiki was tempted. Her shoe was beginning to bite at her swollen instep, and those Metro benches were so skanky sometimes. But she didn't like the way Wayne kept showing up everywhere she went. He'd been calling Kit's house at all hours of the day and night, sending flowers by FTD delivery and effusive, imploring love letters by next-day mail, return receipt requested.

Dearest Kalene,

I am not fit to live on the same planet as you I am such an asshole. I beg you to forgive me. I am a big dumb fuck and if you can ever forgive me and you and me can be a family again I will be the luckiest man on the face of this earth and I will never stop appreciating and cherishing you. I will love you always and I don't think you will ever find a man who will please you in lovemaking sexually as I can. I bet right now you are thinking about me doing it all to you baby and how good it makes you feel when I do that. I want to do that baby if you would just come home and let me kiss you from your tits to your toes Kiki and everything in between if you know what I mean. You are the most beautiful girl on the face of this earth and I was a fucking blind asshole to ever look at anybody else and I swear to you that this will never happen again if you will only come home. Things are OK over at

*the shop. I did Trav Avis's sailfish for him and it turned out real good.
I am such an asshole Kalene but I still love you and I beg you to
forgive me.*

*All my love,
Your Husband Wayne*

"C'mon, Peaches," he said, so soft, "let me take you to
Pappasito's for lunch."

"I'm not hungry."

"You love Pappasito's," he singsonged.

"And I want you to stop following me."

"Ah, Kiki," he soothed, "it makes me feel real proud when
I see you trying so hard. You been very brave. I know you have.
But you made your point now. It's time to come on home."

"I told you, Wayne—"

"Kiki, could you be realistic for a damn minute here? You
got no job experience, no education. The only time you ever
made your own living was when you were a stripper at
Calloway's, and you sure as hell can't do that anymore. Look at
you, girl." He smiled and spanned his hands over her belly.
"Nobody wants to hire some pregnant girl, honey. They know
you won't last, and you'll be fat and crabby and sick all the time
and you won't look good."

"I was not a stripper." Kiki had to talk quietly because her
nose and throat were clouding up with emotion.

"Oh, yeah, I keep forgetting—*performing artist.* I guess
that's why you were so nervous that your mama might find
out."

"I have to go, Wayne."

"Go where? Hmm? Where ya goin', Peaches? There's just
one place in this world where you're worth anything to
anybody, and that's at home with me and the kids. That's
where you belong, honey. I'm the only one who wants to take
care of you. You got nobody else."

"That's not true. I got Kit."

"Yeah, well, I could tell you something right now that would shed a whole new light on your big sister."

Kiki started down the block toward the Metro bench.

"Kalene, I'm more ashamed than I can tell you, but I'm gonna confess to you right here and now because I want to make everything right between us." He stepped in front of her and put his hands on her shoulders, looking right deep into her eyes. "Kalene, your sister has been coming on to me big time for years, and one night while you were in Orlando—down there with your poor mama—and I swear I was too drunk to even know what was going on, but your sister—she was all over me, Kiki, saying how Mel is such a dud in bed and you'd never find out because you're not very smart. And then after—well, I told her how ashamed it made me and how it would never happen again, but I can't stand the thought of you staying under the same roof with her and believing she's your always big sister. It makes me sick inside, Peaches. What she did—it makes me sick."

Kiki stared at him for a long moment and then started laughing.

"Oh, Waynee! As *if!*" she giggled. "Lord, you really are desperate, aren't you?"

"I am! I truly am," he laughed too, but only a little. "I'm desperately lonely at the house all by myself. I'm desperately sorry for hurting the sweetest, most wonderful girl in the world. I'm desperately in love with you, Kalene."

They stood there for a while, and then Kiki said something about how she should head on up to her Metro stop so she could get to her next interview.

"Kalene," he took her face in his hands, fingertips at her temple, "get it through your head. Nobody wants you."

"I know," she whispered.

"You can't mooch off your sister forever. Mel can't hardly support the family he's got without three extra mouths to feed. It ain't fair to them."

"I was thinking . . . I thought I might go on down to my mama's for a while."

"And just how were you planning to get there?" he smiled patiently. "You got some money in your Swiss bank account, Sugar Sweet? Is that it?"

"No."

"I'm sure as hell not gonna buy y'all a round of plane tickets."

"I wasn't even gonna ask you, Wayne."

"Well, your sister don't hardly have a pot to piss in, so I guess you're gonna go crawling to your mama for the money?"

"Just . . . just as a loan."

"I don't know what's happened to you, Kalene," he reproached. "You're not thinking about anybody but yourself. You think your mama wants to hassle with you and the kids right now? The woman just had major surgery, and now she's gonna start all that chemotherapy and all. She's got enough on her without a little birdie fluttering back to the nest."

Rain stung Kiki's forehead, but her face felt warm between his hands.

"But you don't really give a shit about her, do you? You don't care about your sister or her family or even about your own kids sleeping on somebody's floor at night, don't even know where their home is anymore. All you care about is Miss Kalene. You're just being a fat, spoiled, selfish little princess is what you're being. It's all about Princess Kalene."

She bit her bottom lip, shut her eyes, felt cool drizzle on the closed lids.

. . . when he jams with the bass and guitar . . .

"I can't understand you, Kiki. How can you not even care about how you're hurting everybody who loves you? Hurting your own babies? Have you even got a mother's heart in you anymore?"

She screwed her eyes and mouth shut tighter, but two tears and a small sound escaped.

"I know you want to do the right thing. I know you do, Kalene." Wayne folded her in his arms, kissing her forehead and wet cheeks and smooth neck. "Don't cry, baby. I'm not mad at you, Peaches. You just c'mon home now."

❦

"Here's the story of Minnie the Moocher, . . ."

Kit's brush made small back-and-forth nips in the hi-de-ho rhythm of a song her mother used to sing. She glanced up and saw Ander smiling at her.

"This is very strange song to me," he said. "All the time you sing this song when you feel not so terrific."

"Do I?"

"She was rough and tough as frail," he imitated her furrowed brow, her hunched posture, and cramped hand, then expanded to an open-armed baritone, *"but Minnie had a heart as big as a whale!"*

Kit laughed and applauded, which encouraged him to schottische around the room with a plywood cut-out garden gnome, singing "Paul and His Chickens." It was in Swedish, so the only part she could join in on was the *clook-clook-clook* of the chorus.

By four-thirty, it was obvious the hoosier was not going to be done, and Kit gave up any hopes of being home by five. At six, Ander spoke to Ruda on the phone, telling her in Swedish he was going to stay and help Kit finish the behemoth off.

They sat on opposite sides of the cabinet, following the faint pencil marks with their brushes, talking about Morris chairs, mailboxes, and other things they'd like to make someday. Ander laughed at the paint on Kit's nose, and she laughed at his impersonation of the rich lady who'd commissioned the hoosier particularly for a dinner party at which one of the guests would be a Norwegian government official, in Houston for a conference on lutefisk or something.

"Ah, these ferns," Ander nodded, "very good. These ferns

when you freehand them, Kit. Much better than stencil. Better than I do it myself! Nobody can make the ferns like you. You are very best artist of ferns."

Kit finished one off with a Hogarthian curve, just the way Ander had taught her in her very first tole painting class right here in the workshop ten years earlier. By the time she'd waitressed Mel through trade school, and then Cooper came along, a ten-week class at Scandinavian Design and Furnishings was about all she had left of her art school aspirations. Every Tuesday evening, she sat at a long table with several elderly ladies in paint smocks, who worked away at their plaques and planters and made kissy faces at baby Coo, who lay kicking in his infant seat.

Kit was instantaneously infatuated with the colors and strokes. She took to it as if she remembered it from a former lifetime, and Ander guided her hand as if he recognized her from that same incarnation. He praised and challenged her. His expectations gave her confidence. The technique came so easily to her that, at the end of the course, Ander and Ruda offered her a job stencilling and detailing custom-built items. It was only minimum wage at first, but Kit was able to quit waitressing and send a beautifully decorated (though probably useless) letter box to everyone on her Christmas list.

She wasn't alarmed, over the years, when the original infatuation began to spill over onto her mentor, when he started to seem kinder and larger than before, his laughter deeper and his eyes bluer. She came to know and love the fatherly sweetness about him, but there was also something European and arty about his big nose and blunt, blonde ponytail. As he built and stripped and sanded, his body moved with a carpenter's earthy, useful grace. Kit indulged vague daydreams now and then, but she'd read in a magazine that women sometimes develop crushes on their obstetricians, and she thought maybe this was like that: perhaps her attraction was not to him so much as to the new life he coaxed out of her and the gentleness with which he coaxed it.

At seven-thirty, they highlighted the last cherry sprigs on the cupboard's front doors and sat back to survey their work.

"If we let it dry overnight, then you can do the polyurethane tomorrow, let that dry over Sunday, and still be able to deliver by Monday afternoon," Kit said. "But don't forget to take pictures for the book before you take it out."

"This is excellent good job, Kit," Ander told her, leaning against an unfinished chest of drawers. "And very much . . . I enjoy so much to work with you."

"Well, thank you," Kit smiled over her shoulder and went back to checking for blips, blurs, and dribbles. "I enjoy to work with you, too."

"Yes. Is very good. Beautiful."

"Except for . . . that. What is that?" Kit bent over to correct a tiny bobble.

"Hmm," Ander smiled.

"Now—" Kit stood back and nodded. "Is beautiful."

He squeezed her shoulder and rested his hand against her aching back. He was large and comforting, like Mel, almost as tall and just as heavy, and Kit felt a weary impulse to lean back against the cedar smell of his denim shirt.

"You work so hard, Kit. I wish you should have this for yourself."

"Sure. I really need something that costs more than my car in which to store my priceless collection of plastic plates and Snoopy cups."

Ander laughed, but then he dropped his head back against the drawers and sighed.

"This project—all this design of flowers and ferns is making me to miss my country very much these days. I am thinking very much of my friends and music where we go. Ruda and I, we go there with all people in this place. We dance with music, we laugh. I miss this house by the water there. And flowers in this yard. Ruda can grow any flowers in this garden. All colors. And she can be so happy. I am missing this garden of hers where she is so happy, so young. All colors, so beautiful. Perhaps, most of everything, I am missing her."

Kit leaned forward and touched her brush to shade one cherry a little deeper.

"But," Ander shrugged, "what man can marry this beautiful girl and take her far away from all places and people she love, he gives her seven babies to care, and then is complaining, 'What? You can't be happy in this place? You never have a time to give some little kiss?' But, *ah Gott*, I miss that kiss."

"Me too," Kit confided, settling back beside him.

"You? With this big man of yours? Why would he never kiss you?"

"I don't know." Kit took the brushes from her shirt pocket and ruffled them against her hand. "He still loves me. We still—we love each other, of course. It's just . . ." She laid the brushes on the floor and rolled them beneath her palm. "I don't know. I think there must be something wrong with the way I do it."

"I tell you how you handle this husband problem, Kit." Only he said it like "Ket." "You go to video store, rent one of this blue movie."

"What?"

"Blue movie," Ander repeated, trying to enunciate. "This pornography video tape." He cupped his hand to his mouth and whispered, "*Fuck film!*"

"Ick," Kit crinkled her nose. "I don't think so."

"Oh ya," Ander nodded wisely. "You show this movie to your Mel. Then I think he is kissing you all the time."

"Mel's not into that kind of stuff."

"All men love this movie," he said, secure in his expertise. "They go crazy insane."

"Mel's not like that."

"Mel is same as all men. Men in this country, men in my

country, men in ancient times of Greece for paintings, scrolls, carving of stone—all the same. Pigs! Disgusting! They like what animals like. You go to video store, you rent this one movie. Hey, I give you ten dollars if he don't go crazy insane."

"Ya, I tink you crazy insane," Kit mocked and nudged his shoulder.

"Ya," Ander smiled. "Right now I am thinking that, too."

He leaned over, and his nose was *really* big up close. Kit couldn't help but notice, just before he kissed her full on the mouth. Her watch didn't have a second hand, but the kiss lasted an awfully wonderfully long time and felt awfully wonderfully good. Better than in her occasional idle daydreams of him. When he finally drew back, he brushed his fingers across her lips and said, "No, Kit. Nothing is wrong with you to kiss. He is very foolish man." And then he kissed her again, and that kiss flowed into another like rosemaling around a windowsill.

ess
scroll
comma
crescent
fern blossoms   fern blossoms
full splaying orchids

Kit was unable to determine where the kiss left off and the lovemaking began, or where she might have, could have, and should have stopped it, but somehow her head was under the hoosier and his huge Gerard Depardieu nose was between her legs, and then his huge Scandinavian *spunderflägen* was pushing inside her, and his skilled carpenter's hands were roving everywhere, and he never for a moment stopped kissing her.

Kit knew that if she ignored her conscience now, it would wake up howling and hungry in its crib tonight. She knew that she would have to face and fear both Mel and Ruda for the rest of her life and that what she was doing was just flat wrong and her mother might find out and her pants would smell like sex and she was already keeping one horrible secret too many. She knew if she let the next moment flow over her, she'd have a hard time not thinking about it every time she punched in for work. But then nothing mattered, because *sunbursts! squiggletails! cherry blossoms!* she poured and pooled, crystallized and sugared off like syrup.

"*Aaagh . . . ah Gott!*" Ander rasped when he felt it inside her. "Ah, Kit . . . my beautiful Kit . . ."

His hips moving hers in a Hogarthian curve, his tongue stippling and blending florets across her lips, he praised and prayed to her.

"You have so beautiful body, so beautiful breast. I am wanting so very much to do this for very long time."

Kit wasn't sure if that meant he'd been wanting it for a long time previously or wanted it to continue for a long time now, but she was still lucid enough to know that neither was appropriate. And she would have told him this if he hadn't been kissing her and kissing her and kissing her mouth forever, pausing only to allow the licentious colloquy of the Muppet chef.

❦

"*She fell in love with the king of Sweden, he gave her things that she was needin' . . .*"

"Keep singing, Mommy," Chloe tugged at Kiki's maternity blouse.

Glossy magazines lined up in wire racks at the checkout stand, and lifting them reminded Kiki of the game Password, where the magic answer was hidden inside a little cardholder. You'd lift it enough to see the secret, but not enough to take it out.

"*GO GET HIM (Guy-Snagging Moves That Really Work!)*"

Kiki slid a slick issue of *YM* back into the wire rack. Apparently the Y and M stood for *Young and Modern* now. Kiki remembered how it used to be *Young Miss,* back when she and Kit read it, flashlight under the covers, working their way through the bramble of preadolescent turmoil.

"Was My Face Red," Kit would read aloud.

The letters confessed lurid details of how one girl belched out loud in social studies and another tipped over backward in her chair at a birthday party. Then they'd take turns reading articles about what to do if people were calling you "teacher's pet." Or why boys are better at math. Or what might be wrong with you if nobody asked you to the junior high spring dance.

There was much to learn about being female back then, when the idea of inserting a tampon gave her the willies, when the budding of her breasts inside a training bra felt like roses opening, and the telephone rang with all the crisp, light promise of a fortune cookie. But it seemed to Kiki that the general thrust of *Young Miss* was more about being coy and minding your etiquette, as opposed to this outright snagging around on people advocated by the current publication. Or perhaps it was only a different approach to fulfilling the same old expectation. Kiki hoped Chloe would have better luck with it all than she'd had.

"Could you make the check for twenty dollars over, Wayne?" she asked, as the last of the groceries skimmed and blipped across the checkout scanner.

"What for?"

"Well," she hedged, "Kit and me, we might take the kids over to Taco Cabana or something tomorrow."

"You want to stay in this week. You need your rest."

"Well, we'd just be sitting there talking."

"Nah, you're gonna be busy catching up on things around the house." Wayne handed his debit card to the checkout girl, shielding the little keypad with his hand as he input his PIN. Then he turned toward Kiki and stroked her cheek gently. "Maybe in a week or two, okay, baby? Let's give things a chance to get back to normal first."

Kiki nodded and picked up a *National Enquirer.*

"*MYSTERIOUS WEREWOLF CHILDREN OF EUROPE*"

"Daddy, can I get Butterfinger Beebees?" Chloe begged.

"It's almost suppertime—" Kiki started, but Wayne set them on the conveyor belt.

"Sure, Little Muffin," he said. "How 'bout you, sport? Want something to celebrate coming home?"

"No thanks," Oscar said.

"Oh, c'mon, Sport. Sure you do," Wayne said, and he handed the checkout girl a bag of Tropical Fruit Skittles.

Kiki picked up a twin pack of Reese's Peanutbutter Cups for herself, but Wayne gently took it from her hand and set it back in the rack.

"*DOLLY: MY SECRET PAIN*"

With all that money and spectacular hair? It must be something about her childhood. Or maybe her husband beat her. Maybe she couldn't have babies. Kiki tried to remember if Dolly ever had any babies. Tried to remember how she and Kit used to harmonize on the bridge of that "Jolene" song of hers they used to sing.

Jolene Jolene Jolene Joleeeeen I'm beggin' of you please come take my man

Wayne lifted a cellophaned bouquet from an aisle-side water bucket. "Flowers for my beautiful wife."

i'm beggin of you please

"Kiki, honey?"

"Hmm?"

"I said, flowers for you, Peaches." He patted her thigh lovingly. "Sweet as candy, but a lot less calories."

"Thank you, Wayne," Kiki said, and he nodded, satisfied.

"*LIZ AND MICHAEL PLAN PLASTIC SURGERY SPA VACATION*"

Liposuction for her, of course. But what did he need? Maybe eyelids or something about that skin color disease or something horrendously personal.

"Mommeeee . . ." Chloe tugged, "*sing* it *sing* it *sing* it!"

"*She fell in love with a guy named Smokey . . .*"

"*MIRACLE BABY BORN TO COMATOSE MOMMY*"

There was this woman up in Oklahoma, apparently, who got her skull crushed in a car accident and gave birth to a perfectly healthy baby thirteen weeks later, even though she was totally brain dead, and so, of course, they shut off her life support right after the baby was born.

Back in aisle five, they'd walked right under a high shelf of enormous cans. Applesauce, pear halves, fruit cocktail. Those great big cans you'd buy for a family reunion or if you had several foster care kids and you wanted to feed them something sweet after a sensible and nutritious foster care kind of meal. If one of those gigantic cans fell on your head, Kiki mused, if it was just teetering there and tipped off just as you came by, it would probably crush your skull right into your neck, and you'd never know what hit you, probably.

"Again," Chloe rocked and rattled in the seat of the metal cart. "Sing it, Mommy, sing it."

"May I see you home, Miss Ma'am?" Wayne smiled, his hand under her elbow.

Applesauce, pear halves, pork and beans. The cling peaches looked especially close to the edge.

❦

"Must have been quite a project," Mel grumbled when Kit trudged wearily into the kitchen. He leaned on the doorway to the garage, opening and closing some kind of pliers.

"Where is everybody?" Kit asked.

"I guess they decided to work it out. They came and got the kids this afternoon."

"You're kidding me."

"You know how they are," Mel shrugged, "like a trailer house and a tornado."

"Is that why Cooper's crying? Because Oscar left?"

"No," Mel lowered his eyes. "We sort of got into it."

He shrugged again and slunk back to the garage. He lay down on a caster platform and rolled under the car so only his feet were sticking out.

"What do you mean you 'got into it'?" Kit asked, but there was no reply from Mel or his feet, so she went out back and climbed up to Cooper's tree fort.

"What's up, budsky?" she called softly.

Cooper cuddled over to her with his head on her chest, and Kit kissed the top of his head.

"Hmm? What's going on with the guy?"

He ground his face into her shoulder and squirmed onto her lap.

"Did you and Daddy get into it?"

Cooper nodded against her shirt.

"I saw your ball on top of the fridge. Did your ball hit something? Did it hit the car?"

"It was on accident!" he sobbed and held her tighter.

"It's okay, Coo-Coo-burra . . . shhhhhh. You know Daddy's car is very important to him."

"But not as important as me," Cooper said with conviction.

Kit could tell that Mel must have tried to backpedal it already.

"That's right, Coo. You know Daddy loves you more than anything, but you also know you're not supposed to throw your ball in the garage. Right?"

"Yeah."

"Daddy gets kinda nervous and crabby when we go to Grandma's house. He just gets in a big ugly, and it's not your fault, but we need extra good cooperation and behavior, okay? Can you be Dad's big guy?"

Cooper nodded again.

"Are you gonna be my big guy, too?"

"Okay."

She realized sadly that Cooper really was getting big. This

was a rare treasure he was allowing right now, and she cherished it, humming into his temple, stroking his back until he gathered his dignity and wrangled free.

"Girls aren't allowed up here," he told her. "Tree fort rules."

"Not even moms?" She tickled him under the arms.

"Especially not moms!" he giggled, tucking his elbows tight to his ribs.

Kit climbed down and went looking for Mitzi, finally discovering her sleeping in front of the TV, head on the floor, feet high up on a beanbag chair, a box of Lucky Charms spilling across her chest. Like rock, scissors, and paper, Kit relished a righteous stab of annoyance toward Mel, which was immediately squashed by a boulder of guilt, which made her fling the Lucky Charms at the TV screen, accidentally knocking down his high school football trophy that sat on top, which made her feel even more guilty, which made her practically hate him.

He was scrubbing his hands in the kitchen sink.

"I thought we agreed we weren't going to spank them."

"I didn't spank him, Kit."

"Experts say it only shows them hitting is the way to settle—"

"I said I didn't spank him, okay? I grabbed his arm, I yelled at him. I didn't hit him. And maybe if you didn't mollycoddle him all the time, he'd be man enough to take it when somebody looks at him cross-eyed. What do the experts say about that?"

"Did you know she was eating these?" Kit held up the empty Lucky Charms box.

"She was hungry."

"And you were too butt lazy to open a can of soup? It's after nine o'clock, Mel. They should have been in bed an hour ago."

"So where the hell were you? Don't they have a telephone over there anymore? Or were you just too butt lazy to call me?"

"I was—I told you I—I might have to stay late."

"You didn't say you were going to stay till nine-thirty at night."

"You could have at least fed them some supper!"

"I was going to send out for some pizza after—"

"Oh, great. But of course, the car has to come first."

"It's not my fault if the damn alternator—"

"Damn your damn *alternator!* I needed you to take care of a few things for once."

"What you need is to tell ol' Sven and Olee over there you've got a family who needs you at home. You're only supposed to be half-time over there. You put in almost forty hours this week! Christ! This place is a pigsty. Nothing is packed for tomorrow. I don't even have a clean shirt to wear on the way down there!"

"I said I'd get to it, Mel! I'm getting to it! Right now! *See?*" She shook a load of clothes into the washer and brandished the empty basket. "I'll get to all of it! As soon as I get the kids fed and bathed and put to bed and load the dishwasher and pick up the living room and run the vacuum and do everything else that needs to get done around here while you go play with your car and have a brewski and look at 'Baywatch.'"

"Oh, bullshit! I'm just saying they don't pay you enough to own your whole damn life, Kit!"

"*Neither do you!*" She slammed a saucepan on the burner. "But I guess it won't be a problem anymore, Mel. You'll be pleased to know that I just got fired."

Kit was pretty sure that was the gist of what Ruda was screaming in Swedish when she came in and found Ander struggling to get his pants on inside out.

"What?" Mel stared at her.

"I'm fired," Kit repeated. "I'm history. I am no longer employed."

"You've gotta be kidding! After all these years? How could—"

"So are you happy now?" Kit started to cry. "Is everybody happy? Did everybody get what they want?"

"Mom?" Cooper stood in the doorway, his eyes very wide. "Will we still get to go to Disney World?"

"It's okay, Coop," Mel said quietly. "Don't worry about it. C'mon in, and I'll make you a grilled cheese while Mom takes a nice hot bath."

When he rubbed his hand across her back, gently massaging her aching neck and shoulders, Kit felt biblical coals of fire searing into the top of her head.

"Okay, Mom?" Mel touched her face, took the can of tomato soup from her hand.

Kit walked away as quickly as possible. She felt herself losing it and didn't want Cooper to see her sobbing.

Upstairs, she stood in the shower, weeping into a loofa sponge, clutching a bar of Ivory soap against her chest, trying to figure out what the heck just happened, trying to shut out Mel's sympathetic expression and Ruda's heartbroken wails. Ander had babbled and begged, of course, but Kit couldn't understand the language any more than she could understand how, after eleven faithful years, she could betray her husband two times in as many weeks.

Apparently, it gets easier, she figured. Apparently, screwing around on your husband isn't something you do. It's something you are.

I t was a good four hours down to Corpus Christi, and Grandpa and Grandma Prizer lived just beyond there in New Rippy, so Kit was able to get some sleep, dozing with her head hammocked in the shoulder harness of her seat belt.

She'd finished the last of the laundry a little after three, stumbling through the obstacle course of Legos and action figures to fill Cooper's dresser. But she'd left Mitzi's basket on top of her vanity instead of putting things away, so of course, Mitzi had dumped it over on the floor within five seconds of getting up at six.

"I wanted *pink* socks," she sobbed when Kit scolded her for it. "Yellow socks are *stupid!*" Now she sat in the backseat, laboriously sounding out words in a reading workbook. " . . . sssseeeeee t-i-mmmm . . . See tim? See Tim!"

Kit opened her eyes. Port Lavaca, Lamar, and now Aransas? Apparently, Mel was taking the same direct route the Israelites followed on a forty-year trek through a ten-mile desert.

"Seeeee . . . K-i-mmmm . . . See Kim!"

"Hey, guys," Mel called to the back seat. "Should we take the shortcut or the ferry?"

"Ferry! Ferry!" Mitzi squealed.

"Shortcut!" Cooper yelled, only because he knew it would make her shriek, and it did.

"Mitzi!" Kit said, at the same time Mel said, "Cooper!" and then in unison, they said, "Settle it back there."

Kit pushed her sunglasses on top of her head.

"Mel, it's after eleven."

"Just relax, honey," Mel squeezed her knee and went on pointing out landmarks and tourist traps to the kids in a big, overly cheerful, daddy way.

Kit lowered her shades and rested her head against the window, trying not to feel the pleasant little morning-after ache Ander had left inside her.

"P . . . at . . . c-aaaaannnn . . . rr-u-nnn. Run, Pat, run!"

The vague daydreams that had passed through her mind over the years had always seemed so safe. Ander belonged to Ruda. Kit belonged to Mel. That was all. She'd never placed Mel or Ruda in those ambiguous imaginings, never wished them dead nor divorced nor deceived. They simply weren't a factor because the envisioned moment was like a knothole out of a smooth plank, something that swirled dark and circular, separate from the comparatively straight-forward lines of real life.

Kit wished she'd stepped around it, differed and detoured the way the wood grain sways so as not to be interrupted. Sitting with her legs crossed on the front seat of the station wagon, she could still feel Ander's easy, open-mouthed kiss between them. She'd crawled up over him, straddled, and clung like a shipwrecked sailor on a broken mast, knowing even as he floated her upward from the floor that Mel was the dry land she was struggling for. That pleasant little ache was not much consolation when she recognized it was all she had left of a once-solid marriage, two longtime friendships, and the closest thing to a career she'd ever have.

Mel squeezed her knee again, and Kit started crying behind her sunglasses. The most painful thing of all was how his hand made her feel worse instead of better.

"Don't worry about it, babe," he said. "I'll hit the overtime as hard as I can when we get back, you'll hit the classifieds, and something will turn up sooner or later. Hey, that new Albertson's grocery store just opened. And all those places up on 1960 are always hiring."

Yee ha, she sulked. *WalMart pet department, here I come.*

It didn't seem worth the effort to explain to Mel that, while she didn't claim to be an artist or anything, what she'd been doing the last nine years at Scandinavian Design was more than a job, it was . . . whatever.

And now, she had to go face Neeva and Otto for the entire weekend, gagging on cigarette smoke as she picked her way through a minefield of fulminating nerves and volatile chitchat. Along with cheerful reminders of how, now that Kit's mother had breast cancer, she and Mitzi were prime targets for the disease, she'd have to hear the story of Neeva's double radical mastectomy, including a graphic description of every cycle of chemotherapy, how she decorated a coffee can with contact paper and carried it with her at all times, and how all the health care professionals, to whom Neeva always referred in respectful terms like "Dr. Whatsercake" and "Nurse Prissy-face," told her she was sicker than anyone they'd ever seen. (Apparently, they hadn't seen all the dead women.)

With the sensibilities of a tracking missile, Neeva knew the reaction most human beings have to the C word: an amalgam of sympathy, fear, and revulsion; a twisted admiration for the survival instinct and something that confuses respect with an unwillingness to speak ill of the soon-to-be-dead. She held her cancer like a cudgel over the heads of her loved ones. Her martyred breasts had been enormous and beautiful, but she

59

bore her equally oversized prostheses like foam rubber trophies, never hesitating to talk about where she got them, how much they cost, and the fact that 38 double-D's had to be specially ordered. They weren't just a couple of mushrooms off the shelf, like Kit's 36 C's would be. It took a heck of a woman to make Kit feel flat-chested, but Neeva could do it, the same way she could make her six-foot-four, three-hundred-pound son feel like sobbing in his tree fort.

"My mother is very . . . dynamic," Mel told Kit on their first date when she wondered why he hadn't seen his parents in several years. Kit pressed him over the years to get in touch with them and finally convinced him to go for a visit just before Cooper's first Christmas. She saw something broken in Mel's life, and she wanted to heal it. She thought she could do that for him. But she soon discovered that she couldn't, and there were times she wished she hadn't even tried. This definitely was one of them.

When they finally pulled up to the pink stucco house where Mel had spent his childhood, Neeva was standing in the doorway, looking like Texas: all tall and windy and leathered by seventy-four years of too much sun. Otto was in the side yard snipping at a boxwood hedge, his striped walking shorts rising high over his round middle, swallowing him like a python overtaking a dumpling. Each time Kit saw him, his legs thinned a little bonier, and his height diminished a little stoop-isher. Lately, there seemed to be more pants than person, and she couldn't help but envision how his head would eventually converge with his hips, and he would turn into Mr. Potato Head—arms, legs, and eyes all radiating from the same pelvic center with a little straw sun hat perched on top.

"Hey! There they are!" he waved his hat, then went back to pruning.

"Where in the hell have you been, Melvin?" Neeva said in that offhand way she could pass off as joking if Mel challenged her.

But Mel opened his arms to her.

"Scenic route, Ma," he said good-naturedly. "What's for lunch?"

Instead of walking into his hug, she put her hands out and took measure of his middle.

"Good Lord," she pursed, "I think you'd better have a glass of water and some celery sticks."

She'd gotten ribs, fried chicken, and broasted potatoes from Big Jimmy's Bar & Bar-B-Q. Kit was relieved. Neeva's home-cooked meals were blessedly infrequent. It was hard enough choking down take-out food at the grungy table where yesterday's cornflakes were still cemented to the oilcloth with sugar grit and coffee drips. Ashtrays overflowed everywhere, and Kit cringed when Neeva set a full one right next to Mitzi's plate.

"I'll sit here with Miss Millicent, if she doesn't mind."

"Go right ahead, Miss Neeva," Mitzi said in grand tea party style, and they giggled and stuck their pinkies out and clicked their Kool-Aid cups together.

"So," Neeva said, "how's the world of astrophysics, Melvin?"

"It's good, Ma," Mel said, following Kit's admonitions not to let his mother bait him.

"Did your daddy ever tell you he was going to be an astrophysicist?" She leaned toward Cooper. "Always was saying, 'Ma, you know what I wanna be? An astrophysicist!' That's what he always said."

"Daddy, what's a nastro fizzist?" Mitzi asked.

"An airplane mechanic with a brain," Neeva told her, and Kit made a mental note to add "astrophysicist" to Cooper's list of positive affirmations. "So are you still stuck working that graveyard shift, Melvin?"

"I'm used to it," he shrugged. "Lots of overtime. And it's not so hot at night."

"Yeah, it doesn't sound so hot."

"Mel's a foreman now," Kit interjected. "He just got a *gigantic* raise."

"Well, I hope he uses it to pay up his life insurance. Working all night. All that stress. Look at him. He's a heart attack waiting to happen."

"Hey, Ma," Mel said with his mouth full, "we just got these brand new Brazilias down at the hangar—"

"Your brother's doing real well this year," Neeva said. "He moved into outside sales. Avionics."

"Great." Mel rummaged in the chicken bucket and took two thighs.

"You get into that end of the industry, and you're pulling down some real money. And you can bet he doesn't come home with grease up to his elbows anymore, either."

"Good for him." Mel dished himself a helping of peas and passed them to Kit.

"Wears a nice suit every day. He's been flying all over the country. And just last month, he was down in Brazil. Next fall, he's going to Paris, and I mean Paris, France—not Paris, Texas." Neeva picked through the bucket of chicken, drew out two wings, and laid them on Mel's plate. "Here. Now you can fly, too."

"Thanks, Ma." Mel pushed peas onto his spoon and shoveled them up to his mouth.

"Some peas, Otto?" Kit offered.

"Huh?"

"Peas?" she enunciated. "Some peas?"

"Peas! Well, I don't mind if I do."

"He doesn't eat peas anymore," Neeva said, taking the peas from Kit and dishing a helping onto her own plate. "His hands are so *trembly shaky shaky trembly*. By the time he gets the fork to his face, he's got a mouthful of atmosphere." Cooper and Mitzi giggled at that, so she went, "*Shaky trembly trembly shaky!*" and danced her fork up to her mouth, sprinkling peas across the table to make them laugh.

"Eat your dinner, you two." Kit spooned peas onto Otto's plate and passed them back to Mel.

"Would you care for some peas, Miss Millicent?" Neeva asked regally.

"Oh, no thank you, dear," Mitzi said. "I couldn't possibly."

"What? No peas for the princess?"

"No thank you," Mitzi said, less playful when she sensed what was coming.

"Five years old. You have to take five bites of everything."

"She doesn't like peas, Ma," Mel said.

"My boys always cleaned their plates. I saw to that."

Kit tried hard to swallow a mouthful of crispy coating.

See Mel. See Mommy.

"They learned early on that you eat what's on the table or you go hungry."

"Mommy, I'm full!" Mitzi whined.

"You're excused, sweetie," Kit told her, concealing the untouched food on her plate with a crumpled napkin. "Why don't you run outside and play?"

Mitzi can run.

"Millicent Millicent, she's had her fillicent," Neeva made Mitzi giggle again and then shook her head. "Where on earth did you kids come up with that moniker?"

Run, Mitzi, run.

"I got it because of my great-great grandma, Millicent Jane Nolan, a true daughter of Texas," Mitzi recited for the millionth time.

"I've always thought it was cruel to give a child an unusual name."

"Mitzi," said Mel, "Mommy said you're excused."

"You're setting them up to get teased unmercifully."

"What's a mersa flea, Daddy?"

"And nobody ever knows how to spell it."

"Why don't you go outside and swing now?" Kit dipped her napkin in her water glass and scrubbed at the red Kool-Aid stain in the corner of Mitzi's mouth.

"She'll go through life always having to spell it out twice."

"Mitzi, M-I-T-Z-I, Mitzi!" Mitzi spelled.

"Ah ha! Very good, Miss Millicent," Neeva complimented, and they clicked their Kool-Aid again. "I've always thought you should call her 'Millie' for short. Call her 'Mitzi' and people are going to think she's Jewish."

"Mitzi Gaynor was a movie star. In *South Pacific*," Mitzi recited again. "Is she Jewish, Mama?"

"I don't know, sweetie, but there's nothing wrong with being Jewish."

"No, sweetie," Neeva mimicked, "we're all one big, happy, politically sanitized, ethnically balanced, and gender inclusive family. Just like on public television. Now that we've heard from the B'nai B'rith, would anyone care for coffee?"

Mel cleared his throat. "So . . . ummm . . . what's Butchy up to these days?"

"Butchy!" Otto came to life for a moment. It always startled Kit when he did that. "Say now, he's pulling down some real money these days."

"*OTTO!*" Neeva shouted, theoretically because Otto was getting deaf. "*DON'T TALK WITH YOUR MOUTH FULL. IT'S REVOLTING!*"

"Yeah, he's pulling down some real money, all right."

"*I ALREADY TOLD THEM THAT, OTTO,*" shouted Neeva. "*ARE YOU PART OF THE CONVERSATION OR NOT?* He's not even part of the conversation. We might as well have dinner with a lamppost."

"*HOW'S THE FISHING THIS YEAR, POP?*" Mel shouted.

"Say now," Otto's face lit up, but Neeva cut him off.

"Oh, he doesn't know anything about fishing around here anymore. He doesn't go anywhere. Just sits there on the porch glider. *Creak creak creak.* I don't know who needs the WD-40, him or the glider. *Creak creak creak.*"

"*HEY MA, I GOT—*" Mel realized he was still shouting and

lowered his voice. "I got the Falcon running last weekend."

"Oh my God, are you still tinkering with that scrap heap?"

"You oughta see it, Ma. Me and this guy from the hangar, we did the royal blue finish last month. Feels like silk. You gotta see it. I was gonna drive it down here this weekend, but—well, as soon as I get the transmission rebuilt, I'm gonna drive it down." He nodded and wiped his hands on his cutoffs. "This car is so sharp, Ma. It's so sharp it could cut diamonds."

"Well, I don't have any diamonds that need cutting just now, but thank you for thinking of us." Neeva dished potatoes from a carton onto Mel's plate and poured brown gravy over them. "I guess if you kids came down here more than twice a year, there'd be some kind of cataclysm."

"Well, we're pretty busy these days," Mel explained too thoroughly to ring true. "Cooper's got soccer and Scouts, and Mitzi has ballet and . . . Kit's been putting in a lot of extra hours."

Kit felt Big Jimmy's fried chicken decomposing in her stomach.

"Marnie's not working anymore," Neeva said, "with Butchy doing so well, there really isn't any need."

"Mom's not working anymore, either," Cooper piped up. "She got fired!"

"*Cooper,*" Kit and Mel hissed in unison.

Kit felt Neeva turn on her like a T-Rex detecting prey in motion.

"*Whaaaaat?* What's *this?* You got *fired?* From that silly little Norwegian gift shop? Now, how did you go and get yourself fired by some silly Scandinavian herring choker?"

Kit met Neeva's eyes, and there was an odd silence around the table.

The longer they looked at each other, the more certain Kit became that Neeva knew.

She knew everything.

Somehow, with her sharp-tongued, cancer-mother witchcraft, she looked right into Kit's soul and saw exactly what had happened.

"Well." Neeva placed a cigarette between her lips and flashed the lighter in front of her face. "I've always thought immigrants had a lot of nerve. Sure. Come to this country and put honest Americans out of work."

Kit had never heard Neeva speak gently like that. Like a mommy. It gave her the creeps.

"Okay . . . well. If everyone's finished—" Kit stood unsteadily, wanting to either throw her children in the car and head back to Houston or just plunge a steak knife into her heart and get it over with. Gathering plates and cups in a clumsy stack, she stumbled toward the kitchen.

"Do you know what I'm making up in my sewing room, Miss Millie?" Neeva said. "I'm making a little brown-eyed baby doll for a certain little brown-eyed girl I know."

"Me! Me!" Mitzi clapped.

"Tell your mommy to stop fussing with things, and we'll go see it."

"Mommy, stop fussing!" Mitzi commanded.

"You two go ahead," Kit said. "I'll just clear up a little."

"Just give it a lick and a promise," Neeva waved her hand over the greasy chicken buckets and wadded napkins. "We just need a little space to set the cake out. Now," she took Mitzi by the hand and started up the steps to the attic, where she was spending her retirement years piecing intricately patterned quilts with the same obsessive-compulsive precision that had made her a good mechanic in her day. "What color do you think this baby's dress should be?"

Mitzi discussed the possibilities in an animated way that charmed Neeva into relative docility for the rest of the afternoon.

Mel and Otto retired to the living room to finish their coffee, and Kit cleared the table. The dishwasher smelled dank, so she piled the plates on the counter and began running hot water. She flipped the garbage disposal on. Scraping Mitzi's potatoes and peas into the reverberating hollow, she felt an almost irresistible urge to stick her hand in after them.

"Any more coffee in here?"

Mel's voice over her shoulder startled her, and Mitzi's plate clattered in the sink.

"Oh. No, but I could make some," she added, thinking it wouldn't take an astrophysicist to see that she was hoping he'd volunteer to do it himself. Not because of the effort it would take, only so there would be a reason for him to hang out with her a little while.

"Okay." Mel looked around the room, but didn't see any reason to stay. "I guess I'll have some when it's ready."

"Okay."

"If you don't mind."

"Oh, no. No problem."

"Okay. Thanks."

"Sure," Kit nodded. "No problem."

He went back to the living room, and Kit turned back to the dishes.

When she was finished washing and drying, she wiped down all the cupboards, scoured the graying sink, and damp-mopped the thickened linoleum. She took a disposable table cover, plastic forks, and decorative paper plates they'd bought on the way down and spread them out in a fancy way with a fan of paper napkins, leaving a large space at the center of the table for the anniversary cake, and seizing the opportunity to surreptitiously scrub the stained sideboard and wipe the sticky chair backs.

When she was finished, she crept to the bottom of the stairs and sat down with her feet braced against the railing, feeling weary, fingers wrinkled from the dishwater, wishing she was flying down the beach in her old yellow Mustang or anywhere with Ander's arms around her. She closed her eyes and allowed herself to think about him for a moment, but not too much, because she knew she'd have to live off that one encounter for the rest of her life, and she didn't want it ever to lose the potent wave of supple feeling it was giving her now.

Smoke wafted and curled from the sewing room at the top of the stairs. Neeva was trying to teach Mitzi to sew on buttons, but Mitzi was busy sorting spools of thread, poking through the button box, begging for her favorite story.

Kit went back to the kitchen and made frozen fruit punch in the crystal punch set she and Mel had gotten as a wedding gift. When she returned to the stairwell, Neeva was already past the part where Psyche was spirited away to her lover's private castle.

"My other grandma says Arrows, not Cupid," Mitzi corrected Neeva's version.

"Well, I go by Bulfinch," Neeva informed her. "I can't be responsible for what sources other grandmas are turning to."

"And she said he only came home at nighttime."

"That's right. Hand me the scissors there, Midget."

"If it was dark, how did she know it was him?"

"By his—because— She recognized his voice, I suppose. Didn't your mommy teach you to hand someone scissors handle first?"

"Grandma, don't you think that would be stupid if the husband only came around in the dark? 'Cause he would have to mow the lawn in the dark. Or else make her do it in the daytime."

"Well, that's true, Miss Millicent, and Psyche wasn't the last girl to figure that out just a little too late," Neeva said, biting off the thread as she spoke. "Anyway, that was the arrangement. But Psyche was a very bad girl."

"My other grandma says Psyche was a very *brave* girl."

"Well, she was a *bad* girl. She disobeyed the rules. She just had to take a peek. So she sneaked up on him while he was sleeping, and she opened her lantern just a crack . . ."

"And he was beautiful to see, wasn't he, Grandma? And she wanted to give him a little kiss." That made Mitzi giggle.

"Yes, Miss Millie," Neeva sighed, "but a drop of oil from the lantern burned him, and he woke up and flew away."

"That part is silly," Mitzi giggled again. "Husbands can't fly."

"Well, most husbands are too fat and old. But Cupid had wings. Oops! Don't touch the quilts, Miss Millie. Those are just for looking at." Kit heard the clap of Neeva's hands on her lap. "Well. Time for Rush Limbaugh."

The radio clicked and hummed for a moment, then cleared into the complaining telephone voice of a disgruntled dittohead.

Kit stood and stretched and went to the living room, where Otto had turned the TV up to blasting—a blessing, because Mel had eaten way too much and was breaking wind like a bull-horn.

"Mel?" Kit suggested as gently as possible, "Maybe you should go for a walk or something."

"HEY, POP!" Mel shouted. *"WANNA WALK DOWN TO THE STORE? I'M GONNA GO GET SOME ROLAIDS OR SOMETHING."*

"Nah," Otto waved him off, "I don't need Rolaids."

Mel shrugged and sat down in the recliner with a loud *snark* that Kit wanted to believe was the leather squawking.

"Hey, Coop!" Otto clicked the TV off. "Why don't you and me head down to the store and get a Snickers bar?"

"All right!" Cooper would agree to anything if you covered it with chocolate. "Are you coming, Dad?"

"Nah, he don't need a candy bar," Otto said. "Look at 'im! He's bigger'n the house."

As the screen door banged behind them, Kit knelt in front of the recliner and put her arms around Mel's waist.

"Geez," he breathed unsteadily.

"You're doin' good, honey," she said, cuddling him like Cooper. "You're doin' great."

"You, too."

He stroked the back of her head, and she turned her face inward to kiss his palm.

"We'll leave first thing in the morning," he said. "We'll take the kids over to the beach at Matagorda, okay?"

"Yeah," she murmured into his wide hand. "We'll do that, honey. That's a great idea."

Mel let loose a prodigious fart.

"Sorry," he mumbled. "Had to be said."

❧

There were ducks in Mother Daubert's kitchen now, marching in little yellow rows, stencilled with a blue-and-white checkered border above the chair rail, beaks angled open, miming happy quacks above the drone of the dishwasher.

"What happened to the cows?" Kiki asked.

"Oh, Daddy didn't care for them, so I had it redone again."

Mother Daubert tied an apron over the beaded front of a western style jumpsuit that provided the perfect pedestal for her arid Tammy Wynette hairdo. She moved along the counter, adjusting the canisters and can opener and ceramic duck cookie jar in a perfect line, so the shadows just barely touched the imported tile backsplash.

"It was so silly of me. All the girls at the club said, 'How could you have your entire kitchen redone twice in three months?' but I forgot Daddy and his lactose intolerance, you know. He said, 'Mother, it gives me indigestion just looking at all those spots and udders.'"

She pulled a paper towel from the duck-shaped dispenser, polished at the pristine refrigerator, then replaced the magnets, carefully setting them largest to smallest, along the top of the freezer door. Kiki wasn't sure why they were there. Instead of holding up jumbles of grocery lists and phone messages and children's drawings, they clung directly to the sterile white surface like unfertilized eggs laid out for scientific examination. Mother Daubert finished setting them in place, measured with her eye, straightened one or two, and then used the paper towel to open the freezer door, as though she were a jewel thief protecting her fingerprints.

She took out a blue gel Medipac and pressed it under Kiki's jaw.

"Do you know my delphiniums are still blooming?" she said. "Seems like we didn't know the word 'winter' this year."

Kiki slipped a napkin between the pack and her skin, so the pack wouldn't come away sticky from her heavy makeup that apparently was not heavy enough. She prepared to deliver an amusing anecdote about being dizzy from morning sickness, taking a spill, cat under her feet, new high heels, corner of the cupboard. She had practiced it in the shower mirror that morning and visualized it later, in the car on the way over. She was proud of her talent for making it sound funny, her special blend of Erma Bombeck exasperation and Gracie Allen ditz.

"How is your mother doing?" Mother Daubert asked, boosting at her pouffy hair in the reflective door of the micro-wave.

"Just fine. Doing real well." Kiki tried to answer without displacing the soothing cold pack. "Although— Well, I'm a little concerned. I haven't been able to talk with her for a while."

"Well, I suppose, what with the children and church and all your responsibilities," Mother Daubert sympathized. "It's a busy time. First your mother and then your sister being sick and needing you and all."

Kiki nodded and studied the side of the sink where the grout was toothbrushed to a blinding white.

"Maybe you can make another little trip down there when she's all finished with her treatment. Only this time, all four of you. A real family vacation. You could go to Disney World!"

"Yes," Kiki said. "That would be fun."

"I'm sure she'd love to see the children. Nothing to speed one's recovery like having the children close by, filling up the house with sunshine. You know, when our Wayne was little, I had a dizzy spell, and as soon as I got home from the hospital, Lorenza—we still had our Lorenza then—she set me out in the yard with the flowers and a tall glass of ice tea, and I just sat there watching my little Whipper playing in the baby pool, building castles in his little sandbox. He'd find a cicada shell or a magnolia cone or whatever he'd come across, and he'd come running over, 'Mama! Mama! See what I got for you!' He called them 'yard treasures.' And he'd put his arms around me so gently, stroke my cheek—just like this—with his soft baby hands, and he'd say, 'Poor Mama fall down and hurt herself.' I never knew such a sensitive child. Perfect little angel. And smart! Lorenza was teaching us both to speak Spanish, and he could say, 'Mucho gusto en verle!' just like a little señor. And Lorenza . . . You know, without her, I don't think I could have . . ."

Mother Daubert pulled another paper towel free and spritzed spray cleaner on it.

"Do you know, I've been diluting this 409 cleaner half-to-half and it works every bit as well as full strength? There's a little money-saving tip for you," she offered.

Mother Daubert was real big on little money-saving tips, especially for someone who'd never pumped her own gas once in her life. She diluted fruit juice and shuffled generic cereals into name-brand boxes, dealing coupons across the checkout stand like a Vegas high roller.

"I . . . I usually use Fantastik," said Kiki.

"He's still very sensitive." Mother Daubert rubbed around the edge of a drip pan on the stove. "Always bringing flowers and calling me every day. And how many of the girls wish their grandbabies came over every Saturday evening for supper? I couldn't ask for a sweeter son. 'You could not ask for a sweeter son,' the girls always say to me, 'I wish I had a son who was as sensitive and sweet as all that!' and I say, 'It's a blessing is what it is. It's a gift from God.'"

Kiki shifted the cold pack to her cheekbone.

"When I was pregnant with him, I had some trouble, you know. I got dizzy and took a spill. Cracked three ribs. The doctor said, 'If this child is born at all, it'll be a miracle from God' is what he said. He was born almost six weeks early. I bled so bad, they had to take everything. Back in those days, they'd just take everything, you know, and I said, 'Go ahead,' is what I said. I said, 'I've got my little miracle, I don't need any more.' And of course, Daddy was thrilled. He was so dearly wanting a son. He was so in hopes he'd have a son to follow in his path at the law firm someday. He had only girls with his first wife, you know. Just the three girls. That was a great disappointment to him. I'll tell you this," she added in hushed confidence, "I'm not so sure it didn't have a little something to do with their divorce."

Mother Daubert took the cold pack from Kiki and put it back in the freezer. She sat down at the table and straightened the mallard salt and pepper shakers on either side of the grass and cattail napkin dispenser.

"Well," she said. "Isn't this nice?"

Kiki smiled.

"Real nice," Mother Daubert repeated, "real nice. Everything back to normal."

"Mm-hmm," Kiki nodded agreeably, though it hurt her jaw to smile.

"You know," Mother Daubert said, folding her hands in her lap, "I missed our Saturday suppers while you were off visiting. At your mother's, I mean. It's so nice to see you two together. You make such a handsome family. And the children. Wayne was just lost without you, you know. He was just desperately lonesome."

"Yes," Kiki said. "Me too."

"I ask myself what my life would be like if I didn't have Daddy, and I just can't imagine."

"No."

"I suppose you're as busy as can be, now."

"Oh, yes."

"Catching up on things, laundry, garden. Always something to do."

"Mm-hmm."

"A woman's work is never done, they say."

"No, it's true."

The duck-shaped clock ticked its minute wing forward one notch.

"Well," Mother Daubert said.

They sat quietly until it ticked again.

"Well."

She layered Kiki's hands between her own, which were powder soft, except for the cool metal of her spiny diamond anniversary ring.

"You know what we should do?" she whispered.

Kiki shook her head.

"We should sneak those last two pieces of cherry cheesecake."

"Oh. I really shouldn't."

"Could you tell I experimented? I just got silly with it! Can you tell the difference? I made the crust with gingersnaps instead of Nilla Wafers. Can you imagine? Just dropped them into the food processor with some butter and—*kerbingo!* And Daddy said, 'What on earth?' he said, 'What happened to the Nilla Wafers?' and I told him, '*I* felt like gingersnaps!' I said. I said, 'I guess I can use gingersnaps if I feel like it!' And didn't it turn out yummy?"

"Yes," Kiki nodded.

"The gingersnaps really give it that little extra zip."

"Yes. It was really . . . it was delicious, Mother Daubert, but I can't."

"You can afford a tiny sliver," Mother Daubert coaxed, "you're eating for two now. Me—I'm the one who shouldn't. You know how I love my rich desserts, but at my age, those calories go straight to my b-u-t-t!" she whispered naughtily, her hand cupped beside her mouth, still Southern Lady enough to blush and spell. She'd been bred with an invincible brand of careful cotillion charm, and that gentility stood impenetrable to the harsh blurting world. "Daddy says, 'Better watch that girlish figure, Mother.' And I know it plays ping-pong with my blood pressure, but still—I just can't resist a sliver of something sweet in the evening."

Kiki smiled and gazed longingly at the cheesecake.

"C'mon now, I know you want some."

"No, thank you, Mother Daubert."

"Oh, a little corner." Mother Daubert was already unwrapping the glass pie plate from the refrigerator. "Just a little corner?"

"No, really. I can't."

"Just a sliver." She dished a large portion onto a dessert plate and set it on Kiki's yellow place mat.

"Mother Daubert, Wayne won't like it."

"Oh." Her expression was torn, but not confused. "No, of course not, and here I am, tempting you with this awful junk food. I'm sorry, dear."

She snatched the plate back and slid the cheesecake into the garbage disposal, flipping it on and rinsing the sink with the spray gun.

"It's just— He's concerned for my weight, what with the baby and all."

"Of course! He's concerned for your health. That's just how he is. His father was always very solicitous of me that way. Very attentive and concerned. I suppose that's where he gets his sensitive side."

Mother Daubert sat down across from her at the breakfast table and placed her palms on the duck-and-duckling tablecloth. They sat that way as the dishwasher cycled through and stopped, and the clock duck's wing dipped lower and then back up toward the hour. They both glanced up when they heard footsteps on the back porch, and Kiki flinched slightly when Wayne called out to the children, telling them it was time to go.

"Well," Kiki bolted from her chair. "I guess it's time to go."

Wayne called again, telling them to *climb down outa that plum tree and get in the car.*

"I wish they wouldn't dawdle," Kiki fretted.

"Oh, I know how they are at that age," Mother Daubert said. "But they have to learn, don't they?"

"Yes."

"You can't spare the rod."

"No."

"Poor babies. All this—this upset. It's probably . . . upsetting."

Kiki peered into the dusky yard, willing Oscar to swing down from the plum branches, wishing she was hiding with him in the high, leafy silence.

"But everything's back to normal now," Mother Daubert said.

Kiki nodded.

"Everything's going to be fine."

She scrubbed at a spot on the spotless tablecloth.

Kiki nodded again, but she could feel her face turning bleak, the aching muscles in her face too tired to hold up the pleasant expression. Wayne and Daddy Daubert laughed out on the porch.

"It'll be fine," Mother Daubert whispered, and Kiki nodded.

"I know," she said. "It will be. It is. Fine. Only . . ." she searched Mother Daubert's soft gray eyes. "How long—I mean, does it ever . . ."

Kiki impulsively threw her arms around Mother Daubert. Her bouffant hair smelled faintly of perfume, and the embrace was like holding the kind of stuffed animal you might win at the fair: light as sawdust, brittle stitches, an unnatural brightness of color, and stiff instead of soft, like you'd expect it to be.

"There's something I want you to have."

Mother Daubert pulled away and dragged a little folding step ladder from the broom closet, using it to climb up and reach the camouflaged half-cupboard above the oven hood.

"This was part of my mother's tea service," she said, straining toward the back of the shelf. "Sterling silver. I want you to have it. I've been saving it ever since Wayne was a baby. First Lorenza and I . . . and then after she was deported— But I want you to have it now."

Kiki looked at her curiously as she teetered and backed down the stepladder and set the silver sugar bowl on the table. It was large and tarnished, plainly made and not very pretty.

"Oh . . . ," Kiki said. "Why, Mother Daubert, it's just . . . lovely."

"I want you to have it," Mother Daubert said deliberately.

"Well, thank you."

"*It's for you,*" Mother Daubert whispered, pushing it toward her.

"Yes. Thank you so much."

Mother Daubert nodded and pushed it closer.

"Yes. Well. Thank you so much."

Feeling some kind of big response was expected, Kiki took the silver bowl in her hands and held it up to admire it for a moment.

"It's really, really . . . lovely, Mother Daubert," she said, lifting the lid. "Just love—"

She breathed in when she saw the thick cylinder of tightly rolled bills inside.

Turning her back toward Kiki, Mother Daubert busied herself, putting away the stepladder, rearranging the quilted duck-and-tulip pot holders on small silver hooks above the stove, straightening the flatware in the drawer.

"Well, I'm just going to throw caution to the breeze this evening," she said, opening the refrigerator and pulling the Saran Wrap from the pie shell. "Are you sure you won't have just a sliver?"

⚘

Butch and Marnie arrived after six with their four-year-old daughter, Trudy, and Butch's son, Blake. It was a relief to have reinforcements, even though Butch had been drinking and Marnie looked like a gerbil in a cage and Kit was afraid of Blake's influence on Cooper. He was fourteen and only in the sixth grade, the quintessential BB-gun-toting, freckle-sporting, small town Texas middle school bully. But Trudy provided some distraction for Mitzi, and Kit kept reminding herself of tomorrow morning and the blessed thundering quiet of the waves at Matagorda.

"Well, Marnie," she said, moving a gritty ashtray off the arm of the couch, "we didn't know you were expecting."

"Oh, mm-hmm. We're expecting, all right," Marnie said, and she and Kit killed a little time with the standard so-you're-expecting conversation.

"When are you due?"

"Next month."

"How are you feeling?"

"Oh, fine."

"Did you get an ultrasound?"

"Oh, yes. Everything's fine."

"I bet Butch is really hoping for a boy this time."

"Yes, he sure is."

"Do you have names picked out?"

"Probably nothing as poetic as 'Millicent.'" Neeva came in and put the ashtray back on the arm of the couch. "Who wants cake?"

"Grandma," Mitzi tugged on her sleeve. "I'm making you an anniversary card. How do you spell your name?"

"M-U-D."

Mitzi painstakingly wrote it down.

"How do you spell Grampa's name?"

"O-T-T-O! O-T-T-O!" Her voice dipped up and then down. "Same coming as it is going. 'Toot' turned inside out. Ot-to." Her cigarette tipped downward from her mouth, making her look very sad all of the sudden. "That's Otto."

"What number do I put?"

"Zero, Miss Millicent. Put a big fat zero."

"Nooooo," Mitzi giggled. "How many years of anniversary?"

"Fifty-three."

"Oh, no!" Kit cried. "When I ordered the cake, I—I thought you said fifty-four, Neeva. I told them fifty-four. I'm sorry."

"I said fifty-four." Neeva shrugged and lit a cigarette. "I subtract a year sometimes."

"Why?" Marnie asked timidly.

"Because, Marnie dear, some years are better off forgotten." She stubbed the cigarette in the ashtray.

"Let's have it," she sighed and prodded Otto, who was dozing in the recliner. *"OTTO! CAKE!"*

Neeva sat at the head of the table, hacking away oddly shaped servings of marble cake, Kit stood at her elbow slooping out scoops of swiftly melting ice cream, and Marnie focused fiercely on the production of another pot of coffee. Mitzi and Trudy tore around, under the influence of too much sugar. Kit worried about the whereabouts of Blake and Cooper. Neeva opened the tray from Kit and Mel. Otto drew his glasses down to the tip of his nose, examining the check from Butch and Marnie. Finally, there was a moment of silence that felt so void, Kit burst into a compulsive chorus of "Happy Anniversary to You" and then absolutely insisted that everyone have seconds on cake.

Mel and Butch took theirs out on the front porch and sat on the glider. Butch was five years older and it showed, but other than that, the two brothers were virtually identical. They were talking about (what else?) the Falcon, and Butch was giving Mel some pointers on how he might goose that transmission into action.

"Look at those two," Neeva said. "Before and after."

"After what?" Marnie asked, genuinely not getting it.

"I can see we're breeding another generation of Prizer intellect. Jump into the gene pool, honey. Water's fine."

There was boisterous laughter from the front porch. Butch was telling Mel some crude joke, by the sound of it. Neeva stood at the window, smoking and watching them.

"It isn't right," she muttered and shook her head. "It shouldn't be this way."

Kit knew she was talking about Teddy. It usually started toward evening. She hoped Mel would stay out there with Butch. Just stay out there, honey, she willed him, stay out there, Mel.

"Hey," Mel let the screen door bang behind him on his way in, and Neeva's back went rigid. "What are you girls gabbing about in here?"

"Babies," Butch said. "That's all we're allowed to talk about these days. Babies in pink, babies in blue, babies in strollers that cost more than your damn car." He elbowed Mel in the side. "Babies eating lunch at your favorite restaurant."

"Yeah, but you can still enjoy lookin' at the menu, huh?" Mel elbowed him back, and they snickered like they were in the boys' locker room.

"Mel, please," Kit chided. She could tell Marnie wasn't amused.

"Oh, pardon us, Miss Kitty," Butch said. "I guess we're not fit for polite company, little brother."

"Sorry, babe." Mel leaned down and kissed her in an annoying, dismissive, Me-big-heterosexual-guy-you-Jane kind of way. "We just came in to get another beer."

"So go get us a couple o' beers, woman!" Butch hollered.

Kit wanted to smack him.

Mel laughed heartily, and Kit wanted to smack him, too, even though he clapped Butch on the shoulder and said, "I'll get 'em."

"Why don't I?" Marnie offered, grateful for any reason to get out of there.

"You boys better cut yourselves off," Neeva warned, and she wasn't joking. "I won't have drunks out on my front porch."

"Relax, Ma," Butch said. "Nobody's getting drunk on a coupla beers."

"That behavior might be fine for the marines, but I won't have it out on my front porch."

"Don't start on the marines, Ma," Butch darkened. He did sound drunk.

"Hey," Mel cut in, "you know what we should do? We should dig up a deck of cards."

"When did I start on the marines?" Neeva pressed her hand to her chest in innocence. "I have nothing to say about the marines."

"We should dig up a deck of cards and play some cribbage."

"God bless the marines!" Neeva declared, "Semper feeeee."

"I mean it, Ma," Butch warned. "Mel and I did our duty, same as—"

"Fee fi fo fum."

"Hey, Butchie, huh? What about a game of crib?"

"Maybe, they'd have taught him to be a man in the marines," Butch postured, "instead of some pansy-ass—"

"C'mon, Butchy, huh? Remember, Ma?" Mel was begging like a puppy, "Remember how we all used to sit out on the porch and play crib?"

"They teach a man to be a gentleman in the air force," Neeva said. "They teach a man to live with some dignity."

"Did they teach him to die with dignity, too, Ma?"

"Butch," Mel implored.

"Did they teach him that in the precious fuckin' air force?"

"You watch your mouth, young man," her voice quavered.

"But he's a saint, and we're shit because we came home and—"

"*Butch!*" Mel stepped between them. "Enough. Ma, he didn't mean it, okay? Butchy, c'mon. Let's just go outside, man, all right? Let's go on out and have a beer."

He shoved his older brother through the screen door, farting loudly just as it clapped shut behind them.

"Hmm," Neeva pursed her lips in disgust. "Another small country heard from."

"Well," Marnie hedged, "I think we should probably get going."

"You. Just. Got. Here." Neeva gestured with her cigarette as if she were underlining each word on a chalkboard.

"Well, I—I know, but—umm, I've been really tired lately and . . . and my obstetrician said I should keep my feet elevated."

"Here." Neeva pushed an ottoman across the floor with her foot. "Elevation. Sixteen inches above sea level. Probably the highest point in Southeast Texas."

"Thanks."

Marnie shrank back into her chair and gingerly propped her feet up.

They sat, picking at their cake and skiffing noncommittal chitchat back and forth across the coffee table until ten-thirty when Marnie manufactured some reason to be out in the kitchen, and Neeva excused herself to the "little girls' room." Otto was sleeping in the recliner, his top teeth slipping down, forming the off-kilter grin of a skeleton in his slack mouth. Outside the screen door, Butch and Mel were swinging on the glider, Mitzi and Trudy asleep on their laps. They were definitely drunk now, making up limericks and laughing. Being too loud. Kit shifted uncomfortably in the doorway, not wanting to embarrass Mel, but worried that all that base and debasing humor, not to mention the smell of all that beer, might be entering into Mitzi's alpha state.

" . . . he thought he could ride it,
but fell down inside it,
and that's the last dat was seen of da minah!"

Butch cracked up at his own punch line, and Mel fairly
howled, but then hushed, "Shh . . . keep it down, man. Kit's
gonna kill me."

Butch said something she couldn't hear, and they laughed
even harder at that.

"Oh, geez," Mel gasped. "Ah . . . geez."

"Oh, shit." Butch wiped his eyes. He shifted Trudy over to
his other shoulder and rested his cheek on top of her head.
"Christ, Mel. Ma's right. Teddy should be here."

"Yeah." Mel put his hand on Butch's shoulder, and the
glider creaked back and forth.

"God, I miss him sometimes."

"Me too, Butch. And I miss you, too."

"Well, drag your ass down here once in a while," Butch
complained.

"Why don't you drag your ass up to Houston?" Mel countered.

"Oh yeah, Miss Kitty would really love that."

"I'll handle Kit," Mel said as if he did it all the time.

"I bet you will," Butch poked him in the side. "And I bet
you'll like doin' it, too."

"Shut up," Mel snickered and pushed his hand away, but
Butch kept digging his finger at Mel's big stomach.

"Here Kitty, Kitty, Kitty—"

"Knock it off, ya sleazeball."

"Nice pussy, pussy, pussy—"

"I mean it, Butch. Just lay off her."

"I'd rather lay on her."

"I said, shut up!" Mel wasn't playing anymore.

"Geez," Butch made a puffing sound with his lips, "you
don't have to get bent about it."

"I'm not, but geez . . . Don't say that kind of shit about my wife, okay?"

"Fine. Geez."

Butch finished off his beer. Mel took one more swallow off his and set the bottles on the floor below the glider.

"Why don't I give you guys a ride home?" he asked.

"Nah. You're in worse shape than I am, little brother."

"Kit wouldn't mind driving—"

"Christ! No thanks," Butchy waved off the suggestion, and there was an uncomfortable silence until Butch said, "We'll let Trudy drive. What d'ya say, Trudes? Wanna drive the old man home?" Butch waved her lifeless hand and made a falsetto voice. "Shame on you, Daddy! You're shit-faced!" And they cracked up again.

"Seriously though, Butchy," Mel said.

"I know. I know. It's okay. I'll let Marnie drive. Designated preggo."

"Butch," Marnie pushed past Kit and opened the screen door, "you know I hate that word. Especially in front of Trudy."

"Sorry," he mumbled.

His bravado seemed to dissipate somewhat when the light from the living room cracked open the still night air around the swing.

"Butch, I need to go home. Now." Marnie turned wearily to Kit. "Sorry to leave you guys, but I think we're at the saturation point."

"Don't worry about it," Kit said. "You need to take care of yourself."

"We'll see you in the morning, okay?" Butch slung Trudy over his shoulder.

"We're taking off first thing," Mel said, as if he fully expected to be up and functioning hangover-free before noon.

"Yeah, well. Catch ya in the morning then," Butch told his brother.

Kit rolled her eyes in the dark. How many times had she

heard this exchange? Now, Mel would say, yeah, great, see ya in the morning, and then, without ever having to actually say goodbye, Butch and Marnie would leave. But invariably, the following morning, Kit would sit at the kitchen table listening to the coffee turn to acid in her stomach, struggling to make conversation with Neeva while the front half of the day ticked by, and Mel snored like a rototiller upstairs, and Butch and Marnie were nowhere to be seen.

The following morning, Butch and Marnie were nowhere to be seen, but Mel surprised her, nudging her awake a little after six.

It was still dark in the room he had shared with Teddy once upon a time. Books and balls and Tonka trucks slumbered on the dusty shelves. A bas-relief map of Texas was propped on top of the dresser along with a Popsicle-stick replica of the Alamo and Teddy's swimming trophies and Mel's model cars. Mitzi and Coo were still breathing evenly inside their sleeping bags on the floor, and Kit was deep in dreaming something about Ander and the underside of the blue hoosier when she became aware of Mel rubbing himself against the small of her back. She hadn't heard him creep across the hardwood floor, stepping over the Erector Set and baseball bats to sardine himself in with her on the single bed. An old screen door opened in Kit's dream when the metal springs *skreeked* and sagged under their combined weight. As she became conscious, the random creakiness settled into a soft, squeaky pattern. Mel found his way inside her and took up his familiar rhythm. She pushed back to meet him, bracing her hands against the Raquel Welch poster on the wall, and he moaned low in his throat.

Raquel smiled down on them, dressed in a feral bikini, bronzed and beautiful, rising from the spangled blue surf. Her hand was poised in such a way that she might have only just reached out of the photograph to inscribe the blessing beside her sloping hipbone.

"To Teddy," it was signed, "Come home safely. All my

love, Raquel."

But the seductive benediction was not enough for Teddy. Despite all his prayers and imaginings, he was about to get laid by the other kind of bombshell.

He put the poster up during his last leave home and, at twenty-one years of age, was shipped off to Cambodia, never to return. He never again laughed with his brothers on the swing, never played another hand of cribbage on the summer porch, never woke before dawn, silent in the single bed, one hand pressed against the exquisite thigh of the goddess, the other orchestrating a squeaky rhythm, as he envisioned himself doing exactly what Mel was doing right now.

"Honeymoon over already?"

Kit almost dropped her coffee cup. She hadn't seen Neeva sitting at the dark kitchen table, but now she noticed the smell of cigarettes and the wisps of smoke curling up in front of the dawn-lit window.

"I'm sorry," Kit didn't know how else to answer. "Did we wake you?"

"No."

Kit knew they hadn't. As soon as she turned on the light over the stove, she could tell that, if Neeva had been to bed at all, she hadn't bothered to undress.

"Sit on down," Neeva said. "Take a load off, Annie."

Kit sat.

"God, he's getting huge." Neeva drew deeply on her cigarette. "He must crush the life out of you."

Anything Kit could have said in response would have felt like talking dirty out on the porch swing, so she just sipped her coffee.

"Why don't you put him on a diet before he drops dead of a stroke?"

"I can't make up his mind for him," Kit said. "He'll do

something about it when he's ready."

At least, that's what he kept telling her when they argued about it. Two weeks ago, Kit would have said it was the biggest problem in their marriage, though of course, she wouldn't have said it to Neeva.

"I don't know why he listens to Butch about that tranny." Neeva crushed the cigarette onto her coffee saucer and fished another one out of the pack. "Butch doesn't know anything about rebuilding a tranny. But does he ask me? Nooooo. I'm just an old lady. What do I know of things mechanical? Just because I spent all of World War II inside the belly of a B-29 and the next thirty years under an eighteen-wheeler—what do I know about rebuilding a tranny? I was only the best damn mechanic Shankow-Turner ever had." She nodded, and the glow of her lighter cast deep shadows under her eyes. "They got rid of all the other girls after the war. But not me. They knew I was good. They knew I was smart. They kept me on before anybody ever heard of a 'maternity leave.' They kept me on, and they knew why. They might not have admitted it, but they knew. The foreman, Frank Dupuis, told me on more than one occasion. They didn't want me to quit in '74 when I had my breasts off, either. They kept saying, 'She'll be back.' But I knew I wouldn't. I knew I was done." She shook her head, then shrugged. "That was after Teddy. I didn't think I'd live through it, because I didn't want to. But I did," she sighed. "And here I am. And I'd bet money it's the linkage to the transaxle. But does he ask me? Noooooo." She shook her head, bottom lip out. "Nobody asks the old lady anything anymore. But I used to be regarded as a woman of intelligence. A woman of faith. A woman of beauty. I was just like you, Kit."

Kit shuddered at the very thought.

"Men always marry women just like their mothers. That way, they never have to grow up," Neeva went on. "On the other hand, look at Marnie. There's no comparison between me and that mousey little pip-squeak. Butch's first wife, though—

Arlis? Did you ever get to meet her?"

"No," Kit said, though she'd answered that question a hundred times before, and she wasn't sure her attendance was required for the conversation to continue, anyway.

"What—a—bitch," Neeva pronounced. "She had her pruning shears ready when she saw him coming. It drove him to drink. Drove him to see other women. And that divorce was one for the talk shows. Very nasty. Every bit of their filthy laundry flying out on the clothesline of open court. Neither one of them wanted custody of Blake. They asked me to take him, but I'd have sooner brought Charles Manson home and adopted him."

Kit kept wishing she'd hear one of the kids come padding down in their footie pj's, wanting some presweetened, junk-food cereal, dry in a cup, so they could sit on the floor in front of the TV and munch on it while Kit got their things together, and Mel loaded the car, and they could all just get in and go to Matagorda.

"Anxious to get out of here?" Neeva asked.

"No. No, of course not."

"You keep looking at the hallway, glancing around—*glance glance*. He won't be down for hours. Men release a chemical into their bloodstream, you know. Right after. It makes them sleep. Don't say God never did womankind any favors." She gave Kit a confidential sideways look and sucked her cigarette down to the filter. "He'll be down in a couple hours. Then I'm going to make you kids some breakfast. Pancakes."

She nodded to seal the announcement and poured a cup from the Mr. Coffee that nobody could say they gave her.

"You know how Melvin loves his pancakes. 'Your daddy always loved his pancakes.' That's what I told Cooper and Millicent." She held the cup out as if to raise a toast. "Cooper and Millicent. What a couple of bizarre monikers to hang on your offspring. I don't know what you kids were thinking. I told the girls on the bowling league, 'I don't know what those kids were thinking.' Then I reminded myself that I was talking about a Sugar Land girl named Kitten Amaryllis. I said, 'Melvin must have married some flower child throw-back to the 1960s.'" She moved her cup off the saucer to make way for the cigarette butt. "Of course, you're too young to throw back to the '60s, aren't you? I laid eyes on you that first time, I said, 'My God, he's robbed the cradle. She's a baby. May and December. He's fifteen years older than she is.'"

"No," Kit said, "just . . . twelve."

"Oh, well then! What's a dozen years, give or take. Combined with the fact that he's practically begging for a coronary." She lit another cigarette, then asked the lighter, "Which one will be the merry widow?" She set it down and spun it on the table, and it stopped with the click mechanism pointing toward Kit. "You win."

"Wow. Look at the time." Kit got up and set her cup in the sink. "I think I'll just go up and roust my gang out of bed."

"It's only seven-thirty. My God. Good thing you're not in a hurry."

"Well, we were thinking about stopping in Matagorda."

"Fine," Neeva waved her aside. "Get them up. Go."

"Well, I didn't mean we have to leave this second—"

"Obviously, you have better things to do than sit around with the old lady."

"Neeva—"

"*Kit-ten!* Go on! No one's begging you to stay." She closed her eyes and put her cigarette to her narrow lips, cheeks concave with the deep inhalation. "No one's inviting you to come back, either."

"Neeva . . ." Kit sat down and placed her palms on the table. "Why does this always have to be so hard?"

Neeva expelled her smoky breath as if Kit had punched her in the stomach.

"Ask your husband," she said, and it sounded like the air was all in the top part of her chest, sewn in by the scars of the mastectomy. "You just ask him *'why?'* He's the one who took off for seventeen years. Never let me know if he was alive or dead. He's the one who came waltzing back with a wife and kid. *Hey, I'm home! Drop everything and look at me! I'm part of the family again!* But where was he when I had cancer? Where was he the day of his brother's funeral?"

"Neeva, you know it was too late when he found out, or he would have been there. It kills him that he wasn't able to be there!"

"But he didn't have any trouble popping in six months later to pick up Teddy's Falcon. Teddy's first—his *only* car. Into which, I might add, I had just dropped a *brand new engine.*"

"Oh, Neeva, you know that wasn't—"

"He didn't have to go into the marines in the first place! A family sends two boys off to a war—oh, excuse me, a *police action*—and the third one doesn't have to go. He *wanted* to go! He thought the damn jungle was preferable to his own—"

"What's going on?" Mel wandered into the kitchen, scratching his stomach, so disheveled with early morning that even the clean T-shirt didn't look clean on him. "Kit?"

"Nothing. I just—I'm sorry, Mel," she stammered, "I—I said something stupid and upset your mother."

"Oh, no!" Neeva mocked fluttering her hands on either side of her head. *"Oh, my God, Mel! I'm so sorry! I upset the old lady!"*

"Ma, c'mon—"

"I was going to make breakfast for you, Melvin! *Pancakes!* But if you're in such a damn hurry, then just go. Go on! Get out of my house!"

"Kit, get the kids ready to go," Mel said quietly.

"No!" Neeva spun up from her chair and into the kitchen. "I *am* making pancakes!" She threw the refrigerator open, clanged a cast-iron skillet out of the stove.

"I am making pancakes for breakfast, and you are going to sit here and eat them. It's the least you owe me!"

"Oh, yeah." Mel rubbed his hand over his face. "I knew we

couldn't spend twenty-four hours in this house without hearing about what I owe you."

"Did I mention it?" Neeva protested, her voice high and breathy with indignation. "Did I mention it at any time? Why, I thought we'd all forgotten all about it! After all, what's a silly little car in the bosom of a loving family? What does some silly old automobile matter? You went off to live your life, you totaled the car. It's gone. It's all in the history books now."

"Ma, I told you before. If you want me to replace the car or figure out a way to pay you back—"

"How do you propose to pay me back for all the hours I put into that car? And why should you? Why should you pay me back or ask me how to fix your transmission or visit here once in a while?" Neeva started weeping, and it was like watching the implosion of a grand old hotel. "You never think about anyone but yourself. You never have. And I don't know where you got it. Teddy was never selfish that way! Teddy never put a scratch on that Falcon when he was driving it! Teddy never left us wondering where he was year after year—"

"No, Ma, Teddy went and got his head blown off—"

"Oh, Mel," Kit covered her face with her hands.

"—so he didn't have a chance to disappoint you—"

"Mel, please."

"—and you didn't have a chance to drive him out of the house like you did me and Butch."

"And thank God," Neeva cried, "he never had a chance to become a big, fat, boozing slob like you and Butch!"

Kit ran upstairs to Mel's old room. She shoved all their clothes into the overnight bag and dragged Mitzi and Coo out of the Ninja Turtle sleeping bags.

"No," Cooper groaned. "I don't wanna get up."

"Mitzi, run in and go potty. Hurry!" Kit rolled the bags together and tied them with one quick knot.

"Mom," Cooper complained, "you have to zip it shut first. *Mom!* I don't want my sleeping bag touching *hers!*"

"Cooper," Kit warned, shoving the sleeping bags underneath his arm, "I said extra good behavior and cooperation, didn't I? Now you carry these down and get in the car. You obey me!"

"I'm hungry. I don't even have my clothes on."

"Mitzi?" Kit rapped on the bathroom door. "Mitzi, c'mon. Hurry up."

Mitzi opened the door, rubbing her watery eyes, fly-away hair going every direction.

"Daddy's yelling at Grandma," she said. "You told us they weren't going to fight today."

"I know, honey. C'mon. Let's just zip this up and hop in the car."

"You said fighting is naughty. You said people can't sass their mother."

"C'mon, guys. We'll stop and get dressed in a little while. We'll stop and eat and get dressed, okay, Coocaburra? C'mon. Daddy needs his big helpers right now."

"Dad said a bad word," Cooper whispered. "He said the F word."

"He did not," Mitzi defended him.

"I heard him, ya stupid little gnat. I guess I know what I heard."

"You're the stupid one! You big stupid lying . . . stupid . . . *poophead!*"

"Mitzi, that's enough! Coo honey, please, just take the sleeping bags down to the car. Okay, sweetie?"

"I'm not touching her bag! I don't want her smelly naked butt germs!"

"*Shut up!*" Mitzi shrieked.

"*Millicent Jane!* You *hush your mouth!* Cooper, stop devilling her."

"You didn't do it right, Mama!" Cooper struggled with the contorted sleeping bag. "It's all tangled up now!"

"Coo, it doesn't matter, honey. I'll straighten it out later."

"You can't! Now the zipper's off the track!" He threw the bag to the floor. "You're so stupid! You just break everything!"

Kit grabbed him by the arm and put her face very close to his.

"As you value your life, little boy," she menaced through gritted teeth, "you shut your mouth and get on down those stairs! *Right now!*"

With the overnight bag over her shoulder, Kit dragged them into the hallway. Mel and Neeva's voices were still escalating in the kitchen, but they were both shouting at once, so Kit hoped it would be a little more difficult for the children to understand what they were saying. She whisked them out the back door and stuffed them into the backseat.

"Buckle," she commanded. "I'll be right back."

She crept to the kitchen with Mel's dilapidated sneakers in her hand.

" . . . because it's not like you get a choice, Ma. It's not a fucking travel agency. I was a seventeen-year-old kid! They told me to go to Guam. I went to fucking Guam. I did my duty. I served my country."

"—and never gave one thought to Teddy or anyone else who was over there where the real war was going on—"

"It wasn't a *real war*, Ma! It was a *police action!* And I'd have gone there if I'd got sent there, but I didn't, and there's not a goddamn thing I could have done to help him if I had!"

"Mel?" Kit tried to be small, to stay out of the cross fire. She handed him the sneakers, and he pulled them on without any socks.

"Jesus Christ! You think I don't know you wish it would've been me instead of Teddy who came home in a box? You think *I* don't wish it would've been me instead?"

It twisted Kit's heart to hear him say it out loud.

"Are the kids in the car?" he asked her, and she nodded.

"No! No!" Neeva was weeping again. "You can't take them yet. You can't take them away without their pancakes!"

Mel pushed Kit out the door, and they got into the car.

"Ah, damn it! Shit!" His hands were trembling, and he dropped his tangle of keys on the floor.

"I wanted to make *pancakes!*" Neeva wailed from the kitchen steps.

"Oh, no! Ma, don't! *Ma!*"

Splakk.

A raw egg hit the windshield.

"Oh, *man* . . ." Mel threw the keys on the dashboard. "God *damn* it!"

Twisted shell, globulous yolk, and clear, viscous white slid down the outside of the glass toward the wiper blades.

"Go," Kit said. "Just go, honey!"

"I wanted to make them for *you*, Melvin!"

Splakk.

"Mel!" Kit seized the key and jammed it into the ignition. "Go!"

Gripping the wheel, Mel slammed the station wagon into reverse. It jerked back and to the side. One wheel cut up onto the lawn, and then they lurched forward and sped down the street to the end of the block. Ignoring a four-way stop, Mel steered toward the highway, eyes forward, jaw locked tight.

The backseat was silent.

Kit just breathed. She would wait a while, let him put some road into the rearview; then she'd slide across the center of the front seat to stroke his neck and speak gently to him about the sun sparkling like sequins on the water at Matagorda.

"Dang," Mitzi sighed. "We never get our pancakes."

❧

Kiki told them to pretend they were camping out, but Oscar didn't buy it. She told them how, if you slept in your clothes, you'd be ready to jump right up and play the next morning, but that didn't explain why she put their shoes in her purse or why she dumped the schoolwork out of their backpacks and put in favorite books, toothbrushes, Barbies, and action figures. She kissed them and came back later to close their bedroom door so they wouldn't hear the karaoke machine.

"*Diamonds . . . ooo I said diamonds . . . yes, diamonds are a girl's best friend . . .*"

She didn't do it only so he would fall asleep.

It was partly because she wasn't sure if anyone else would ever want to hear her sing or watch her take her clothes off and dance in nothing but a necklace. She wanted to please him, wanted him to please her.

Just a sliver of something sweet.

*K*iki traced the cursive neon with her finger, but it wasn't quite hot enough to burn.

Vivica Talent, it said, pinker than lip gloss and underlined with purple just in case there was a shadow of doubt left in anyone's mind.

Pressing her résumé and demo tape against her chest, Kiki walked the perimeter of the circular reception area, studying the pictures of people Vivica represented.

Pubescent blonde actresses and spokes-models beamed from their framed head shots. Pammy Thomas-Trent. "You watched her grow up on TV's 'My Neighbor Kate.' Now look for her in this year's action-adventure blockbuster 'No Prisoners!'"

There was a beaming mariachi band called El Cumpleaños, a beaming, blonde country singer named Cammi Terrell, the painfully clean-cut Dave Rossy Trio, beaming along with an entire wall of bright-faced children with ice-white teeth and eyes like polished obsidian.

Xylo Haines and the Euphonious Brethren: Fusion, Blues, and Shades of Jazz. Winner of the Deep Hot Award at the 1998 Rio Rialto Jazz Festival.

The ensemble members stood, streamlined and shiny as the highly polished xylophone that spanned horizontal on the floor in front of them. They wore skinny ties and a profusion of rings that looked like solid gold, even in the black-and-white photograph. Their trapezoidal suits angled downward from padded shoulders to narrow hips and pants so sharply creased the lines flowed into the reflective contours of the brass instruments as if they were all cut from the same metallic fabric.

They did not beam. They appeared to disdain beaming. They appeared to be the kind of guys who drank Drambuie and used the term "hep cat." Their hair was slick and luxurious as a freshly waxed Mercedes, and they were all thin as pencil lead. Bending toward the camera like jackknives, they appeared to be daring any nightclub owner who came into possession of their demo to "be there or be square."

But as Kiki leaned toward them, she noticed that Xylo's eyes seemed less calcite than the rest of the office gallery, his enthusiasm more ingenuous, his smile less brittle. He stood at the center of the group, his arms open in front of the others, both mallets in one hand, only his open palm in the other. At first, he looked as if he were displaying the xylophone on a game show, but on closer inspection, it was more like he was offering it as a gift to Baby Jesus.

Kiki smiled Mary's smile and started to reach toward the love offering but snatched her hand back when the inner-office door opened, and Vivica's assistant came out.

"She'll see you now."

Kiki nodded, adjusted her facial expression, and went in.

Vivica was on the phone, but she pointed to a chair with one long red-nailed finger. She rolled her eyes, making a quack-quack-quack gesture, opening and closing her hand. Kiki smiled and nodded. She laid her tape on the desk, trying not to notice how tiny Vivica looked in her big executive chair.

"The only problem is, he's put on a few pounds since the last time you used him. Well, enough to make a difference. No, I have absolute confidence in him, but I want you to take a look before we sign anything, just so . . . Mmm-hmm. That would work. Uh-huh. Here in Orlando, if it's all the same to your people. Right. Hmm? How is—which thing was that?" She slid a pencil under the edge of her Zsa Zsa Gabor wig and scratched it up and down a little. "Oh, that thing. It's going fine, but the whole process is slower than the mills of the Lord's justice, so . . . No, we aren't counting any chickens yet. Hmm? Oh, you're sweet, but really, I'm fine. Sure. Sure I'm sure. Absolutely. So okay, sweetie. Oh, I sure will. And you watch out for those grandbabies while you're out scootin' around in that golf cart. Okay. You, too, sweetie. B'bye. Yes, I will. You, too. Uh-huh. B'bye, now. Okay. Bye, now. You, too. B'bye."

She clacked the phone down before another word could sneak through the wire and snag her back. Raising one finger in a hang-on gesture, she pressed the intercom button with the eraser end of the pencil.

"Estelle, call Phil back. His audition is on for tomorrow at two." She pressed again. "Tell him not to embarrass me."

She released the button and clapped her hands together.

"All rightee!" she said, smoothing the front of her turquoise silk blouse. "Finally. Let's hear it, shall we?"

She dropped Kiki's demo in the deck and turned the volume up. The intro brassed up, and Kiki came on.

"Ol' man rivah, that ol' man rivah . . ."

Vivica drew bodily away from the speakers.

"Oh. Oh, dear," she pressed her fingertips together to form a little tent in front of her face. "Where on earth did you dig that up?"

"I—I had it from . . . before."

"Oh. Oh, my." Vivica pushed her red lips together as if

someone were trying to make her taste fried monkey. "Oh, my God."

"He must know sumpthin' but don't say nothin'," the canned Kiki sang.

"Oh, sweetie," Vivica said, punching the stop button, "nobody's going to book this. I can't sell this. I'd be embarrassed to try."

"Aren't you even going to look at my résumé?" Kiki pleaded. "I had it typed."

"Everything on this résumé took place before you got your first period."

"No! I was in *Hello, Dolly!* When I was sixteen. And I was Minnie Fay. *Minnie Fay!* I had solos!"

"Community theatre. I'm talking about professional stuff."

"I was a professional singer." There were tears in Kiki's voice. "And I'm gonna be a professional singer again. I don't care what you say."

"Oh yeah, that's very professional," Vivica chided.

Kiki started sobbing in earnest.

"Oh, now, don't do that, sweetie. Sweetie, c'mon. All right," Vivica sighed. "C'mon over here."

Kiki went around the desk as though she were still eight and nobody in third grade wanted to play with her because her hair was bleached platinum blonde and all teased up like Annette Funicello. Vivica scootched over in her large leather chair, and she was so thin, there was plenty of room for both of them. She smoothed Kiki's hair back and kissed her temple.

"Goodness, Moon Pie," she said, stroking her quivering arm and warm, wet cheek. "You're just like me. I always got so emotional when I was pregnant. When I was expecting Kitten, I used to set aside a half hour every day, just for weeping. Your poor daddy didn't know what to make of it."

"I'm sorry. But geez, Mama! You could have looked at my résumé!"

"Alright, sweetie, I'll look at it. See? Looking. Looking at it right now." Vivica picked it up, waving it to prove her good intentions. "But, honey, it's the tape that gets bookings, and you don't have one. And you don't have backup, and you don't have clothes, and you're pregnant. Honestly, I don't understand why you're so hot to do this all the sudden."

"Mama, I don't know what else to do." Kiki blew her nose into the Kleenex Vivica handed her. "I'm not going back to Wayne. I'm not."

"Well, you know you and the kids can stay with me as long as you need to. Just stay here. We'll sit by the pool. We'll talk. We'll go to Disney World. Now, you'd like that, wouldn't you, sweetie?"

"Mama, I'm talking about making a life for myself. What kind of life is that? Hanging out by the pool and going to Disney World and mooching off my mama?"

"Sweetie, I built this business on top of you and Kitten. Your hard work. Your talent. Every connection I started with was somebody calling here looking for you two. I think the least I owe you is a little safety net now and then."

"You were the one, Mama." Kiki nuzzled the most familiar place in her world. "We'd've never done any of it without you. You were the one who taught us everything and made our dresses and hustled every gig."

"I did hustle, didn't I?" Vivica smiled, and her eyes went nostalgic. "Hustled my buns off. And if you two had kept it up once you got old enough to do nightclubs, with those voices—and those figures! Mm-mm-mm." She fanned her face with her hand and repeated, "Mm-mm-mm."

"I wish I had, Mama. I wish I'd never quit. I wish I'd never married Wayne."

"Now, don't say that." Vivica pushed her back so she could look her sternly in the eye. "He gave you Oscar and Chloe, and that's worth anything. Anything, sweetie."

"Yeah." Kiki nodded and looked away. "But, Mama, I

can't stay married to him. I feel like I don't even know him anymore."

"Personally, I think you two need to consult with a good marriage counselor. Have you thought about that, Moon Pie? Because single motherhood is no picnic, I promise you."

"He went with that woman and had sex, Mama. Had sex with somebody other than me."

"That's a biggie," Vivica conceded. "I'm always amazed if a marriage bounces back from that one."

"And it's not just that, Mama. Sometimes he . . . he scares me."

"Scares you?" Vivica asked seriously. "Scares you how?"

"He—when he gets real mad—it's my fault because I always make a mess of everything, but then he gets so angry and . . . and he—he . . . yells at me."

"Oh, Kiki, for heaven's sake," Vivica looked relieved. "You might not remember Daddy ever raising his voice, but let me tell you what, he and I had some humdingers."

"Did you?"

"Oh, yeah." Vivica seemed to enjoy remembering it. "We had some real lulus."

"But he never . . . Did he ever . . . scare you?"

"The only thing I was scared of was losing him. But," she said, making her face solid again, "I survived that, too, didn't I?"

"I'm not like you though, Mama. I'm not tough like you."

"Oh, *pfff!* I think you girls are plain spoiled. Honestly, the way Kitten talks, you'd think Mel is the ogre under the bridge, and you're apparently too thin-skinned to yell back when someone yells at you." Vivica straightened Kiki's posture with a hand against her shoulder blade. "You need to learn how to yell right back. Make him respect you. Let him know you won't tolerate any more of his shenanigans. You just yell right back at him! What's he gonna do about it?"

Kiki didn't say.

There's a particular rise, southbound on 45, where the skyline suddenly reveals itself, and that view of Houston always made Kit feel like she was standing at the gates of the Emerald City, ruby slippers on her feet, heart full of belief in something greater than herself. Traffic surfing around the Pierce Elevated, she passed the honeycomb of high-rise apartments, the twin monoliths that reminded her of *2001: A Space Odyssey*, the giant blue icefall, and a great green glass phallus.

It seemed more appropriate, somehow, to take this bold step among the glass and granite of the city, where the wind soared between steel structures that sheered right up into the clouds like tall sailing ships. She felt stronger here than she did among the low roofs and ceiling fans of the suburbs, where privacy fences and manicured hedges blunted the breeze, and strip malls stretched out like afternoon cats. Suburbia was a lifestyle too lazy for the country, too chickenshit for the city. This brazen gesture required the sophisticated danger of downtown.

Besides, Kit reminded herself, the last thing she needed was to bump into someone from church or PTO.

When she pulled off Fannin into the parking lot at Cinema Star Video, her face was already flaming. She meandered through the children's section, scanning the shelves for something the kids hadn't seen fifty-five times already. She picked up *The Fox and The Hound, Goonies,* and some cheap foreign animation version of *Gulliver's Travels.* She wandered over to the comedy section and picked up *Ace Ventura: When Nature Calls,* a movie she hadn't allowed Cooper to see previously, even though he protested to her that everybody except stupid little kindergarten babies had been allowed to see it, and she was just being mean.

Toward the back of the store there was a plywood partition with swinging shutter-type doors and a sign that said "NO

ONE UNDER 18."

Kit looked over her shoulder and sidled in that direction.

"Can I help you?" A tiny Korean lady appeared from around the corner, and Kit practically jumped out of her sandals. "You finding everything okay?"

"Yes. Oh, yes. Fine. Thank you."

"Okay." The Korean lady stood there smiling.

"Just fine." Kit repeated. "Thank you."

"You ready to check out now?"

"No. No. Not quite," Kit browsed pointedly at the documentaries on the shelf. "Still looking."

"Okay." The Korean lady kept smiling.

"Right . . ." Kit glanced over her shoulder at the swinging doors. "Okay. Well, I guess this'll do me," she said and followed the lady to the counter.

At the place on San Felipe, she came out with *The Sound of Music* and the place on Old Katy Road provided *Squanto: A Warrior's Tale.*

Kit was getting disgusted with herself. They couldn't afford this. The kids were going to be home from school in an hour.

Is this a free country, or isn't it? she demanded of the rearview mirror. *Am I over 18 or not?*

She strode into the place on Post Oak, stepped over to the desk, removed her sunglasses, and said, "Excuse me. Do you have pornographic movies here?"

The guy shook his head at first, thinking she was some Baptist or something, but when she seemed disappointed, he guessed she was more likely a desperate housewife.

"However," he said, "we do have *adult features.* In there."

He pointed to the same swinging doors and sign that must be marketed through some massive fuck film outlet supply catalogue.

Porno-R-Us, Kit mused.

She nodded and went over to the doors, veering off at the

last second toward the children's section. She looked at her watch and sighed. She went out to her car. She looked back at the store window. The guy was smirking at her.

Head high, purse clutched primly under her arm, Kit strode back into the store, passing the new releases, ignoring romance and drama, pushing through the swinging doors. The room had that basementish skanky-carpet-and-air-conditioner smell born of sustained deep South humidity. The walls were lined with plastic boxes bearing pictures of heavily made-up women bending over things—their eyes closed, their lips open.

The films were all cleverly titled with double entendres like *Wet Nurses* and *Between a Cock and a Hard Place* and *Tits a Wonderful Life.* Kit picked up a box that said HOT! HOT! HOT! across the top. The woman on the front was bending over the hood of a vintage Ford Falcon. Royal blue.

It felt like an omen.

Kit turned the box over. The woman's tongue protruded, tip touching the erect shaft of a shiny steel ratchet.

"Triple T & A Auto Club: Mr. Good's Wrench

XXX 75 minutes

Gentlemen, start your engines! The Triple T & A girls are back in their nastiest, fastest, most motor-revvingest adventure yet! When a nosy neighbor schemes to shut down the only all-gal garage in Peter-ville, Candyapples, Pussywillow and Miz Pistonpumper treat him and his horny henchmen to the lube job of their lives!"

Kit wasn't sure why they would want to do that or why it would be particularly off-putting to henchmen with an announced predilection toward horniness, but—what the hey. The overall theme seemed like something Mel might be able to relate to, and chances were, he wouldn't pause to question the commercial stratagem of three businesswomen named Candyapples, Pussywillow, and Miz Pistonpumper, particu-larly when they were uniformed in excruciatingly short bib overalls with no shirts underneath.

Kit tucked it under her arm and hurried out.

"Find everything?" the guy at the counter smiled.

He looked dangerous in a handsome young Hispanic kind of way. Kit put the plastic box face down on the counter, and he ran it across the scanner. There was an electronic chirp and "*Title: T & A: Good Wrench*" flashed up on the computer screen.

"That's a great one," the guy said, to Kit's horror. "It's a classic."

She couldn't imagine what she was supposed to contribute to this conversation. A lady with two Care Bears cartoons stepped in line behind her.

"Adult features are two-for-two," the guy said.

"I'm sorry?" Kit whispered, hoping to bring his voice down.

"Adult features. Two-for-two," he repeated impatiently and even louder. "You rent two adult features for two days—five bucks."

"Well, I just . . . I just need the—the one," Kit stammered.

"Well, you might as well get another one, 'cause I have to charge you the five bucks either way."

"No, really. I—I—because, see—I'm actually just getting it as a joke on my cousin . . ."

"You got two days to watch 'em. Two-and-a-half, in fact, 'cause adult features don't have to be back till midnight."

Kit felt the woman behind her giving her the Care Bear stare.

"Just charge me the five dollars," she hissed. "I'm in a hurry."

"Geez," the guy looked hurt. "I guess you are."

※

"She's white," Xylo Haines repeated.

"Yes," Vivica nodded. "You know, I noticed that about her when she was born."

"She's a white girl."

"So is Peggy Lee."

Kiki shrank back into the semicircular booth, quiet as instructed, letting Vivica do all the talking.

"And she looks . . . she looks . . . *pregnant*," Xylo whispered the last word toward Vivica, as if Kiki might not know this about herself.

"I'd noticed that, too," Vivica whispered.

"You're killin' me, Vivica. Killin' me here."

"We'll get her something with a princess waistline," Vivica said. "She's still got a terrific set of pipes."

"What are you trying to do to me?" Xylo tried to turn aside to avoid hurting Kiki's feelings. "Ain't no little white girl gonna *sing* like Ramonica did, and ain't no pregnant lady gonna *look* like Ramonica did."

"Maybe not, but Ramonica's gone, Xylo. We've already canceled out of six very decent gigs, and if you want to do this thing in Buena Vista at the end of the month, you're gonna need—" Vivica gestured toward Kiki as if she were the prize on a game show, "—a girl."

"Think about the repertoire, lady. No way she's gonna be hip to the repertoire."

"You guys don't have a repertoire without a female vocalist," Vivica countered. "I'm sure you could sing 'Oh my man I love him so,' but this isn't The Flaming Flamingo."

"And it ain't the cocktail lounge at the Ramada Inn, either. This is a blues gig in a blues establishment frequented by those who are able to distinguish blues from elevator music. Don't even try to tell me this girl is gonna sing 'Suitcase Blues' and sound like Sippie Wallace."

"No, Xylo, she's going to sing 'Suitcase Blues' and sound like Kiki Smithers, and you'll be damn lucky to have her."

He started to say something else, but she raised her hand and continued.

"Sweetie, I guarantee you, this girl knows every song that ever passed the lips of Billie Holiday, Koko Taylor, and Cleo Laine. Not to mention Peggy Lee. And what she doesn't already know, you can teach her, Xylo. She's very bright. And it's the obligation of the old master to pass his knowledge on to the next generation." She cued Kiki and gestured toward the stage. "At least listen to her. One number. Something easy. Something quick. Say . . . oh . . . 'Gloomy Sunday'?" She suggested it as though she'd just thought it up off the top of her head and hadn't actually been coaching Kiki on it for three days. "Just give me 'Gloomy Sunday,' hmm?"

Xylo rolled his eyes and trudged up onto the stage where Kiki waited now, smiling a bit too brightly, microphone held up to her pink mouth.

"Gloomy Sunday," he mumbled. "Yeah, I got a gloomy Sunday for you, lady . . ."

But then he looked at Kiki, and even though he still seemed irritated, his features mellowed slightly.

"Good afternoon, Miss Kiki," he said, his voice low and slow like deep water. "In which key do you prefer your 'Gloomy Sunday'?"

"Could we do it in A minor?" she asked timidly, hoping Xylo hadn't noticed how the microphone trembled in her hand. "'Cause I . . . I practiced it in A minor. If that's no trouble."

"A minor it is," he shrugged. "A minor, my brothers."

The rest of the Euphonious Brethren drifted onto the stage, and the stand-up bass started an easy rhythm. The drummer fanned out a pair of brushes over the cymbal and snare, and Xylo squeezed in between the electric piano and his xylophone, picking up the intro on the keyboard. After a moment, he looked over his shoulder.

"You gonna sing the song or what?"

"Oh. Sorry."

"It's cool," he softened a bit, "just jump on in when you're ready."

"Okay." Kiki smoothed her hand over her dress, eyes forward like she was timing her way into a twirling jump rope. "Now?"

"Do it, girl."

"Sunday is gloomy . . . my hours are slumberless . . ."

Kiki stumbled a little, but then she smoothed it out. She felt safe with Billie Holiday. She'd been listening to the lady sing the blues since she was a child and practiced this song a million times in front of the mirror, polishing the pouty mouth, the droopy eyelids, the tragic trill.

"Dreaming," Kiki belted over the bridge, *"Oh, I must have been dreaming . . ."*

She looked down and saw Vivica tugging on her earring, the sign for "you're trying too hard." Kiki pulled back and tried to relax the straining muscles in her cheeks.

She sensed Xylo looking over his shoulder.

"Gloomy—Sunnnnn-daaaaaaaaaaaay," she finished with her arms extended wide above her, microphone tipped down, chin tipped up, and then her hands arched gracefully down as the bass trailed out.

Vivica stood, applauding vigorously.

Xylo sat on the piano bench with his hands at his sides.

"Viv," he said without turning to face her, "I don't want to hurt nobody's feelings or nothin', and the lady has a powerful instrument there, but . . . she's a white girl, Vivica. She might have all the words memorized, but I'm sorry. She don't know nothin' about singin' no blues."

"Okay. Well . . . ," Kiki nodded and replaced the microphone in the stand. "Thank you, Mr. Haines, for your time and . . . and everything."

"Wait a minute, wait a minute," Vivica strode forward. "C'mon, Xylo, you can't base this decision on one number. Let's call that one a warm-up, all right?" She patted Kiki's hair back into place. "How about 'Them There Eyes'? She'll knock you dead on 'Them There Eyes.' Kiki, get back up there."

"It's okay, Mama, really," Kiki whispered.

"No, it isn't!" Vivica whispered back. "You think you're going to get anywhere giving up that easy? You were just a little nervous. Now, shake it off."

She took Kiki by the shoulders and spun her back toward Xylo.

"She was just a little nervous. She's fine now."

"I'm sorry, Vivica," Xylo repeated, "but she don't know nothin' about singin' no blues. She was smilin' and muggin' the whole time like the damn Miss America pageant. She's all lookin' like 'Star Search' or some damn thing, makin' them plastic Barbie-doll hand gestures. I don't know who's been tellin' her what, but that microphone up over her head, she look like a widemouthed bass comin' up to take the bait off a hook."

"Vivica?"

A soft voice came from the doorway before she had a chance to come back. It was Estelle, her assistant from the agency, and she had Oscar and Chloe by the hand.

"I'm sorry, Viv, but I had that appointment, remember?"

"Oh, damn. No, I forgot, Estelle. I apologize. Just leave them here with me." She pointed at Kiki and said, "I've got 'em. You sing." Then she pointed at Xylo Haines. "'Them There Eyes.' Key of D."

She took the children from Estelle and parked them at a table near the front of the stage with the very same air of authority while Xylo's mallets danced a tinkling upbeat intro and Kiki started singing.

"I fell in love with you the first time I looked into . . . them there eyes . . ."

She tried to move around the stage a little, but she bumped an amp cord, and her mike fed back on her with a shrill beam, so after that she stood still, focusing on Oscar and Chloe, singing it to them the way she always did.

She decided at the last second to tag a more casual ending onto it this time.

"Oooooo, baby . . . themmmm . . . them there eyes."

She looked hopefully over at Xylo, who closed with a rhythmy upward canter.

"Much better," he nodded with those kindly eyes. "Kiki, you're a beautiful woman, and you got a beautiful voice, and that was real nice, but . . ." He shrugged uncomfortably at Vivica, pleading, "You got nobody else to show me?"

"Nobody."

He shrugged again and shook his head.

"Your loss," she shrugged back.

"I'm sorry, Miss Kiki, I wish you the best of luck."

He took her hand, not to shake it so much as to embrace it between both of his. Kiki focused on his long fingers, pale palms, and ebony smooth forearms. The small gesture awakened a part of her that had forgotten grown-ups could touch with the tenderness of a child, and that part of her hated to let go.

"All right then, Mr. Haines." Vivica snapped the catches on her briefcase and opened it on the small round table, pushing aside the round candleholder and making room for a stack of contracts. "I've been holding the paperwork on these bookings, but I have to believe that your signature on the bottom line here means that you will be there to perform, come what may. Kiki, do you mind waiting? It'll just take a minute."

"That sure is a fine xylophone you have over there, sir," Oscar spoke up from his grandmother's elbow.

"Yes, son, it surely is that," Xylo said with grandfatherly patience.

"It starts with an X, you know—not a Z, like it sounds."

"Well, this one over here," Xylo smiled, "actually, this one starts with a V."

"Mama," Chloe said, "I have to go potty."

"C'mon, then," her mama smiled.

It was a relief to move toward the ladies' room with Chloe's familiar hand in hers. Kiki was having a hard time keeping her okay face on.

"In point of actual fact," Xylo's voice faded behind her, "this here is what you would call a vibraphone . . ."

Kiki let Chloe into the stall and then sat on a wooden chair by the door, listening to the muted voices and music on the other side. There was laughter, a lush, upward interpolation, then a blunt yelping from the instrument. Kiki smiled and guessed correctly that Xylo was giving Oscar a turn.

"Mommy, there's no toilet paper in here," Chloe called.

Kiki reeled some off in the neighboring stall and passed it under to her.

"Got it?"

"Yeah. But somebody put a cigarette on the floor in here."

"Well, don't touch it. It's yucky."

The toilet flushed, and Chloe came out.

"Wash your hands, honey," Kiki said wearily.

She realized she was always saying that. She even made it into a little song to remind them as they were getting potty trained.

Wipe! Flush! Wash and dry your hands off . . .

She was always saying the same things over and over, knowing nothing would ever change. She was running out of money. Wayne had canceled her credit cards. In a tourist town like Orlando, she figured, there must be some kind of work for her. But the thought of auditioning turned her cold. She knew from experience that not everyone in the business shared Xylo Haines' reluctance to hurt anyone's feelings. Kiki wasn't sure she had it in her anymore, the ability to bounce back. And with the baby showing already, there wasn't much hope of being hired anywhere else, even if she were to discover something she was qualified to do.

Chloe waved her hands under the air-dryer for a moment, then came over and wiped them on Kiki's evening gown.

"Do you think Daddy remembered to feed the fish?" Chloe asked.

"I'm sure he did, sweetie."

"And Miss Calico?"

"Miss Calico can make her own way in the world," Kit told her. "She can run fast and catch mice to eat. She can climb trees to get away from dogs. And she has nine lives. She'll always be okay."

"Do you think the baby birds are still there?"

"Oh, I hope not, sweetie. I hope they got strong and brave and flew away as free as the wind."

Chloe nodded, but her expression was one of great sadness, the expression of someone struggling to understand. Kiki pulled her little girl onto her lap and rocked her on the wooden chair, thinking about what she could say to Wayne on the phone. Wondering if he'd send her the money for plane tickets. Wondering what he'd be like if she went back.

"Hushabye, don't you cry . . . go to sleep my little baby . . ." she sang and stroked the bridge of Chloe's nose, an almost hypnotic gesture that had been soothing her since she was a baby. *"When you wake, you shall have all the pretty little ponies . . ."*

He'd keep a pretty tight lid on her for a while. Whenever she'd try to leave and then come back, he'd watch her like a hawk the first few weeks, counting the money in her purse and comparing it to the grocery receipts, calling and hanging up to make sure she stayed in the house all day. She could handle that for a while, she figured.

"Blacks and bays . . . dapples and grays . . ."

She could handle the other stuff once in a while, too, as long as he didn't hurt the kids, and he never did. Just her. Somehow that seemed not so bad. And it wasn't really like a beating if somebody just slapped you or shook you by your shoulders. Maybe he really didn't know he was pushing hard enough to knock her down, and it wasn't his fault if she bumped into the wall or the cupboard or something. And then he was always so sorry and solicitous about it later.

"One by one . . . see them come . . ."

She just wouldn't make him mad. She wouldn't give him any reasons. She wouldn't say "no" to anything he wanted.

And she would cook nice dinners for him and have everything perfect when he came home from work.

" . . . *dancing for my little baby* . . ."

She would be a good wife and keep everything nice. She'd keep her dang mouth shut and not aggravate him. She wouldn't screw up or do anything stupid or ask him where he'd been or where he was going. She'd make the kids be quiet and make herself look pretty, and she'd go down on him just the way he liked it, on her knees in front of him, her hair twisted like a rope around his hand. Kiki closed her eyes, accepting the image without gagging on it the way she used to.

"When you wake, you shall have all the pretty little ponies."

The bathroom door creaked open, and Xylo Haines stood there, dark eyes wondering, full lips slightly parted.

"Now *that*," he spoke softly so as not to wake Chloe, "is blues."

⚘

"What's with all the movies?" Cooper asked, and Kit whisked the bag out from under his hand right at the last moment.

"I thought it would be fun to have a . . . a home . . . cinema . . . party!"

"What does that mean?" Cooper looked suspicious.

"This!" Kit whipped out her *Ace* in the hole, and Cooper whooped and grabbed it out of her hand.

"Allll rrrright!" he exclaimed. "Dad! Look what Mom got!"

"Yeah, I see." Mel looked suspicious, too, but kept on stirring the spaghetti sauce with a wooden spoon.

"I'll let you watch this on two conditions," Kit stated to Cooper. "One: no Jim Carrey imitations. I don't want to hear any of his crude jokes repeated in this house. And two: you go to bed without arguing at nine o'clock."

"No way!" he protested. "On a Friday?"

"Never mind, then," Kit shrugged and dropped *Ace* back in the bag.

"Okay already! Nine."

Cooper stomped off, well aware he was being manipulated.

Mel picked up the bag and poked through the stack of plastic boxes.

"*Goonies?* They've seen that a million—" He stopped, and when Kit turned around, he was staring at the back of the *HOT! HOT! HOT!* box with sort of a confused half smile. "What's this?"

"What . . . that?" She couldn't really read the expression on his face, so she started babbling. "It's . . . it's . . . oh, you know what happened? I—somebody—I guess they picked up my bag, and I picked up their bag and—geez! Can you believe that thing?" A short little laugh tripped out of her throat. "I mean—I can't believe somebody would actually rent something like that, you know?" She took two forks and furiously tossed the salad. "Geez! I guess they'll be surprised when they get to the ol' stag party and find *Care Bears: The Movie.*"

"Yeah." Mel laughed a little, which Kit thought was good, but then he said, "You should complain to the manager when you take these back tomorrow."

He shoved the box in the bag and his hands in his pockets.

"Nice car, though. On the front there."

"Oh. Really?" Kit said and displayed great interest as he showed it to her.

After cleaning up the dinner mess, Kit sat at the table and played Chutes and Ladders with Mitzi while Mel and Cooper watched *Ace Ventura*. When that was over, she agreed to let them stay up long enough for *Gulliver's Travels,* but Mitzi was asleep within ten minutes, and Cooper decided to climb into bed with a book, complaining that the Lilliputians' mouths weren't moving in time to the dialogue.

On her way down from tucking them in, Kit froze on the stairway. She distinctly heard the words "torque wench" from the darkened living room.

" . . . as long as you don't mind getting a little slippery," someone giggled.

Then she heard Mel laugh.

She flattened herself against the wall and crept down far enough to look through the arched doorway. Mel had shucked out of his sweats and was sitting in his boxers, as he usually did after Kit put the kids to bed, but instead of lolling back with his arms outstretched on the back of the sofa, his ankle propped on his knee, he craned forward on the couch cushion, as if Miz Pistonpumper had him by the front of his T-shirt. The light and shadow of whatever was happening flickered across his face.

Kit hurried back upstairs, piled her hair on top of her head, whirled under the shower, and thrashed through a drawer she hardly ever opened, mining for some flimsy underwear. She unearthed a midnight purple G-string unit from some prehistoric weekend trip to New Orleans and pulled her bulky bathrobe on over it.

"Hi," Mel grinned, embarrassed when she came in and found him staring. "I um . . . I was just checking out that car."

"Oh?" Kit sat beside him on the couch.

"Sorry. I'll turn it off."

Mel started to get up, but Kit seized his wrist and said, "No!"

He looked startled.

"I mean . . . Well . . . did they show it yet? The car?"

"Yeah," Mel admitted.

"Oh."

"But only for a second," he hastened. "They might show it again, and then—then you could see it, too."

"Right. Sure. I'd like to."

Mel sat back on the couch, leaving a formal distance between them. The horny henchmen were receiving what Kit guessed was the fabled lube job.

"So . . . do you wanna play Scrabble or something?" He

asked casually, though he sounded a little short of breath.

"Not really," Kit sidled over to him. "Let's just hang out."

"I should have tried to go in to the hangar tonight," Mel said. "We'll need all the extra hours I can get if we're going to go to Orlando in June."

"You're entitled to a day off, Mel," Kit tensed. "You're not some kind of robot. And the kids need to see you once in a while, too."

"Well, right, but—I just thought . . . Never mind."

When they stopped talking, the squeaking and churning and yelping from the television seemed to get louder and louder. They sat in the midst of the sound effects.

"Would you like some coffee?" Kit asked suddenly.

"Oh—um . . . no," Mel startled and pointed the clicker at the television set, subduing the volume.

"Are you sure? 'Cause I could make some."

"No, don't—don't bother. It's too hot for coffee, anyhow."

"Yeah," Kit offered him a sly smile, "it is getting kind of hot in here."

"Is the air on?"

"No," she deflated. "Remember, we were going to try to cut down until summer hits?"

"Oh. Yeah."

"I could turn it on, though. If you want."

"No, no. That's okay."

"Are you sure?"

"Oh, yeah. Sure."

"Because, you know . . . I could turn it on."

"No. It's . . . it's fine."

The henchmen were duct-taped to their chairs now.

"This music is so bad," Kit commented.

"*Bow-ba-dit-dow-buppa-dip-a-dit,*" Mel imitated the sleazy synthesizer, and they laughed together, relieved for a moment.

The garage gals had shed their overalls. They were kissing each other and playing with their tools, making a noise Kit only came close to when she was walking barefoot on blazing hot sand.

"Oh," Mel said, "there's the umm . . . the . . ."

"Car?"

"Yeah."

"Wow," Kit said, "it's really . . . nice."

"Yeah. Yeah, very nice. Nice car."

"Yours is nicer, though."

"Well, yeah, because mine is a '62, and that right there . . . that's a . . . a . . ."

"69?" Kit quipped, and Mel laughed nervously.

They stared in silence until the action relocated to the business office of the garage, and the Falcon could only be seen in fleeting glimpses through a window, between Candyapples' upraised stilettos.

"So . . . ," Mel picked up the remote, but didn't hit REWIND or STOP.

"So . . . what?" Kit said, touching one finger to the back of his hand.

"So, that's it. So, I guess . . ."

She let her finger drift up the side of his wrist.

"Can I make a confession?"

He nodded, and she opened the front of her robe to let the midnight show.

"I didn't really get somebody else's movie. I rented it."

"You . . . umm . . . ," Mel laughed nervously. "You're kidding."

"I thought you might like it." She traced her fingers up his sleeve to his shoulder and then turned her nails down to scratch him gently. "Do you?"

He didn't say anything. Just swallowed, nodded very slightly.

"I thought you might find it kind of . . . exciting." She slid her other hand up the baggy leg of his shorts. "Hmmm. Evidently, you do."

"Yeah," he whispered hoarsely, "kind of."

"Oh, look, there's the car again," Kit teased her foot up and down his shin. "And that must be Miz—oh. Goodness. Those are certainly . . . impressive."

"Yeah." Mel shifted on the sofa and looked into Kit's face. "Yours are nicer, though."

He cupped his hands beneath her breasts, and she smiled, wanting him to lean forward and kiss her, but instead, he leaned back, wanting her to go down. And she did. She closed her eyes and opened her mouth. But he hadn't quite worked himself out of his underwear when the phone started ringing.

"Dang!"

"Let it go!" he whispered, thrashing free of his BVD's.

"What if it's Kiki?"

"She's a grown woman, Kit! She's not your baby sister anymore."

Kit glanced toward the doorway as Mel dove down the front of the purple teddy. He freed her from the lace and ribbons with a frenzied, bomb squad dexterity and planted his mouth with the urgency of the unweaned. Kit felt a tinge of excitement fizz from her tailbone to the roof of her mouth. She groped below, and Mel moaned when she closed her hand around him. He lifted her onto his lap, hooked the G-string aside, and just that quick, was in clear up to there.

Kit interlocked her fingers behind his neck and touched her forehead to his, concentrating on the connection between the two of them. With her back to the TV, she could almost block out the wheezing of the videotape synthesizer, but that dang-bastard telephone would not shut up. She tried to focus on Mel's mouth and his rhythm and the adroit placement of his thumb, but after a few more rings, the guilt and the jangling got to her.

"Mel, honey, can we—"

"No." He tried to hold her there. "Don't go!"

"Mel, I'm sorry, honey. I can't just ignore her."

"Kit, please don't leave."

"I'll only be a minute, I promise."

She stood up and pulled her robe closed.

"Kit, for Christ's sake!"

"I'm sorry, Mel, just—please!" She took his face between her hands. "Hold that thought, okay?"

In the kitchen, she snapped on the light and stood in the glare for a moment before picking up the shrilling telephone.

"Hello."

"Kit!" Only he said it like "Ket."

"Ander!" she hissed. "What are you thinking? Mel's right in the other room!"

"Kit, I want so much to be with you again—"

"No! How many times do I have to tell you? I can't."

Faint background sounds of traffic told her he was at an outside phone booth, which made it seem all the more clandestine and seedy.

"I am having so great a desiring for you."

"No!"

She stepped inside the broom closet and closed the door the way she did when Mitzi and Coo were being too noisy for her to hear the bill collector's threats.

"Ander, this can't happen. You have to stop calling me."

"But I love you, my beautiful Kit. Years now, years! I wait for days you come to my store, and I watch you working—your beautiful hands. I build things I know you have to paint, so I can make you come to be with me any little more hours I can have you. And always I am thinking in the night of kissing you, and then I can kiss you, and I see these beautiful breast at last, and I need to touch this beautiful woman again. To make love to this lady I care so much."

A feeling Kit couldn't recognize or put a name to—what it was to hear these things said to her—it was substantive enough to sway her on her feet, and she had to lean against the closet door.

"Ah Gott, Kit, I feel like crazy man. My mind is going crazy with these many desiring thoughts of you, of touching your skin. I am so very, very much so love with you. I am wanting you more than my own life!"

"Ander . . ." There was a long silence while Kit tried hard not to feel the luxury of it, tried to face the closet interior and focus on the shelf-papered reality of its contents. "Ander, it's not right."

"Is not right to love someone you know and have respect and work by the side of this person and laugh with them years and years? Do you say is right to have lovemaking with this person, but then say you don't love them? Do you say you don't love me, Kit?"

"No," she spoke quietly into the cache of Resolve and Lysol and Love My Carpet. "I don't say that."

"Ah, thank you, *Gott!*" he breathed. "Manne tusen täg."

"But Ander," Kit kept her voice as even and slow as she could, "one of the things I love most about you is that you cherish your family as much as I cherish mine—"

"Kit, please—"

"—and I know you don't want to lose that, Ander, do you?"

"I want to be with you. I must to be with you. You don't know what is this burning I feel."

"I do." She leaned into the hanging brooms and mops. "I do know. But I'm not going to let myself think about it anymore. I'm not going to jeopardize my family like that ever again. It was wrong and stupid, and I hate myself. I'm just going to do my best to find another job and make it up to Mel as best I can, and I think you should be trying to do the same for Ruda. I can't imagine what she must be going through."

"Ah, Gott." His voice crumpled with emotion. "I am never wanting to hurt her. And to hurt you, Kit. I am so very much sorry. I never want you to be not working here anymore. You are most talented artist. Most talented of students in all my life and wonderful painter, and I always want to see you every day."

She couldn't answer him.

"Now I mostly miss you," he whispered.

"Ander . . ." Kit stood there for a moment, aching with her own desire to change things. "Don't call here again."

Biting her lip, she stepped out of the closet and hung up the phone. She got a drink from the sink and sat down at the kitchen table, just on the edge of the chair, clutching her robe as high on her neck as she could, too bleak for tears, too weary to want anything more than water. She wished Kiki were here, and that one simple thought of missing her engulfed Kit in a sudden riptide of loneliness. They'd never gone this long without talking. Eleven days. But Kit was afraid if she called Orlando, and Vivica answered, her mother would have that maternal psychic insight into everything Kit had done.

After a while, she heard a telltale rumble from the living room. The movie had run out, and Mel was snoring in front of the blue screen, an afghan across his lap. She hit the REWIND button and touched his shoulder.

"Mel."

He snorted, opened his eyes, and squeezed the back of his stiff neck.

"Who was on the phone?"

"Kiki."

"She okay?"

"Yeah. She just needed someone to talk to."

"I can't tell you how glad I am to hear it."

He handed her the afghan, and she felt a damp spot on it.

"I'm sorry," she said.

"That settles it," Mel took hold of the wide lapels on her bathrobe and pulled her over to him. "First thing tomorrow, I'm gonna go out and buy us an answering machine."

Kit smiled up at him and nodded.

"Are you coming to bed?" he asked.

"I've gotta toss in a load of towels first," she said, because neither of them wanted to admit they were out of the habit of sleeping together, and it was really more comfortable if one of them just happened to fall asleep on the couch. Kit figured it was her turn.

"Fine." Mel figured the same. "See you in the morning."

He trudged up the stairs, and Kit picked up his boxer shorts from the living room floor.

Just Kiki. Just needed to talk. Just gotta throw in a load of towels. She couldn't remember when it started being so easy to lie to him. Perhaps when he lost interest in the truth; when the truth started to weigh on him, but a lie slid off his back as easily as a bead of sweat.

The VCR started making a grinding noise. She ponked it on top with her fist, administering the Mel-chanical "RCA Field Maneuver." The machine stopped grinding and flashed PLAY.

Kit knelt and turned the volume very low.

Miz Pistonpumper was saying something about inspecting the Falcon. Camera angle at her backside, she leaned in and over the engine, dragging her breasts across the gears and belts until her tight T-shirt was streaked with motor oil, so of course she had to drag it off over her head. She languored like an ermine through the interior, bent between the bucket seats, caressed the upholstery, licked the steering wheel, straddled the manual transmission, and pleasured herself on the gear-shift, squinting, sighing, quickening, lips parting and pursing in rhythm.

The light and shadow of it played across Kit's face.

&

" . . . and the sunlight kisses earth . . ."

"Too much."

" . . . and the moonbeams kiss the sea . . ."

"Not enough."

" . . . but what is all this sweet world worth . . . mmmm . . ."

"Watch it, watch it now."

"... *if you don't kiss—MEEEEEEEEE* ..."

"No!"

" ... *eeeeee* ..."

"Better. Now, ride it just a little while."

" ... *if you-oo-oo* ..." Kiki ad libbed, " ... *if you don't kiss me* ..."

"Take it home."

"Oh, babe, you've got to ki-i-isssss mmmmmmmmeeeee."

Albert's flute tangled up around her, and Zeke's soft-brushed Zilgian cymbal hushed the samba rhythm to a close.

Kiki looked over her shoulder expectantly.

"I'm outa spit, man," Albert said. "Break time."

The rest of the brethren agreed and mumbled toward the doorway, digging in their pockets for cigarettes and lighters. Kiki sat on her stool behind the microphone and self-consciously sipped at her water bottle.

"I'm afraid everybody's getting mad at me," she said meekly.

"You'll get it," Xylo shrugged.

"It wasn't my intention to make y'all practice a bunch of extra. I really thought I could just ... you know—do it."

"Oh, you could do it all right. You look real nice, and it's like I told your mama, you got a powerful instrument there. You could walk outa here and do this gig right now. And most people would probably like you just fine."

"Then I don't understand," Kiki said irritably. "Why are we still here?"

"I ain't most people."

Kiki went over to the piano and tried to look as if she were flipping through the binder of lyric sheets. As badly as she'd wanted this job, she was beginning to doubt that it could ever work out. Gravitating between Zen master and muleskinner, Xylo yelled at her if she stopped in the middle of a song, pounded on the piano if she kept going, criticized her for being too soft, too loud, too slow, too fast, too timid, too confident, too interested in appearing to be not interested enough in appearing disinterested. They'd been either at the club listening to other acts or in the upstairs rehearsal space hashing over his sacred repertoire until eleven-thirty every night since her audition. Oscar and Chloe were happy enough at Grandma's house, but the rest of the Euphonious Brethren were beginning to chafe.

Xylo startled her with his hand on her elbow.

"Nuances," he said. And Kiki repeated, "Nuances?"

"Nuances." This time he illustrated, both with the shading of his voice and a gesture of his hand.

"Suggestions, allusions, intimations. It's the nuances that tell the story, don't you see? And it's the story that separates the performer from the artist."

He pulled his piano bench from behind the keyboard and over to where she sat fidgeting with the mike stand.

"See, Miss Kiki, you were brought up to be a performer. You were taught to strut your stuff all over the stage and blow everybody away with your powerful pipes and seduce everybody with your dazzling smile. And you did that so good, you got so much applause for that, well it just got easy to let that ol' story slide, and pretty soon, it's forgotten. But I need you to remember now, Kiki. I need you to remember the story."

"Okay," Kiki said, because she had no idea what he was talking about. "I remember but—well, maybe you could . . . remind me?"

"Oh, I suppose I could, but I'm not so sure your mama wants me to!" Xylo laughed the same way he played—in easy, open chords and broad ranging melody. "No, Miss Kiki. Nobody can teach you to be who you are. But they sure can teach you not to. That they surely can."

"So, all I have to do is unlearn something that nobody didn't teach me," Kiki sulked, "and then you'll be happy."

Xylo shook his head and smiled. "Kiki, you know what a red hot mama is, don't you?"

"The front woman for a jazz band," Kiki nodded, adding with as much modesty as she could, "I was the official red hot mama of the Fort Worth Jazz Festival in 1980. I won a contest."

"I can believe you did! I bet you delivered that package and blasted the doors off the place. Because that's what a red hot mama does. She sings it out loud, she struts it out big. But the cool blues mama, Kiki, the cool blues mama, she just tells the story. She just gets born and falls in love and does what she has to do. It ain't no performance, it's her life. She knows what's in her soul, and when she lets it go—"

Kiki's eyes were starting to sting, not because she didn't understand, but because she did.

"I don't think I can do it," she told him.

"Oh, I think you're gonna work out just fine."

"I'll try," she managed to mumble.

"No," he said gently, "that's your problem right there, Kiki. You got to stop *trying* to sing—and just sing. Stop *trying* to make everybody love you. Stop *trying* to give everybody what they want. Stop giving away everything except the story."

"Yo, Xylo," Zeke said from the doorway, "if I ain't home by ten o'clock tonight, my old lady is gonna show me the wrong side of the door, man. She's gonna show me down the hall."

"I don't even know if I got an old lady anymore," Rueben grumbled. "I might as well be sleepin' at my mama's."

"Nah, that's Albert sleepin' at your mama's," Zeke ribbed, and Rueben threw a phantom punch at him.

"Yeah, fuck you, man. Your mama's so ugly, she got to open a homeless shelter to get somebody to sleep at her house."

"Go home, my brothers," Xylo smiled. "I believe our work here is done for this evening."

They packed up their instruments and sound equipment with the usual banter and jabs.

"Bus leaves at five o'clock P.M., gentlemen," Xylo reminded

126

them as they headed out the back way. "We don't want to be late and embarrass Miss Vivica."

"Yeah, just like she don't want to embarrass us!" Albert called over his shoulder. "Remember the Alamo, man. Remember the Alamo!"

Kiki looked at Xylo. He was laughing again, doing some kind of elaborate secret handshake with Albert, but he noticed her quizzical expression.

"Why don't you walk down to the end of the block with me, and I'll tell you all about it," he offered. "Looks like Jackie's Diner ought to be open for another half hour."

"Oh," Kiki looked down at her stretched leggings and oversized shirt. "I'm not dressed very—"

"You look fine, Kiki, just fine. I'd be most pleased to share your company. Shall we?"

The night was warm, but Florida never felt as stifling to her as Texas in the summer.

"Last time we were booked in Buena Vista," Xylo told her as they walked, "your wonderful mama, whom I love like my own, booked us into the saddest gig known to the industry: the Alamo rental car office."

"What?" Kiki giggled. "How do you play a rental car office?"

"Oh, it's done," he assured her, "this was an ongoing situation, although our predecessors were mostly of the country and western variety. See, the people come over on a bus from the airport, all unsuspecting how sometimes they're gonna have to stand in line for quite some time to get them wheels. I guess the good people of Alamo want to prepare them for the herd mentality of Disney World. But to soften this cruel blow, they provide live entertainment."

"Music to stand in line by?"

"That is correct, Miss Kiki, and these are not happy people. They're standing in, standing in, standing in the line one hour, two hours, more, getting all hostile and uptight. And we're doing our best to play the music, saying, 'Damn, this is one tough room.' And these guys in their hangin'-out-over-the waist, one hundred percent polyester Sansabelts, Hawaiian luau shirts, big ol' cameras hangin' all down around their necks, they're calling out, 'Hey, y'all boys play some Jimmy Buffet. Play that honky ol' Margueritaville song. Hey, don't y'all boys know some Willie Nelson?' And I'm saying to Zeke and Reuben, 'Man, I play Willie Dixon, Willie Cantrell, and Blind Willie Johnson, but I'll go to my grave a happy man without playing no Willie Nelson.' But ol' Jethro Clampit and his kinfolk, they start getting a little bit of bile up. They don't appreciate being forced to stand in no line listening to the sounds of blackness, and then they all get their shorts in a big ol' festival 'cause Albert starts making some speculations about their lineage, specifically their uncle and/or cousin and/or father being one and the same individual, and pretty soon the management requests rather emphatically that we go on and leave, and we oblige in such a rush, we go and leave all the patch cords from the sound system laying on the floor. Damn. Had to go buy new ones on the way to the next gig."

Kiki couldn't stop laughing long enough to comment.

"Girl, I love your mama like I love my own," Xylo said, "but that was one evil gig."

"Obviously," Kiki giggled, "you never played the Purmela Pork Festival."

"Sweet Lord!"

"Or the Ledbetter Convalescent Home. Or the Karnack Bikerama."

"Lord help us all."

"Or the Louisiana State Penitentiary."

"Oh," Xylo cried, "now tell me my own sweet Miss Vivica never sent her precious babies into the Louisiana State Penitentiary!"

"A riot broke out right in the middle of our Streisand medley."

"No, girl!"

"It's the truth! I swear upon my mother's cell phone."

Xylo pulled open the door of the coffee shop. Kiki realized people were staring at them. Because they were laughing so hard, she supposed. She tucked her hands under her arms and tried to be quiet as she slid into a booth across from Xylo.

"We're closing in a few minutes," the waitress said, setting a sandwich and fries in front of an elderly man at the counter.

"Ah," Xylo nodded.

"Can I give you something to go?"

"Oh, we were just going to have a quick cup of coffee," Kiki volunteered, but Xylo placed his hand on hers.

"That would be most kind," he said to the waitress. "We'll have two coffees to go. One black, one cream and sugar."

"So," Kiki giggled, "as long as we won't be playing any penitentiaries or rental car offices, I can handle just about anything."

"I can promise you, I have no intention of going there. But as you know, your mama isn't always as selective as we might hope."

"She used to tell us, 'If they've got enough money, they've got enough class.' So I've done my share of evil gigs. And then, of course, there was Calloway's. But I got myself into that one."

"Calloway's? *Hi-de-hi-de-hi-de-ho*," Xylo sang. "That don't sound too bad."

"Oh, not Calloway's as in Cab Calloway. Calloway's as in Frank Calloway. It's—I guess it's what you'd call a cabaret. Or a men's club. I mean, it's not a strip joint. It wasn't like—well, it was, sort of, but—anyway, I guess it's hard to picture. The idea of me being an exotic dancer—the way I look now."

"No," Xylo said. "I don't have a hard time with that at all. Only thing I have a hard time with is the idea of a lady like yourself casting such precious pearls before swine."

The waitress brought the coffees in a bag and wordlessly set them on the table with their bill. Xylo handed her three dollars and thanked her, holding the door open for Kiki. There was an office building with benches and a fountain out front just a block or so further, and before he sat down next to her, Xylo handed Kiki her Styrofoam cup.

"To gigs better forgotten and better gigs in the future." She lifted her cup and touched it to his. "Remember the Alamo."

"To the story," Xylo said, "and a cool blues mama about to be born."

❦

"Today," Ricki Lake announced, "*I Had SEX with My Boss AND My Sister's Sleazeball Husband!*"

The audience writhed with one twisted expression of hatred and condemnation. Despite the heat of the studio lights, Kit shivered in her midnight purple teddy.

"She's a hussy, pure and simple," said an audience member, "and that Wayne person should be castrated."

Applause, and Ricki directed a meaningful glance to the camera.

"I can't understand it," Mel said sadly, "I gave her everything. Two great kids, a three-bedroom house, two bathrooms, double garage. We just got a new microwave."

"Kit," Ricki wondered, "what was Mel not giving you that you hoped to find with another man?"

"It wasn't Mel, it was—"

"How long have you been in love with Wayne?"

"I'm not in love with Wayne! I don't even *like* Wayne!"

"Then it was pure sex? Raw animal pleasure?"

"No! No, it—it definitely wasn't that at all! It was—it was—I don't know. It . . . it all happened so fast."

"So Kit," Ricki said, holding a handful of notecards in front of her, "from the beginning. What happened?"

"Well, you see, there was this big storm, and Kiki was in Orlando visiting our mom when she got out of the hospital on account of she had to have this double radical mastectomy,"

Kit started meekly, but had to speak up to be heard over the hue and cry. "I want to say that I never meant to hurt my little sister."

Her voice was drowning in the tide of righteous indignation.

"I didn't!"

"Kit has always had difficulty in her relationships with men," said the clinical psychologist. "Her father, who favored her, died when she was young. Her mother plainly preferred her younger sister, who is smaller, prettier, more talented—"

"Would you stop with that?" Kit cut in. "I happen to be very talented."

"At what?" An audience member leaned into Ricki's mike. "Screwing?"

"*Ya, ya,*" Ander nodded. "She is most talented."

"She really is," Miz Pistonpumper added. "We've invited her to join the union."

"I think she should let her sister slap her across the face as hard as she can," another audience member was telling Ricki, "and then just move on."

"Closure," Ricki nodded wisely.

"But Wayne was the one who came over here! See, Chloe is really scared of thunder, and she was just screaming, going '*mommy mommy mommy,*' and so Wayne calls me up, and he's going, 'She won't knock it off' and 'couldn't we please just come over there' because, you know, it's a trailer house and all, and there were tornado warnings, and he just— And then he asked if it would be okay if the kids could sleep over, and I said sure, that they could sleep over with my kids, but then after I got them all tucked in and all, the power went out, and the roof was leaking, and somehow my shirt got wet from emptying the drip pans . . . and I told him to stop it, but—but he wouldn't stop it."

"So, she invites him over in the middle of the night," Rush Limbaugh stepped in, and Kit's microphone suddenly shorted out. "His wife is out of town, her husband is conveniently at work, she's strutting around braless in a wet T-shirt. Now she cries rape, and all the feminazis rally round to condemn this poor guy she lured into her spiderweb."

"I told him to stop! I kept telling him, but—"

"But does she call the police? Does she tell her husband or her sister?"

"How could I? He—he was crying and—and he said he was drunk and he didn't mean it and it would destroy her and that it was all my fault because—but I tried. I tried to make him stop."

"Funny, I don't see any bruises," Rush said with huge mock amazement. "She must have really put up a hell of a fight."

"I didn't want it to happen . . ."

"Did you fight him, Kit?" Ricki asked. "Did you give him a sharp knee to the groin?"

The audience was very quiet, waiting for the correct answer, but Kit couldn't think of a way to explain to them how he could hold both her wrists in one hand, how he kept telling her to be quiet or she'd wake the babies, how impossible it is to defend something that has no value.

"C'mon, Kit. A knuckle to the eye socket? Anything?"

"No."

"Then it *was* your fault."

"Yes."

A howl went up. Kit looked away from Mel's injured expression and into Kiki's tearful one, which was worse. Even Ricki looked annoyed at this point.

"I—I just want to say that I never meant to hurt my little sister. And—"

"*Awww!*" the audience derided, blasting gales of it toward the stage.

"I didn't!" Kit turned to the clinical psychologist, pleading for some support. "Tell them I didn't. Tell them I wanted to hurt myself, not her."

"Kit, we have a special surprise for you today." Ricki referred to her hand-held cue cards. "Let's welcome to the show Mrs. Vivica Smithers, Kit and Kiki's mother!"

"*No!*" Kit blurted aloud, startling herself awake, sloshing bathwater onto the floor.

It had gone cold, but rather than try to warm it up, she got out and sat on the bathroom rug, arms wrapped around her legs, her legs tight together, trying to breathe evenly, trying not to remember how she let him climb on top of her like that.

The things he was saying that night gave her the same scalp-crawling sensation she'd felt listening to the backwash of looped blue movie voices. She had resisted when he came up behind her and slid his hands inside her shirt and then down. The bourbon on his tongue tasted acrid as the vomit that now scratched at the back of her throat. He was skinny and workish, not large and warm, like Mel. He was the Anti-Mel. There was no trace of human comfort in his carefully groomed physique, in the technique he substituted for touch—only proclivity and function and the smell of beer.

He pierced into her like the lancing of an abscess: disruption, injury, but an end, or at least, a different brand of infection. She knew she'd be left blood-rusted and ruined, but no longer, at least, what she had been. There was no need to struggle anymore. A wooden feeling, a great leaden sadness she'd been fighting for a long while now, went to her hands, and they dropped to her sides, and he mistook this for the seduction of her.

Lying inanimate between his writhing and the clean kitchen floor, Kit observed the broken dark of the bay window, the hushed ticking of the sunflower clock. From there, she could see accumulated deposits of grease and grime on the underside of the range hood that looked so shiny clean from the usual upright perspective.

She focused on the endless turning of the ceiling fan, the

imperfect tulips stencilled on the doorjamb, a glass tumbler that teetered at the very edge of the table. It wobbled slightly in response to the repeated pulse of her knees, pushed apart, apart, apart like a mechanical butterfly between the table leg and the white wainscoting.

More than the possibility of loss, it was the suspension Kit found unbearable; watching the glass hang there at the edge, knowing it must eventually hit the floor, must explode, expel. The only thing that could prevent it now was the end of the world. But it held there, against the laws of nature.

As Wayne groaned and jerked his final spasm, Kit grasped the bottom of the checkered tablecloth and wrenched it toward her. The tumbler tipped and gratefully gave itself to gravity, turning in the air, milky-hard ice and cold-stung water spiraling outward like the cataclysmic birth of a galaxy. And then, such relief at the sound of shattering.

A jagged crescent skittered across the linoleum, and Kit closed her hand around it, letting her blood, losing her innocence, breathing again.

*T*he droning motor of the tour bus lulled Kiki to a nodding doze as it lumbered down the highway toward Tampa Bay's Azure Club and her twenty-sixth gig in thirty days.

She lay across two seats, dreaming of Oscar and Chloe, catching brief glimpses of them as they dove and tadpoled between the surface of the water and the fathoms of her fitful sleep. She wished she could float up from the bottom of Vivica's pool to surface beside them, kiss them over their air mattresses, taste the chlorine on their cheeks, feel them hugging back in their clammy, neon-colored swimsuits. From under-water, she could see Vivica coming out onto the patio, bringing them juice boxes and animal crackers, her pink lips chatting at the cell phone, telling someone how her daughter pulled off a kamikaze audition with a stroke of musical genius and a bit of bathroom reverb.

"Kiki?"

Xylo's soft calling drew her deeper until the water pressure became one with the droning of the motor. She didn't open her eyes yet. She wanted him to call her again. Maybe even bend down and touch her shoulder. She felt guilty for wanting that. She was still a married woman, after all; Wayne hadn't yet responded to her lawyer's fat envelope of paperwork. She was a mother. She was about to become another mother. She was trying to make her way in the world for the very first time in her twenty-nine years. She had to set priorities.

But she couldn't help it.

When Xylo said her name like that, it made her feel silky all over.

"Kiki?"

She smiled, and her smile made the sound of "Hmm?"

"Zeke wants to know if he should pull into the rest area."

"Y'all don't have to blame me for every rest stop." Kiki sat up and pushed her hair away from her eyes. "Doesn't anyone else ever use the bathroom around here?"

Xylo folded into the seat next to her, sitting cross-legged like Oscar would or Gandhi or a Hopi medicine man.

"The Brethren have been known to do some prodigious micturition, particularly subsequent to some legendary libationary intake," he told her proudly. "However, we are sensitive to the diminished bladder capacity often associated with your delicate and oh-so-womanly condition."

"Okay," Kiki laughed. She had no idea what he'd just said, but she loved the sound of his language. It made her think of when her mother used to read to them from the old *Bulfinch's Mythology* or the heavy brown *Complete Annotated Works of William Shakespeare* that spread open across their three laps and featured elegant etched illustrations protected by a layer of tissue paper.

"In other words," Xylo said sideways, "does the lady got to pee?"

"No, I'm OK."

"Hallelujah. It's a miracle."

"I've been trying not to drink anything. It wasn't my intention to put anybody out."

"No such thing, Miss Kiki." Xylo rested his head on the seat back. "Don't you go depriving yourself. We're most pleased and privileged to be put out by you. And adequate hydration is essential to vocal strength."

Kiki rested her head back, too, so that if they were living on a plane of reality tipped perpendicular to this one, they would be lying down together.

Up front, Reuben was bar-chording a rumpled rhythm with his guitar, spreading it out like an unmade bed under Albert's restless flute. The reedy melody tossed and turned, tangled itself in the sheets. When Zeke swerved to miss a bump in the road, it made Xylo's shoulder lean against Kiki's, and neither of them moved to make it not be so.

Two days unshaven, the gray in his beard had become more evident. Kiki studied the lines at the side of his eye, the etching at the corner of his mouth as elegant as the images of the Old Globe.

Reuben eased into a minor key, and the tangled bedclothes spread out over them, the surface of the sound rising and rolling with the motion of all the life that lay below. When Albert laid his flute aside to pick up his clarinet, Xylo hummed and scattered a line that quietly crossed and countered the alto strand, though he kept his voice low, a voyeur at the keyhole.

He turned to Kiki, his mouth close to the curve of her ear.

"You see it, don't you?" he whispered.

"What?" Kiki whispered back.

"Mazzini called music 'an echo of the invisible world.' But some people see it. You see it, don't you, Kiki?"

Silky, silky, silky as her red spaghetti-strap gown swaying back and forth on the costume rack.

"I see it, too," Xylo nodded. "Always did."

"Even when you were little?"

"It was my destiny. My mama knew it the day I was born.

She made me take piano and play organ in church, but I wanted to play brass. I wanted to blow like Louis or Dizzy. I thought blowing a note like that would feel like flying. I thought I'd hit that note someday, and my feet would leave the earth."

"Why didn't you?"

"That was not my destiny," he shook his head. "Adam and his kind, we got to reach out to the hand of God and allow the light to guide us."

"Why'd you start playing the xylophone?" she asked him, and he smiled.

"You sound like Oscar." Kiki took that as a compliment, even when Xylo laughed and parroted Oscar's inquisitive tonality. "'Why'd you start playin' that xylophone? Why you got such black dark eyes? Why you got that scar on the side of your face? Why you not married when you so old?'"

Kiki laughed too, but then she said again, "Why?"

"I signed up to play the cornet in the marching band at George Washington Carver Junior High School on 87th Street in Detroit, Michigan. And when I arrived for the first day of summer band practice, I walked into that beat-up, high-ceiling, paint-crackin'-off-the-walls band room, and I saw a beam of sunlight streamin' in between the metal bars on the window, fallin' down in a golden ray that exploded into a long row of silver streaks like the fingers of angels all lined up shining on the keyboard of God's piano. And that was the xylophone. Layin' up there on a big ol' wooden box in the percussion corner. All the sticks and mallets and screws scattered on the floor. All kinds of 'fuck you' and 'shit' and 'Delbert love Loretta' and 'white man die' was written all over the tympani and the trap set, and they scratched up, dented up, kicked in the old glockenspiels and wood blocks and hanging chimes. But that xylophone—that was like the Ark of the Covenant. They never dared to touch it. I stood there like I was Adam on the ceiling of the Sistine Chapel, the finger of God reaching down to me, telling me, 'Zephaniah Haines, you gonna live or else. You gonna get on outa this bad-ass neighborhood, and you gonna build your mama a decent house, and you gonna play this thing to the glory of God until the day you die.' And right then and there, I traded in my cornet, and I took my place high up in the far corner of the percussion section. And the moment I lay my hand on that radiant silver surface, I knew I was touching the hand of God. I knew I was to become an instrument of His peace."

"Your destiny," Kiki murmured.

"I surely did know it. I went home that day and told my mama, 'I am going to be a blues impresario.'"

"I wonder what my destiny is," Kiki said, settling deeper into the seat cushions.

"To sing . . . ," Xylo traced the curve of her throat with his fingertips, "to have babies . . . ," and touched the swell of her stomach. "To be innocent . . . " He pressed his lips to the back of her hand, "and beautiful . . . ," and kissed the front of her wrist. "To love . . . ," he nuzzled her cheek, "and be loved." He brushed his soft, full lips against hers in a gesture too gentle to even be called a kiss. "To feel joy."

When Xylo breathed the word against her mouth, Kiki could almost feel herself speaking it and believing.

The music soaked up the last of the moonlight, leaving a vacuum that drew flat against the tinted windows everything that is always just before dawn. The bus rolled on toward the coming day, and Kiki rolled with it, yearning toward the newly perceptible nearness of her Creator, striving to open her eyes wide enough to allow the light.

⁂

"Shut that light off!" Kit croaked, squinting and shielding her eyes with her hand, but the sudden shaft pierced straight through to her gray matter.

"Mom?" Cooper ventured.

"What do you want? Get out of here. Go back to bed."

She pulled the blankets over her face.

"There's somebody at the door," Cooper whispered. "I was watching 'George of the Jungle,' and somebody knocked on the door."

Kit's hand emerged from the wadded sheet and dragged the alarm clock into her floral cocoon.

"Six seventeen on a Saturday morning," she moaned. "What kind of Neanderthal jackass—"

"It's Mr. Anderson," Cooper said.

"*What?* Are you sure?"

"I pulled a chair up to the peephole."

"Oh, god*dang!*" Kit threw off the covers and clapped her hands over her face. "Coo, be my big boy for me? Go on down there and tell him—just tell him . . . oh *dang.*" She kicked out of the bedding and ran for the bathroom. "Tell him I'll be right down."

There was nothing for it.

He was down there at the door with his carpenter's hands and his blue eyes and his lilting mouth. Kit caught a glimpse in the mirror. Good. She looked like complete and utter hell. He couldn't want her like this, and that would make it easier. He would be revolted and draw back and never return. She pulled Mel's bathrobe over her dowdy sleep-shirt to make it even dowdier, splashed cold water on her blotchy face to make it even blotchier. She pulled on some socks from the laundry basket and shuffled down the stairs.

Ander stood in the entryway, talking with Cooper about the Houston Rockets' shot at another NBA title. When he saw her, he smiled in a way that encompassed his whole head.

"Kit," he said. "Ah, Kit."

"Cooper, go on in and watch TV now," Kit said, wishing for both their sakes she'd taken a moment to swish some Scope through her mouth before she left the bathroom.

"Ah, Kit," Ander said again when Coo had disappeared back into the family room. "Kit. Hello, Kit."

"Hello, Ander."

"Ya. Ya, hello, Kit. Hello."

He was fidgeting with his hands, as though they wouldn't do what he wanted them to. Or he wouldn't let them do what they wanted to.

"Ander, what are you doing here?"

"Oh Kit. I—I am . . . *ah Gott*. This is so good to see you."

"Ander, I told you before—"

"No! Yes, I know, but I—I am only coming to—to be bringing this to you."

He pulled a letter out of his pocket. It was stamped and addressed to Kit in Ruda's handwriting. It had obviously spent several days in the pocket, knowing full well it was morally obligated to a mail box, but unable to resist fantasies of hand-delivery.

"Is your pay," he said, thrusting it forward. "For the last week of working and . . . and the extra for the—the painting of—of . . . that day."

"Yes. Okay. Fine. Thank you." Kit took it and pulled the door open without looking at him. "Goodbye, Ander."

"Kit—"

"Goodbye."

He sighed heavily and dropped his chin down to his chest.

"Ya, okay, then. Goodbye, Kit."

He stepped past the door, but when she started to close it after him, he blocked it open with his outstretched hand.

"Kit—" His face was earnest, but he wasn't pleading, only telling her. "You are very beautiful lover to me, beautiful, beautiful Kit. And I am never forgetting you forever. I am very much remembering you. Nothing can ever be same for me any more."

Kit allowed herself to look at his eyes, blue and brimming as the fjords. She nodded and tried to swallow the burning in her throat, but her voice came out scratchy and staccato.

"I know. I'm sorry, Ander. I never meant to—"

"No. No, of course not. And I never did also."

They stood for a long moment, recognizing how that didn't change anything.

"Goodbye, Ander."

"Goodbye, Kit."

She closed the door and went back upstairs.

She stood crying in the shower a while, then pulled on her bathrobe, sat down on the bed, and picked up the phone.

"Hmm . . . mm-hmm?" Vivica murmured.

Kit realized a moment too late how early it was and was about to hang up, but her mother said, "Kit?"

"Hi!" Kit said cheerfully, trying not to show how it weirded her out when her mother did that. "Did I wake you?"

"No, I had to get up and answer the phone."

"I'm sorry."

"It was a joke! Really, it's all right. I'm a steroid insomniac these days. My eyes look like empty wallets, but I'm getting a lot of paperwork done."

"How are you, Mama? Are you okay? How's the—the chemo . . . thing?"

"Worse than the dentist, not as bad as the IRS," wise-cracked Vivica.

Kit laughed for her and tried to make it sound genuine.

"All in all, I think we'll make it."

"I know you will, Mama."

"They say that which does not kill us makes us stronger. I've decided to go with Plan B."

Kit found herself waiting for the rim shot when Vivica delivered this sort of stand-up comic line, but it was getting harder and harder to be the appreciative audience.

"Mama?"

"What is it, Bitty Kitty?" Vivica sounded concerned or maybe just tired; Kit couldn't tell.

"Well, I was just thinking. You know, if you need me to, I could drive down there and stay for a couple weeks. To help out, you know?"

"You're sweet, Kitten, but I've already got Kiki here, honey. I'm not sure I'm up to having any more help than that right now."

"Oh, right," Kit said, "I just thought—"

"Is something wrong, sweetheart?"

"No, of course not. Everything's fine."

"What's going on?"

"Nothing! Nothing is going on, Mama. Why would you think something is going on? Isn't it possible that maybe I just wanted to come down there and—and be with you and help you get through this and take care of you?"

"Well, don't get upset, Kit. I'm just being concerned."

"Well, I'm just being concerned about *you!* And I think I've got more reason to be concerned about you than you've got reason to be concerned about me being concerned . . . about you."

Kit listened to herself protesting too much, knowing her mother could see right through it, hating it that neither one of them could come right out and say so.

"Mama, I—I should go. I'm sorry. I didn't mean to wake you."

"Honey, wait—"

"Mama, would you tell Kiki to call me when she gets up?"

"Actually, she's out of town for a couple days. Tampa Bay through the weekend. I'm lining her up in some delicious venues," Vivica confided, "and she is in good voice, Kit. Very good voice."

"That's great," Kit said. "I'm really glad for her."

"You know, sweetie, if there's something wrong, and you need to come down—"

"There's nothing wrong, Mama. Everything's great."

"In fact, why don't you? Actually, it does sound like a good idea. You know, I really could use a hand, and I'd love to see you, Bitty Kitty. You know you're always welcome."

"I know," Kit whispered.

"You and Mel and the kids are still planning to come down here next month, aren't you?"

"I don't know."

"Well, *I'm* still planning on it! I'm looking forward to it. I told them all down at the torture chamber I was holding off that cycle—"

"No, Mama, don't do that. The most important thing right now—"

"Yes, yes," Vivica said, "I already got that lecture from the home health nazis, but this is my body, and I'll decide where it goes and when it goes there."

"I know, but—well, anyway . . . We won't be—I mean, we still want to come, but we won't be able to spend the week like we planned."

"Oh, now don't you kids ruin your vacation plans on my account."

"No, it's not that. It's just . . . I mean, we were—we *are* concerned, and we just decided to make it sort of a . . . a weekend thing."

"Nonsense! Everybody knows you can't do Disney World in one—"

"I know," Kit hedged, "but I decided to take some time off from work, so you know, budgetwise . . . "

"Time off? What for? Are you feeling all right?"

"Yes, fine. I'm fine."

"How much time off are we talking about?"

"All of it."

"What?" coughed her mother. "You quit your job? Kitten, why?"

"Mama, please don't start."

"Kit," she started anyway, "someone as intelligent and talented as you—"

"What? You don't think it takes intelligence and talent to raise children and manage a household?"

"I never said that."

"But you think it, Mama, you think it all the time. You think I wasted my whole life."

"I most certainly do not."

"Just because you chose to be—"

"I didn't *choose* anything! I never had a choice! When Daddy died, he left nothing. I *had* to support myself and you girls, and I had to do it with an educational background of charm school and tap dancing lessons. But you had a choice, Kit, and you chose to be an artist."

"Oh, artist *shmartist!* I faked and copied and stencilled other people's art on tasteless little bric-a-brack and white elephant furniture. I hated that job!"

"Baloney. You loved that job, and you were damn good at it. I always said that if you'd gone to art school—"

"But there's one more thing I failed to do. Go to art school and be a painter. Go to college and be a music teacher. Go to technical school and be a paralegal. Did you have any other great ideas for me, Mama?"

"Yes! Millions of them. I had hopes and dreams for you, too. So shoot me. Don't you have hopes and dreams for your children?"

"Yes, but I'm not trying to shove it down their throats."

"Oh, don't *even!*" Vivica sounded wide awake now. "When you wanted out, you got out. Just like that. I never said word one about it. And not because it didn't kill me to let you go! Sometimes—oh, I *tell* you!—when I think what the two of you could have accomplished—"

"Yeah, I know, I know. We could be opening for everybody from Wayne Newton to the Lord God Himself by now, but instead, I got married. And since Kiki has to do everything I do, she got married, too. So of course, it's all my fault. I disappointed you. I'm just a big ol', stupid ol', fat thighs, unemployed disappointment."

"*Kitten Amaryllis Smithers.*" Vivica could still send her to her room, even when Kit was in her own house a thousand miles away. "I don't know what's going on with you today, but I am really not up for this." Kit curled up at the corner of the bed and rested her head against the wall. "Kit?" She didn't make a sound. "Kitty, why are you crying?"

"I'm not," she denied tightly.

"Sweetie, tell me what's wrong."

"*Oh, God, Mama. I'm sorry.*" Kit audibly dissolved. "I'm so . . . I'm so *stupid!*"

"You most certainly are not."

"I am! I break everything. I hate myself! I wish *I* was the one with cancer! I wish I was *dead!*"

"Stop it!" Vivica said sharply. "Don't you ever say that. Not ever."

"I'm sorry, I'm sorry. I don't know what's wrong with me, Mama. Lately, I can't—I can't even—" Kit left off, crying harder, struggling to breathe.

"Honey, shhh. Calm down now. Try to relax," Vivica soothed. "Kitten, what on earth is this all about? Is this about Mel?"

"No," she choked. "At first I thought it was, but it's not his fault. He always—he only does what's right, and I always—I don't know . . . "

"Kitty, what on earth is going on?"

But Kit just cried.

"Tell me what happened with your job," Vivica pressed. "Honey, why would you go and quit your job?"

"*Because they fired me!*"

"Oh, dear."

"And I m-miss K-kiki and I'm—I'm worried about y-you and we don't have any money and everything is rotten and it's—*all—my—f-fault!*"

"Now, wait a minute," Vivica said. "I hate to interrupt the flagellation fest, but let's just take a deep breath and look this thing in the eye for a minute. First off, you are not stupid, and whatever that damn Andrew—"

"*Ander.*"

"Whatever. It's his loss. Nuts to him. You *are* talented and intelligent, and if that job was out there, there's a better one right around the corner. Now that you've had nine years of experience—"

"I didn't have nine years of experience," Kit sniffed, "I had one year of experience nine times."

"Well, then," Vivica stood firm, "it sounds like you're ready for something new. Just shake it off, honey. Now's the time you've gotta keep your wits about you. You've gotta take that ram by the horns. Have you made any inquiries or applications?"

"Not really."

"Well, there. You see? Once you start putting yourself out there, opportunities will crop up, I guarantee it. They'll jump out and bite you when you least expect it."

"Yeah, right."

"I mean it! Just keep your eyes open. Stay awake, be ready."

"Okay."

"And in the meantime, enjoy being home for a while, sweetie. You've earned a little time off." Vivica softened the coaching tone. "Funniest thing, down at the chemo ward? There are plenty of regrets, but I haven't heard a single person say, 'If only I hadn't spent so much time with those damn kids!'"

"Mama . . . "

"I mean it. Being a mommy isn't the only thing you'll ever do, but it's the most important, Kitten. It's the one thing in my life I wish I could have done better."

"Mama, you did fine. You did . . . amazing."

"All I'm saying is—enjoy it while you can."

"I do."

"I know, Bitty Kitty. You're a wonderful mother. And you're beautiful and smart, and Mel Prizer is the luckiest bastard on the face of this earth."

"Mama, I should go. The kids are up, and they make a big mess if they end up getting their own breakfast."

"Kitten—"

"Mama, would you tell Kiki to call me when she gets home? When she gets back, I mean? Gets there?"

"Of course. I'll tell her," Vivica promised. "Kitten, you know I love you, sweetie, and if you need to come down here—"

"I love you, too, Mama. I'll . . . I'll talk to you soon."

Kit set the phone down and pressed her warm forehead and swollen eyes into the cool pillow. By the time the pillow sham began to feel damp and warm, she knew what she had to do.

It wasn't even seven yet, and Mel was planning to work overtime till ten. Kit got up and pulled on jean shorts and one of his old T-shirts. In the kitchen, she opened the under-sink cupboard and pulled out rubber gloves, paper towels, and a bottle of all-purpose spray cleaner.

Starting at the back door, she worked her way around the kitchen, leaving everything spotless. She opened the refrigerator and took out every last item, scrubbed the shelves, and soaked the crisper drawers in antibacterial dish soap before reassembling the whole thing. She bent over backwards to scour at the grease and grime on the underside of the range hood until it shone as white as the top facade.

"You two go on out and eat your cereal on the patio," she shooed Mitzi and Coo away from the table. "And shut that door! We're not air-conditioning the state of Texas!"

She moved through the living room like a cyclone, creating a Mitzi pile and a Cooper pile to carry up to their rooms, stacking newspapers and magazines to jettison into the recycling bins, then vacuuming everything from the carpet up to the couch cushions and even the dust bunnies on top of the drapes and the cobwebs above the ceiling fan.

By the time she finished scrubbing both bathrooms from grout to showerhead, the sun was moving over the windowsill, and Kit was sticky with dust and sweat, but she attacked her and Mel's bedroom and didn't stop until every item was in its proper place.

Looking finally around the immaculate house, she was breathing hard, but feeling oddly heroic.

Yes, she was guilty, but she would atone. She would redeem herself. She would systematically eliminate every bad thought from her mind, expunge every stray image. She would reclaim Mel from the winter of obesity and indifference and chronic fatigue that had engulfed him by providing him a place of comfort, a tower of strength, meals fit for a god, and a toilet that shone like an ivory chalice. Arrayed in lace and stilettos, she would entertain him like a mechanical she-devil. She would be a good wife, and she would never, never, never question or break a rule or betray her husband again.

She put in a load of laundry, then took another shower. She tied her hair back with a yellow scrunchy, put on a summer dress, and hung little sunflower earrings on to match. She made Mel's coffee and laid the *Houston Chronicle* on the table for him.

Then Kit sat on a kitchen chair, waiting for the grating garage door opener to trumpet the arrival of her destiny.

☙

It struck Kiki as odd that the pictures were in color. Because in the movies, pictures of this sort were always composed of stark black/white contrasts and grainy telephoto grays.

But the blend of Xylo's hand on her bosom was explicitly clear and actually more coffee and cream than black and white. His palm partially covered the rose-mauve tip of her breast, as if to safeguard her modesty, defend her honor. Her upraised eyes shone blue as pool water above her soft ruby smile, and the strap of the red silk dress trickled down her arm. In the second photo, her head dropped forward, spilling golden hair against the sea-green satin of Xylo's shoulder. His hand had disappeared inside the dress, but now his full lips shielded her nipple from the lens.

"Well, Mrs. Daubert?" Wayne's lawyer said, and Wayne just stood there grinning.

"Well what?" Kiki slid the eight-by-tens back into the manila envelope. "I don't know what I'm supposed to say."

She stared out at the patio where Oscar and Chloe huddled next to Mrs. Quintantilla on the pillowed chaise lounge.

"She doesn't get it." Wayne wasn't even bothering to promise and plead with her like he usually did. He seemed disappointed that she wasn't upset by the packet he'd presented to her the way Miss Calico might proffer a gory trophy. "She doesn't know what we got here."

"Well, I guess you got . . . I mean, this must be grounds for divorce," Kiki said. "Don't you want a divorce?"

"No, Kalene, I do not want a divorce," he replied. "I want y'all to come on back home and get everything back to normal. I want you to settle yourself down and be just like you always were before this jigger-boo come along and put all kinds of ideas in your head, and I warn you, Kalene—"

"Wayne," his lawyer mumbled and made a let-me-handle-this gesture. "What your husband is saying, Mrs. Daubert, is that he still loves you. He forgives you and is willing to take you back, if you're willing to come home and work toward a reconciliation."

"No. I'm not going home with him." Kiki could see nothing in this man's eyes that seemed open to her side of the story. "I told you, sir, he drinks, and he went off with another woman and he . . . he scares me."

"Scares you?" he said patiently.

"He . . . hurts me." She swallowed and straightened her shoulders. "He beats me."

"Bullshit!" Wayne exploded. "You're the one running all over the country, hangin' out in bars, screwing around with that nigger—"

"Wayne, " the attorney repeated the gesture.

"If anybody's gettin' beat on here, it's me!"

"*Wayne. Please.*" He sat down in the middle of the sofa and motioned the two of them toward the wingback chairs at either end of the coffee table.

"Now, Mrs. Daubert, it's not uncommon for a woman to make all kinds of wild accusations, including infidelity and spousal abuse, in order to gain financial and custodial leverage in these situations, so please understand if I'm a bit skeptical here. How is it that you've never mentioned any of this before? I notice the grounds you cited for wanting a divorce were . . . " He consulted some paperwork. "Ah, yes. 'Irreconcilable differences.'"

"He knows what he did."

"Do you have any evidence? Anything at all to back up these allegations? Photographs? Videotapes? Affidavits from any of these alleged other women? Hospital records pertaining to your supposed injuries?"

"Yes! I—I had to get stitches one time. There must be a record of that!"

"Your chart reflects that you told the attending physician," he consulted the paperwork again, "that you 'tripped over the cat and struck your chin on a cupboard.'"

"And—and another time, I had a broken finger—"

"And you said you closed it in the car door."

"He knows. He knows that is not true."

"Well, that would be for a court of law to decide."

"And I . . . Last year, I had a miscarriage."

"Kalene, you shut the fuck—"

"*You know, Wayne Daubert, Jr.! You know what happened!*"

"*You shut the fuck up, Kalene!*"

"Enough! Wayne, that's enough. Mrs. Daubert, please." The lawyer gestured them back to their chairs. "That's enough. Both of you. There's nothing to be gained by this."

"Please, sir," Kiki started, "don't make me—"

But he focused his eyes away from hers. He dropped his pen and fumbled with his papers uncertainly for a moment, but then he smoothed them out over the top of his briefcase and nodded to himself.

"All right. All right now, Mrs. Daubert," he said. "Of course we cannot nor would we want to force you to return to Houston against your will, but we have obtained a court order enabling us to take the children—"

"What?"

"—back to the home they know and love—"

"*No!*"

"—with the father who has always provided for them so well."

"I won't let you, Wayne." Kiki stepped between him and the patio door, as if that would stop him. "They don't want to go with you, and you know it."

"Mrs. Daubert, these are minors, far too young to make their own decisions regarding custody and placement."

"That's right, sir. They're young. They are. They need their mama."

"Not if their mama is 'unfit.'" Wayne poked his index finger toward her, proud of all he'd learned about legal matters in just one plane ride from Houston to Orlando.

"Unfit?" Kiki repeated, not even knowing what to deny. "I am not unfit."

"Mrs. Daubert, in addition to the fact that your income is extremely unstable, we have evidence that the children have been subjected to some very unwholesome influences while in your custody."

"Dang unwholesome," Wayne concurred.

"Wayne, why are you doing this?" She tried not to sound scared. "Why won't you just let me go?"

"Mr. Daubert is simply concerned for the welfare of his children."

"That's right," Wayne nodded.

"His children?" Kiki almost laughed, "Where do you think his children were while he was—"

"Do you or do you not routinely take them into bars and nightclubs?" Wayne's attorney asked, his proficient calm feeding off Kiki's intimidation and panic.

"No! No, of course not! Unless you . . . well, just—just during . . . See, sometimes while I'm rehearsing, but—but that's always during the day, and they're not even open."

"And are they not routinely left behind without adequate supervision while you travel out of town for several days at a time?"

"No! Not—not *several*. Just . . . just two or three maybe, and they're with my mother—"

"Who dumps them on her secretary while she runs a busy office."

"No, she—sometimes they stay home because—"

"And where did you say your mother is today?"

"Well, see, she had a bad time with her chemo this month and—and her white count got too low, and she had to stay in the hospital for a couple days, but Mrs. Quintantilla—"

"Who doesn't speak English."

"Well, not fluently, but—"

"In addition to which you have now been photographed carrying on lewd behavior in a public place, openly engaging in a sexual affair with some transient lounge performer."

"*Lounge performer?*" Kiki burst out. "He happens to be *a blues impresario!*"

"He also happens to be a convicted felon."

"No . . . " It took a moment for that to sink in. "That's not true."

"Oh, it's true, I assure you, Mrs. Daubert. Your friend spent fourteen years as a guest of the state of Michigan, which I'm sure gave him plenty of time to work on his music, but tends to be very troublesome to a jury. And we haven't even mentioned the . . . shall we say, 'cultural differences' that may cast a very bad light on you."

"That means," Wayne explained to her as if she were Chloe, "how you're a white girl and good ol' homey there is a goddamn—"

"I know what it means, Wayne!"

The attorney didn't even bother gesturing. He was focused, closing in on his favorite outcome to his favorite game.

"It could be argued that this entire situation has already caused lasting emotional harm to the children."

"We are not having a sexual affair, Wayne. I have never been with any man but you. Not in my whole life!"

"Mrs. Daubert, the photos would seem to indicate that you are lying."

"Well, yes, it—they *seem*— But that's all! We never—"

"If you insist, Mrs. Daubert." The lawyer brushed her denials aside and snapped his briefcase closed on Vivica's end table. "Your attorney can certainly contest this order, but the children would most likely be placed in foster care while that decision is being made. And that can take a long time, Mrs. Daubert. A very long time. But your attorney can best advise you on that."

Kiki's attorney had answered the phone when she responded to an ad that read "Divorce $80!" in the *Penny-Wize Shopper* classifieds. He wore a bad toupee and spoke with some sort of clicking, glottal speech impediment.

"Mrs. Daubert?" prompted the attorney.

"Sir," her voice quavered, "I am a good mother."

"Then act like it, Mrs. Daubert. Your husband is being very generous here. He's willing to overlook this indiscretion. He's merely asking you to return home and serve the best interest of the children." He took both her hands in his and smiled with a sudden Machiavellian fatherliness. "Kalene, I know y'all two have your differences. But Wayne here is prepared to go to counseling and work those differences out. Now, don't you think it'll be best for everyone if you come on home with your little ones to Houston and resume your place in a happy, Christian home? And then y'all can just forget that any of this unpleasantness ever took place."

Kiki knew there was nothing else for her to do. Daddy Daubert had paid out a significant amount of money to fly this man down here and finance the private investigation firm that followed her to Tampa Bay and took those pictures. He kept a tight grip on his money; when he spent it, he expected results. And he got them. Because he wouldn't stop until he did.

Kiki wished now she'd listened to her mother and used an attorney Vivica dated occasionally: a slashingly well-dressed man who wore suits as gray and sleek as shark's skin and whose TV commercials portrayed a self-professed "legal hammer." She wished she'd cashed out the cards before Wayne had a chance to cancel them. And gone somewhere Wayne wouldn't have thought to look. She wished she was back on the bus with Xylo and Zeke and the rest of the Euphonious Brethren.

She wished Xylo had been willing to make love to her, as long as she was getting blamed for it now, anyway. But he wouldn't do it. He said it was too soon. That she was still married. He said that he wanted to know her better, wanted to know how to spell her middle name, and who her first-grade teacher was. He wanted to see each one of her scars and hear how she got it. He wanted to know what she looked like sleeping and what she felt like inside, but he would wait, he said, until she was free of all the negative energy Wayne was exerting over her, and then he would celebrate the essence and beauty of her in a proper and conducive setting, not on the dirty backstage floor of the Azure Club.

Kiki wished he hadn't said that. She would have preferred having Xylo once on a dirty floor to never having him at all, but as she stared at the manila envelope, he sank back into his invisible world, taken on the tide of Albert's disconsolate clarinet.

The Second Trimester

Biology is her destiny.
Anatomy is her fate.

Mary Hugh Scott

*T*he pressure of the takeoff made Chloe scream because of her swimmer's ear, and she cried, on and off, until they reached Houston, but there were little video game screens built into the backs of the airplane seats, so the flight couldn't have lasted long enough for Oscar.

When they stepped into the jetway, the heat and humidity enveloped Kiki, intensifying the forces of gravity and leaving her feeling even more earthbound. They walked wordlessly to the long-term parking lot where Wayne had left the station wagon. He unlocked the doors and loaded the luggage.

"I've got a surprise for you." Wayne reached over and squeezed her knee as they came down the circular ramp of the parking tower.

Kiki nodded slightly, and they drove on in silence until they came to the gravel drive outside the double-wide. Wayne pulled the car into the translucent green shelter of the carport, but they all sat silent, even after he'd shut off the engine.

"Oscar!" Kiki said suddenly. "You know what you should do?"

He looked up, startled, and their eyes met in her visor mirror.

"You should call Cooper. You should call Coo and tell him all about those little video game screens, you know? You know how Coo loves video games?"

"Could I, Dad?" Oscar asked. "Just to tell him about the games?"

Wayne put the car in park and rested his palms on the steering wheel.

"Maybe next week," he said quietly. He turned to Kiki, and his face was full of regrets and pleading. "Next week, Peaches, okay? Please?"

Kiki dropped her eyes guiltily.

"Give me a chance, Kiki. Give me a chance to show you I can make you happy again."

She nodded, and he broke into a grin.

"Come and see your surprise."

He leapt out and dashed around the car to open Kiki's door for her, pointing out the freshly mown lawn and tidy flower-beds that gave her that odd coming-home feeling of never having been gone.

He led her by the hand all through the house, excited as a child. He'd had someone come and clean. He'd made window boxes and installed them outside the living room and kitchen. There was a new entertainment center with a new game system for Oscar and Kiki's karaoke machine installed alongside a big-screen TV. A pretty porcelain doll that looked like Shirley Temple had been added to Chloe's collection.

"Okay now," Wayne delighted, "no peeking."

He stepped behind Kiki and placed his cool hands over her eyes, guiding her, his body against her back, toward the back door.

"Surprise!" he said, and she found herself standing in the middle of the patio, facing the hanging bougainvillea.

"*Oh!*" she exclaimed softly when she glimpsed the soft brown back of the mother dove. "They're still here!"

But as she carefully approached the basket, the dragging gravity she'd felt in the jetway began to take hold of her again.

"Stuey and Dad both said it's some of the best work I ever did," Wayne told her, too modest to say he thought so himself. "They said it was as good as anything in the natural history museum."

"*Oh . . .*" Kiki said again.

"It's the perfect little family." He led her closer with a gentle hand at her elbow, tenderly adding, "You were my inspiration, Kalene."

The mother dove arced gracefully over the babies, holding a small bread crust above their open mouths. The eager young ones craned toward the morsel, downy necks extended, delicate wings slightly open, as the daddy dove perched on the edge of the basket, looking proudly on. They didn't look frozen; they were still the same brushed brown and alabaster, not iced white or tinged blue. They didn't even look dead, really; the still life was dynamic with the asymmetry of artistic motion.

The scene was one of such serenity. There was no echo of screeching or fear or frantic flapping; no memory of the moment when all their terror became this perfect peace. It took Kiki a long moment to realize there was no life there, except the uninterrupted blossoming of the bougainvillea.

❦

Kit had become the perfect wife.

Mel's favorite dishes hit the dinner table every evening at six, and the leftovers traveled to work with him in neat Tupperware containers. He came home each morning to a clean house. His underwear was being folded for the first time in his life, and Kit voiced no complaints about his Dorito-munching, night-off TV habits.

She was waiting tables at Chef Carleone's, making more in tips than she'd ever earned at Ander's shop. She came home after her midday shifts to drill Coo on his multiplication tables and stayed up late, sewing summer jumpers for Mitzi to wear in Orlando.

Though it hadn't worked exactly the way Kit planned, Miz Pistonpumper and her ilk had burst a dam of unspoken fetishes and untapped libido that Mel had apparently been hoarding for Lord knows how long. He'd come home in the morning and shoo the kids out to the swing set, coaxing Kit upstairs, suggesting things she'd never even read about.

He began bringing home a blue movie every Saturday night, and costumed in satin, lace, or the altogether, Kit sat beside him as the same cheap synthesizer wheezed out equally cheesy sound tracks, *bow-ba-dit-dow buppa-dippa-dit*, orchestrating the same condemned-to-repeat-itself scenario that played out over and over in slightly different lingerie.

Delivering the same breathy dialogue from varying shades of red lipstick, the interchangeable women filled stereotypical roles: Candy the Mechanic, Nancy the Nurse, Stacy the Secretary. With a sad, sleazy sense of kinship toward them, Kitty the Housewife imitated their strained sounds and practiced facial expressions, their orgasmic toe-pointing and teeth-gnashing, as deftly as she used to imitate a watercolor fruit bowl. That was her art now.

"Show time," she'd sigh inwardly, poking through the laundry basket for her scant, lacy getup.

The poor production values didn't bother Mel. The absence of character and story line was immaterial. After a while, his response became so autonomic, Kit suspected he'd get a hard-on watching Wilbur kiss his wife in front of Mr. Ed, and she sadly realized that instead of reopening a clear channel to his heart, she'd tapped into an electric undercurrent that enabled her to flip his erection up like a toggle switch. Instead of redis-covering the Mel of the yellow Mustang, she found herself alone in a phony blue Falcon, where she was obligated to play Miz Pistonpumper, pleasuring herself on his gearshift.

In the casting and waning shadows of the television's glow, Mel's features became flat and two dimensional, like the women who lay prone and panting on the screen, like the audi-ences she and Kiki used to pretend were only paper dolls, knowing she and Kiki were only paper dolls to them. As Kit's cargo of guilt dragged more and more heavily, she tried to think how she might atone for this dehumanization of him but couldn't think of anything except to giggle and coo and give him what he seemed to want.

Mercifully, they rarely had to sit through the entire feature. She was usually able to hit REWIND, gather their hastily discarded underwear off the floor, and trudge up to bed twenty or thirty minutes into it. Once, they didn't even make it through the previews, cleverly slated as "Coming Attractions."

Now, Kit wasn't sure if she should pack the silky under-things for Orlando, or if she could call it intermission and wear comfy cotton briefs. She put in two pairs of each and punched the redial button on the phone for the third time.

"Kiki," she said when the answering machine kicked in again, "I know you're home. Kiki, pick up! Oscar told Coo you weren't allowed to talk on the phone. That's craziness, honey, that is not normal. Kiki? Kalene Smithers, you pick up that phone right—"

"*Kitty, stop!*" Kiki rattled onto the line. "You gotta stop calling me!"

"Kiki! Thank God. What on earth—"

"You're getting me in trouble. You're making Wayne mad at me. He checks to see if this line is busy, and when it is— Well, it just better not be."

"I don't understand this, Kiki. How can you let him boss you around like that? He treats you like one of the kids."

"No! He's—he doesn't treat the kids like that," she said, meaning it to be in his defense. "And anyway, just wait a couple weeks, and everything will settle down. Everything will get back to normal, and we'll get together and have lunch and stuff like always. Just leave it alone for a week or two, okay?"

"Kiki, listen to what you're saying! What is the matter with you?" Kit stopped folding and packing and took hold of the phone with both hands. "Sweetie, Mama and I are worried about you. She says she's left a million messages, and you haven't called her back. You've been home for ten days, and I haven't even seen you." There was a long, empty moment. "Kiki? Are you still there?"

"I'm not sure," she sounded very far off.

"What?" Now Kit was really worried. "Sweetie, what does that mean?"

"Nothing."

"Kiki, let me come over there and pick you up."

"No! No, don't do that. It's all right, Kitty. Really. Things are a little awkward right now, but we're getting marriage counseling from the pastor over to the Church of Christ, and it's all gonna be fine. It was even Wayne's idea to go there, and he's trying real hard, Kit. And he's real nice, the pastor is. Everybody calls him 'Reverend Doo' for a nickname."

"Well, what is he saying about all this?"

"He says I've been struggling against the will of God all my life, Kit, and that's why things have been so hard for me. And I think he's right. If I could just—if I wasn't so— You know, I think Wayne wouldn't get so mad at me if I was a better wife to him."

"Kiki, that is such a load of crap," Kit said bluntly.

"It's true, Kit! It says in the Bible for women to obey their husbands."

"What? It does not either!"

"Oh, it does, Kit. It does so. Right there in First Corinthians, chapter seven, verse four." Kiki recited it like a Sunday school lesson. "'*The wife hath not power of her own body, but the husband.*' And Ephesians 5:22—'*Wives, submit yourselves unto your own husbands, as unto the Lord.*' And Colossians chapter—"

"Oh, well, that is just so very convenient, isn't it? Now Wayne is a born-again Christian when it suits him? Or has he got so good at what he does, he can even stuff and mount Almighty God in whatever pose he likes best?"

"Kit! It's the *Bible!* You can't argue with the *Holy Bible!* It's the inspired word dictated by God!"

"Well, it might have been dictated by God, but it was written down by men," Kit said, resisting the urge to check over her shoulder for lightning bolts. "Gee, what motive do you suppose a man might have for saying his wife ought to obey him like he's the Lord?"

"I just wanna do the right thing, Kit."

"Did you tell Reverend Doodoo-head that Wayne won't let you call our mama on the phone? That he won't even let you come and meet me for a lousy little lunch at the Taco Cabana?"

"He says Wayne's insecure on account of I've been—the way I've been. And if I can rebuild his trust in me—"

"Well, he's wrong," Kit said flatly. "Wayne is never gonna be anything but what he is, a lying, rotten—"

"*Stop!*" Kiki cried. "You don't say that about him!"

"It's the truth, Kiki, and you know it!"

"He's been good to me since I came back, Kit. He's been trying real hard. And I have to believe that this is gonna work and everything's gonna be okay because—because if I leave again, I can't take Oscar and Chloe with me, or I'll get arrested and go to jail for kidnapping and have my baby in prison alongside malefactors and murderers and prostitutes, so that means I can't leave." Kiki's voice cracked and gave way to crying. "Do you understand, Kit? I cannot leave here. I have to stay and make it be okay, and you are not helping when you keep on making the phone line busy and saying bad things about my husband and blaspheming against God!"

"Okay, okay. Shhh," Kit hushed her. "Don't cry."

Kiki cried anyway.

"I'm coming over there," Kit said. "Right now. I'm on my way."

"No! No, don't do that or he might—"

"He might what?"

"Just don't, Kitty, please."

"*Why not?*"

"Because! He'll—he'll—"

"*What?*" Kit pushed. "What will he do?"

Kiki took a jagged breath and said very softly, "He'll hit me."

"*Oh, God!*" Kit anguished, crumpling forward as if she'd been struck in the stomach, and they both breathed a moment, recognizing the vast uncharted sea between spoken and unspoken.

"That bastard," Kit finally said. "That rotten, lousy, goddang—*I knew it!* I tried to tell Mama, and she said I was just—*damn* him! *Damn* him and his stupid truck and his stupid little stuffed piece-of-shit deer heads!"

It didn't make Kiki feel particularly good to hear Kit as she went on cussing and deploring him, but there was a sudden openness in her lungs, as if the act of confiding in her sister had lifted a physical restraint from her chest. She felt calm now. She was sad, but she saw very clearly where she was, and she was not entirely alone. Kit's voice was like a keyhole of light in a locked door.

"I am coming over there, Kiki," she concluded the tirade. "I'm coming over right now, and you're coming home with me, and we're gonna call Mama and ask her what she thinks you should do."

"I told you, Kit, I can't leave. And Mama understands. She knows that having Oscar and Chloe—that's worth anything."

"You can't stay there. You can't let that rotten—"

"I don't let him, Kit. He just does it," Kiki said, and even that small measure of self-defense felt good to her. "But it's like I said. He's been okay since I came home. And what with the counseling and all . . . Maybe he really is . . . I really think it's all gonna work out okay. So right now, I just want to keep things normal and not make any trouble, and it's okay, Kitty."

"No, it isn't. It isn't okay. Please, let me come get you. You can go to Orlando with us. We can get a lawyer."

"That won't help, Kitty. And it won't help if you tell mama when she's so sick, so please don't tell her, okay? And don't tell Mel. Promise me."

"Kiki—"

"Promise, Kit. Please? Anything you try to do to help is only gonna make it harder on me."

Kit covered her mouth with her hand. She sat rocking on the edge of the bed, clutching the phone as close to her cheek as possible.

"So . . . when are you guys leaving?" Kiki asked after a little while.

Kit cleared her throat and whispered, "Tomorrow morning."

"Well. Well, that's great. That should be fun."

"Yeah."

"I hope y'all have good weather down there. They're saying thunderstorms around here all weekend."

There was another bleak silence.

"Kiki, I have to tell you something," Kit started, but Kiki said at the same time, "Kit, I have to go."

"Kiki—"

"It's okay, Kitty. It's fine. And by the time you get home, everything'll be back to normal."

Storm sounds obscured the rumble of the pickup truck, but headlights beamed across the living room wall like searchlights in a prison yard, creating a mural of reflected rain and announcing Wayne's arrival on the parking pad.

Oscar sat perfectly still, one hand poised above his tumbler of milk.

"It's him."

"All right, you two," Kiki said, "in your room."

She took the brownies out of their hands, flung them in the garbage, and scrubbed a dishcloth over the table.

"Mama!" Chloe objected, but Kiki held up her hands.

"No! No fussing! You know Daddy doesn't like fussing!" But Chloe kept on until her mother carved another brownie off the baking sheet and thrust it at her. "Here. Oscar, take her in there and keep her quiet."

"Yes, ma'am," Oscar nodded gravely behind his spectacles.

"Mama, I'm ascared of the thunder—" Chloe started, but Oscar teased the brownie in front of her, backing down the hallway toward her room.

"C'mon, Chloe. I'll read you some more of *Dr. Doolittle*."

"That's my big boy," Kiki blessed him with a kiss as they passed by.

The wind cranked the door back, screeching the stop-chain.

"Shit crackers!" Wayne burst in. "It is *something* out there!"

"Wayne!" Kiki cried as he fought the front door shut. "Thank God you're home. There's tornado warnings on TV, and the Abernathys and Pearsons all went over to the high school."

"Oh?" He handed her his dripping hat and set two brown paper bags on the end table. "Did they?"

"I didn't answer the phone, Wayne," Kiki started fluttering and explaining, "but Mrs. Abernathy came, and—and I just talked to her through the window. And she thought maybe the kids and I should go with them on account of . . . well, you weren't home yet."

"Why didn't you go?" he asked quietly.

"I didn't think I was . . . allowed."

"That's my girl," he touched her under the chin. "They're a bunch of old ladies, anyhow. Think this house never sat through a thunderstorm before?"

He opened his rain-wet denim shirt and withdrew a bouquet of yellow roses wrapped in cellophane, handing them to her with great ceremony.

"Flowers for my lovely wife. And . . . *ta-da!*"

He reached into the grocery bag and pulled out a bottle of wine.

"Oh, honey. That's very sweet, but—" She placed her palm on her stomach.

"Oh, I know, but it's your favorite. That white zinfandel you like. One little glass won't hurt."

"But don't you think we should maybe take the kids over—"

"A little white zin for my girl, a little of the ol' Southern Comfort for me," he danced her to his music, the bottles between them. "Aren't you even gonna say 'thank you'?"

"Thank you."

"Where is everybody?"

"I—I thought I was supposed to have them in bed when you got home."

"Well, for pete's sake," he laughed. "It's not even eight o'clock yet."

"Oh, well . . . I just . . . they were real tired and . . ." She looked at him wide-eyed, not sure which way to take it. "Should I get them up?"

"Nah, that's okay," he shrugged.

"Because I could get them up, and we could go."

"Oh, I'm not going anywhere tonight, babe. Stuey and I stopped off for a couple beers on the way home. And then Stuey always gets going on the tequila shooters, you know. I probably shouldn't of been driving home even. But just try to get a ride from anybody in this weather," he called from the kitchen, where he was putting the wine in the refrigerator. "Hey, Peaches, have you seen my binoculars?"

"Your . . . your what?"

He meandered back to the living room with his hands in his hip pockets, and Kiki stood there with her flowers.

"Binoculars," he repeated. "Why don't you run and put those in some water and then check the utility closet for my binoculars, okay, hon? They gotta be in there somewhere. I already looked out to the shed in my hunting gear."

He took off his shirt and looped it over the brass coat tree, surprised to see her still standing there when he returned.

"Well, go on now, Peaches."

"Wayne, they said on the news—they said tornado *warning*, not just *watch*. They said it's not safe in a mobile home."

"They're talking about some little ol' rattletrap trailer house, Kiki, not a double-wide manufactured home. A trailer's not sitting on a solid foundation like we are. Nah," he waved it aside, "I'm stayin' right here where I got a bird's-eye view. Let 'er rip!" He flopped into the recliner in front of the bay window, his boots up on the sill. "Just get the binoculars, and c'mon over here, Peaches. It's a wild night, and you and me," he spanked her playfully, "we're gonna ride it out together. Just like the old days. Just like Sugar Land."

"Wayne, please. We need to take the kids and go to the high school, honey. I can drive—"

"Kalene, I told you. We are staying here." His voice low and controlled, he made a gesture with his hands facing each other like solid walls. "Now go and get the *goddamn binoculars*."

Kiki nodded and took the flowers to the kitchen. She took a vase from under the sink and arranged them in it without adding water.

Outside the window, the patio was a playground of scattered furniture and broken pots. Chloe's rocking horse was on its side, its head wedged between the flapping folds of the collapsed beach umbrella. The ground was strewn with pink bougainvillea petals, and the basket with the little family lay on the floor, still poised and tranquil, beneath the swing that strained and twisted on its chains.

She took a can of cola from the refrigerator and went back to the living room.

"Hey, honey?" she cracked the can open and set it next to him on the end table. "Would you—would you like me to turn on the TV?"

"Funny, Kalene, this does not look like a pair of binoculars to me."

"I could turn it on so you could—you could see the warnings, Wayne. You could see for yourself."

"*Kalene . . .*"

"Because they said, Wayne! They said—"

"Kiki, don't do this now!"

"I'm sorry. I'm sorry." She immediately backed off.

"Ah geez, no, I'm sorry, baby. I shouldn't of yelled." He pulled her onto his lap and smoothed her shirt over her stomach. "I just want to be here and have a glass of wine and watch the lightning with my best girl. Remember how we used to go down home and sit out on my daddy's porch and watch the lightning, Kiki? I just want it to be like that. Is that so much to ask?"

"No, but . . ."

"Now, I let you come home. I forgave you. I'm trying to let things be like they were before," his voice took on a certain edge. "All I'm asking from you is a little cooperation here. All I'm asking is for you to make an effort."

"I'm trying to—to do it, Wayne. I'm trying to make it up to you. But Reverend Doo said you ought not to drink anymore."

"Shoot me," Wayne grinned. "I'm an evil backslider."

"And he said that you oughta listen to me, and I oughta tell you what I think."

"Okay, Peaches," he said patiently. "Tell me what you think."

"I think we gotta get outa here!"

"And I disagree," he smiled. "Anything else?"

Encouraged by his open expression, Kiki grasped the arm of the chair and struggled to stand up in front of him.

"I think I should be allowed to drive the car, Wayne. I should be able to go to the store and stuff."

"I see." He got up and shuffled over to the fireplace, tapping at the andirons with the pointed toe of his boot. "Anything else?"

"Well, it seems like—I guess . . . I should be able to use the phone."

"So you can call your boyfriend?"

"So I can call my mama!"

"Honey," Wayne said, rubbing his fists against his eyes, "I want to let you drive the car. I want to let you talk on the phone. But how can I let you do these things when I can't trust you?"

"You can, Wayne. You can trust me, I promise."

"You betrayed me, and that's gonna take some time to forgive. It's gonna take some time to get over the way you hurt me."

"Hurt *you!*" Kiki blurted a broken laugh.

"It's not funny, Kalene!" He seized her arm and wrenched her toward him.

"I'm sorry, Wayne! I didn't mean it!"

"You em*barras*sed me in front of the *whole* goddamn *town!*"

When he slapped her, certain syllables rang against the side of her head.

"And now you wanna call everybody up and run all over and show everybody how I'm being so goddamn mean to poor little Princess Kalene."

When he let her go, the back of the recliner caught her in the stomach. She dropped to her knees, and his boot caught her in the side before she could scuttle away, scattering the clattering andirons and fireplace utensils as she tried to get around him.

"Wayne, *no! Not by the baby!*" She stopped short of begging him to hit her in the head, but she used her arms to cover her belly instead of her face.

"Ah, shit. Kiki . . . are you—I didn't mean to—ah, shit." He knelt down and caressed her shoulders, pleading. "Please, baby—don't make it be like this now, Kalene. Christ, why do you always make it be like this? You know I don't want to hurt the baby! And if you cause me to hurt the baby, I don't know what I'll do, Kiki, I just don't know."

"I'm sorry, Wayne," she whimpered, "I . . . I'll be—I won't—" She couldn't think of what she was supposed to be promising. "*I'm sorry. I'm sorry . . .*"

"I know." Wayne folded her to his chest. "Baby, I love you so much. I wish you wouldn't make it be this way for us. Stop that caterwauling now, baby. Kiki, honey, stop that now. I said, *stop that crying, Kalene!*"

He pulled her head back, raising his hand over her, but when she bit her lips and made no sound, he folded her to him again.

"Okay, shhh. That's better. That's my girl." He kissed her swelling mouth and burning cheek and closed his hands softly around her throat. "I think I know what your trouble is," he told her, moving his lips directly against hers. "I guess I know what my sugar wants, don't I?" He stroked his thumbs across the front of her neck, repeating, "Don't I, sugar . . . don't I?" stroking more and more firmly until she answered, "*Yes.*"

"That's right. I guess I do." He eased her back onto the carpet, caressing her breasts and heavy stomach. "Sometimes my girl likes to play a *liiiittle* bit rough, doesn't she?"

"Wayne, stop it . . ."

"Right here," he unzipped his jeans and removed his flaccid penis. "Isn't this what you wanted?"

"No."

"Oh, I think it is. I think you're playin' with me."

"*No!*"

"But see, I know it is," he crooned. "I knew what you

wanted soon as I walked in that door, didn't I? You just kept at me till you got it, so don't you give me one of your little tantrums, Kiki. Shhhh. You don't want to wake up the kids . . . 'cause right now, Mommy and Daddy need a little privacy."

His hands crept, delicate as spiders, pulling down her maternity shorts and panties. He eased a pillow under her hips and pressed her knees apart.

"I know what you been missing. Or did your jigger-boo boyfriend eat your pussy for you?" His tongue flickered against her clitoris and the insidious ripple of involuntary response was a more painful betrayal than the throbbing in her cheekbone. "Except I bet he didn't know how to do it just the way you like it, did he? Just like *mmmmm* . . . like that. And there it is. There's my sugar. Now we got some honey."

Kiki wasn't sure if she was listening to the wind, or if it was still the ringing in her ears. Wayne eased his fingers in to spread the moisture that wept out of her, and she covered her face with her hands, struggling to keep the choking sobs below her throat.

"Yeah. Listen to you. You love that, don't you, Peaches?"

He set her ankles on his shoulders, priming himself with one hand, still stroking her with the other. Branches battered and scratched outside, twigs raked like fingernails on the screens and siding.

"Here it is . . . *here* . . . *here* . . . *here* it is . . . something great big for that sweet little pussy . . ."

Pinecones cantered on the roof of the shed. Its aluminum walls clamored in and out in a warping, metallic respiration.

"I bet your skinny little nigger boyfriend didn't give it to you this good, did he? He didn't know all your sweet spots, did he?"

Kiki watched from a distance, observing through the eyes of the wind at the window. She watched his mouth moving, his eyes drifting closed, his face turning out toward her ankle. His tongue and teeth lightly teased the delicate bone there, and a

174

current of sensation established itself between that point and the place where his first two fingers made a small circular beckoning. Kiki came closer and closer to a brink of feeling she feared more than anything else he did to her. Betrayal, betrayal. It was the undoing of herself, and she refused to feel it from him, here, now, like this. She would have wanted the world to end rather than have him take away that last sweet sliver of herself. Her hands reached out for anything, found the iron utensils that lay on the floor.

She stayed silent, but he read something in her mind, heard something in her truncated thoughts that made him open his eyes just as the poker swung toward his head.

"*Shit!*"

He instinctively raised his arm, and the hook bit into the flesh just below his elbow. He grimaced and swore, twisted the poker from her hand and hurled it against the wall. And then he rained down on her in torrents of hands, fists, epithets, and the ramming of his erection.

Kiki crossed her wrists above her head, shielding her face and crying against her forearms until Wayne became so distracted by the ramming, even his cursing fell into its compulsive gait.

The back screen door banged open and closed. Lawn chairs writhed and folded in seizures on the patio.

Clenching the front of Kiki's shirt, Wayne finally reared and groaned at the back of his throat, spurting a white stream of ejaculate across her stomach and spending the last of his energy with it. He shuddered forward with his hands on her shoulders, and blood trickled down his arm onto her neck.

"Damn. That hurts," he breathed heavily, "Fucking . . . god*damn* . . ."

He lifted her shoulders and slammed her back against the floor.

"You little *cunt!* I can't believe you fucking did that!"

Open palm, backhand, open palm, his arm whipped back and forth like the sheets out on the clothesline.

"You should not've done that, Kalene."

He staggered to his feet, pulled his T-shirt over his head, and wrapped it around his elbow.

"You shouldn't . . . you shouldn't've done it."

He picked up the poker and stood over her, panting, looking down on her from a great height, a far distance.

Kiki rolled onto her side, legs drawn up, arms wrapped around her stomach, making herself fetal, her face close to the pointed toe of his boot, waiting for it to draw back and swing forward, wanting him to kick her hard enough to turn everything dark, longing for the serenity of the still-life birds.

miracle child: comatose mother gives birth to healthy baby

"Shit . . ."

Wayne swayed, stumbled back on his feet.

"I think I'm gonna puke," he mumbled and lurched toward the bedroom, dragging his pants up from the middle of his thighs.

Kiki lay listening to the wailing at the windows.

After a while, she gingerly rolled up to her hands and knees and pulled herself into the easy chair. She used her panties to wipe away the trickle between her legs and the stickiness on her stomach, then unsteadily pulled her shorts on.

In the kitchen, she pressed a wedge of ice against her cheek before dropping it in a glass. She poured red Kool-Aid from a Tupperware pitcher, but it had settled to a sickening artificial nectar that smelled thick and syrupy when she raised it to her lips. Kiki bent over the sink and threw up, heaving vocally, moaning with the mimosa trees that leaned and foundered in the yard.

When she could breathe again, she turned on the water and cupped it, cool, up to her mouth with her hand. She washed her face and neck and forearms with the dishcloth, then used the sprayer to rinse everything toward the drain.

The garbage disposal flushed away the vomit and water, cleansing, eliminating, disposing, disappearing everything, grating its familiar and immediate relief. Kiki fed in a brownie, then the rest of what was left on the baking sheet. She took Wayne's dinner out of the microwave and slid the meat and potatoes off the plate, followed by the tiny cubed carrots mixed with peas. She fed in the roses from the vase one by one, petals and stems, and a soft breath of fragrance echoed back to her from an unknown place where it was cool and damp and dark.

She pulled the phone book across the counter, tore a page out, fed it down. It frenzied for a second, then disappeared. She reached for a slender, long-stemmed glass from the cupboard and dropped it in. It danced, whistling and shringing, spitting shards of crystal, but in a few moments, the rim was gone from sight. The grinding sounded angrier then, less accepting, but still efficient, familiar, relentless.

Kiki made a closed fist and pushed it past the triangular rubber safety flaps. She felt the vibration in her whole arm, and dancing bits of crystal tingled between her hand and the metal chamber, but at the moment the rotating blades began to graze her knuckles, there was a deafening rock of thunder. Lightning cast a brief, piercing glare across the countertops and stove, and then everything fell to darkness.

The disposal ground to a halt.

The refrigerator wheezed once and stopped running.

Kiki stood in the brittle shell of the kitchen, waiting for her home to explode, acutely aware of the glassy feeling of her face, a veneer of numbness over deep blue pockets of pain.

"*Mommeee!*" came Chloe's voice, thinned by terror and made smaller by the storming.

Kiki followed the plaintive strand and found Oscar and Chloe both crying in their bedroom.

"The light went off," Chloe whispered when Kiki took her up in her arms. "Oscar is scared."

"Oh, don't be scared, my sweeties. Shhh. Don't be scared. It can't last much longer." Kiki sat on the beanbag chair between their beds, and they huddled close on either side of her. "Shhhh. That's just a lot of angels singin' the blues. That's what my mama used to tell me." She settled her bruised cheek into the cool sateen of Chloe's pink ruffled bedspread. "Something made 'em sad, and that's the crying in the wind. Something made 'em mad, and that's the thunder booming. Shhh. Listen."

Through the fusion of wind and rain, a low, collective thrumming could be felt. Chloe strained forward, tearstained and intense.

"*They're coming,*" she whispered.

"Yes, baby. Just close your eyes."

"Is it a tornado, Mama?" Oscar asked.

"Maybe," Kiki said vacantly. "Maybe it'll pick us up and take us to the land of Oz. And we'll go spinning . . . far away to the Emerald City."

"But what about the witch?" Chloe cried.

"Oh, yeah," Kiki lifted her head. "I forgot about the witch."

Climbing up onto the bed, she pushed aside the Pooh curtains and looked out. At first, she wasn't sure what she was seeing. It seemed like a tear in the tenuous fabric of her own vision, a stain dribbling down the far-off clouds onto the distant horizon. But then it retracted. And then it extended downward again, an angled finger poking through the turbulent sky, pointing at Adam and his kind, threatening them to live or else.

"*Oh, Jesus,*" Kiki whimpered. "*Jesus, please help me.*"

"Mama," Oscar peeked over her shoulder, his big-boy voice pockmarked with tears and panic, "we should open the windows. And we should get in the tub. In the middle-est part of the house."

"What?"

"They said," he nodded emphatically. "On Discovery Channel."

Kiki gritted her teeth to keep from telling him that this thing would either kill you or not, as it wanted to, but when she turned on him, he put his hand out of his pajama sleeve and stroked her cheek.

"They said, Mama. On TV, they said."

"All right. Okay." She nodded and swallowed. "Okay, that's what we'll do. We'll open the windows, and we'll get in the tub, and we'll be safe."

She made the bathtub soft with towels on the bottom before they stepped in and let her legs dangle over the side, so they could hide their faces in her lap as she stroked their heads and sang softly to them.

"I see the moon and the moon sees me under the shade of the old oak tree . . ."

But the lullaby was taken by the storm on the roof of the carport, lacerated with sheets of rain, strangled with the sound of leaves and pine needles choking at the gutters. Kiki's ears popped, and the sudden, unpleasant overclarity made her realize how the pressure inside her head had been building without her even noticing. The walls thrummed with the same painful hollow as her skull.

"Stay right here."

"No, Mama, don't go!" Chloe squealed and tried to hold her there, but she dragged herself forward onto the edge of the tub.

"You stay here, Chloe! You stay! Oscar, you make her sit there. I'm gonna go wake up Daddy."

But Oscar caught her hand as she stood.

He didn't speak it out loud. Didn't want the angels to get any angrier. He just looked up at Kiki with his wide, wise eyes, and shook his head.

Kiki felt like she was going to throw up again.

"Stay," she said, and drew the shower curtain across their small, frightened faces.

In the bedroom, Wayne lay asleep, his arm across his chest.

Blood was seeping through the white shirt on his elbow, and he breathed with a congested rattle.

Kiki lightly pressed his shoulder with the heel of her hand.

When he made no sound or movement, she bent down and picked up the poker from the floor where he'd dropped it. She balanced it in her hands for a moment, then laid it carefully beside his head.

She picked up two pillows and propped them, one on either side of his face, tucked snugly over his ears, then located his jeans in the rumpled bedding and rifled the pockets for the car keys, shaking them, straining to hear the blessed tinny sound of metal on pocket chain. She skimmed her hand over the bedclothes to see if they'd fallen by his side, whispering *"Dang! Dang it!"* when she couldn't find them.

The wind was shrieking now, the trees in the yard bowing and cracking like an old woman's hips. She ran back to the living room, where the curtains flapped furiously at the open windows, lace sheers knotting and unknotting, drapery legs flailing against the wall. Yanking the cushions off the couch and easy chair, groping beneath and between every section, Kiki prayed for the solid keys to come into contact with her trembling fingers.

Brother go find your brother. God please please please Jesus help me.

"Dang!"

She squeezed her forehead between her hands and realized he must have left them in the truck.

"Oscar! Chloe!" She dragged them out of the tub and threw their blankets across her back. "Let's go. C'mon!"

"I need my glasses," Oscar protested.

"No! We'll get another pair, sweetie, just the same, I promise. Now c'mon!"

When Kiki opened the front door, it tore away from her hand, snapped the stop-chain, and flattened itself against the wall of the house. The little redwood deck was gone—potted geraniums, garden angel, and front steps with it.

The tornado stood before them, curving down like a spine to the northwest of the highway, half a mile away. Dust and debris swirled up in a Dorcas dance around the base—twirling, worshipping, orgiastic. Cars, trees, and tar paper roofs forgot what they were and flew into the air, intoxicated by the dizzying current, sucked into the whirling center of the funnel. They rose, ecstatic, not knowing as Kiki did the price that must be paid for any such moment of weightlessness. They soared, cast outward by centrifugal force, then landed—splintering, bellowing, indignant.

The noise was enormous, celestial, so far beyond thunder, it surpassed sound and bordered on the west side of silence.

"Jump!" Kiki seized Oscar and Chloe by their wrists, not trusting the grasp of their small, frantic hands. "One! Two! *Three!*"

They leaped into the wind, hit the mud, and fell to their hands and knees. Straining into the suffocating gale, she dragged them to their feet and headed toward the drainage ditch thirty feet away. The children hung from her hands, barely touching the ground. They screamed, and Kiki screamed with them, voices unraveling like threads, stinging in their throats when they could no longer hear themselves.

There was water in the bottom of the culvert. Kiki couldn't see it, but razor-bright droplets scoured her face. She pulled Oscar and Chloe to the ground, her body covering theirs. The blankets caped and soared, as she spanned her wings out over her young.

Kiki felt herself at the center of all things: the lashing weeds, the ragged cobweb of voices, the tangle of wind-flown hair, the thundering, the silence, the twisted powers of anger and chaos and love. She raised her face to the heaving green sky, wailing in convective harmony with the violent troposphere. The psalm keened out of her, *gloria matri,* exalting every moment of her survival within the house of Wayne Liam Daubert, Jr., rejoicing in the life she'd brought to its hollow core, celebrating her exodus and its destruction, rising higher, higher, until the howling army of angels encompassed her, and every temporal thing in their path was taken up toward heaven.

🙐

The spinning world became surreal. There was a feeling of being lifted, dissipated, taken away. Looking up brought a torrent of rushing images and colors, focusing downward brought a scalp-raising pressure, and all the while, there was the endless screaming of the children.

Kit felt nauseous.

Clinging to the sides of the pink teacup as it hurtled round and round, she silently cursed Walt Disney, a man whom, until this day, she'd loved as dearly as she loved her own father.

"Crank, Mommy! Crank! I wanna spin!" Mitzi shouted, heaving with all her might on the wheel between their laps, but her small hands and slender back were not enough to affect the forces of physics.

"No, sweetie, that's enough spinning," Kit murmured, doubtful that her diluted voice would be heard through the joyful music from above and the mechanical whirring from below.

How much longer can this go on? she wondered, and in answer, the ride ground down to a circling stop, and a wholesome young man in leiderhosen stepped over to help them out. Mel and Cooper climbed out of their yellow teacup, and Mitzi danced over to them.

"Again, Daddy! Again!" she squealed, but Kit held up her hand.

"You okay?" Mel asked. "You look a little green around the gills."

"To tell you the truth, I feel a little queasy. Could we just—"

"Off to Mr. Toad, then!" he declared, consulting *The Complete Guide To Disney World,* his Bible, as he planned every joyful step of one perfect day on the immaculate streets of The Happiest Place on Earth. "Says here that's a pretty tame one, honey. Maybe you can sit a little while we wait in line."

"Oh . . . well . . . okay."

She took his elbow, and they headed in that direction, Mitzi and Coo chanting, "Mr. Toad's Wild Ride! Mr. Toad's Wild Ride!" over and over again. She expected the feeling of dissociation to wear off with the dizziness, but even after another twenty-five minutes in line, the altered state persisted.

When they came to the front of the line, Mel and Kit got in the backseat of the boxy, old-fashioned car. Mitzi and Coo sat up front, where a Disney engineering genius had placed two nonfunctional steering wheels, on the off chance that little siblings might argue over who gets the driver's seat.

The doors spanked closed behind them, and the car lurched and swerved on its track, bumping through solid walls, narrowly avoiding disasters. Mitzi bounced and clapped, squealing with delight. Kit wanted to tell her to sit still, but a cartoon bank robber leaped out and caught her attention away from her mother's hand on her back. Mel laughed and pointed, his features exaggerated and dimensionless as the caricature hoodlums, dogs, and demons populating the black-lit inner world of Mr. Toad.

As they paused outside on the immaculate sidewalk, Mitzi and Coo got autographs from Chip and Dale, and Mel crossed another ride off his list.

"Okay, I think we've hit most of the biggies. Pirates of the Caribbean?"

"Check!" Mitzi and Cooper had been going over the list all day.

"Big Thunder Mountain Railroad?"

"Check!"

"Swiss Family Tree House? Mad Hatter's Tea Party?"

"Check and check!"

"Small World?"

"Not gonna happen!" they chorused in Mel-speak, and he rewarded them with a thumbs up.

"Alien Encounter?"

"Check for me and Dad!" Cooper called, adding, "That was so rad."

Mitzi clouded over. She hadn't measured up to the inflexible line on the height restriction podium, but Mel quickly came back with extra enthusiasm especially for her.

"Dumbo's Flying Circus?"

"Check me, but not Coo!" she clapped and brightened, bouncing on the blistering hot concrete.

"Let's see. It's two-twenty. We still want to hit Space Mountain, Hall of Presidents, Haunted Mansion—"

"Haunted Mansion!" Cooper begged. "Haunted Mansion next!"

"Mel, maybe we could get some lunch pretty soon," Kit said, but that brought up a disappointed chorus.

"How about right after the Haunted Mansion?" Mel suggested.

"Sure," Kit nodded.

She was giving in on everything these days, feeling that she'd used up all her brownie points and no longer had the right to an opinion.

"You're not going to be too scared, are you, Mama?"

"I don't know," Kit said. "Sounds pretty scary."

She reached down and grasped Mitzi's sweaty hand to keep her from dancing and prancing off all her energy. She didn't want Mel to have to carry her in this heat.

There was a little shade at the entrance to the Haunted Mansion, and as they crowded into it, Kit felt Mel's hands on her shoulders. She let herself lean back against him. The plain largeness of him was so comforting sometimes. He made her feel like she was living in a solid brick house with a firm foundation, which of course she was, because Mel was working overtime to pay the mortgage.

"Are you okay?" he asked her again.

"Fine," she said. "Just hungry."

"We'll get lunch right after this, I promise."

"We could try that cafe with the alien lounge singer," Kit suggested.

"Hey now," Mel teased, "let's leave your sister out of this."

Kit *tsked* and swatted his arm. He kissed the back of her neck, and she leaned into him again. Thinking of Kiki made her feel so sad. The line moved forward somewhat. Mitzi and Coo bounced with anticipation.

"They're gonna sleep like rocks tonight," Mel whispered, wrapping his arms around her, allowing his thumb to discreetly caress the side of her breast. "Then you and I can take a nice long shower."

Kit nodded. She didn't care, as long as he kept feeding her regularly.

She started to feel a little better when they got inside the cool dark of the great Victorian house. They entered a large room filled with foreboding music and listened to a spooky narration tape as the floor descended. Or perhaps the roof was rising, Kit wasn't sure, but the portraits on the wall began to transform.

Slowly, the frames around the stolid faces elongated to reveal the frightening and ridiculous secrets of the archetypal family. A gentleman in his dapper waistcoat gradually exposed bright-colored boxer shorts, then the fact that he was standing in this state of undress on the shoulders of another man. A frilly young woman was discovered to be walking on a tightrope; then the frame dropped even lower to unveil a ravenous crocodile just inches below her dainty feet. With the disclosure of their imperiled bodies, the complacent tintype expressions took on the tragic quality of grotesque theatrical masks, beneath which writhed a host of inappropriate emotions.

When it came time to get into the shell-shaped cars, Mel made Mitzi and Cooper share.

"Nope," he raised his daddy-hand to halt their objections. "I'm sitting with my best girl on this one. She might need to grab onto somebody, and I want to make sure it's me!"

He laughed his big Mel laugh, large and hearty.

Kit felt the clammy breath of the crocodile beneath her sandals.

As the car rolled slowly through the gloom, past tombstones and ghoulies, Mel put his arm around Kit's shoulder and nuzzled her neck, whispering more about her and him and the hotel shower. Phantom dancers holographed by below, their skirts silent as cobwebs, weaving in and around each other, past a banquet table of long-withered flowers and the decayed remains of a great feast. Kit closed her eyes, listening to Mel's voice mingled with the sinister music until Mitzi's scream jolted her back to herself.

Before them was a mirror. Kit saw herself and Mel in the shell-shaped vehicle, but seated between them was a greenish specter, leering and waving in the glass. Kit inhaled sharply.

"Gotcha, didn't they?" Mel laughed. "It's okay, Mitzi," he called into the darkness. "It's just pretend. It's almost over."

Back outside again, the sunlight pierced even more brilliantly, and the heat was that much more oppressive for the cool of the air-conditioned exit. Kit retraced their steps in her mind, trying to calculate how long it would take before she would be sitting down with food and water in front of her. Mitzi and Coo had been tanking up on cotton candy and other vacation extravagances all morning, so they weren't begging or whining yet. Kit hoped she could depend on Mel's formidable appetite to spur them on, but there was a show being performed on the stage in front of the castle, and then Pooh and his friends and Minnie and finally Mickey Mouse himself strolled by, gathering crowds of autograph seekers.

Mel waited patiently, camera in hand, for Mitzi and Cooper to get close enough to hug each character.

Kit shifted her heavy purse from shoulder to shoulder.

Move your ass, Tigger, I'm dyin' here.

By the time they reached Tomorrowland, it was going on four o'clock, and Kit was woozy with sunburn and longing. A drink of water. A sandwich. A chair. Anything.

"Hey, look!" Mel pointed. "There's hardly any line for Space Mountain!"

"Mel, I thought we were going to get something to eat."

"Well, yeah, but—are you guys that hungry?" he asked the kids. "Wouldn't you rather go on Space Mountain first?"

"Yeah! Space Mountain!" they shrilled. It was like offering them a game of Go Fish before bedtime. No contest.

"Let's do it!"

Mel strode toward the line, and Kit followed, gazing, yearning, toward Cosmic Ray's Star Light Cafe just beyond the entrance. The line looked a mile long to her.

Mitzi measured up to the height requirement.

Dang.

At least it was cool inside.

They snail-paced through a winding futuristic passageway lined with windows into outerspace until they finally came to a great room where the line of people twined back and forth like ribbon candy, and those who lived long enough were loaded into rocket cars for the ride. TVs blared clever space-comedy above their heads, but Mel was busy striking up a conversation with the family just ahead of them.

He'd been doing that all day. Greeting people, being jolly, introducing their family as "the Prizer Gang," evangelizing from his guidebook Bible, sharing his newfound expertise. He now had more pals in Disney World than Goofy did.

". . . and this is my wife, Kit. Honey, Midge and Bob Pillerman. From Bethlehem, Pennsylvania!"

"Hi," Kit smiled wanly.

They indicated an adolescent, Bob, Jr., over here, and little Heather hanging upside down from the metal dividing bar. Midge was planning to get off with Heather at the last escape, because of course, she couldn't go on a roller coaster, being five-and-a-half months pregnant, you know, and poor little Heather—well, she was just plain terrified.

Mitzi seemed to lose a bit of her nerve when she heard that.

"I want to sit right behind Mommy," she said.

"Mitz, you don't have to get on if you don't want to," Kit told her. "We could go out and wait for Daddy and Coo."

"Oh, c'mon, Kit, stop babying her," Mel chided. "You'll be fine, won'tcha, Mitzi-noodle? You liked Big Thunder Mountain Railroad, didn't you?"

"Well, kind of . . . ," Mitzi shrugged a noncommitment, drawing a circle on the floor with the toe of her red maryjane.

"See? She's fine. She's Daddy's big girl."

Mel congratulated Bob and Midge on the impending Pillerman, and the standard pregnancy conversation segued into Midge describing what a terrible time she'd had with Robert Junior. Placenta previa. Vomiting. Migraines. Toxemia. Edema. Ankles swelled up like tree trunks.

"Kit always had an easy time of it," Mel said, though this was certainly news to Kit. "Never had morning sickness or anything. She worked right up until the day the kids were born," he bragged, and squeezed her shoulder, so proud of The Little Woman. "And she looked fantastic three days after."

"I was in labor for thirty-two hours with that boy," Midge was saying. "They induced me Monday morning, and he wasn't born until 2:23 A.M. on Wednesday."

"Oh, you don't even want to hear how long Kit was in labor," Mel said.

Kit didn't want to hear it either, but he went chatting right on like some PTO mommy girlfriend.

"With Cooper, Kit's sister barely got her to the emergency room, and with Mitzi, her water broke while she was grocery shopping, and the baby was born right there in the super-market! It was incredible! Her picture was in the *Houston Chronicle*," he added proudly, "and the Fiesta store gave us a year's worth of diapers, six cases of formula, plus all the groceries Kit put in her cart before she went into labor."

Midge cooed in awe, knowing she'd been one-upped, and Bob Senior shook Mel's hand.

Mel beamed at Kit. Kit plotted his death.

This was one of his favorite anecdotes. Probably because he wasn't there. All he remembered were the free diapers and the Hallmark card of congratulations signed by all the checkout girls and stock boys. But Kit remembered the towering wall of canned goods, the horrified onlookers, the agony, the panic, the terse voice announcing, "Cleanup on aisle seven."

Two wholesome Disney employees stepped up and directed the Pillermans to their loading spots. They all wished one another a great vacation, and Midge smiled and waved as the two Bobs sped away. Then it was the Prizer Gang's turn, and wholesome employees were helping them into the rocket car, placing Kit in the very front.

The car moved smoothly at first, hissing down a tube of pulsing blue lights. After that, Kit found herself in a cool, dark place—the vast nonatmosphere of outer space—staring up at endless stars and a distant, familiar planet. As she ascended, nearer, nearer, and the continents and oceans separated and became clear, Kit reached out her hand to touch the face of this world, but in that same moment, her own world dropped away beneath her, and she hurtled downward, upward, side-to-sideward, sledding past nebulous blue nebulae, rushing toward the turning eye of the galaxy, spiralling, flying, above, below, and between the stars that shone like sequins.

Then, just when the wonder of the flight was almost more than she could bear, she descended, down into a warm and private expanse of pitch black, from which she was squeezed through a pulsing red narrow and delivered out into a bright light.

The unexpected earth stretched tangible and true along metal tracks and fixed walls. A wholesome young man hurried over to help her disembark. Kit took his hand and stepped out of the car onto the platform, but the concrete floor was too physical for her feet. They were still in outer space, it seemed. The straight lines of the wide hall began to bend and blur, and the next thing Kit knew, she was looking up at the ceiling and Mel's concerned face.

"Kit? Kit? Don't cry, Mitzi," he said over his shoulder. "Mommy's okay. She just got a little dizzy from the ride. She's okay. Everything's okay."

Kit was cognizant of wanting milk. Wanting to suck it right out of a gallon jug.

"Kit?" Mel tapped her cheek softly. "Honey? Are you okay?"

"No," she whispered as realization rose up and clobbered her the same way the floor had risen up to slam her in the back of the head. "I'm pregnant."

"Let's all sing like the birdies sing, tweet tweet-tweet tweet-tweet . . ."

Kit could hear the melody ingraining itself in Mitzi's brain. She knew that for months to come, they'd hear this song sailing over the shower curtain, being sung by the tub toys, and reeling out from the high side of the swing, twittering in time to the crinkling chains.

" . . . sweet sweet-sweet sweet-sweet . . ."

"I can't believe it," Mel whispered and laughed out loud for the millionth time in the last forty-five minutes. "I just can't believe it."

"Me neither."

He was hugging and kissing on her, grinning like an idiot,

beaming down at her in the dappled half-light of the Enchanted Tiki Room.

"It's just so incredible," he said. "Things have been so great lately, and this is just . . . it makes everything . . ."

"Perfect," Kit said grimly.

"Yeah," he squeezed her hand. "I can't believe it!"

"You wanna know what I can't believe?" Kit shrugged away from him in annoyance. "You! You're the one who said we should give up on it. You said two kids were all we could handle. You said we couldn't afford it. You said you were too old to have another baby, and that was three years ago! Now it's the worst possible time, and you're all sunshine and happiness?"

"I know it sounds corny, but it's like . . . like a miracle or fate or something. After all these years of trying and not trying and trying to pretend to be not trying—"

It must have been Ander.

"Oh, man! I can't wait to see the look on a certain Dr. Jane Poplin's face! Talk to me about 'poor sperm motility' now, huh?"

Ander and all that prolific Swedish seed of his. The other possibility was more than Kit could stand to think about.

"I guess I can get 'em where they need to go. I guess my little guys can swim upstream when they need to," Mel nodded, leaning back and propping one foot on the bench in front of them as if to accommodate his ponderous testicles.

Kit made a small sound with her fist pressed to her mouth.

"I'm sorry, honey," Mel said sheepishly. "I didn't mean to make it sound like that. It's just—when she told us—when we couldn't get pregnant again after Mitzi, and she said it was my fault, it felt like . . . like—I don't know, but that's why I said I didn't want any more kids, Kit. I felt like I was shooting blanks or something. Like I was disappointing you. And the last thing I ever want to do," he whispered into her hair, "is disappoint you."

"I know."

"But I'm not taking any credit for this. This is you. It's just you being miraculous and wonderful, and geez, I love you, Kit. Only you could give me a gift like this. Only you."

"*Oh, God!*" Kit choked. "*I don't know if I can do this.*"

"Oh, c'mon, Kit. You do it great. And you're doing it now. What else *can* you do?"

"There are options."

"You're not serious." His ridiculous grin faded.

The carved figures on the wall began a relentless drumming, lush bowers of lilies and nasturtiums sang in a high minor key.

"I don't know," Kit started crying softly. "I don't know, I don't know."

"Ah, honey." He pulled her to his large, warm body, stroked her hair, and kissed her forehead and cheeks. "C'mon, babe, it's okay."

"I'm so sorry, Mel. I never meant for any of this to happen."

"Well, geez, Kit. Don't say that, honey. We'll work it out. I know it wasn't in the plan, but the plan is adjustable." He stroked a tear away from her nose and planted a kiss in its place. "C'mon now. It'll all work out. Everything's gonna be okay."

He held her just enough away to show her his eyes, show her how he really meant it.

"Don't be sad, Kit." And he laughed like Cooper on a slick skateboard ramp. "You can't be sad. We're gonna have a *baby!*"

S weet Lady of Joy and Blues,
    I refuse to believe that the tides and eddies of this universe, having brought you now to me, will take you away without me touching you again. I refuse to know that I will not taste the smooth dark circle, the silk-lined chamber, the birch and ivory skin that drew my mouth and hands like a climbing vine to your strength. Nothing is right within my life since I know how you been hurt. Nothing grows from out my hands, nothing changes in its season.

When you came to me, the body and heart of my youth were born. For I was chained, you see, when it was my time to be an explorer in this world. You brought with you what I lost when I lost my freedom. The longing I learned to keep and control through years of anger and fear, it was returned to me tenfold in the form of fire, in the rhythm of an undiscovered music, in the thought of all your silk surrounding me.

There was a beautiful woman by my side last night, but I was an old man for her. The will and willingness of a young body are gone with you to whatever place you are. And until you return, I will not

*have all myself. I will have only that which was allowed me by my
captors. Hunger, thirst, and this profound silence.*

That's all that was in the top drawer of the little desk built
right into the wall of Kiki's new breakfast nook. No ink marks
or pencil shavings or anything else. It was perfectly clean and
empty, except for that sweet letter from Xylo and a tablet of
blank paper that kept looking like it expected her to reply.

There was something comforting about that empty drawer.
And about the clean carpet that spanned seamless and soft gray
throughout the apartment. And how you could see every
square inch of it because she didn't have any furniture yet.
There was nothing on the plain white walls except the drawings Oscar and Chloe made in art class at their new school.
Even the cupboards were fresh and smooth and virtually
empty.

Kiki liked that. She liked the flawless sky-blue countertops
and pristine porcelain toilet in the bathroom, the kitchen
surfaces all immaculate and free of nicks and scratches, the
snug-fitting window screens, the gliding closet doors. There
was a brilliant new lightbulb in the spotless refrigerator, and
the drip pans on the electric stove top shone like Olympic
medals. The doorknobs, the miniblinds, the drain stopper in the
tub—everything was new and untainted. She was the first
person ever to live there, since the Cypress Tree Manor apartment complex was still under construction. Hers was the first
building finished. Building A. And apartment 4A was her
apartment.

She had no idea when she would be able to pay Vivica back
for the security deposit and first month's rent or Kit and Mel for
the groceries and clothes for her and the kids and everything
else they had paid for after they rushed back from Orlando to
pick her up at the Red Cross shelter. But it was worth feeling
like the stupid, needy, little sister yet again to feel her bare feet

on the fresh new floor of the slate-colored hallway where Oscar and Chloe each had their very own room.

"Wake up, Winken and Blinken," she called. "Put on church clothes. We're going to visit Daddy."

Oscar came out in his nightshirt, his face all rumpled and soft from sleep.

"I don't wanna go."

"You're going."

"No, I ain't."

"Ain't ain't a word, so you ain't supposed to say it." Kiki turned up Bonnie Raitt on the radio and tried to get him to dance with her. "*All I got was a mouth full o' feathers,*" she sang along, "*little birdie got free*—C'mon, Oscar, how 'bout a little footsie tango?" He put his feet on top of hers, and they clasped hands wide out to the side. "*I guess my love's got no business no business*—say, you're not gonna go and get too big for this someday, are you?"

"Mom," he said, and he rubbed his head against her huge stomach, "I don't wanna go there."

"Why not?"

"It smells weird."

"I know, Punkin, but Grandma Daubert's going to be there today, and she's very anxious to see you."

"She smells weird, too."

"Oscar!" Kiki admonished. But she had to laugh.

She smiled again just thinking of it later, and she put her arm around his shoulder as he trudged unhappily down the hall at the care center where Wayne was moved once they decided to write it on his chart that he was in a persistent vegetative state.

When Kiki quietly opened the door, Wayne's mother was bent over the bed, gently shaving under his nose. She squealed with delight when she caught sight of her grandbabies.

"There they are! There they are! There's my darlings!" She

handed the razor and towel to Kiki and threw her arms open for them. "Come here, you *sweeeeeeet* things!"

"Hello, Mother Daubert," Kiki said, but Mother Daubert was busy kissing Chloe and Oscar and smooshing them into her billowy bosom and pulling their heads into her high-teased, blue-tinted hairdo, sandwiching her heavily made-up face between their fresh, cool ones.

She led them over to Wayne's bed, holding their hands as if she were taking them into the traffic.

"Say hello to your daddy, sweet things."

"Hello, Daddy," they said.

There was a long silence.

"Well," Mother Daubert finally said, digging into her gigantic white purse and producing two KitKat bars, "I'll just take these little monkeys out to the trees where they belong. I thought the two of you might like to be alone."

"Oh. Sure," Kiki nodded. "Y'all go along with your grandma now."

They went, hushed and reverent until they were out of the room. Then Kiki could hear them chattering, their school-shoe feet scattering down the hall toward the glass door, their grandmother calling out for them to walk, to wait, to keep their voices down. Kiki came over and sat beside Wayne's bed, her feet on the floor straight beneath her, her purse held between folded hands on top of her big stomach.

"Oh," she said after a while when she noticed she was still holding onto the shaving things. "Okay. Well, hold still, honey."

She lifted the razor and began skimming it over the soapy patches.

"So . . . how have you been?"

She swished the razor in a basin of water and wiped it on a towel.

"We're doing fine. Really fine. The kids are doing good in school, and everything's just going along fine."

She drew the razor up the front of his neck, stroking away the last of the lather.

"Kit and Mel are helping me out. And Mama sent money for plane tickets for me and the kids to come to Orlando again next month. So I can help her with her chemo and all. Drive her to her treatments and everything. And I might even be helping around the agency a little. She thinks I could be good at that. She said she'd pay me and everything."

She patted his face all over with the hand towel.

"There you go. How does that feel?"

Wayne's hands were beginning to draw up to the sides of his chest, shriveling toward the empty clutch of a dead bird. His mouth was open just slightly, and his atrophied legs twisted to the side.

"Oh, by the way," Kiki told him, "you know those Lamberts over there by the highway? Their house got wrecked by the tornado, too. I just saw Lavina Lambert in the Fiesta store the other day, and she said they got so much insurance money, they're building a real house over in this new subdivision just off Katy Freeway."

She straightened the sheets and smoothed the corners and then sat down in the easy chair.

"That's what she told me. Yeah, that's what she said. And I figured you must have had some insurance on that house, Wayne. You're way smarter than Ray Lambert. You must've thought of that. And Mel said they make you have insurance when you have a mortgage, and all I have to do is call and tell them the house is gone, but I don't know who to call, Wayne. Did you even have a mortgage? Me and Kit, we went over to the house, but we couldn't find anything in that mess. Everything was pretty much smashed up and wet and blown all over. Oh! You know that big brown chair you got at Star Furniture Outlet last year? Well, it went up and set down right on top of the karaoke machine. Can you believe it? No more karaoke. They found your bedroom TV clear over in Tom and Brenda Berry's backyard."

Humming a little, she got up and straightened the sheets on the other side of the bed, then went back to her chair.

"We went down to the shop and had a locksmith drill the door open, you know, but there was nothing in there but some old dead animals. And the electricity had gone off during the storm, so the freezer was off, and it smelled real bad, Wayne. Mel paid somebody to go over there and clean it out. Some guy came to get some head off of something—a sheep or goat or something that he shot up in Montana, but they'd gone and thrown it in the dumpster already. He was awful mad, but— oh, well."

Kiki shrugged and pulled her feet up underneath her.

"So, anyway. I keep calling that lawyer of yours, but he's always in meetings or out of the office, and he just never calls me back. I don't understand it. It's been—what? More than a month now, and he still hasn't called me. But I figure maybe he knows something about that insurance and everything."

She drew a lock of blonde hair over her shoulder and started making loops with it.

"Yeah, so Lavina said it was just their starter home, anyway, and I told her, us too. We knew we couldn't stay there forever."

Kiki rested her head back, trying to tip her plane of reality.

"Remember when we moved out there, Wayne? It was right before Oscar was born."

The respirator next to the bed made a steady *shah-sigh,* and Kiki let her own breathing fall into rhythm with it. It made her feel sleepy.

"They brought the house on two big trucks, half and half. Like that Barbie dream house you can open up and see inside. And I was so worried that it wouldn't fit together right. That if we didn't walk real careful and jump over the cracks, it would just break apart. And you laughed at me for being silly, but then you said we had to make love every night for a week when we moved in, to make the house have good luck. And it must've worked, because then we had Oscar."

She stroked her hand over her warm, turgid stomach.

"We put the Christmas tree in the playpen so he couldn't get at it, remember? You said, 'I ain't gonna cage up my child just so a tree can have its freedom.' You said, 'Let the kid run, Kiki-peaches; put the dang tree in the cage.' I remember you saying that. And we were laughing. We were laughing all the time back then," she said, and it made her laugh a little now. "I guess we'll have to do that again for a couple years. Put the tree in a cage. Just when Chloe got big enough. Won't be long though, and this one'll be big, too. Time goes by so fast now. It's not like it used to be."

The baby turned and settled in her abdomen, not a kicking, just a gentle swim: the slow and inevitable growing, the deep whale-song evolution that draws the living being from the seed in a uniquely sexual, uniquely powerful, uniquely female process that began the instant her golden hair caught a flash of lightning that illuminated Mother and Daddy Daubert's back porch in Sugar Land.

"Now, that's fireworks," Wayne had breathed close to her ear, drawing her back against his chest. He'd stroked her hair and caressed her body as they lay together on the wooden swing.

"*I'm the sheik of Araby,*" he sang, softly teasing, gently rocking, "*your love belongs to me.*"

And Kiki had reached back over her head to pull him closer, touching his face, letting him warm his hands underneath her shirt, forgetting everything, forgiving him again.

"*At night when you're asleep, into your tent I'll creep,*" and he'd walked his fingers downward, under the waistband of her skirt like delinquent boys stealing under a fence.

Kiki put her legs over the side of the chair and laid her head on the bed beside him. From behind closed eyes, she followed the lightning to the touch, to the insemination, germination, unfolding, going forward.

She let herself touch the smooth-shaven side of his face.

"I'm the sheik the sheik the sheik of Araby . . ."

That she could still remember him that way, that she could miss and mourn him, this was something she could not understand. She wondered if she would have felt any satisfaction if she'd bashed his head in when she had the chance, when she had him right there and the poker in her hand.

But it was the moment she laid it down that she felt the power; the moment she remembered she'd fallen in love with Wayne not because she was stupid, but because there was a loving and good part of him that could be separated from the rest—the part that looked like Oscar sleeping and sounded like Chloe when he laughed.

Kiki could feel that part of him growing inside her now. Now that he was sleeping peacefully with all the rage withered from his half-open hands and all the hard words evaporated from his slack mouth.

sha-sigh sha-sigh

"Wayne," she whispered, her lips touching the rim of his ear, "I forgive you."

The flow of the feeling was so powerful, she fully expected him to open his eyes.

❦

Kit was unaccustomed to the sound of Neeva's voice on the phone.

On the rare occasions she heard it, there was always a weird moment of unbalance before she realized it was her mother-in-law and not some kind of prank call. Neeva never said "hello" or "hi, this is Neeva" or anything plain and civil like that. "Prizer residence," Kit would cheerfully pick up, and Neeva would launch right into something like, "Well, I suppose they're sending out those damn Easter seals even as we speak. Now I can't even breathe without feeling guilty." As if the conversation were already in progress, but Neeva had picked up the phone to dial in a second party as an afterthought.

This time it was more direct.

"And where the hell have you been?"

But it still caught Kit off guard as she grabbed the phone and tucked it between her shoulder and ear so she could continue cooking Mel's breakfast.

"Umm . . . hello?" she stammered. "I beg your pardon?"

"I should send you my answering machine for Christmas, since you're never home and nobody ever calls me."

"Oh. Well, hi, Neeva," Kit tried to sound like she wasn't cringing. "How are you today?"

"Same as I was four months ago. I'm not aging that rapidly."

"Wow," Kit said, "has it been four months already?"

"Time flies when you're too busy to pick up the phone," Neeva said. "I told the girls in the bowling league, 'Well, I thought they were coming for the Fourth of July, but apparently the Second Coming is more likely than theirs.'"

Kit twisted the phone cord around her hand, trying to stay cool, to think what she should say and not say.

"Well . . . umm . . . it's been a real busy summer is the thing and . . ."

"Have you made plans for Thanksgiving?"

"Oh . . . Thanksgiving? Wow, umm . . . we really haven't looked that far ahead, but . . . we'll see how things go, you know, with everything. But I guess maybe— Sure, you know, yeah. We could make a—a tentative plan for that . . . tentatively."

She'd eat Thanksgiving dinner at Jack-in-the-Box before she'd force her family to choke down turkey roll and tater tots at Neeva's, but she decided to go along with it for now. The holiday was still months away, leaving plenty of time for Kit to either kill herself or come up with an excuse.

"Have you found another job?" Neeva moved on.

"Well, actually," Kit said evasively, "Mel is doing so well now, there really isn't any need."

"You're pregnant," Neeva stated without a shade of emotion or shadow of doubt.

"*No!* No . . . don't be silly."

"You most certainly are."

"Well, I—I mean, there might possibly be a—a *remote* . . . possibility."

"How far along are you?"

"Four months. But we really aren't telling anyone yet, so—"

"Well, I guess it's easier than working."

"That isn't it at all! We've been—we wanted—I'll be going back to work as soon as . . ."

Kit gave up her protests. She knew she was double damned on this topic. Neeva dismissed stay-at-home mommies as lazy and condemned corporate mommies for abandoning their offspring like lotus-eaters.

"When I went into labor with Melvin," she said, "I was flat on my back under an eighteen-wheeler. Barely finished changing out the bearing before my water broke."

"Really?" Kit tried to sound appreciative and resisted pointing out that Neeva's generation of mothers took a ten-day "lying-in" at the hospital, while modern HMO mores told women it was *hoo-hoo-hee* and back to the rice paddies.

"You never bounce back from that third one," Neeva went on. "That third one leaves your stomach looking like an empty kangaroo pouch." Kit moved her hand to her abdomen, just to make sure she could still contract the muscles there. "I don't know how many times I wished I'd stopped with two."

"Well, considering Mel is your third, Neeva, I'm personally grateful you didn't."

"Do you know that according to Jacques Cousteau, every

major environmental problem on this planet can be traced to the overpopulation of the human species?"

"No, I hadn't heard that."

"It's true," Neeva assured her.

"Well, hopefully someone old will die and make room," Kit said baldly.

"Wheeee," Neeva whistled, "sounds like those hormones are kicking in already."

"Who's on the phone?" Mel asked, strolling into the kitchen, and Kit answered his question by holding up a raw egg.

"I'm not here!" he mouthed.

"Would you like to talk to Mel?" Kit offered. "He's right here."

"Hi, Ma." Mel took the phone, then covered the receiver with his hand and whispered, "One of these days, Alice—straight to the moon."

Kit giggled and opened the refrigerator to put away the milk and margarine.

"No, we're really excited about it," Mel was saying, but then an odd expression crossed his face. "So? Why should I care what some French fairy scuba diver says about it? Well, I wish him good luck with that, but I'm gonna keep swimming upstream just the same." He covered the receiver again. "Would you knock that off?"

She had the egg and was miming a slapstick pitcher's windup with it.

"How's Butchy?" Mel said. "Yeah, I hear it's great over there. I'm sure he'll do fine. How's Pop? No. Yeah, just working. Same old same old."

He grabbed Kit's hand as she moved to drop the egg down the front of his sweatpants.

"No, she's . . . yeah, I know you did, Ma, but Kit's . . . No, it's not that at all. She is, Ma. Well, taking care of the kids and all that, and—and she's doing some painting. Something on the corners of the kitchen cabinets. I don't know, little fruit things or something. She has fun with it. It's a little something to keep her occupied."

Mel made a face at her when he noticed she'd quit goofing around.

"No, but . . . I know, but there's always somebody hiring. She won't have any trouble finding some kind of work."

Kit went to the kitchen table and picked up Cooper and Mitzi's cereal bowls, stacking them in the sink.

"The Falcon? It's umm . . . it's—it's fine," Mel was saying. "No, turns out it was a linkage to the transaxle. Yeah, that would be great, but I can't. No, I won't be able to drive it down after all. I just, you know, I wanna keep it close to home, just in case. Well, you know. Yeah, I guess maybe, but— What? You mean this weekend? Well, I'd have to check with Kit on that. No, Ma, but she still has things to do."

No no no, Kit shook her head, making forget-it, no-way, and absolutely-not gestures with her hands.

"Yeah, Ma? Kit says this weekend would be great."

🕸

There was a gentle hand on Kiki's shoulder, and that's what awakened her, but the moment she smiled and pressed her cheek to it, the real world displaced the sounds of Sippie Wallace and the hum of the tour bus returned to the sigh of the respirator. Instead of the velvety back of Xylo's hand, Kiki felt the spiky brightness of a diamond anniversary ring. She opened her eyes and noticed for the first time how much Mother Daubert had aged lately.

"Were you sleeping, dear?"

"Mm, just drifting a little," Kiki said.

"Sweet dreams, I hope."

"Yes," she told the truth.

"Oh! I almost forgot. I brought a little something to brighten up the room." Mother Daubert drew a small, rolled up

poster and a roll of Scotch tape from her purse. "Precious Sentiments. Don't you just love Precious Sentiments?"

"Oh, yes," Kiki said. "They're so . . ."

"Precious!" Mother Daubert supplied with a giggle.

She carefully centered the poster above Wayne's bed. "A
little angel is watching over you," it said in soft printish letters
beneath a large-eyed child who held a moppy little puppy with
wings tied on its back.

"It made me think of our little angel," Mother Daubert
patted Kiki's stomach, and her voice broke with emotion. "It
made me think how—how they might be together right now,
just on this side of heaven . . ."

Kiki managed to smile and nod, then moved quickly to the
window while Mother Daubert pillaged her purse for a pink
tissue and daintily blew her nose.

"This must be a very difficult time for you," Mother
Daubert solicited.

"Oh, well, it's probably harder for you." Kiki smoothed the
front of her shirt. "Because he was . . . you know."

"My baby," Mother Daubert nodded, and her dangly
earrings swayed beside her sad mouth. "My only child."

She rested her fingertips on Wayne's forearm, stroking
from his constricted biceps to the wrist he kept drawn up to his
chest.

"He very well could come out of it, you know. That's what
it means when they say 'higher brain function.' That means he's
still here."

"Yes," Kiki said. "That's what they told me."

"It would take some time. It would take some effort, but he
could be as strong and vital as he ever was. I listen to their
predictions and their statistics, and I say *Pff!* They don't know
my Whipper, that's what. They don't know what a dynamic
person he is."

"No."

"Such an active little boy. Oh, he used to run Lorenza

ragged!" Mother Daubert laughed, relaxing into the nostalgia. "When we had our Lorenza," she smiled, "those were happy times. She and I would take him to the park and the swimming pool. Why, we could barely keep up with him once he learned to swim."

"Mm-hmm," Kiki nodded, trying not to drift toward the window.

"We taught him to swim, Lorenza and I. Do you know what we did once? We took him *camping*." She covered her coral pink mouth with her dainty hand, eyes shining with the long-kept secret. "Daddy was in Atlanta for ten days. No one was ever the wiser! We took him to the state park in Huntsville, and oh, oh my, we had such a time!" She laughed again. "We sang, and we paddled the canoe, and we lay on the sleeping bags with the tent flaps wide open, and the air was so full of jasmine at night. I was afraid Daddy might put up that tent next time he was out hunting and still smell the jasmine."

Mother Daubert fell silent, and a long time went by before a nurse came in and fussed around Wayne's bed a little and left with only small hellos spoken between them. Kiki noticed that Wayne's nails had grown. She wondered if she was supposed to trim them or if the nurse would do it.

"And then, of course, he was so athletic in high school," Mother Daubert suddenly picked up an invisible conversation. "Outdoors all the time with his fishing and his hunting. Just like his daddy. Vital and vigorous. You see how vigorous Daddy is yet today. Seventy-seven he is, and he's as vigorous as a man half his age. Twenty-one years older than I, but he'll probably outlive us all. He'll probably—oh, what is it, dear?"

"Are Chloe and Oscar still outside?" Kiki craned at the window.

"Now, you just relax, honey. I can see them just fine from here." Mother Daubert went to the window and raised the blinds. "It's actually a lovely view they gave him."

"It is nice here. Do you know . . ." Kiki hedged. "I mean, is it being paid for by . . . somebody?"

"Oh, good heavens, don't you worry about that," Mother Daubert said. "Daddy doesn't permit me to worry myself over any such thing. I'm sure he's seen to it."

"Oh," Kiki said. "'Cause I thought maybe there was some insurance or something like that."

"Well, I'm sure there is," Mother Daubert raised her eyebrows as though it hadn't occurred to her.

They stood side-by-side at the window, watching Oscar struggle to boost Chloe onto the low branch of a crab apple tree.

"He's so gentle with her," she said. "He wouldn't hurt her for the world."

"He's a good boy," Kiki said.

She envied them out in the sunlight and wondered how much longer Mother Daubert intended to stay and how much longer she expected Kiki to stay with her.

"It'll be so much more convenient for you to bring the children now that he's here, as opposed to the hospital," her mother-in-law went on. "It's just too bad you won't be able to go back to Orlando for your mother's—Oh. You weren't still planning to go to Orlando now, were you, dear?"

Kiki started to stammer denials and reassurances, but Mother Daubert was at the window again, waving to the children.

"They grow up so fast," she said. "I remember when you and Wayne were first married. So young. So full of hopes, so much in love. But so young. Even so, he was a good father. He was so happy when Oscar was born, happy and proud." She pushed into her purse and came up with another tissue.

"He was," Kiki struggled out of the chair and went over to her mother-in-law's shoulder. "He was a good daddy."

"Women just don't understand the pressure and—and that a man has needs and for such a young man to have so much responsibility—"

"Mother Daubert—"

"But he supported his family. Even at the age of twenty-three. He accepted that burden like a man."

"Please don't cry."

"And he's a creative person. An artist, really. Creative people have their moods. You have to understand the artistic temperament."

"Mother Daubert," Kiki said, "he was a good boy."

"He was!" She seized Kiki's hand. "He was a good boy."

"Of course." Kiki tried to pull away, feeling alarmed, trapped by the sigh of the respirator and the unexpected strength of this tiny woman's grip.

"Why did you have to come back here?" Mother Daubert demanded in a strained whisper.

"Ma'am?"

"Why?" Mother Daubert asked again. *"How could you be so stupid and weak?"*

"Mother Daubert, I . . . How can you say that? I—I only—"

"If you'd only gone and never come back. None of this would be happening! He didn't want to hurt anybody. He was a good boy!"

"Yes, Mother Daubert, he was a good boy."

"And he was a good man."

"Yes. Yes, he was a good man," Kiki affirmed.

"You weren't afraid of him."

"No! No, of course not!"

"And he never purposely hurt you, Kalene. Not purposely."

"Mother Daubert, please stop this . . ."

The gentle lady shook her head, her face full of grief and something else Kiki couldn't even begin to identify.

"Please," Kiki repeated, standing firm, supporting her belly with one hand. "I don't want you to remember your son that way. I don't want my babies to remember their daddy that way. He was a good boy, and he grew up strong and handsome, and that's how we should always remember him. Now please, please don't upset yourself any more."

Mother Daubert nodded and freed another pink tissue, offering one to Kiki. She looked out over the grassy yard, gently pressing instead of wiping the tissue under her eye so as not to smear her makeup. Oscar was leading Chloe by the hand, back toward the breezeway where there was shade and a water fountain. She waved again, and Oscar waved back.

"He's a good boy," she said.

Kiki felt nauseated and afraid. The scent of Mother Daubert's perfume mingled with the antiseptic smell of the hospital hallway. Outside, Oscar tried to lure a squirrel with a walnut shell he'd found on the ground.

"Wayne always loved animals that way," Mother Daubert said. "I guess that's why he went into taxidermy. He had such an appreciation for the beauty of living creatures."

Kiki couldn't quite follow *that* line of logic, but she nodded anyway.

"That was his art," Mother Daubert said.

sha-sigh sha-sigh sha-sigh

"I saw a movie once," Kiki said after a bit. "There was this guy, see, who was in a car accident, and he got hurt real bad and went into a coma for five years. And then when he came out of it, he was like a whole different person."

Mother Daubert stood staring at her, lips slightly parted.

"See—before—he was real mean, like a gangster or something, but after he came out of it, he was nice," Kiki explained. "Only he had amnesia and this big old scar on his head. And I think he might have had telekinetic powers."

Mother Daubert just stared. Kiki fidgeted with the front of her maternity blouse.

"But other than that, he was a real nice person . . . afterward."

Mother Daubert turned away and stroked Wayne's arm. She traced his eyebrow with her fingertip.

"I believe you get one chance in this world," she said finally. "If you throw away the one chance you're given, then you're alone. People come. Friends, household help, passing acquaintances—oh, by the dozen, there are people you know. But not one of them knows you. When the person you love is gone, then you know what it is to be alone."

Her face had fallen to a shadowed painting. Heavy makeup stressed the lines and cracks in her expression and tinted sallow the dark circles beneath her eyes.

"Mother Daubert?" Kiki said gently. "You're not alone. I'm here."

She realized as soon as she said it how much it sounded like a big-eyed Precious Sentiments cliché.

"Oh," Mother Daubert glanced up at Kiki. She seemed surprised to find her still in the room. "Well, that's very sweet of you, dear. Very sweet. I guess what I meant was . . . well, I guess I'm just being silly today. I apologize, dear. I had no business . . . I . . . "

"It's all right, Mother Daubert. I understand."

They passed a few more minutes in silence.

"Well," Kiki stood and tucked her purse under her arm, "I think I'll run down to the ladies' room for a minute."

Heading down the hall, she wished she could just leave, collect Oscar and Chloe, get in the car, and go home, but her bladder was the size of a walnut now, and she knew she'd never make it. She wished Kit would hurry and get back from New Rippy. She wished her mama wasn't too sick to talk on the phone. She wished, oh, she *wished* she had just one flat, smooth-faced card—an ATM card or a VISA. She longed for that unconditional love, that sheltered feeling of friendly clerks and universal acceptance.

At their favorite little toy store in Old Town Spring, that nice lady looked down at Kiki with surprise and disappointment as Chloe begged for a porcelain doll for her collection. Chloe didn't know yet that the wind god had whisked away all those sweet china faces and ruffled Edwardian frocks. The entire dolly society had flown away with all other evidence of the life they'd left behind. Kiki had no money to buy the doll for Chloe and no experience at explaining that fact to her.

"It costs a lot of money, Chloe," she struggled. "I don't have that much money today."

"That's okay," Chloe smiled up at her, not upset yet, thinking her mommy simply needed a little reminder of where things come from. "You can use a credit card."

Perhaps, if Kiki could have traced for her the backward process, the waning of what had been them together and her by herself, it might have made sense, how it had all come to nothing now. If she could have told Chloe that when she met Wayne, she was still working, that she and Kit were still performing together at country clubs and upscale bars in nice hotels. She was earning her own money. Driving her own car. Saying her own name. Right up until the day they stood on Grandaddy Daubert's back porch, reading their handwritten wedding vows from three-by-five-inch cards.

"Husband, I will nurture this precious seed you have planted inside me, and I myself will grow in the fertile ground of your love."

But she somehow started shrinking instead. Her first pregnancy made her feel vulnerable. Just as she reached the world of womanhood, she became childish again, giving up her strength to his solicitude, her power to his protection, and so it went over the years, until even her voice was confined inside a metal box on the entertainment center.

"I promise you, my lovely wife, that I will love you and be faithful to you and gently cherish you and always provide you a good home."

But one night Chelsea, the seventeen-year-old babysitter, needed a ride home, and his faithfulness was gone. And then Kiki lost a baby because his gentleness was gone. One by one, even the small promises disappeared, until all she had left of her covenant with him was the accordion sheath of plastic faces hoarded in her handbag, the smooth magnetic strips that confirmed he was still her caretaker, if no longer her love. They imprinted on her a code of acceptance, issued a statement of her place in the world.

Mrs. Wayne Daubert, Jr.: Approved.

Standing in the toy store, looking around this plateau in her life, Kiki felt a longing and aloneness such as she had never known.

"I can't use a card, sweetie," she whispered. "I don't have one."

"Well then," Chloe darkened, "you can write a check."

"I'm sorry, Tweetie Bird . . ."

And then the reality set in, and the grieving began.

❦

Kit had never known Neeva to look so beautiful.

Her widow's peak ascended in a soft wave from her forehead, her cheeks were gently flushed, and her soft smile blushed with a careful touch of lipstick. She was wearing a pastel blue skirt suit instead of her traditional white work shirt and khaki Bermudas, and there was an opening yellow rose in her hand.

That was a nice touch, Neeva's sister Alice commented, as they lowered the coffin's sleek black lid, but Kit was remembering something she'd read one time about how they glue your lips shut. The morticians. She was wondering if they'd glued Neeva's lips shut. Wondering if they'd argued over who would get to do it.

Butch and Mel stood in their dark suits, dry-eyed and grim, with Otto weeping between them.

"Fifty-four years," he sobbed, "fifty-four years."

Kit didn't know if he was mourning the duration of their marriage or the fact of its passing. When it came time for each person to pass by the open casket, he gazed down at his late wife and bawled loudly, "There's so much to say." But then he sat down without saying anything.

It bothered Kit how he bent down to kiss Neeva's cheek. He never would have dared that when she was alive and kicking. She'd have bitten the nose right off his face.

Kit and Mel had both noticed, as soon as they arrived in New Rippy, how Otto's hearing had miraculously regenerated. He seemed reborn, making his own coffee and talking with Mel about airplanes and fishing and the Falcon. He was the life of every conversation and stood at the head of the funeral parlor receiving line, shaking hands with old friends and being hugged by the neighbor ladies and telling everyone the story of how Neeva had been cutting pieces for Mitzi's birthday quilt when she looked over at him and said, "Did you hear me?" and then fell right down dead, the scissors still in her hand.

The chaplain was a young man. The funeral parlor had him on a list of references for people who didn't go to church during their lifetime and weren't about to start now.

According to Mel, Neeva had been a Southern Baptist early in her life, doggedly devout and inviolately unforgiving— "Calvinism in a chignon," he said. But when Mel was about Cooper's age, she'd suddenly done a complete one-eighty, refusing to set foot in the First Baptist sanctuary again, and from then on was harsh and judgmental simply for her own entertainment.

Kit remembered her saying once that she wanted her funeral to be in a bowling alley. She said the league girls should each take a turn rolling the ball at her urn of ashes.

"I'd like to share with you a portion of the thirty-first book of Proverbs," the chaplain said. He took a sip of water and lifted his Bible in his hand.

"'Who can find a virtuous woman? For her price is far above rubies.

The heart of her husband doth safely trust in her . . . she will do him good and not evil all the days of her life . . .'"

Mitzi crawled onto Kit's lap, and the cool of her soft round cheek made Kit realize that her own face was burning.

"'She riseth also while it is yet night, and giveth meat to her household . . .

She girdeth her loins with strength, and strengtheneth her arms . . .

She stretcheth out her hand to the poor; yea, she reacheth forth her hand to the needy . . .

She openeth her mouth with wisdom; and in her tongue is the law of kindness.'"

Kit and Mel exchanged an uncomfortable glance.

"'She looketh well to the ways of her household, and eateth not the bread of idleness.

Her children shall rise up and call her blessed; her husband also, and he praiseth her . . .'"

Otto honked loudly into his handkerchief.

"'Favour is deceitful and beauty is vain; but a woman that feareth the Lord, she shall be praised.

Give her the fruit of her hands; and let her own works praise her in the gates.'"

Okay, then, Kit prayed silently, give her the fruit of her hands. At least give her that.

But there was no mention of Shankow-Turner or the B-29's. The young chaplain had never met Neeva, and Kit wondered if anyone else in the room knew her any better than he did. As he delivered the brief, generic eulogy, a desolation swept over Kit, a bereavement. This is what it is to be dead, she understood. To be never met, never even known well enough to be forgotten. To ask, "Did you hear me?" To glide past and past as the banquet table decayed to dust.

They traveled with their lights on to the graveyard, and then Kit made Mel stop at the store on the way back to the house so she could buy plastic plates and cups and some paper napkins.

She hovered quietly between the dining room and kitchen, making coffee, slicing bundt cake, shushing the children, and fetching fresh tea bags for the bowling league ladies, until all the customary baked beans and lemon bars and hot dishes of death had eroded to crumbs and leftovers. She plastic-wrapped and aluminum-foiled things to send home with people, making sure Mel thanked each one of them for coming as they migrated out into the quiet street.

"Is there anything we can do to make things more comfortable for you, Otto?" Kit asked after the last neighbor left, but she immediately regretted it.

"Well, things around here need to get cleaned out," he said. "That would be something for you girls to do, I guess."

Kit and Marnie exchanged horrified glances when Aunt Alice concurred, "Yes, I think that's something for the daughters to do."

Mel tried to suggest that maybe they could come back in a couple weeks, and Butch pointed out that Marnie was in no condition to be doing heavy housework, but Otto was adamant that all Neeva's things had to be removed from her room, and indeed, from every room in the house, in order for him to stay there by himself. When it came down to the point that the old guy was either going to have his way or come home with one of them, Butch and Mel stopped short of volunteering to do it themselves.

"Kit, I hate to do this to you," Marnie pulled her aside in the kitchen, "but I've been having contractions since we got back from the cemetery."

"Oh, Lord! Are you okay?" Kit put her hand on Marnie's elbow and pulled a chair across the linoleum. "Did you tell Butch?"

"No. He's not having a very good day. I was hoping it might just be Braxton-Hicks, you know?"

"Do you want Mel to drive you?"

"Would you mind?" Marnie hedged. "Butch had a couple martinis earlier and . . . oh. Oh, boy. Here it goes again."

"How far apart are they?"

"About five minutes," Marnie checked her watch and winced at the internal pressure. "Oh, dang! I can't believe this is happening today."

"It's all right. Just breathe. Relax." Kit stroked Marnie's shoulder, holding her wrist so she could follow the sweep of the watch's fine gold second hand. "How is it?" she asked after another minute.

"Over. It's over."

"That was a pretty good one. I think you're going for it."

Marnie nodded. She looked haggard already, and knowing what sort of evening lay ahead for both of them, Kit drew her sister-in-law into a hug.

"It's okay, Marnie. You sit tight while I get Mel. It'll be okay."

"Yeah, okay."

"C'mon now," Kit coaxed, setting her hands on Marnie's shoulders. "You can't be sad. You're having a baby!"

"Yeah," Marnie still sounded uncertain, but she smiled. "I guess I am!"

"Hey, can I tell you a secret?"

"Oh, Kit! Are you?" Marnie cried, and Kit nodded. "Kit, that's wonderful."

"Yeah," Kit said, "I guess so."

And she realized that, even under the circumstances, she couldn't be completely sad, either. Like her other babies, the one inside her was a little time bomb, ticking with the combined promises of disaster and delight, melancholy and mayhem, sleepless nights, joyful days, and eighty years of God only knew what.

"You guess so?" Marnie said gently.

"It's just—we didn't exactly plan it."

"Us either. I hope Mel is handling it better than Butch did."

"Oh, Mel's on cloud nine. He's gone absolutely sappy." Kit laughed a little now, though it tore a hole in her heart every time he knelt down in front of her to press his cheek to her stomach or said how much he loved her or surreptitiously deposited another effusive love letter in the mail box.

"So, there you go," she sighed.

"Life goes on," Marnie agreed.

As they drove away in the rain, Kit waved from the window. Then she turned toward the kitchen, her heart sinking. It was filthy, lacking even the superficial skiff of house-keeping Neeva breezed over it before family visits. Kit rolled up her sleeves and looked under the sink for trash bags.

She decided to attack the refrigerator first. She opened the door and peered inside, half expecting to find Jimmy Hoffa in there. It was wedged full with unidentifiable remains mummi-fied in foil or entombed in Tupperware, almost-empty bottles and corroded jars, fuzzy cheese, green lunch meat, a drawerful of slimy produce.

Kit closed the door and decided to attack the cupboards first. When she unlatched the one at her feet, a large brown roach startled out and scuttered across the floor. Kit shrieked, cussed, stomped on it, and wiped her shoe on the dingy braided rug.

She decided to attack the bedroom first.

Neeva's door creaked open, allowing the same sad sigh with which her coffin had creaked shut. The blinds were drawn, the windows closed, and Kit was afraid to open them, even though the stench of cigarette smoke was overpowering.

She crept to the dresser and eased the top drawer open. Bras. Dozens of them. All white. She extracted a trash bag from a cardboard box and gingerly dropped them in, one by one, discovering a trove of unlikely items among the strained elastic and voluminous cups. A bag of jelly beans. An alarm clock. A thick-handled plastic spoon. A Band-Aid box full of nickels. A petrified Hostess Ding-Dong wrapped in cellophane and secured with Scotch tape.

The second drawer was full of underwear. All pink. There

were five or six old threadbare panties, obviously laundered and worn for years, and sixteen identical packages of new ones, ordered from J. C. Penney, apparently over the course of thirty years, but never opened. Beside those were several authoritative girdles, another Ding-Dong, a slide rule, something that looked like a wooden turkey baster, a *Roget's Thesaurus,* a letter opener with John Wayne's head on the handle, and a Danish Butter Cookie tin.

Kit pulled the lid from the tin and discovered old letters and newspaper clippings. There were black-and-white snapshots with crimped edges, one picture of Mel as a two-year-old, wearing nothing but a pair of cowboy boots and a great big grin. Kit laughed out loud, partly because he looked exactly like Cooper, and also because she remembered Neeva telling her once, "I never took naked pictures of the babies. Isn't there enough smut in this world?"

Kit opened the closet door and felt for a light switch. Not feeling one, she passed her arm back and forth across the expanse of the walk-in, hoping to touch a string hanging down. Her hand came in contact with something that felt like ribbon. She tugged gently, then jumped back as the entire wall collapsed forward in a Fibber Magee of tumbling boxes, breaking glass, and a choking billow of dust. Blessedly, something snagged on the string that yanked a bare, dangling lightbulb to life.

Kit found herself knee-deep in gaily wrapped and ribboned packages of all sizes. Christmas, Mother's Day, Happy Birthday—the paper ranged from fairly recent angel foil to kitschy aquamarine flowers, dusty and brittled by age. Kit recognized her own poinsettia paper from last year on one bundle. She recognized her own carefully tucked corners, as distinctive as her own handwriting on several of the tags.

Sliding her finger beneath one of the corners, she uncovered the word *Vid-tek.* The tape rewinder from three Christmases ago. Inside the angel paper was the large-number, extra-volume telephone they'd sent the following year. She tore open the end of another bundle and discovered an afghan just like the one Marnie had crocheted for her and Mel five years earlier.

In a sad antithesis of Christmas morning, Kit opened the packages one by one. Robe. Slippers. Tea cozy. A pair of garden angels. Jenga. Isotoner driving gloves. Clap on, clap off—The Clapper! Not knowing what else to do, she piled the gifts into the Salvation Army box on the bed.

After a while, Mel returned from the hospital with news that Marnie was doing fine, but Butch was terribly sick to his stomach. He now had Trudy and Blake in tow, and Kit's heart sank even deeper.

"Mel, I know this is a tough day for you," Kit said, "but honey, I can't take care of all these kids and do this thing, too. I can't."

"Well, I have to take Aunt Alice back to Corpus. And Pop is going to need some supper." He looked at her helplessly. "What am I supposed to do?"

"All right. Okay. This'll be fine." Kit tried to think of a way to make that true. "Okay, here it is: I'll keep Mitzi and Trudy. You take Cooper, Blake, your dad, and Alice over to Corpus Christi. Take them all to a restaurant, feed them, and drop Alice off. Come back to New Rippy, drive through McDonald's for Mitzi and Trudy, drop it off here, leaving Cooper and your dad, then take Blake back to his house. He's plenty old enough to be by himself. We'll keep Trudy here just in case he decides to set the place on fire or something."

"Okay," Mel nodded numbly. "I got it."

"Wait!" Kit called as he headed down the hall.

He turned back, thinking she was going to kiss him.

"Bring trash bags," she said.

*S*weetest, most coveted love,
　　　Please don't let me hear your voice again. Every
time you feed me, I know I'm slowly starving. It's not
ours to take, but I lie at night, tangled in a wanting of you that
breathes deeper than my silent prayers. I used to watch you working,
alive with desire for your hands, your mouth, your voice on the phone,
your eyes like cigarette smoke over sky, like deep water. How did
boundaries that were always so clear become so blurred?

　My room is still and hot tonight, and as always, I'm alone. I'm
thirsty. I brush the back of my hand across my mouth and imagine the
nape of your neck, the curve of your spine. I push my dry tongue
against the roof of my mouth and feel the color of your nipple—pale
brown as it comes erect at the slightest small tease. I love that you
never push my head down. You let me go my own way, finding
forgotten nerve endings at the back of your calf and thigh. When I say
something that makes you laugh, I feel the sound against my soft
pallet, a vibration, like someone calling my name under water. You're
lazy, letting me tease around the ridge to the tiny eye, lifting your hips

221

like a bowl of honey-milk. But sometimes, I'm so thirsty. I want too much. I go too fast, too hard. My lips begin to feel bruised and swollen, a slight tinge of blood where I tried to protect you from my teeth. If you kiss me now, you'll taste it. So kiss me now. Please, kiss me, stroking and saying, easing, entering in. I'll cross my ankles and confine your stroke just there. Whisper something, anything, private things, until I feel myself resolving—nipples, fingers, the soles of my feet, the internal expansion that pulls my head back, opens my mouth, forces the air from my lungs. This is the moment I'm most afraid. I'm alone unless you're willing to reveal something. Confide secrets, extract promises, speak profanities. I used to pray to be forgiven, to forget how you revived my dry hopes, my dismembered senses, but now, I beg for one more opportunity to trespass and be trespassed against. Oh, Lord, let him touch me. Christ, let him kiss me. Jesus, let him lie over me like a cross against the back of the crucified. Oh, God, let him fuck me, let him fuck me, let him—

"I'm back," Mel opened the back door, startling Kit and letting in the sound and smell of a summer thunderstorm as he tromped into Neeva's clean kitchen a little after three in the morning. Kit hastily folded the floral notepaper and shivered it back into the envelope.

"Kit?" His wet sneakers squeaked across the linoleum.

"In here!" she sang. She tried to vault over the Salvation Army box to cram the letter inside *Roget's Thesaurus* or chuck it into the now empty bra drawer, but Mel was coming down the hall, so she snatched the Danish Butter Cookie tin on top of the armoire and stuffed the missive inside, clanking the lid down tight against all that stroking and saying and blasphemous, ankle-crossing bliss.

"Well, it's a boy," Mel announced from the doorway.

"Lord help us," Kit said, leaning casually on the dresser. "This world really needed another Butchy Prizer." Mel laughed, and she asked, "Is everybody all right?"

"Yeah. Marnie's pretty wiped out, but Butch slept for a

couple hours while she was in the labor room. And the baby! Ah, Kit, the baby's just beautiful." He stroked his hand across Kit's stomach. "The whole time, I couldn't stop thinking about—"

"I'm glad everybody's okay," Kit broke away and busied herself back at the boxes, intently resorting the contents. "And I got a lot of work done. Took four huge bags of trash out of the kitchen and six or seven out of here."

"Come across anything interesting?" Mel asked, shaking out Butch's raincoat.

Kit motioned toward the trash box, and he knelt beside it with a soft, slow whistle. He used a yardstick to stir the contents, dislodging a 1967 New Rippy High Armadillos seat cushion, two miniature sombreros, a set of Myrtle Beach salt-and-pepper shakers, and about twelve years' worth of those little plastic squares that hold bread bags shut, all clipped onto a length of clothesline rope.

"Hmm," he said.

"Mel, I'm afraid your mother was a few flakes short of a piecrust."

"Yeah." He sat down on the edge of the bed and then lay back with a long, deep sigh.

"Are you okay?" Kit sat close beside him and stroked his forehead.

"Yeah."

"Do you miss her?"

"I missed her forty-four years ago," he shrugged. "Or she missed me."

Kit thought this was the saddest thing that could be said in epitaph for a mother, and the stinging in her eyes was as close as anyone came to crying that day. Crying for Neeva, anyway. She lay down and put her arms around Mel, drawing her leg protectively across him, wishing she could have made at least one good mommy in his life. The tension in his body seemed to melt a little when she laid her hand over his heart.

"Thanks for doing this, Kit," he said. "This and everything else."

"Don't say that."

"No, it's true. You do everything that makes our life work. You always have. And I never tell you, so you think I don't know it. But I see it, Kit. I know. I appreciate it. And I'm gonna show you how much. Just you wait and see."

"You don't have to show me anything, Mel." She tried to get up, but he held her there.

"I've got something for you," he tantalized against her neck. "And I think you're gonna like it."

"Mel, not here."

"Not that," he grinned, "but it's almost as good."

"What is it?"

"It's a surprise. And you don't get to see it until you come home from the hospital with the baby."

"Like the baby isn't surprise enough?"

Mel laughed and kissed her, and he tasted like summer rain.

"God, I love you," he said. "You're my whole life."

His words lay on her chest like an anvil. Kit thought if she stayed one second longer, she was going to start bawling.

"I love you, too," she mumbled, and headed for the bathroom.

It was a long, hot drive home.

"How much longer?" Cooper kept asking until Mel finally barked at him that if he asked that question one more time, somebody's father was gonna pull this car over to the side of the road, and then he'd see just how much longer it was. Nobody really knew what all that meant, but Mel's tone of voice could be pretty intimidating, so they drove on in silence.

"Do you want me to drive for a while?" Kit asked when the

stars began to appear and Mitzi and Cooper were both asleep in the backseat.

"No, that's okay," Mel said. "You must be wiped out."

"Kind of," she shrugged, "but I could take a turn."

"Is there something wrong with the way I'm driving, Kit? Am I annoying you in some way with my driving habits?"

"No, I just thought—"

"Then let me drive, okay?"

"Okay."

"Okay?"

"Okay, already!"

"Good."

"Fine."

Mel rubbed his eyes and squeezed the bridge of his nose, and Kit bit her lip to keep from telling him he was right smack on the bumper of the truck in front of them. And way too close to the center line.

"I sure wish we could afford to stop at a motel," he said.

Kit bristled on her side of the seat but didn't say anything.

"But I guess Kiki's happiness is worth more than anything else in the world," he continued. "And we are responsible for all her needs."

"Mel, do we have to—"

"After all, it's not like she's a grown woman or anything."

"I told you, I will replace the savings account."

"Yeah, I heard. Are you gonna hold up a liquor store to do that or just sell one of your mink coats?"

"As soon as I can start working again, I will, Mel. I was thinking I might wait until the baby's born, but what the hey! I'm sure a lot of people are anxious to hire a pregnant housewife who dropped out of college on account of she was working two waitress jobs in order to send her husband to vocational school."

"Oh, forgive me, Kit! I actually forgot for five seconds how I selfishly robbed you of your education just so I could provide silly little extravagances like shelter and food for our family. I forgot that I forced you to be a waitress with no education when *what the hey!* You could have been a waitress with an Art History degree!"

"You're right, Mel. An Art History degree is worthless. I'm much better off with nothing. I mean, this way, both the food service and housekeeping industries are wide open to me. Why, I bet there's a million career opportunities ready to jump on up and bite me, so you know, any day now, I'll be out there shakin' that moneymaker, all right?"

"Geez," Mel mumbled guiltily. "Forget I said anything."

Kit was impossibly caught between seething wrath and the compulsive urge to beg his forgiveness. She knew they couldn't afford it, but she couldn't turn her back on Kiki. Not now. She knew she should have never left for Orlando. She should have been there for Kiki all along when this weirdness with Wayne was going on. A thousand tiny details—bruises explained away a little too easily, glib stories about trips and mousetraps and scatter-minded accidents, long periods of silence, the violence of Chloe's Ken doll whenever Barbie wasn't quick enough jumping into the Dream Car. And then there was that night. The rain. The broken glass. As soon as she learned what he was capable of, Kit castigated herself, she should have forced Kiki to admit what was going on and get out of the house for good. When Kiki finally did blurt it all out over the phone from the Red Cross tornado shelter, Kit wanted to kill the bastard herself. She wanted to be part of the wind that ripped his stupid head off and pounded him into the ground.

After they rushed back from Orlando to get her, Kit took Kiki shopping, purposely avoiding the discount stores where she always bought clothes for herself and Mel and their own kids. Kiki and Oscar and Chloe were accustomed to better. Kit combed the newspaper and apartment guidebooks, paging past the low income complexes and insisting to their mother that Kiki needed the security of a gated community. At the furniture store, she emptied the last of their savings account with the fervor of someone purchasing an indulgence from the pope, but the images still haunted, and the knowledge still nagged. She couldn't get around the fact that someday, somehow, Kiki was going to find out what happened, and Kit would lose something that had been precious to her all her life. Lately, she found herself separating from Kiki in preparation for that day, unable to bear hearing her voice on the telephone, making excuses to avoid the Taco Cabana, not wanting to think about the ten-minute drive to the apartment complex, even though she missed her sister painfully and knew her sister painfully missed her.

According to Dr. Jane Poplin, Kit's obstetrician, the only way to determine for sure who the baby's father was would be through amniocentesis and DNA testing, and for that, she'd need blood samples from the two possible . . . here Dr. Poplin had used the word "subjects." Kit had been tearing her mind apart, ransacking for some way to obtain the samples without facing the "subjects" or having to explain the whole thing to Kiki. As much as the idea of sneaking into the hospital and slashing Wayne's throat appealed to her, she figured she might have a problem getting a sitter while she went to prison for fifty years. And the idea of Ander's expression when confronted with the possibility of yet another child—Ag! sadaesten dröeker!

The baby grew inside her, day by day, and the burden of guilt expanded with it. Kit spent her days waiting for punishment to descend, knowing that whatever was coming, it wasn't bad enough. There wasn't a shower hot enough or a communion wafer dry enough to absolve her. Mel wasn't the kind of man who would beat her, so she did her best to beat herself.

He pulled into the driveway a little after midnight. Each bundling a child into their arms, they carried Mitzi and Coo up to their beds and tucked them in come-as-you-are—jean shorts, dirty feet, and all.

Kit came down to the kitchen and measured grounds into Mr. Coffee. As she headed back up the stairs, she heard Mel out in the garage, clanking his tools on the cement floor, whirring his electric drill.

The garage was now off-limits to everyone else in the family, including Kit. She caught fleeting glimpses of the Falcon as Mel came and went through the kitchen door; it was now swathed in an enormous blue drop cloth, a divine sculpture awaiting its grand unveiling by the Michelangelo of mechanics.

Kit carried the suitcases upstairs and stretched out on the bed. Reaching into her bag, she brought out the Danish Butter Cookie tin and spread the antique-smelling contents on the comforter. The letters were still sealed in their pale blue envelopes, neatly addressed beneath brittle virgin stamps, and they all began the same way.

Sweetest, most coveted love . . .

Sometimes the handwriting became too erratic to read, and Kit had to strain to decipher those lines that were scored through by the deeply creased folds.

. . . when I get there that day because I told you I would forbid nothing. The tacit invitation, the permission, I bow away from you, presenting like a mare. (Oh, I know! And I am sorry for the image, but I long to lead you back from your civilized mind to an ancient, bestial self.) This isn't something I can give you. You must be strong enough to take it. Don't be afraid. My cry isn't so much pain as intensity. I deliver myself to your gentleness, I believe in your willingness to go slowly, just a centimeter more each time I breathe out, until I'm pliant and wet and open and you're able to pull back and slide forward as freely as when you faced me.

It was like staring into a solar eclipse. Kit couldn't resist. Her eyes felt large and dry, her chest constricted, scarred, as she carefully slid the John Wayne letter opener across the top of another envelope and pressed the notepaper open on the bed.

. . . *while my fingers find the precise circular motion that brings on my little nova. I do my best to hold back, but now? Please, now. The dissolving is such that all my being is wracked and weakened and taken under. Whose name will you cry out at the last moment? Mine? Your wife's? Jesus Christ? I don't care as long as I'm the one to hear it. Flood and overflow me. Or let me lay back to receive your warm white milk across my nipples and mouth. Oh, I want that, please. I'm so thirsty. I'll share the salt taste with you in a kiss, drawing you on top of me, inside me, to comfort you, to let you sheath your sword. You've just slain Grendel's mother, my love. You are mortally wounded, though you laugh every time I tell you that.*

How could a harpy like Neeva have written any such thing? Who was her sweet, coveted love, and why did the letters lay there unsent for all the years that had gone by since you could send a letter for just five cents postage? And how could Otto have been oblivious to something that so profoundly affected her? And who the heck was *Grendel?*

Aching between empathy and a heartbreaking, targetless anger, Kit bundled the letters together and foraged deeper into the tin.

Frank Dupuis's carefully clipped obituary typed out his simple life in no more than a couple of column inches: born in San Antonio, Shankow-Turner foreman, father, grandfather, great-grandfather, dead. He wore horn-rimmed glasses and a gentle-humored expression, softened further by the grainy beige of the aged newsprint.

Next, Kit excavated a curled photograph of three women on the loading dock at old S-T. You could tell it was the late forties because of the way they all had their bangs rolled up in sausages above their foreheads. The other two had their hair pulled back with those big bows that remain timelessly in style, but Neeva stood in the center, dark hair draped over her shoulders like a velvet curtain. Her head was thrown back laughing, those big ol' breasts of hers riding all the higher and prouder for the tight-cinched waist of her coveralls. At the edge of the great corrugated steel door, there was the blurred image of a man, features distorted by motion just a heartbeat ahead of what the camera could capture. But even as he turned, it seemed that he was laughing, too.

Kit turned on the shower and slowly undressed, thinking of Neeva embalmed in clothes she'd never have worn. "Wouldn't be caught dead in," Neeva might have said. Kit drew the plastic curtain and imagined what it would be to lie closed in with the dark and the flowers and all the coming decades of glued-shut silence. Hidden in the hot water, she cried, mourning all things unheard, unhad, unwritten, and unread. The steam on the window reminded her of cigarette smoke over sky. The slippery soap made her think of stroking and saying and the sort of dissolving that could wrack your entire being.

No wonder Neeva couldn't sleep nights.

This Kit understood, because lately, after Mel went off to the hangar, she'd find herself pacing, obsessively cleaning things or sitting at the table staring. Her bed was too empty to retire to. Her inner landscape was changing with the slow, sure swelling of her belly, and her middle finger could no longer access that one specific place or capture that precise circular motion that used to release her enough to sleep. There was no little nova for her anymore. Not with the repugnant mental residue of Wayne crawling over her skin and the guilt-ridden images of Ander crowding out her familiar store of romance novel fantasies and pleasant memories of Mel in his worn jeans and Semper Fi T-shirt. On his nights off, Mel made slow, quiet love to her, cherishing her breasts full of milk and her belly full of life, and Kit tried to deliver herself to his gentleness. She trusted his willingness to go slow. But so much hung so heavily between her and her self now. There was just no joy in it anymore.

"Do you want coffee, Mel?" she called from the kitchen, but Mel's head was under the car. He couldn't hear her. "Mel? I made coffee."

She poured a cup for him and a cup of tea for herself and set them on saucers with Oreos.

"Mel?" She backed out the kitchen door, balancing the cups in her hands.

"I told you not to come out here!"

The wheeled platform squealed out from under the jacked-up body of the vehicle, and Mel conked his head on the bottom of the door.

"Ouch! Dang it! Shit!" he gritted, and then pointed a socket wrench at her, placing the blame for his throbbing head and his mother's death and everything else that was broken in his life. "I told you I don't want anybody out here!"

"Mel, why don't you come on in now? You've had such a long day." He rubbed his head sullenly.

"What do you want?"

The easing and the entering, she longed to tell him. *I want you to be my sweetest, most coveted love.*

"I made coffee," she told him instead.

"Thank you." He took it from her and blew on it, taking a drink and then looking at her as if she was supposed to be satisfied and go.

"Mel, fixing that car couldn't bring him back," Kit said carefully. "And it's not gonna bring her back, either."

"That's not what this is about."

"Then what is it about, Mel?"

"It's about the restoration of a classic automobile—"

"—that just happens to be exactly like the automobile your dead mother restored for your dead brother? C'mon, Mel!"

"It's a car. Spare me the deep-seated psychological bullshit."

"Your mother didn't care about the car, Mel. She just wanted someone to acknowledge her. To ask her. To hear her."

"Well, maybe there are a few things you don't know about my mother."

"And maybe," Kit countered, "there are a few things *you* don't know about her."

"Like what?"

"Nothing." Kit backed off and picked up a wrench from the tool bench.

"Like Frank Dupuis?"

"You *knew* about that?"

"How could I not know about it, Kit?" Mel took the wrench out of her hands and laid it back on the bench. "I was ten years old. I wasn't stupid. I heard people talking."

"But you never mentioned it."

"It didn't exactly come up in conversation. 'Oh, by the way, my mother spent eight years getting porked by her boss.' I didn't think it would really improve your relationship with her," he said, adding, "That's the kind of thing you'd never understand."

He sat on the steps, twisting together a cable that would connect something automotive to something vehicular.

"One Friday morning, when I was about Cooper's age, she left. Like she was going to work. Like usual. Only she didn't come home that afternoon, and when my dad called, they said she'd called in sick. And so had Frank."

"What happened?"

"They found him parked by the side of the road up north of Nacogdoches, hammered as a two-penny nail. He was supposed to meet her in Texarkana, but . . . I don't know. He didn't. Lost his nerve, I guess. Maybe because he and Pop were friends. Or maybe he decided to go back to his wife or something."

"Then what happened?" Kit knelt down in front of him, ashamed that she was more transfixed by curiosity than concerned for his pain.

"He gave Pop the number of this hotel where she was at.

Where he was supposed to meet her. Pop called the pastor of their church, and the pastor called her."

"And what did she do?"

"She did the right thing," he shrugged. "She came home."

"No," Kit shook her head. "It wasn't right. Not for her. And I'm not even sure it was the right thing for you, Mel. I mean, what did she really give to you after that?"

"You can't blame that on Frank Dupuis. She was never willing to give anybody anything."

"Yes, she was! She was willing to give everything! She would have given it to your father if he wasn't such a—a *lamp-post*, and she'd have given it to Frank if he'd had the guts to take it. But maybe when he left her like that, she couldn't risk it again. Maybe she wasn't willing to risk taking anything or giving anything ever again. That part is her own fault. That was her choice. But Mel, that guy was an idiot to let her go. And with or without him, she should have never looked back."

"How can you say that? She had a husband and kids. You don't just abandon your family!"

"No, you don't." Tears were stinging Kit's eyes and nose. "You just abandon yourself. You just do what they tell you because they say that's what God wants you to do, and you don't know who God is anymore. You just accept whatever half-assed effort someone's willing to put out because you think you don't deserve anything better. And you think, well, it's better than nothing."

"What? What are you talking about?"

"You just keep all your thoughts to yourself because nobody can hear you anyway. You just kiss your own hand and pretend you believe it's wrong to want anyone to touch you. You just turn your back on the one person who could have given you some happiness—and I don't mean your husband or some lover—I mean *yourself!* And then you just get old and angry and bitter until it consumes you like a cancer, and then you just die!"

Mel stared at her for a moment and then laughed nervously.

"Okay." He turned back toward the toolbox. "I think somebody's mommy hormones are running a little rampant tonight."

"Don't you dare dismiss me like that!" she shrilled at him, startling them both.

"I'm sorry!" Mel got up and started chucking his tools in the squeaky red drawers of the top box. "Geez, can we please get off this subject?"

"Fine. Don't think about it. That'll make it go away."

"No, Kit," he wheeled on her, "she's dead! *That* makes it go away. So can we please let it go away now? Please?"

"Fine."

"I'm sorry. I just don't want to talk about it. Okay?"

"I said fine, didn't I?"

She took a sip of her tea, but it was cold and oversweet now.

"Why did you even come out here in the first place?" he grumbled.

"I was just trying to help."

"Yeah, thanks, honey. You've been helping me become a better person in so many ways lately."

"What's that supposed to mean?" she defensed.

"Kit, you've been on my back for some reason or other every damn minute since we got back from Orlando. If it's not my weight, it's money or my laundry or razor stubble in the sink or newspaper on the floor or the way I put syrup on the kids' pancakes, for God's sake!"

"Every dirty sock under the bed, every syrup dribble on the floor, it takes away from me that much, Mel," she measured a minute quantity with her thumb and index finger. "Just that much. What you don't understand is that all of it together adds up to my life! But that doesn't mean anything to you. You never had a concept of what I did at the shop all day, and you don't have a concept of what I do around this house. You don't know. You don't *want* to know. You don't *care!*"

"And what do you know about what I do, Kit? You have no concept of what goes on at the goddamn airport all night. Have you ever even thought about it?"

She thought about it now, while he finished putting his tools away and straightened the blue tarp.

"Mel, this is not about housework, it's—"

"No, look . . ." He rubbed his hands over his face, leaving a black mark that made him look even more weary. "I'm sorry, okay? Let's not fight."

"No, *I'm* sorry. I have been on your case, but I—"

"You've been great." He sat next to her on the steps, pulled her head over to his chest, and whispered into her hair, "I'm the one who's sorry."

"Mel," she pulled away, "you have nothing to be sorry about."

"I know what's bothering you, and I don't blame you for being mad at me about this baby thing. I know it's my fault."

"Your fault? How is it your fault?"

"Well, I knew I was supposed to go back and have another sperm count done every year, but geez . . . The whole process is so—geez!" He wrinkled his large nose in childlike beets-and-broccoli distaste. "I just didn't want to. It was easier to assume that Poplin was right, you know? She goes around acting like she's always right, and she seemed pretty sure that nothing could ever happen, so to—to use something or get a vasectomy or whatever, it seemed like there wasn't any point." Mel got up and moved away, embarrassed by both the concept and the conversation. "But now, it's too late. And I know you're not thrilled about the timing, and I'm sorry, Kit."

"Would you please stop saying that?" she begged him, because the anvil on her chest was starting to feel more like a branding iron.

"I'm gonna make it up to you, Kit. I swear, I'm gonna be

more help to you than I was with Cooper and Mitzi, and I'm gonna work every bit of overtime I can, so we can afford for you to stay home—"

"Do I ever get to be the one who makes the mistake or causes the problem or takes responsibility for anything? Is it ever my fault? Is it even necessary for me to be here? Because, obviously, if you've caused all these problems, then you're the one with the ability to fix everything, aren't you?"

"Kit," Mel coaxed. "C'mon, honey. Stop this."

"No, Mel, you stop it! Just—stop it stop it *stop it!*"

She pushed against his chest, but he was immovable as the foundation under her feet. That branding iron finally penetrated the thick, dry shell in which she'd encased her heart and lungs, searing into the last part of her that was left.

"I can't do this anymore! I can't stand it! How can you be such a big, stupid ox? How can you keep acting like everything's fine? *It's not!* Get with reality, Mel! Dr. Poplin *is* always right! Hasn't it occurred to you, hasn't it once crossed your mind that maybe this is not your baby?"

"No," Mel said mildly. He even laughed a little. "No, of course not!"

And Kit knew that it hadn't and couldn't and wouldn't, even now. She went away from him, and facing into the corner like a little girl, covered her face with her hands and started sobbing.

"Honey, what is it?" Mel was immediately at her side. "What's wrong?"

"Oh, God, Mel! I'm so sorry. I'm so . . . so very sorry."

"Why?" Mel sounded hollowed out and scared.

"I didn't mean for it to happen. Any of it."

"Kit, please . . . don't do this."

"It was all—it was a terrible, horrible mistake."

"*No!*" He stumbled away from her. "I won't hear this!"

"Oh God, oh God!" she wept, "I wish I were dead." And she could almost hear the coffin slamming shut, denying her the work of her hands and the praise of the gates and every-thing she had ever wanted, worked for, and loved. "I wish I'd never been born."

"Kit, I don't understand what . . . what . . . I mean, if—if it's not . . . whose baby is it?"

"I don't know."

"What do you mean, you don't know? How could you not know?" She could feel the air around him escalating like a thunderhead. "What the hell is going on?"

"It's not going on," she tried to tell him, "it just . . . happened."

"Happened? How does that just *happen?* Happened with who?"

"Oh God, oh God!" She covered her head with her arms as if the debris crashing all around her were something tangible.

"Ander. It was that goddamn Ander, wasn't it? Was it him? Or . . . What? Are we talking about—about neighbors? Delivery men? *Strangers?*"

Kit shook her head, grieving, sobbing, seeing herself as he was seeing her now, sleazy sound track, stilettos, and all, as she opened the front door for the pizza man. *Come in and bring that big, luscious pepperoni with you. My husband won't be home till morning.*

"Kit, why?" Mel held out his hands to her, begging her for something. "Why would you do this to us?"

"Why would *I?*" Kit's jaw clenched hard enough to hurt. "You better ask yourself that question, Mel Prizer, because you did this to us as much as I did!"

"I have never fucked around on you, and you know it!"

"There's more than one way to betray somebody, Mel. You left me drifting. You couldn't find fifteen seconds for me! You couldn't take care of your own body half the way you do this damn car! You just let go, and you lost me!" The shame and remorse that had been eating a hole in her stomach for the last four months were suddenly eclipsed by plain white rage. Kit was snow-blind with it. "You *lost* me!"

The closest thing at hand was Cooper's Louisville Slugger, and she brought it down on the blue plastic tarp with all her might, knowing full well she couldn't have hurt Mel any worse if she'd kneecapped him with it.

"*You—lost—me!*"

With more force than she knew she had, Kit swung, flailed, flogged on the car. The side window and then the windshield gave way, sucking the tarp toward the interior.

"You *lost* me, you lazy *bastard!* You *lost* me!"

The hood groaned, a headlight exploded, the chrome side mirror clangeranged on the floor along with the hood ornament and one side of the bumper.

"You lost me . . . you lost me . . ." Kit sank down on the red picnic cooler, sweating, breathing hard. "So just you go ask yourself *why*, Melvin Thadeus Prizer. Why'd you have to go and lose me?"

She rested her hands and forehead on the baseball bat and cried like the newly born.

Mel stood in the corner, not speaking. Just standing still. After a time, he knelt down and picked up the hood ornament. He weighed it in his hand, then hurled it through the window, shattering one pane, spidering the other. He brought both fists down on the hood of the car, dragged the tarp aside, and flung it against the wall.

"Surprise," he said bitterly.

Kit stared in disbelief at what was left of the taxicab yellow Mustang.

"*Oh*—" She felt like her whole soul was caught in her throat. It was her old '69. It had black vinyl seats. Kit could almost hear the Gulf of Mexico reflected in the windows. "*Mel*—"

His eyes were red-rimmed and full, his mouth twitching

slightly. After a little while, he began gathering wrenches and sockets in his airport toolbox.

"Mel, please. Don't leave."

He just shook his head.

"*Please, Mel!*"

He had to blink and swallow hard and even then, he could only speak the words one at a time.

"Fuck . . . you."

He stepped over her legs to the door and closed it quietly behind him.

A little time later, there was the gun and roar of his truck starting outside in the driveway. Kit listened until the engine gave way to crickets, and then she listened to the crickets until the night chirring gave way to the long predawn silence, gray dawn birds, early-morning traffic, and then she got up and went into the kitchen.

"*O*h, yeah." Neeva's lighter flashed in front of her face. "I'd say the honeymoon's definitely over."

"Go away," Kit mumbled. "I don't have to put up with you anymore."

"Then why did you keep the letters?" Neeva asked.

"Why did *you?*" was Kit's retort, but Neeva wasn't listening.

"She just had to take a peek, didn't she?"

"Oh, shut up," Kit dragged the pillows over her head.

"She couldn't keep a lid on it. So, he gets burned."

"Is there something I can do for you before you *GO?*"

"Oh, just give it a lick and a promise."

Neeva tipped her coffee can and dumped the lentils and beans, the millet, barley, vetches, and wheat in a seemingly endless shower, down over the worn bedroom carpet, but somehow through the sound of their falling, Kit distinguished the humming rise of the garage door.

She was standing in the middle of the room before she was truly awake, struggling for balance, grasping for her robe, pitching toward the stairs. She realized as she reached the kitchen that the robe was inside out and that's why she couldn't get hold of the sash, so she pulled it closed in front of her, one fist clenched at her pounding chest, the other below her distended stomach.

"*Mel!* Thank God!"

But Mitzi and Coo were quicker and had already surrounded him with squeals and hugs by the time she reached him.

"Hey! Heckle and Jeckle," he boomed in his big Mel voice, "what are you guys doing out of bed?" He dropped to his knees, bear-hugging and kissing Mitzi and Cooper and looking at them as if they'd grown six inches, and kissing them again, saying over and over, "Geez, I missed you guys. Geez, I missed you so much."

Kit stood by the table, feeling like an intruder. Mel was avoiding her eyes. He looked like he hadn't slept or shaven in the three weeks since he walked out the kitchen door. She hung back, hoping he would notice her eyes were swollen and dark-circled, too.

"Dad!" Cooper cried. "Where were you?"

"Hey, Buzz," Mel skimmed his hand over Cooper's fresh crew cut, smiling a little too broadly. "I had to go on up to Dallas and work for a couple weeks."

"Mom said El Paso." Cooper wasn't fooled for a minute. "And she keeps crying in the bathroom."

"Cooper . . . ," Mel tried to think of what to say.

"Dad," Coo swallowed, "are you divorcing us?"

"No! No. Geez. I was just—I had to . . . to go up there and work."

"That's a lie!" Cooper charged, and it was all the proof he needed. "You *are* divorcing us!"

"I'm not divorcing you, Coop, I'm right here." Mel pulled him into his big arms. "I'll always be right here, right with you, Coo buddy. Only, I have to stay at another house for a while."

"No!" Cooper was crying now.

"Yes, Coop. I have to. And it's gonna be okay. I promise."

"Why can't you stay at our house, Daddy?" Mitzi asked in a small voice.

"I need to help somebody out for a while is all. Somebody whose grandma is in the hospital. And while she's in the hospital, I'm taking care of her house for her. And I mow the lawn and water the plants and take care of the gardens. Oh, Mitzi-girl, you should see all the flowers Mrs. Garza has. And I fix things and make sure her car is running okay. But it sure is a lot of work. I sure wish I had some helpers sometimes."

"I could help you, Daddy." Mitzi seemed even smaller when Mel put his wide hand out to her.

"Yeah, right." Cooper wiped a dirty palm across his cheek. "You're not big enough, ya little squat doggy."

"Hey now. Shhh," Mel soothed in between them before she could start screaming. "Sure she can help. She can help me take care of Mrs. Garza's flowers, can't you, Mitzi-bitsy?"

"Big deal," Cooper sulked. "You can't pick flowers that's growing at somebody else's house."

"Well, you can if it's your job, right?" Mel pulled Mitzi into the hug along with Cooper. "That'll be Mitzi's special job. She can pick flowers, and we'll put 'em on the table for Mrs. Garza. And I was thinking maybe I should start a terrarium for Mrs. Garza. There's lots of lizards in that garden of hers, Coo, and I bet she'd like some of those lizards in a terrarium. But I'm gonna need help catching some of those lizards."

"Can we, Mom?" Cooper asked, and Kit nodded because she couldn't speak. "Okay, I guess I'll help with the lizards."

"That would be great, Coop," Mel grizzled them with his new beard, and they had to giggle and pull on it. "We'll get all our work done, and then we'll go to Checkers for lunch. Get a

Checkerburger and some fries? And then maybe we could go to the movies."

"Okay," they said, wanting and willing to be taken in.

"Okay!" Mel stood up and clapped his hands together. "Okay, then. That's the plan. I'll be here first thing in the morning. I'll be here so early, y'all won't even notice I didn't sleep here."

But Kit knew with great certainty she would notice. The house had been like an echo chamber to her those last three weeks.

"Now, c'mon, you two, back to bed."

They protested until Mel chased them up, pretending to be a monster who professed to eat the digits off any children caught out of bed after ten. When he came down from tucking them in, he pulled his raincoat out of the closet and took up the extra toolbox he always left in the garage. He tipped the empty baskets in the laundry room.

"Where's some socks and underwear?"

"It's all done," Kit told him. "It's all put away."

He seemed to find something bitterly amusing about that. He went back upstairs and came down with a garbage bag full of clothes.

"Well," he sighed. "My checks will keep going in the automatic deposit. I'll use the cash machine, so you can keep the checkbook."

"Mel, please—"

"Mrs. Garza is the grandmother of one of the day-shift mechanics at the hangar, and their caretaker quit on them so . . ."

"I've been worried out of my mind."

"I've got an apartment over the garage, and there's plenty of room for the kids to stay, so I'm going to keep them over the weekend."

"Please sit down and talk to me," Kit pleaded.

"I'll bring them back Sunday afternoon."

"I don't know if you can ever forgive me or if I can ever make you understand—"

"Kit, we've got an airplane coming in at midnight."

"—but you have to know that I love you and—"

"Do you mind if I take a quick shower here in the morning?" he asked, as if she hadn't even spoken.

"Of course not! This is your home!"

"Right. Well, I gotta go to work."

"Mel, please—"

"Just have them ready in the morning, all right?"

"But when are you going to sleep? You're already exhausted."

"I'll handle it," he said curtly. "I don't need you to pretend you're suddenly all worried about me."

"I'm not pretending anything. I love you!"

"Oh, yeah!" he laughed the same way he did when he saw the empty laundry baskets. "Yeah, that's great."

"Mel, listen to me—"

"*No!*" With his hand he made a gesture that widened the space between them. "I'm not gonna listen, and I'm not gonna talk. Because right now, I'm so—*God!*—I'm so pissed off, I can't even . . . I can't even stand to look at you, and—and I'm afraid I'll end up saying something that—" He shook his head and grasped the toolbox. "I'm going to work."

There was an awkward moment because he almost stepped forward to peck her on the cheek out of habit, but the toolbox came unlatched, and wrenches and drill bits and sockets clanged on the kitchen floor. Kit stooped to help him gather them, but he held up his hand.

"Just leave me alone. Go back to bed or—whatever."

Kit stood hugging her arms tightly across the front of her body as he clanked the tools into the box and slammed it shut. He opened the door but paused for a moment.

"Look—" he said, though his anger and hurt made it sound

like the shame-faced admission of a great personal failing. "I love you, too, okay?"

"Okay," Kit breathed.

"Okay," he repeated and stepped out into the rain.

❀

The bathroom in Attorney Poole's office had a genuine leather toilet seat. Or at least it looked like genuine leather. Kneeling on the floor, Kiki could smell the upholstery smell, even with a wet paper towel over her face.

"Mrs. Daubert?" Attorney Poole rapped impatiently. "Are you all right?"

Kiki stood up and flushed again and rinsed her hands and opened the door.

"I'm sorry, Mrs. Daubert, I know this all must be coming as somewhat of a shock to you."

"Actually, it's just morning sickness," Kiki said. "I'm all right."

"Please allow me to express the sincere condolences of everyone here at the firm. Wayne was a valued client, and his father has been a good friend of mine from the club for many years, of course." He pushed a chair she was positive had to be real leather close to the front of his desk. "I was gratified to hear that you two were working out your differences. That makes this terrible tragedy all the more . . . tragic."

"Yes," Kiki murmured.

"Are you sure you want to continue?"

"Well," she said uncertainly, "I'm not sure there's any point."

"No," he admitted, "between the credit cards, medical and funeral expenses, and the small claims judgments against his business. And then, of course, there's the matter of his account with our firm here . . ."

"Of course," Kiki said. "The thing is . . . I guess I still don't understand how this could have happened."

"Well, it was pretty much like I told you, Mrs. Daubert. She came in and requested the paternity test; the phlebotomist came and drew the blood. A short time later, she was seen leaving, and shortly after that, it was discovered that the respirator had been disconnected from the wall outlet."

"And they think she did it."

"The investigation is pointing in that direction."

"She's been under a lot of—of stress lately, and she truly is a good person inside. Mr. Poole, surely they won't . . . they won't, will they?"

"The investigation is still ongoing. Hopefully, there won't be anything beyond this very circumstantial evidence that's already come to light."

"Will you represent her, Attorney Poole?" Kiki leaned forward, her hands on the edge of the desk as if she were a supplicant to the great and powerful Oz. "If it happens, I mean? See, her husband—they're separated now, and she's not used to being on her own, and I don't have any other money right now, but whatever's left in Wayne's estate, I'd gladly give it to you."

"Oh, it's not a question of money, Mrs. Daubert. I'm simply not a criminal attorney."

"*Criminal?*" Kiki swallowed.

"If it's discovered that she did indeed terminate your husband's life support when the most recent tests clearly showed higher brain function— Yes, it's likely she'll be charged with manslaughter, possibly murder."

"Mr. Poole, my mother-in-law is not a criminal."

"Of course not. They'd just like to check her fingerprints. In order to clear her name, you see. So if you have any idea where she might be—"

"No," Kiki said again, quickly producing the facial expression she used for innocence and denial. "No, I can't imagine where she might be."

"Well," Attorney Poole smiled the fatherly smile he'd

smiled at her in her mother's living room. "I'm sure this is all a tragic error, and the investigation is just a smoke screen. In fact, you may decide to pursue a wrongful death claim against the facility, in which case—" He pondered that pleasant prospect for a moment. "Well, now that's something I could help you with."

"Paternity test?" Kiki wondered. "Why would she ask for a paternity test? And how could they do a paternity test without something from me? From the baby, I mean?"

"Well now, I don't know," Attorney Poole consulted a manila file folder. "Let's see. Yes. It was requested by Mrs. Daubert, Sr., and results were to be conveyed to . . . here it is. Results were to be conveyed to a Dr. Jane Poplin." He closed the folder, pondering again. "You know, Mrs. Daubert, your father-in-law—well, not to be crass, but there are some considerable assets there."

"Dr. Poplin?" Kiki echoed.

"Now, he's been in possession of these letters from South America for some time," Attorney Poole continued, "and they clearly refer to this inappropriate relationship. Plain evidence of her mental instability. I believe we could show there's a liability there. So if we were to pursue him *and* your mother-in-law on the matter of wrongful death as well as the facility, why, we'd be in a very good position whichever way the investigation goes."

"Excuse me, sir," Kiki said. "I think I'm gonna be sick again."

❧

"Okay." Kit checked her facial expression in the rearview mirror and started again. "There's something we need to discuss and . . . and . . . okay. There's a—a matter of some urgency. Shoot. Okay. Ander, let's face it, you seem to be a very . . . um . . . fruitful, a very fertile . . ."

Kit ran out of road. She had to pull into the parking lot and stop the car in front of the ornate window she herself had painted with ferns and fiddleheads and the words *Scandinavian Design.*

C'mon, you can do this, she told herself, *one down. You did one already.*

And that wasn't an easy one, either.

It was a simple plan. On a day she knew Kiki wouldn't be there, she would just go and explain the situation to Wayne's mother, and she would sign for the test, and Kiki would never have to be the wiser. But when Kit arrived at the nursing home, Wayne's mother was sitting next to him on the bed, singing the same little song Kit herself had sung to Cooper on a thousand summer evenings.

" . . . *ragtime cowboy, talk about yer cowboy, ragtime cowboy Joe . . .*"

She brushed her fingers up and down his atrophied arm, humming in time to the respirator's syncopated rhythm.

"Mrs. Daubert?" Kit broached, "I don't know if you remember me . . ."

"Why, Kitten! Of course! Of course, I do. And even if I didn't, well, my goodness, you girls look like twins. Anyone would know you're Kalene's sister." Mother Daubert embraced Kit and kissed the air at the side of her cheek. "It's so sweet of you to come. And you're expecting! Kiki told me, and she was so delighted."

"Mrs. Daubert," Kit swallowed, not at all sure she was going to be able to go through with this, "that's sort of what I— I need to talk to you about."

Mother Daubert's face solidified to a pleasant mask. Her soft gray eyes took on the heavy-lashed look of a porcelain doll's. Kit tried to breathe enough to speak. She told her as gently as she could. Then, there was a dry quiet in which the respirator clicked and sighed.

"I see," Mother Daubert nodded, taking Jane Poplin's card with the courtesy and composure of a charity function hostess.

"So, if you could . . ."

"Yes," she said, her coral pink lips quivering only slightly and only for a moment.

"Mrs. Daubert, I can't tell you how horrible I feel about—"

"Perhaps you should go now, Kitten."

"It's just that Kiki has so much on her mind right now. I didn't want her to be . . . to have any unnecessary . . ."

"Yes. Yes, I definitely think you should go, dear." Mother Daubert tucked the sheet over Wayne's atrophied arm. "They'll be bringing his Jell-O soon. He loves to share his Jell-O with me in the afternoon."

Kit left as quickly as possible, blinking furiously, determined to drive directly to Scandinavian Design before she lost her momentum.

In the space of that afternoon and the two weeks since, Kit had driven past the ornate sign at least twenty times.

From the parking lot now, she could see Ander through the wide front window, chatting with a customer she recognized. They both looked up at the sound of the door chimes.

"Why, Kit!" the customer declared. "We were just talking about you!"

"Oh . . . Mrs. Lu. It's nice to see you again," Kit said, trying not to notice that Ander's mouth was hanging open and his eyes were riveted to her stomach. Perhaps this was going to be easier to explain than she thought.

"I was so sorry to hear you aren't working anymore because—well, as I was telling Ander—I've had so many compliments on the armoire with the mimosa ladies," said Mrs. Lu.

"Oh, yes. The mimosa ladies. And the little house and orange blossoms," Kit went on, not wanting Mrs. Lu to leave. "And it was over a—a nice black lacquer, wasn't it?"

"Yes, very high gloss," Mrs. Lu nodded enthusiastically. "I came in because I've been wanting to have some companion pieces done—a vanity and a little ottoman, perhaps, and two little night tables? But I understand you're no longer available."

"No. I . . . I'm taking some time off."

"Well, Ander made it sound so final! I didn't know this was just a maternity leave," she said in a congratulatory way that made it all seem even more ironic. "When will you be back?"

"I won't be back, Mrs. Lu."

"Oh?" she said in a way that inflected the unspoken *why not?*

Kit had never considered herself particularly quick-thinking, and it pleased her, even in the moment, to know how proud Vivica would be of what happened next.

"Because, you see," she blurted, "I'm working out of my home now. Because, well, actually, I—I just recently, I've gone into business for myself! And . . . and very recently, in fact so . . . I mean, I don't even have business cards yet, but here, let me give you my number because I—I'd make you a great price and—" She dragged her checkbook out of her purse and ripped the address part off a deposit slip. "Oh, I'd be so happy to do it for you, Mrs. Lu."

"I'm so pleased!" Mrs. Lu beamed. "Why don't you prepare an estimate for me, and I'll give you a call first thing tomorrow so we can discuss when and delivery and all that."

"Okay. Yes. Wonderful," Kit nodded and agreed and nodded some more.

"And I want you to give me some of those business cards the moment you get them because I have so many people ask me about that armoire."

"Oh, that would be just—just wonderful, Mrs. Lu. Thank you!" As she grasped the fine lady's hand, Kit felt her bleak future suddenly opening up like a magnolia right in front of her. "Wonderful. And—and you have a real good day now."

The door jingled with porcelain chimes as she went out, and Kit turned to Ander, who was still staring, slack-jawed at her abdomen, not aware or caring that she'd just stolen his customer.

"Ah *Gott*, Kit! My *Gott*," he stammered. "Is . . . is . . . ?"

Braced and emboldened by the lingering sting of Mrs. Lu's diamond-ring handshake, Kit stuck out her hand with Dr. Poplin's card in it.

"There's only one way to find out," she decided to be blunt. "You need to have this blood test so they can tell. Will you, Ander?"

He nodded.

"Right away? Tomorrow?"

He nodded again.

"Okay," she said. "Good."

"Ya," he echoed, "Good. Right away tomorrow." But he still didn't take the card.

"Well, that's all I needed . . . so . . . thank you." Kit laid the card by the cash register and started to go, but Ander suddenly broke free of whatever force was holding him behind the counter.

"Kit! Kit, wait!" He bolted over the top and caught her elbow before she reached the door. "Ruda . . . She take the girls, she leave the boys. She is gone back to Kristianstäd."

"Oh, no."

"She say to me that she is wanting good reason to leave for very long time now. She say she never want to learn this English speaking, she never want her children to listen on this rap music. She only want to be back in her one home." His blue eyes were reflecting, close to spilling over. "She is getting divorce with me."

"Oh, no."

"Ah *Gott*, Kit. I never am so alone in my life."

"Ander, I'm so sorry." Kit put her hand on his elbow.

"Don't say you are to be sorry. Is my fault all completely."

"If it makes you feel any better, Mel and I are . . . Well, actually, Mel. He left."

"Why would this make me feel better?" Ander anguished. "You think I want for you this unhappiness I have?"

"No! No, of course not." She put her arms around his big middle. "It's just an expression."

"You must believe I never want for you any unhappiness."

When he hugged her, Kit's eyes welled up. Partly because he felt so much like Mel, and partly because she realized how much she missed having Ander as her good friend, laughing with him, planning, dancing around to "Paul and His Chickens."

"I miss you," she said against his denim shirt.

"Ya. Ya, I also am missing you, Kit. Missing you very much." He took her face between his broad, roughened palms. "Kit, if I am father of this baby, then you don't worry. Nothing could make me so happy as to take care of you."

"Ander . . ." Kit pulled away from him. "I don't want anybody to take care of me. I just need to know." She picked up Dr. Poplin's card and pressed it into his hand. "Okay?"

"Ya," he nodded again. "Is okay."

"Okay," she repeated and stepped out into the sunlight.

❦

Six weeks later, as Mrs. Lu's teenage sons carried out the two small night tables and brought in two highboy dressers, Kit tucked the check into her shirt pocket and rolled out the sketches on the kitchen table.

But Mrs. Lu wasn't even looking.

Her neck craned back, her eyes traveled the trailing vines that sprouted up from the wainscoting and tendrilled up and around the ceiling, draping above the cupboards, whose doors now windowed a French cafe. Twining past the ceiling fan, whose blades hung heavy with leaves, pears, glockenspiels, and lingonberries, the foliage wound round each switch plate and electrical outlet, whose corners ticked and popped with dots and dashes and curlicues, blossoming at the base of the bay window in a profusion of orchids, harmonicas, and day lilies, some of which burst up through the sill and painted their morning colors directly onto the glass.

"I am stunned," Mrs. Lu said for the fourth time. "Absolutely stunned. My goodness, Kit, this is just . . . so . . . stunning."

"I've had trouble sleeping the last couple months," Kit said, because in her mind that explained it completely.

"I have truly never seen anything like it." Mrs. Lu pressed her hands together and then held them wide apart. "Have you photographed it for your portfolio?"

Kit stood with her sketches in her hand. She'd never thought of herself as having a *portfolio*. Like an *artist*.

"Not yet. But soon."

Mrs. Lu looked at the sketches, loved them, and left, just as Mel's truck pulled into the driveway.

Kit was a little anxious when she saw him getting out instead of just dropping the kids off as he usually did, but knowing he'd eventually have to come inside the house again, she'd been bracing herself for his reaction.

"Holy shit!" He seemed to be as stunned as Mrs. Lu.

"I've been having trouble sleeping," Kit sounded even smaller than she felt.

"It looks like a cuckoo clock exploded in here."

"I was just going to do a little something on the pantry door, just to match the cupboards."

She tried to stand in front of the lazy Susan where Gene Kelly lunched with George Gershwin, but Mel was already pointing at it, his speechless mouth opening and closing like a fish on dry ground.

"Then about two o'clock in the morning, see, I was listening to *American in Paris,* and it just started . . . growing."

Mel followed the wandering ivy to the doorway.

"Hey!" he startled and then bounded back to confront her. "What the hell? You tore the carpet out of the living room!"

"Well, see, the garage was still full of all that—you know . . .

everything. And I need to work in the air-conditioning, anyway. It's really too hot out there and—and the stuff doesn't dry on account of the humidity, and I can't hear the phone. And the carpet was old, Mel, it was practically worn out, anyway."

But Mel was back in the living room, his voice echoing off the empty walls.

"Where's the furniture? Where's my chair? What have you done with my chair?" He wheeled on her, pointing his finger like Hercule Poirot, accusing, "You threw it out! You always hated that chair!"

"Calm down, Mel. It's in the garage."

He'd already discovered the sofa scrunched up against the wall in the dining room, but, "Hey—hey—*hey! Where's the TV?*"

"Well, actually, I took it down to Cash America."

"You took our television to a pawnshop?" he cried, as though it were one of their children. "You *hocked* it?"

"Well, right. Because I forgot to ask for a deposit on the first couple jobs, and so I needed the money for brushes and paint and a T-square and—and things."

"Have you completely lost it, Kit? Are you . . . are you . . . You are! You're crazy." Mel circled the concrete floor as if the coffee table were still there. "You've completely lost your grip."

"Mel, I've already made over six hundred dollars! See, Mrs. Lu, she has this friend whose sister owns this specialty shop down on Montrose—"

"What's that in the hallway?"

"It's . . . primer." Her small answer inflected upward like a question.

"Primer? What d'you mean, 'primer'?"

"It's a base coat for—"

"I know what primer is! Why is it splattered all over the hallway I just painted last winter?"

"Well, I haven't decided exactly what that's going to be yet. But now I have to do these dressers first, anyhow. And Mel," she looked at him expectantly, the way Mitzi would offer a beautiful bouquet of weeds, "I'm getting four hundred dollars for the dressers, Mel. Two hundred a piece! And all I have to do is a little ivy down the sides and a little bunch of violets on each drawer."

"That's great, Kit. That's very nice. But how much do you think it's gonna cost to repair all this?" He rubbed at a spatter of green paint on the woodwork. "Has it occurred to you that we might be trying to sell this house sometime soon?"

It hadn't. And Kit didn't even know how to respond to the idea, now that it had. She was wearing a pair of Mel's old overalls she'd cut off for maternity clothes, and she pushed her hands into the deep pockets.

"Sell this house? I don't want to sell this house."

"Okay, okay." Mel pushed the heels of his hands against his eyes. "I don't want to fight. You were upset. You just—you know, you always get a little wiggy when you're pregnant, so you did this and that's okay. We can fix it. I'm not mad. But don't do anything else without asking me, okay?"

"Asking you?" she said. "You mean like . . . permission?"

"No! I mean like—"

"Mel, I'm the one who's always taken care of this house—"

"And I'm the one working his ass off to pay for it!"

"I'm trying to make something of my life so I can pay my own—"

"*Fine!*" Mel erupted. "Tear the goddamn place down! What difference does it make? You trashed our marriage, you trashed the car! Why the hell should it bother me if you destroy our home right along with it?"

"I didn't destroy—"

"You did, Kit!" he bellowed. "You destroyed everything! And God damn you for it!"

"He already has!" Kit bellowed back at him. "Along with you and Mama and *Good Housekeeping* magazine! I guess you all would have been happier if I'd just gone on destroying *myself!*"

She let him absorb that while she pulled the drawers out of the highboys, stacking them where his recliner used to be.

"Well, I am *so* sorry, Kit. I had no idea your life was so fucking terrible."

"I know you didn't," she said bitterly. "And God damn *you* for that."

He stepped between her and the highboy.

"If we end up getting divorced, Kit, this house is gonna get sold."

"It's my house," Kit faced him in his own pants. "I'll sell it or stay in it as I please, and I'll do it without your permission."

"I don't believe this!"

"Believe it, Mel," she said unsympathetically and stacked another drawer against the wall.

"So, that's it?" he said. "We're over? We're—we're getting divorced?"

Kit stood still by the wall. "Isn't that what you want?"

"No! I want—I want— I don't know what I want. But it might be nice to see a little *remorse* on your part!"

"*Remorse?*" Kit almost laughed, "I have been *hemorrhaging* remorse for the last five months, and yes, it might be nice if you could see that."

She stripped masking tape off a roll and started laying it on the edges of a dresser drawer.

"I realize it now, Mel. I was being just as blind and deaf as you were. You never did a thing to me that I didn't do to myself first. But after a while, all I could see was my own misery, and then something horrible happened and everything just . . . just . . ." Kit spanned her hands in front of her, searching for words. "Everything *shattered,* and I couldn't fix it no matter how hard I tried."

Mel sat on a color-spattered kitchen chair and rested his forehead on his fists.

"Mel, I've torn myself up over it every night, all night, ever since you left. You think I'm glad things turned out this way?

Think I'm proud of what I did? That it's not tearing my heart up to see you drive away with my kids every weekend? You think it doesn't hurt and humiliate me how—after everything we've been to each other for the last twelve years—how you won't even speak to me, let alone look at me or—God forbid!— touch me? But that's not enough for you. I'm supposed to sit here in sackcloth and ashes for the rest of my life."

She set the drawer down and braced her hands on either side.

"Every time you come here, I beg and plead and apologize, and I'm done with it, Mel. Yes, I did wrong, and yes, I feel like shit about it, but I'm still entitled to a life. It didn't erase everything good I ever did, and it shouldn't drown out everything good that I am."

Mel passed her another drawer. "I never said it did."

It was like seeing a photograph of a long-forgotten friend. Her first thought was to be amazed at how much she missed him now; her second, to wonder how she could have missed him even more when he was living with her.

"I am sorry, Mel. I am so sorry I hurt you. Because I do love you. But can you understand? That's what made it so hard? That first time—it was like—like being forced to drink poison. And with Ander . . ."

Kit turned back to taping the edges of the drawer.

"What? You love him?"

"Is that allowed?"

"You know it isn't."

"But what if I can't help it?"

"I don't know." Mel shook his head as if it suddenly felt very heavy. "Christ, I can't understand any of this."

Kit took his hand, and she held onto it, even though he flinched.

"Me neither," she said. "But I'm trying to get it sorted out."

The Third Trimester

There ain't no answer.
There ain't gonna be any answer.
There never has been an answer.
There's the answer.

Gertrude Stein

*H*eat waves sweltered up from the patio and filled the air with rattlesnakes. Even above the sounds of the children running in the sprinkler, they buzzed and chickered, seeped through the voices of the book Kit was reading, permeated the sun and blood-red darkness when she closed her eyes.

It crossed her mind that she could get up off her low-slung canvas deck chair and step into the wild, cool spray, but the oppressive weight of the afternoon humidity drained her even of her will for water. As she lay listening, the heaviness of the day settled to her breasts, sagging them aside. The baby rolled over, pushing a foot into her diaphragm, forcing her to sigh a deep, involuntary sigh.

Hello there.

The foot moved to the bottom of her rib cage, and through the murky amniotic fluid, Kit could see the baby smiling in her sleep. She allowed herself the pleasure of it for a moment, sinking deeper into the deck chair, cradle in cradle.

"It's that third one, you know." A Cricket lighter chirped through the din of cicadas, and the smell of smoke invaded the summer scent of wet grass and cocoa butter. "Leaves your stomach looking like an empty kangaroo pouch."

"Go away," Kit said. "I hate you."

"A so-called 'healthy tan,'" Neeva commented, "actually represents an injury to the skin."

"Leave me alone."

"Do the two words 'skin cancer' mean anything to you?"

"Do the two words—"

"And how are you planning to turn over on your stomach? Drill a hole in the pavement?"

"*What?* What do you want from me?"

"But I guess it's easier than working."

"I'm working!" Kit defended herself. "Just take a look at that beast in the living room!"

"Oh, yes. That's quite a project," Neeva said. "How much did you fleece that art lover for?"

"Mama?" Mitzi's patty-cake-hand on her shoulder brought back the smell of cocoa butter. "Mama, wake up. I have to go potty."

"Just go in and go," Kit murmured without opening her eyes. "Be Mommy's big girl."

"*Ma-maaaa,*" Mitzi whined, pulling on her shoulder. "I can't get my suit off when it's wet. It gets all twisty!"

"Okay," Kit sighed and rolled up off the chair.

She took Mitzi in and helped her peel down the swimming suit and struggle out of its clammy cling.

"Next time," she advised, "remember to go potty before you get wet. You'll never get this thing on again."

"Can I wear my purple one?"

"No, let's dry off now. You're starting to look a little pink on the cheeks."

Kit was amazed when Mitzi went along with this without a tantrum, especially since Cooper and the rest of the neighborhood kids were still out there dancing and whooping like a war party around a bonfire of cold, hissing hose water.

"Knock knock," Mitzi baited as Kit toweled her off.

"Who's there?"

"Interrupting cats."

"Interrupting cats wh—"

"*Meow!*"

For some reason, this struck both of them as about the most hilarious thing they'd ever heard.

"Oh, you're funny," Kit snuggled her close and pulled a T-shirt over her head. "But looks aren't everything."

Then she made a big raspberry on Mitzi's tummy, and they were still giggling as Kit spread out paper and watercolors on the living room floor.

"Okay, Peanut, here's your project," she said, laying brushes and napkins nearby. "You work over here, and I'll go over there so we don't get in each other's way, okay?"

Kit tried not to look at the enormous sideboard she was supposed to be doing for a new restaurant called Mon Petit Chou, focusing instead on the finishing touches to the cedar chest Mrs. Sheehy planned to present to her deb daughter on the night of her coming-out bash. She let her mind go with the strokes, responding mostly with monosyllables while Mitzi chattered on about . . . whatever that was she was chattering on about.

"But what are those puppies called?" Mitzi asked, swooping great washes of free-flowing blue and purple across her tablet.

"Hmm?" Kit drew her brush down to complete the trailing stem of an orchid.

"Those puppies? What are they called?"

"What puppies?"

"You know. *Those puppies.*"

"No, sweetie, I don't know." Kit brought a stroke of sunlight across the face of the flower.

"Those puppies that go *ab! abb-ab-abb!*" Mitzi pierced, making barking mouths with her hands. "Daddy's puppies."

"I'm sorry, Mitzi-pop, I don't know. Maybe you could ask Cooper."

"No," she sighed. "I'll ask Carmen."

A petal wilted under Kit's startled brush. "Who's Carmen?"

Mitzi's eyes got wide.

"It's okay." Kit sat down and brought Mitzi onto her lap. "Did Daddy say not to tell?"

"He said what you don't know won't hurt you," Mitzi nodded. "Are you hurt now?"

"No, of course not. The truth never hurt any—" Kit realized midsentence what a crock that is and decided to rephrase. "You can always tell me anything that's on your mind, Mitzi-pop."

"Nothing's on my mind." Mitzi gave her a quick squeeze and started to skip away.

"Wait!" Kit snatched her back, layering on her best technique. "How 'bout a Popsicle, Popsicle?"

"Okay!" Mitzi cheerfully agreed.

"So," Kit said, once she had her cornered at the kitchen table, "is Carmen nice?"

"Mm-hmm!" Mitzi nodded enthusiastically.

"Is Carmen . . . pretty?"

"Yeah, but not like you. Nobody is pretty as you, Mama."

"Well, thank you, sweetie." Kit pecked her on the cheek.

"She's not as big as you, either."

"Great." Kit moved to the sink, swishing at the faucet with a dishcloth. "Does Carmen visit very often?"

"Oh no. She lives there."

"Where?" Her hands felt colder than the tap water.

"At Daddy's house."

"What?" Kit turned on her. "Since when?"

Mitzi's eyes got wide again, but Kit abandoned any

pretense of trying to shield her from this particular emotional scar and started pumping for hard information.

"Mitzi, since when did Carmen live at Daddy's? Did she just move there?"

"No, she was there before."

"Before what?"

"Before Daddy. Mrs. Garza is her grandma. Only she calls her 'Ah-bay' 'cause it's in Spanish when you say—what do you say for grandma?"

"*Abuela*," Kit told her bleakly.

"'Ah-booo-ay-la,'" Mitzi repeated, loving the lay of the word on her foreign tongue.

"Mitzi, does Carmen live in Mrs. Garza's house or at Daddy's apartment?"

"Her and Troy and Sarah live upstairs in the house," Mitzi told her.

"Oh," Kit laughed out loud with relief.

"But last week, we all had a big slumber party!"

"*Oh.*"

"Where are you going, Mama?"

"I just remembered—" Kit hoped she could keep from crying until she got upstairs. "I gotta call Grandma and make sure she's okay."

She dug through a stack of stencils and sketches on the counter and retrieved the cordless phone she'd bought for her work space. She stumbled up the stairs and closed herself in her bedroom closet, pressing in Vivica's number with trembling fingers.

"Hello!"

"Mama?"

"You've reached 555-6262. Leave a message at the tone or call the Vivica Agency at 1-800-555-VIVA!"

"*Dang!*" Kit clicked the phone off and threw it in the corner. "Don't even say it!" she told Neeva, though she knew Neeva wasn't there.

She didn't have to be. Kit was well able to point out to herself that what's good for the gander is blah blah blah and taste of your own medicine and all that crap.

Dang. *Carmen* . . .

Euta Mae, Kit could have handled. Or Beulah or Baleen or Mavis Louise or any other toothless white chick of East Texas, but *Carmen*? They'd only been separated for two months, and Mel had already upgraded to a *Carmen*?

Carmen Miranda.

Carmen Sandiego.

Carmen get it.

Kit's head hurt. She realized she was shivering in the over-conditioned inside air. Dragging one of Mel's flannel shirts from its hanger, she wrapped it around herself and rested her head on the foot of the closet organizer.

What goes around comes around.

Carmen law.

Carmen Punishment.

⁂

The problem with Ramonica Deets was not that she had enormous breasts and a flat stomach or that her fingernails were lacquered long and wine-red by the Vietnamese lady down the street or even that she wore a deliciously taut version of Xylo's coffee-colored skin. The problem was that she could deliver *Billie's Blues* better than Billie, and this is what Vivica was trying to explain to Kiki, whose head was halfway in the toilet because, going into her ninth month, she still had the morning sickness, and all in all, it was making for a not-very-good day.

"Sweetie, you shouldn't be working anymore, anyway," Vivica soothed, stroking the back of her neck with a cool cloth. "All that cigarette smoke isn't good for the baby, and frankly Moon Pie, you don't look that good."

"Thank you, Mama. I feel better now."

Kiki wasn't being sarcastic. She was genuinely grateful to have that bowl of Fruity Pebbles out of her system. She sighed and sat on the bathroom floor. Vivica had the pale blue tile covered with an extra-thick area rug the color of Pepto-Bismol, and it comforted Kiki's stomach just looking at it. She laid her palms on the clean, pink pile.

"I figured he'd have replaced me by now. I just thought I'd ask."

"That's the nature of the biz, honey. People come and go. You know that." Vivica freshened the cloth in the sink and pressed it to Kiki's forehead. "And what did I always say to you girls about getting romantically involved with musicians?"

"You said 'don't.'"

"But do you listen? Think of some of those losers Kit ran around with before Mel came along." Vivica sat down close to her and leaned back against the tub. "Anyway, after the baby comes and you get back in shape, we'll find you another band. Who knows? The way Ramonica and Xylo have their ups and downs, she might be gone again in a few months."

"Oh, I hope not," Kiki said. "Xylo needs someone to love. And I just can't do it, Mama. I'm scared to be in love anymore. It makes you forget too much."

She lay down on the floor, her head in her mother's lap, and they stayed that way for a while.

"Aren't you glad I came down here to take care of you, Mama?"

"I sure am, Moon Pie."

Kiki sat up and took the lukewarm cloth from her face.

"Are you okay, Mama? Or are you just pretending?"

"Oh, both, I guess. My energy's down, I'd have to admit that. Mostly, I'm mad at myself for letting it go so long. I felt the lump almost a year ago, but I didn't want to think about it. I knew I should be getting the regular mammograms, but I felt fine, and I was busy. I was—"

"Scared?"

"Stupid."

"No. It wasn't stupid, Mama. That's what everybody does. As long as things are basically tolerable, you just keep going. You keep walking around doing what you usually do and . . ."

"Dying."

"Oh, Mama, don't say that! Don't even think about that!"

"Most days, I don't. Most days, I think about staying alive. Other days . . . but that's normal. According to Jim Bagjani, Guerilla Oncologist, it's also normal for the side effects to accumulate. He warned me after three or four cycles, things might get ugly. And I certainly did."

"You did not, Mama. You're still beautiful."

"Well, I finally dropped those ten extra pounds, anyway."

"Does it bother you about your hair?"

"As soon as I found out about this whole thing, I went to Giovanni and said, 'Buzz it, sweetie.' Sort of like, 'You can't fire me. *I quit!*' Then when it did fall out, it wasn't so bad." Vivica sighed and scratched at the back of her head. "I am getting sick of the wigs, though. This latest one cost me almost eighty bucks, and it makes me look like Edith Bunker. I think I'm going to switch to the Gloria Swanson look for a while. You know, head wraps are *trés charmeuse* for aging prom queens. Liz Taylor—prime example. Takes a bad hair day, plops a turban on it, and *voilá!* White diamonds."

"Maybe you could get a few tips from one of those female impersonators you represent," Kiki giggled.

"You know, that's not a bad idea." Then Kiki really laughed, but Vivica protested. "No, I mean it. You gotta learn from the pros. That's what I've always tried to tell you girls." She put her arm around Kiki's shoulders and pulled her close again. "But did you girls ever listen?"

"We tried, Mama. We really did."

"Look at the two of you. Both of you. Pregnant, on your own, broke. You never could put a dime away for rainy days, either one of you. Thank God your Mee-ma Kelsey isn't around to see this. She thought the two slickest sleigh rides to Hell were divorce and show business. You two must have her spinning in her grave."

"What do you suppose is wrong with us?"

"Oh, I don't know," Vivica sighed again. "Maybe it was all that applause you started out with. All those people loving you, telling you how pretty you were, how special. It's gotta be sort of tough for one man to top that kind of affection."

"I suppose."

"But all those people, Kiki, they only had to love you for one hour at a time."

Kiki nodded.

"Falling in love is so easy." Vivica pressed the cloth to her own temple. "It has to be accidental, or it doesn't happen. But then you try to sustain that feeling. That's not so easy.

"Frankly, I wasn't all that surprised to see things turn out badly with Wayne. But Mel? He's so much like your daddy. I really thought Mel Prizer was the last genuinely good man on the face of the earth. Now, poor Kitten." She shook her head, but Kiki couldn't say anything about that right now. "She was a mess by the time she got me on the phone the other day. Apparently he's already seeing somebody else."

Kiki couldn't say anything about that either, so she just squeezed Vivica's hand and said, "Don't worry about us, Mama. We'll be okay."

"You will, you know." Vivica nodded, resolute.

"Mama?" Chloe came to the door, and Kiki and Vivica both answered, "Yes, sweetie?" and then looked at each other and smiled.

"Did you throw up again?" Chloe asked.

"Yes, but it's all right, Cinnamon," Kiki reassured her.

"Call me next time, so I can watch," Chloe said.

"Why?" Kiki wrinkled her nose.

"I wanna see when the baby comes out!"

Kiki and Vivica exchanged another look, burst out

laughing, and pulled Chloe down, sharing her across their laps. She giggled with them. She didn't need to know why, only that it felt good.

"Play 'take my arms.'" Chloe lay across their laps and pulled their hands over her like a quilt. "Sing it! Sing it!"

"*All of me*," Kiki sang, "*why not take all of me*," tickling and pretending to steal each part of Chloe as she sang about it, eating it up or putting it in her pocket. "*. . . You took the part that once was my heart . . .*" Chloe scrunched in Kiki's lap and both of them supplied the big finish. "*So why naaaaaaaht—take all of meeeeee!*"

"Again! Again!" Chloe cried.

"No. You go get your swimsuit on. Go tell Oscar, okay?"

She skipped away, calling for her brother, and Kiki and Vivica sat quietly for a while.

"Say!" Vivica suddenly sat up and snapped her fingers. "You know what we should do?"

Kiki didn't have the vaguest idea.

❦

Carmen Garza stepped out of Mel's pickup with a large watermelon in her arms and such a flowing water-for-chocolate exotica, Kit could actually feel her own stomach and hips inflating beneath her frumpy K-Mart maternity moo-moo.

"Hi. You must be Kit."

"Hi."

"I'm Carmen Garza. Mel is working as a caretaker for my grandmother?"

She was wearing an infinitely smaller version of Mel's Industrial Air coveralls, only she had the top unbuttoned with a tank shirt underneath and a cinchy red belt that made them look like Barbie clothes.

"You're a mechanic," Kit said, demonstrating that what she lacked in looks was dwarfed by her dearth of personality.

"Yeah," Carmen smiled with her perfect small teeth,

exuding the *Wild Juniper and Herb* scent of someone privy to Victoria's most intimate secrets.

"Umm . . . are you with the C-check crew or . . . ?"

"I was on the line side, same shift as Mel for about six years until—well, my husband and I—we split up last spring, and then after my grandmother's stroke, the night shift thing got to be sort of a child-care dilemma."

"Oh yeah. I suppose."

"Yeah. So I bid over to days then."

They stood uncomfortably for a moment.

"So . . . you have kids?" Duh. Kit could plainly see them scrambling over the tailgate, following Mel to the backyard, calling for Mitzi and Cooper.

"Yeah. Boy and a girl." Carmen smiled again. "Troy and Sarah. They're the same age as Mel's. Yours. You guys's."

Kit just stood there, breathing in all that juniper.

"Well," Carmen said.

"Hmm." Kit nodded and smiled.

"So, this is pretty awkward."

"Oh yeah," Kit empathized, but couldn't offer any help.

"I didn't mean to bother you. But my truck ditched a seal over at Willowbrook Mall, and Tank—that's my ex—he wouldn't come get my kids, and I've gotta be back to work at two, and Mel didn't want to be late picking up his own kids so . . ."

"I see." Kit motioned toward the watermelon. "Were you needing that to be . . . umm . . . refrigerated or cut or something?"

"Oh! This. No. In fact, it's for you." She held it out, but retracted it when they both noticed it was smaller than Kit's abdomen. "We passed a guy selling them off his truck on the way over, and Mel—"

"It reminded him of me. How sweet."

"He's a thoughtful guy," Carmen laughed, and that surprised Kit for some reason.

Cooper ran around the corner of the house with Carmen's son.

"Dad said to tell you he's gonna take a shower," he told Kit.

"He said to tell you he'll be down in twenty minutes," Troy told Carmen.

"Well," Kit sighed, feeling the mores of modern love pressing heavily on her shoulders. "Why don't you come in and have some ice tea while you wait?"

"Oh, no. No thanks. I don't want to bother you, Kit. We'll just wait in the truck."

"Don't be ridiculous. You'd roast out there. C'mon in. Let the kids play on the swing set a while."

They were already doing it, anyway, oblivious to the unofficial turfs and territories and self-effacing etiquettes of these matters. Kit pulled the screen door open, and Carmen followed her into the kitchen.

"Oh, wow! You did all this?"

"I've been having trouble sleeping," Kit nodded, as if it made perfect sense for an insomniac to get up and put Muddy Waters in a giant bowl of green chili with Annie Lennox instead of, oh, taking a Tylenol or something.

"'Naked Soup?'" Carmen marveled at Muddy's place above the wainscoting. "This is amazing! The way Mel described it— This isn't what I envisioned at all."

She bumped into the corner of the cupboard because her head was tipped back to see the ceiling fan.

"Truly amazing!"

"Thank you."

Kit didn't let her own envisioning of Mel's description detract from the satisfaction she was beginning to take in showing people what she could do.

"'House of Blues,'" Carmen peered into the dimly lit nightclub on the pantry door and read the neon above the stage. "Lena Horne, right?"

"Yeah," Kit nodded again, pleased that Lena turned out to be recognizable. "And there's k. d. lang and Peggy Lee."

They sat in the audience sipping black coffee, moonin' all the mornin' and mournin' all the night.

"You painted a blues bar in your kitchen," Carmen said, studying Kit closely. "Lena Horne is on your pantry door."

"Well, I was listening to that university jazz station at about three in the morning," Kit tried to explain, "and she just . . . materialized."

"Cool," Carmen said. "Very cool."

"Come and see Mitzi's room."

They went up the stairs, where aspen trees had grown up behind the banister and down the hall, which now had a smooth marbleized floor and was in the process of growing a Max Parish environment. They walked past his hallmark deep blues and high columns on the way to Mitzi's room, where unicorns and castles were just faintly visible through a fine purple mist over the moss-green forests. The knights and dragons destined to live in Cooper's room were still jousting in Kit's imagination, but she had outlined the stonework over the top of his windows.

Kit's only intention in opening the door to her own bedroom was to show Carmen the dune-colored desert she slept in now, but Mel was standing naked in front of the understated saguaros.

"Kit! Geez!" He yanked the spread from the bed, but she shut the door before he could cover himself.

"Oops," she cringed and then called, "Sorry."

"Nice ass, Mel!" Carmen rapped her knuckles against the door, then asked Kit, "Who's the guy in the white suit?"

"Over by the window? That's Leon Redbone."

"Oh yeah," Carmen said, "Like *diddy-wa-diddy*. Very cool. Kit, this is all very, very cool. Mel doesn't know what he's talking about."

It was getting harder and harder to hate her guts.

Kit decided she may as well offer her some watermelon instead.

They sat in the kitchen with their feet up on chairs, spitting seeds into a mixing bowl, discussing the comparative merits of the local school districts, swapping single mommy war stories.

"Bottom line is—I'm doing it," Carmen remarked. "I'll survive. And ultimately, I'm gonna be a whole lot happier."

"I don't know if I'm ready to say that yet," Kit said. "I'm not even sure about the survival part."

"I was always so buried in stuff I was *supposed* to do," Carmen tried to explain, "I never had any time for stuff I *wanted* to do. And then, it was like I just realized one day—hey, that *is* what I'm supposed to do. Stuff that matters to me. Carl Jung: '*The greatest sin is to be unconscious.*'"

"But how do you do that without coming off as completely selfish?" Kit asked. "Am I supposed to take a break from folding the laundry in order to paint a little or take a break from painting to fold a little laundry?"

"Haven't you figured it out, Kit? You're damned no matter what you do. We're the first ones to live on the flip side of 'having it all.' The Thomas Hardy rule of thumb is still in effect: mothers are not allowed to have lives, the clitoris is Satan's earlobe, and strong women must be punished. But if you don't earn a full-time income, you're lazy."

Kit nodded and refilled their glasses.

"I think the key to survival is knowing the difference between ministry and servitude," Carmen said. "Nurse the baby, make love to the man, run the household—that's ministry. That's you giving something no one else could have given. But picking up the socks of somebody who is perfectly capable of picking up their own little socks—that's servitude. In addition to which, you're taking away from them the gratification of doing it for themselves."

"Wow," Kit stared at her.

"Oh, I'm into Mary Hugh Scott right now. *Passion of Being Woman*. You should read it."

"Maybe so," Kit said.

"Sorry." Carmen suddenly seemed embarrassed. "My husband always tells me I read too much. 'Oh, boy,' he always says, 'bring out the soapbox. Here comes Alexandra Firestein. *Traditional marriage is the daily rape of womankind,*'" she wryly imitated his imitation. "You probably think Mel's hooked up with some kind of nut."

"Not at all," Kit reassured her. "But I can't quite picture him participating in this type of conversation."

"I don't know. Maybe he was just trying to get me in the sack," Carmen laughed, but when Kit didn't, she added, "He might be a little more open-minded than you thought."

"If he is, I wish he'd have let me know it before," Kit said. "Maybe somehow it could have all come together—the laundry and the lovemaking and the painting. Maybe if we'd given each other a chance to be something other than what everybody else expected us to be."

"*'Life can only be understood backwards; but it must be lived forwards.'*" Carmen rested her chin on her hand. "Who said that? Kierkegaard?"

"Yeah, I think it was," Kit said, wondering who the heck Keer Kergarg was.

"Maybe it's not too late, though. Maybe you guys will work it out."

Kit glanced up at her in surprise.

"Oh. Huh-uh," Carmen shook her head. "Don't look at me. Mel's great. I love him. We've been buds for a long time, and he was a godsend for Abee. And since we've been . . . I mean, since we started . . . this last couple weeks, he's been just what I needed when I really, really needed it, but . . ." She shook her head again. "I just got out from under one man. I don't intend to give that kind of control to anybody ever again."

"Me neither," Kit said, and she meant it, though she hoped that didn't mean she'd never again feel a man on top of her.

"I'm heading out to Albuquerque," Carmen said, with firm resolve and only a little fear. "I got an offer from one of the regional airlines out there. I'd have been there already, but it won't be long now for Abee. I want to stay close until then." She used a spoon to poke a lemon slice deeper into her ice tea. "I am gonna miss the man, though. I'll admit to that."

"Me too," Kit confided.

"The thing that's so amazing about Mel," Carmen said, "I mean besides . . ."

"Right."

"It's the way he's so neat and tidy. I never knew any guy who picked up after himself and did his little laundry so nice, and he's always busy with projects instead of loafing around watching TV or whatever."

"Mel?" Kit said skeptically. "Mel Prizer? Big guy? Receding hairline?"

"And he's so cute, the way he's so involved with the kids." Carmen took another watermelon wedge and dabbed a few seeds away with her finger. "He always packs my lunch for me, asks me how it's going, and he's actually interested. He talks to me like he has some respect for what I do."

For the first moment since they met, Kit felt a sharp stab of jealousy. She had almost adjusted to the idea of this woman having and touching Mel's private body, but the idea that he freely gave her the respect Kit had never bothered to hope for— that hurt.

She suddenly knew how Mel must feel, watching that guy from the hangar drive around in the shiny blue Falcon, hearing the motor purr like a panther, knowing he'd traded it all for a mashed apart Mustang. He must be mourning those four years he spent closed up in the garage, working away at the wrong end of the drivetrain.

"He is the sweetest, most sensitive man I've ever known. But I guess you know," Carmen concluded, "that's just Mel."

"That's *Mel?*" Kit echoed. "*My* Mel?"

Carmen shifted uncomfortably, and Kit caught herself.

"I mean, he's not *my* Mel, he's—he's—I guess he's pretty much his own Mel these days. But I've got to tell you, Carmen, the last person I would describe as 'thoughtful and sensitive' is Melvin Thadeus Prizer."

"*Thadeus?*" Carmen giggled. "That's so cute! I can't stand it!"

"I think his mother was trying to get him back for leaving her stomach like an empty kangaroo pouch."

"You know what Tank's middle name is? Wilmer. Timothy Wilmer is his name. How could you not love a guy named *Wilmer?*" Carmen traced one finger around the rim of her glass. "That's the other reason me and Mel would never work out," she sighed. "We're both still hung up on our exes."

Mel cleared his throat near the back door.

"Are you ready to go, K . . . Carmen?"

"Oh umm . . . I guess." She turned to Kit, not really expecting her to invite them all to stay for lunch, but looking like she possibly was hoping. "Yeah. I'm ready." She got up from the table and set the mixing bowl by the sink.

"Well," Kit said, "this certainly has been . . ."

"Yeah. It was great meeting you, Kit. So maybe sometime, if you wanted to umm . . . well . . . It was great meeting you."

"Yeah." Kit took the strong, slender hand Carmen extended. "Maybe sometime though. That would be great."

"Okay," she smiled with her perfect teeth.

They started out, but Mel turned at the doorway.

"I fixed that upstairs toilet. It sounded like it was running."

"Thanks," Kit nodded.

"So, I guess I'll see ya Sunday," he said awkwardly.

"Yeah. See ya then."

A long moment of silence followed.

"So . . . ," Carmen broke it. "Mel?"

"Kit—" he blurted suddenly, "that whole thing up in the bedroom with the sand dunes and cactus and Redbone and all, it's really . . ."

"Cool," Carmen supplied, "Very cool."

"Yeah," Mel sounded surprised and a little sad. "I didn't even know you could draw a camel."

Kit smiled and shrugged.

"I like it," he told her.

"I'm glad. Thank you for saying that."

"You're a muralist is what you are," Carmen told her. "You should be doing walls of whole buildings and office lobbies and restaurants and stuff like that."

"What I get paid for, though, is kitchen chairs and baby furniture." Kit realized she hadn't yet thought beyond that.

"'We work to become,'" Carmen quoted philosophically, "'not to acquire.'"

"Well, I should get back to work, before I become bankrupt."

"See ya Sunday," Mel repeated and pulled the door open.

"Oh, Mel, wait!" Kit caught his hand. "What's the deal with the puppies?"

"Huh?"

"Those puppies Mitzi likes. What are they?"

"They're um . . . they're called the jabber puppies," he mumbled.

"What?"

"The jabber puppies," he enunciated. "Jabber. Puppies."

"I don't get it," Kit said.

"Because they go, they go like jabber jabber, you know?" He looked the same way he had when they opened the door and saw him naked.

"C'mon, Mel, do it," Carmen prodded. "I love it when he does this."

"They just go like *Jabber! Jabber-jabber!*" Mel's bark was

even more shrill than Mitzi's, and the sound brought her bursting through the door.

"*Jabber!*" He made yapping mouths with his hands, and they nipped and tickled on her rib cage. "*Jabber-jabber-jabber!*"

"Daddy!" she giggled and squealed in delight. "Do it to Sarah! Do it to Sarah!" and the puppies jabbered and yapped and chased both little girls out to the truck.

"I can't stand it." Carmen turned to Kit at the doorway, exuding one last breath of juniper. "He is so *cute!*"

❦

"I haven't been sleeping," Kit told Ander as he traced the trailing vines with his fingertips. "Would you like to see the dining room? It has an ocean now."

Deep beneath the surface, Bette Midler could be seen singing, "*shiver me timbers, I'm sailing away,*" and swishing her mermaid tail, the Harlettes harmonizing at her side.

They walked through the house, room by room, saying nothing, and Kit felt, as she pointed to each place and person she'd projected onto the walls around her, that she was seeing it all for the first time.

"What's that noise?" she wondered again as they climbed the stairs.

But Ander only breathed in the aspen trees, whose leaves guttered and trembled and showed their white sides, predicting rain. He paused at each of the Max Parish columns, examining the spiraling ivy that clung and climbed to the blue ceiling, peering into the distance to see the Count Basie Orchestra set up on the other side of the shimmering water.

"You gave me this," Kit said. "You taught me how, made me believe I could."

"No," he shook his head. "No, Kit, this all is not from me."

"I don't know how I'll ever thank you, Ander. You don't know what it means to me now, that I have something to be."

"No." He touched the cellos and violas that flew on golden wings above Basie's head. "All this is only from you."

"Ander," she stepped over to him, serene as the geese gliding out onto the water behind them, "would you like to see the bedroom?"

Ander nodded with the willow tree that swayed over the head of Lightning Hopkins, who sat cross-legged in the grass with Janis Joplin and Ella Fitzgerald. The breeze raised the branches around them in the same easy way with which Ander lifted Kit's spring-green maternity dress over her head.

She swung the door wide to see Mel standing naked before the saguaros, his wide hands supporting Carmen's hips, her slender brown legs locked around him. Beyond Carmen's back, as it arched and rounded, Redbone tethered his camel in the sun-shy cool of the desert dusk. Kit looked up into the stars on the ceiling, not wary, not wondering how Ander could be behind and below and around her, cupping her breasts and nuzzling between her thighs and teasing across her lips all at once. Hands and mouths crossed paths. A delicate tongue darted down her leg.

Mel made life to her, plain and big and honest. Ander penetrated her with colors, ways, and visions. Kit had always thought that when two women press their hips together, there must be a great emptiness between them, but Carmen whispered the thousand things that fill it up, taking Kit's nipple between her perfect pearl teeth. Kit responded, softened, gave over to the quickening, the colloquy, the juniper, and the familiar rhythm.

But that noise, she wanted to tell them. What is that noise? It buzzed like a cicada just beyond her eardrum, and with each stroke and moan and tremble, it came closer and closer until it touched the back of her neck like ice water . . . *bowm-pa-dip-dowm-bumpa-dippa-dit* . . .

"*No,*" she said, and then spoke louder so as to be heard over the whining of the synthesizer, "No! That is not what I do!"

"Love's not something you do," Redbone shrugged, "it's something you are."

"*Hnuh!*"

Kit sat up, drenched in sweat, nightshirt clinging to her body, hair plastered to her cheek, air wrenching out of her lungs.

"Whoa . . . geez . . ."

She groped in the dark at the side of her bed, searching for the lamp switch, but she strangled a shriek as it glared to life.

"Thirsty, Kitten?" the camel asked.

Neeva smiled, and her lighter flashed.

Kit screamed and flamed and was immolated.

*T*he climb up to the tree fort was getting tougher each day. Towering six feet above her head, the structure was a redwood monument to all the seemingly impossible tasks she was faced with these days, and Cooper had been taking full advantage of the sanctuary.

"Cooper," she called, hoping to avoid the ascent. "Cooper Theodore Prizer, you get on down here, and I *mean* it!"

There was no answer, but she could hear him crying quietly through the whispering rush of leaves. Mel had nailed ten two-by-four remnants to the trunk of the tree for a ladder, and Kit pulled herself up the first few before threatening, "I'm coming up there!"

"Go away!"

"I will not!"

"I hate you! You're always on *her* side!"

"I am not," Kit said. She didn't have to yell because she was on the eighth two-by-four now, her elbows on the floor of the fort. "I'm on both sides. But I am mad at you right now. You know it's hard for me to get up here, what with the baby and all."

"Then stay down there. I don't want any girls up here. Or any babies."

"Cooper, you watch the way you're talking to me."

He sat sullen with his back to the tree trunk.

"Yes, ma'am," Kit prompted.

"*Yes, ma'am,*" he exaggerated.

"And when I tell you to come down out of here, you do it."

"Yes, ma'am."

"That's better."

Struggling her way through the trapdoor onto the floor, Kit tried to think of what she was supposed to say to him next. Fortunately, it took her a long moment to get her breath.

"Coo," she said finally, "we can't keep on like this. You making trouble every minute, me being mad and yelling. It's not doing anybody any good. You and me, Coo, we need to stick together and help each other. We need each other."

"I don't need you," Cooper pushed the heel of his hand across his cheek.

Kit nodded and scootched over to lean against the tree beside him.

"I won't bother to argue with you on that. We both know you do need me. And we both know this isn't about me being on Mitzi's side. And we both know you have no excuse for throwing a dead lizard on her, Coo. That was just plain mean. You get some kind of kick out of being mean to people?"

"Just her."

"Why?"

"Because I hate her! She's stupid."

"That's not true, Cooper. You love her. And she's smart. This isn't about her at all. This is about you being sad and scared and mad at me and Daddy for messing things up, and you want to do something with this great big ol' ugly blob of rotten feelings you have inside. You want somebody else to feel as bad as you do, and Mitzi's an easy target. You're bigger than her, and you know just how to make her unhappy, so you don't have to be unhappy all alone. But that's not right, Cooper. That stinks. It's wrong and mean and rotten, and I don't think you're a mean rotten kid. I think you're a good kid. So, stop acting mean and rotten before Dad and I have to do something we don't want to do, okay?"

Cooper sat digging the stiff tip of his shoelace through a hole in his sock.

"Okay?" Kit repeated, trying to make it sound strict.

"Whatever," he mumbled.

"Your daddy's gonna be here soon. You don't want him to see us fighting, do you?"

"I don't care."

"What are y'all doing this weekend, anyway?"

Cooper shrugged.

"I bet it'll be something fun," she tried again.

Another shrug.

"Coo . . ." Kit didn't know where to take it. She'd never felt this kind of distance between them before. "I sure wish . . ."

"Whatever," Cooper said, as if that settled the matter.

The matter didn't exactly feel settled to Kit, but the over-whelming weariness that overtook her about this time every day was dragging at her shoulders. She closed her eyes, letting her head lay back against the tree trunk. The murmur of the leaves, the chickering of the cicadas, the almost imperceptible sway of the tree itself became an ocean, a ray of light, a womb.

Suddenly, Kit jolted awake. Cooper was down the ladder, running across the lawn, and the trapdoor had slammed shut behind him. It took her a moment to realize he'd left the dead lizard on her chest, it's stiffened forelegs tickling the sensitive sun-browned skin above the scooped neckline of her maternity shirt. She shrieked and batted it away, struggling to her hands and knees.

"*Cooper Prizer!*" she bellowed and yanked the trapdoor open.

But he was already around the side of the house, tormenting Mitzi with cold water from the garden hose spray gun. Kit cussed and started crying and let the trapdoor bang shut again. It caught her knuckles as it came down, and she cussed again, raising her injured fingers to her mouth, sucking the blood away. The stinging sensation was not nearly enough punishment. She'd failed at marriage. Now she was failing at motherhood.

And to put the frosting on the cake, Mel was pulling into the driveway just in time to see her clumbering down out of this goddang tree. She'd managed to maneuver her burgeoning bottom half through the trapdoor and locate a two-by-four with her toes when he wheeled the lawnmower out of the shed below.

"Need help?" he called.

"No, thanks. I'm fine."

"You sure?"

"I'm sure."

He ripped the starter cord on the mower as Kit struggled the rest of the way to the ground.

"*I CAN DO THIS MYSELF, YOU KNOW,*" she shouted over the roar.

"*WHAT?*" Mel shouted back.

"*I SAID I CAN MOW IT MYSELF, MEL!*"

"*I KNOW,*" he boomed, "*JESUS CHRIST, AM I ALLOWED TO BE NICE?*"

Kit nodded sheepishly and pushed the side gate open for him. Out front, Cooper was rubbing marks on the driveway with a white rock, and he looked nervous as she approached.

"I got your little present," she said.

Cooper ground the rock in a wide arc across the pavement.

"Guess what I'm gonna do with it?"

He glanced up, startled to see her dangling it by its tail.

"What?" he said with guarded curiosity.

"Art project," Kit told him casually. "Wanna do it with me?"

"I hate art. It's stupid."

"Ah," Kit nodded. "Well, this is actually kind of a combination art project/science experiment sort of thing."

He looked skeptical.

"I'm gonna frame this lizard's skeleton like a picture. I think it might be kind of pretty. Plus we can, you know, observe it and stuff."

"How can you get all the guts and skin and everything off it?" Cooper asked, and Kit eased herself down onto the curb, patting the space next to her, inviting him to come and sit close.

"I'll do like Psyche," she said.

"What does that mean?"

"It's a story my mama used to tell me. She let the ants help her, and that's what we'll do. You run in and find a piece of black construction paper, and then we'll lay the lizard on it, and while you're gone over to Daddy's this weekend, the ants'll come and clean off everything but the bones."

"No way!" Cooper's eyes lit up with new interest.

"Way. And then when you get home on Sunday, we'll very carefully spray some fixative on it to make it stay, and then we'll frame it."

"Can we hang it up in my room? Can we hang it on my poster wall?"

"I suppose," Kit said. "If you don't mind looking at some stupid art all the time."

Cooper rolled his eyes, and Kit realized he was of an age where she'd either have to be a little bit more subtle or just come right out and tell him things.

"Go get the paper," she told him, and he disappeared into the house, letting the screen door bang shut behind him.

"What's being detected on the ultrasound," Dr. Jane Poplin explained with a carefully trained gentleness, "is a condition known as anencephaly."

"Right," Kit said, "but I don't know what that means."

"It means the baby's brain has not physically developed beyond the stem."

"Oh . . . God . . ."

"Because the cerebral hemispheres are severely malformed or missing, the anencephalic infant has no function beyond the very basic autonomic responses and consequently dies within a short time after birth, usually a matter of hours, sometimes a few days, but never more than a week or two. Which is a mercy, because there is no possibility of any development."

"Then is it better to . . . to terminate the . . ."

"I do advise that if the condition is detected early in the pregnancy, or if there's a threat to the mother's health or future fertility, but . . . ," Dr. Poplin shook her head. "Your sister's obstetrician will have to advise her on that. The body of the anencephalic child can be healthy and normal with the exception of the malformed skull, so often organs can be harvested for transplant. She might want to consider that. And I understand she's almost to term, anyway. As difficult as the next few weeks will be for her, I believe it's usually better to let nature take its course."

"Oh, God." Kit started crying.

"As far as you flying down there, Kit, I have some reservations. Your life is bogged down with some pretty stressful circumstances right now. The headaches, the insomnia, the nightmares—these are indications that it's affecting you, emotionally and physically."

"I have to go," Kit wept. "Our mom, she just finished chemotherapy, and she's in the hospital. And it's not even the same hospital. Kiki's going to be there all by herself! She can't do this all by herself."

"She will do this all by herself," Jane Poplin said, "even if you're there. She's the one going through it, and there's nothing you can do to take that away from her, no matter how much you want to help. But," she sighed, "I have a little sister, too."

She put her glasses back on and looked at Kit's chart.

"You're still a good fourteen weeks from delivery, so I think it's safe to fly. Just be aware of how you're feeling, and Kit, you've got to be ruthless. Your baby is healthy, and we want to keep it that way. You come first. I know that flies in the face of everything a good mommy or a good sister or a good daughter is supposed to do, but with this history of extremely short labor, you can't afford to be noble."

"I understand."

"I'll give you the name of an OB down there, and I want you to call him if there's anything at all that feels like it could be labor—indigestion, lower back pain, anything, okay?"

"Okay," Kit said obediently.

"I've seen you through three pregnancies," Dr. Poplin smiled. "I think it's only fair if I finally get to attend a delivery."

Kit nodded and lay back, listening to her second heart, throbbing like a locomotive in the stethoscope.

❧

"You came," Kiki said over and over. "You came."

She was pale and groggy with painkillers.

"Of course, you goose!" Kit said too cheerfully. "Of course I came!"

And of course she had. Straight from the airport to the hospital, her stomach roiling with indigestion, her lower back clenched in spasms.

"But what did you do with your kids?" Kiki worried.

"They're with Mel. They're fine. Mitzi's loving Mrs. Garza's swimming pool, and Cooper is—well, when he's willing to speak to me these days, he seems like he's doing okay. They miss you."

Kit opened her purse and gave Kiki the construction paper cards they'd made for her.

"Oh, I miss them, too," she sighed. "And I've missed you, Kit. I thought you were mad at me over the money or something because—Kit, that money, did that money have anything to do with you and Mel?"

"Oh, Kiki, of course not!"

"I've been feeling so guilty for taking it. I knew I shouldn't."

"Would you stop this, please? Kiki, that money is the least of our worries right now. I don't even want you to think about it. I don't care if I ever see it again. Don't you know that?"

"Well sure, Kit. But I care. Don't you know that?"

"Shhh," Kit made her lay down again, and the nurse readjusted the monitor belt around her middle, measuring contractions on graph paper that streamed out in a roller coaster of peaks and valleys.

"Don't you know, Kit, that I get awful tired of being your baby sister? My whole life I've been trying to look as good as you or sing as good as you or—I don't know—be as good as you at *something*."

"No! I don't know any of that! It's ridiculous. Look at you! You're beautiful and sweet and good and you're . . . ," Kit noticed the peaks climbing higher on the graph paper.

"Oh . . . *oh Lord* . . . ," Kiki groaned and rolled onto her side as another contraction wrapped around her. Kit pushed her hand against the small of Kiki's back and stroked her forehead.

"Whoa!" Kiki whispered, returning to the valley. "They're getting bigger."

"I know, sweetie. That's good, though. That means it won't be long."

"You're five centimeters dilated," the nurse concurred, "ninety percent effaced."

Kit stroked Kiki's arm and pressed ice chips against her dry lips.

"The reason I haven't called—I haven't been mad at you, Kiki. I've been mad at me. I've been feeling so guilty."

"Guilty?" Kiki paused until the nurse left the room, then asked, "What for?"

"Because I've been so wrapped up in things. I haven't been there for you, and I haven't been there for Mom and . . . Kiki, ever since we were little girls, I always—I got so jealous of you sometimes, and—and it just made me treat you not very nice and everything."

"Hmm," Kiki said. "I thought you meant for having sex with Wayne."

"Oh, Kiki," Kit breathed. "How long have you known?"

"He told me a long time ago. But I didn't believe him. When I got back after Mama's mastectomy, I could tell something was eating on you, but I never thought—Anyway, later, I found out about the paternity test."

They sat quietly together.

"Kiki, I want to tell you—"

"No! No, it's okay, Kit. Because I figured it out. I figured he must of been drinking, and he thought you were me. And maybe you had an epileptic seizure, or—or maybe it was real dark, and you were real sound asleep, and you thought it was a dream. A beautiful dream about Omar Sharif. You would've made him stop if you knew it wasn't a dream. And he didn't mean it to hurt you, Kit. He wouldn't—he could never do that to you. It was an accident is all. Wasn't it, Kitty? Isn't that the way it happened?"

"When he . . . I was . . ."

Kit felt twin chasms of damnation yawning to either side of her but recognized she didn't necessarily have to drag Kiki down with her.

"Yes," she said, "that's—that's what happened."

"Thank you." Kiki clasped her hands together like a prayer.

"I don't want it to burn a hole in your heart, Kitty. But right now, that's what I have to think. I need to remember him as the father of my babies. Of this baby." She closed her eyes as if to concentrate on that very hard.

"Do you still want me to be here?" Kit asked, when she couldn't stand the silence any longer.

"Of course I do! I can't afford to lose you, too! Wayne's gone and Mama . . . Kit, she's so sick, it scares me. And now I'm gonna lose my baby. It would be too hard if I lost you, too. I need you to be my big sister. Because I can't feel anything right now, Kit. I can't feel a thing. So somebody else has to be here who can love him. Because that would be worse than anything, wouldn't it? To never be loved even a little?"

"I'll try," Kit promised.

"You don't have to try, Kitty. Just be here."

Kiki put her arms around her to the extent she could, and their turgid bellies pushed together.

The organ harvest person came with a support group woman who told Kiki about how she'd given birth to an anencephalic child, and she even had pictures of the dead baby all fixed up in christening clothes. She told Kiki how having given that gift of life was all that made it bearable. They told Kiki about the babies on the waiting lists and the healthy heart and corneas and kidneys she held like hoarded treasure inside her, like money in a mattress, like the gift of the magi, all dressed up with no place to go. They talked about what great good could come out of this tragedy, as if that decked the tragedy out in sequins and made it something noble.

Kit urged her to sign the papers, thinking that would make them go away, and they urged Kiki to listen to her sister.

Kiki took the pen in her hand.

"I would have named him Luke," she said. "If he was mine."

She signed, and they blessed her for caring. They left, and Kit blessed them for leaving.

Two more hours passed, Kiki sweating and groaning through the contractions, Kit offering a cold washcloth for her to suck on, singing softly in her ear, tucking her into the starchy sheets as if they were back in their own ruffled bed.

"But Psyche was a very brave girl," Kit said, stroking Kiki's bangs back from her damp forehead, telling her the story she'd always begged for when they were little and less little. "Very brave. Just like you. And she went to Aphrodite and asked her what she should do."

Kiki drifted on the waves of pain and painkillers and the sound of her mother's voice.

"'If you wish to redeem yourself,' the Chatty Cathy doll warned, 'you shall do it by dint of industry and diligence!'"

The ring of her pull-string made a scabbard for a sword whenever she played the stern mother goddess.

"What's 'dint' mean, Mama?"

"Yeah, Mama. And what's 'digilence'?"

"Well, I'm not sure about 'dint,' but diligence means that you stick to it. *Anyhow*," the mommy continued, raising Chatty Cathy's hand, "Aphrodite set forth three impossible tasks for Psyche to accomplish. First, she made her sort the seeds and grains with which she fed the doves that drew her golden chariot. But the king of the ants took pity on Psyche and brought all his armies, and they sorted the piles for her, seed by seed and grain by grain."

"I bet she didn't step on ants anymore after that, huh? Or spray 'em or anything."

"The next day, she had to gather the golden fleece of the ferocious rams who grazed in the field."

Two fuzz puppies, brown heads nodding, were set out in the field of rose-colored carpet, and the little girls gave them voices of such ferocity that poor Skipper Psyche hid, shivering, by the blue jean leg river.

"But Psyche was a very clever girl. She waited until the

rams were asleep in the afternoon sun, and then she gathered the bits of fleece that clung to the bushes."

The puppies had to sleep sitting up because their heads fell off if they lay down, but the fleece was finally gathered and laid at the feet of the goddess.

"'Now,' said Aphrodite, 'you will journey to the underworld—'"

The little sisters giggled, because "underworld" always made them think of "underwear."

"'—and tell Persephone to fill this box with a little of her beauty.'"

"This can be the underworld!" The little sister draped a beach towel across two chairs, and they all three put their heads inside.

"Can she have the flashlight, Mama?"

"Yeah, Mama, that can be her torch!"

"Okay. Here she goes. Where's Persephone?"

A Barbie in a Kleenex toga was placed among the souls of baby dolls and stuffed animals who wandered the shadows, and Psyche ventured past their grasping paws and pitiful wailing.

"'My mistress must have a little of your beauty,' said Psyche, and the sympathetic Persephone gave it to her, admonishing, 'Take care that you do not open the box!'"

"That's what they told Pandora. That never works."

"No, Bitty Kitty, I guess it's just not in a girl's nature to do as she's told," the mommy sighed. "Because on the way back . . ."

"'Oh dang,'" the littler sister wrinkled her nose toward a tiny accessories-sold-separately foil mirror. "'I'm not having a very pretty day today.'" She dipped Skipper's hand into the empty Band-Aid tin. "'I better take a tiny bit to make myself look pretty for my husband.'"

"But when she opened the box, she discovered it was filled with a powerful sleep that came over her like—"

"Oh, God, Kit! Help me! Kit, it hurts . . ."

"Can you breathe, Kiki? Kiki, look at me. *Hwee hwee hwee*—like that."

Kit pushed her hand against the small of Kiki's back.

"You're almost there, Kiki," the nurse encouraged. "You're doin' good."

When the time of transition came, Kiki didn't scream or swear like some women. She didn't curse or cry. But at one point, she grasped Kit's hand hard enough to hurt.

"Don't you think they could give me something to make me go to sleep?" she whispered. "Please, Kit! I want to go to sleep. Couldn't they just take it out of me while I'm sleeping?"

And then another contraction was on her, and her obstetrician came and determined that she was fully dilated and it was time to push.

"Oh, no! No, I can't do this! They have to knock me out, Kit. They have to!"

"Yes, you can. You can do this, Kiki. You can," Kit mantraed and affirmed. "You are strong and brave and beautiful. You are Kalene Olympia Smithers, Professional Singer."

Someone gave Kit a pair of blue-green pants, enormous gown, face mask, paper shoes. She followed the gurney down the hall to the delivery room, where another hour blurred by as she stood, feet numb and back aching. She clutched Kiki's hand, telling her she would be okay, telling her what a good little trooper she always was, telling her that it was almost over now, truly wanting it to be over for Kiki's sake, but secretly dreading the moment the changeling would emerge, deformed and inert.

As it came, Kit focused on her sister's face, unable to go any further with her, but willing her to know how much she was loved.

Kiki had no more ability to cry than the infant. She was calm as they delivered the placenta, severed the cord, asked her if she was ready. She wanted to hold him. She wanted to, but was seized by the terrible trembling that sometimes accompanies shock and childbirth, and the nurses moved swiftly to cover her with oven-warmed blankets.

"Bye-bye, Luke," she said, and when she kissed his forehead, her mouth came away painted with her own red blood and the baby's delicate white vernix.

They gave her a shot of something, and she slept as the doctor sutured her episiotomy.

There was such a quiet in the room then. Silence radiated outward from the tiny form as he was passed through the necessary hands, being washed, measured, swaddled in a small, soft blanket, and when Kit received him into her arms, she understood the nature of it. It was a peace that eludes all living creatures with the precious exception of those born to it; the unattainable *om* aspired to by the Zen master and cloistered nun in all their deepest days of prayer, but beyond the reach of any spirit encumbered by presence of mind, by floor beneath feet, by the memory of an insect—even by the thought of thinking nothing—shifting the consciousness, if ever so slightly as a drop of rain on the surface of an ocean.

But for Luke, there was no ripple on the face of the deep; for Luke, there was nothing, and so everything: eternity and abyss. He existed, omniscient, unconscious, in the unclouded iris of God.

Kit held him until he died, kissing his flawless chin and sweet forehead, touching each graceful finger and perfect toe, sharing the breath from his bow-shaped mouth and tiny nose. She was acutely aware, in those hours, that all this was for her own blessing, since he had no knowing of it. And with that awareness came the enormous revelation of all she had received while calling herself the giver. For the first time in her life, she knew what a privilege and gift, what a decadence it is to give love.

She cried then, but in the wake of a most unexpected joy. She'd expected an aberration, not a miracle, preparing herself for something neither human nor complete. And instead, here was Luke; resonating against the swell of his unborn cousin, warming Kit's arms with his life, filling her heart with his peace beyond knowingness.

Even after they took him, his beauty stayed with her.

i *could wile away the hours conversing with the flowers . . . dee doot dee doodly doot*

The ditty kept rewinding like tape on a reel, and Kiki let it scritch across and across her forehead like ninth grade irony, like fingernails on aluminum siding. She let the last line turn her stomach over like a nauseating little rise in the road, like pushing on a bruise, lemon juice in a paper cut. She kept hoping the small torment might eventually reactivate the numb nerve endings that webbed and cocooned her body now. Or maybe she'd get lucky and get hit by a bus. If the dull wound was cauterized by some spine-smashing, skull-crushing shock, she might be able to feel Chloe in her arms again. She might be able to stand for Oscar to touch her.

i would be bright and merry life would be a dingaderry if I only—

"Well, we're a couple of sad cases, aren't we?"

Vivica tossed an extra pillow over and eased onto the hammock next to Kiki, thin and pale as a wisp of smoke. Her hair was beginning to grow back—a white, fine stubble that stood out from her delicate head like a dandelion halo. It made Kiki feel afraid to breathe by her.

The poolside phone *brreeped* again; Vivica was subject to a constant stream of well-wishes from her ten thousand close personal friends. It was beginning to make Kiki nauseous, listening to her mother's upbeat, Molly Brown bravado. All that Og Mandino, Zig Ziglar, positive attitude "when life gives you lemons" crap. Vivica was a commercial for pluckiness, marketing her survivorship like a Cherry Coke every time she picked up that stupid phone.

Kiki pushed one ear into the pillow and covered the other with her palm. She turned her face away from her mother, mouthing the words, silently mimicking. *Hi! This is VIVica!*

"Hi! This is Vivica," Vivica proclaimed.

I'm still here, sweetie! How are YOU!

"Still here, sweetie! And how are you?" She stroked Kiki's rumpled bangs back from her face. "Oh, she's doing great. She's a real trooper. She looks fabulous. Been working on a gorgeous tan. Oh, well, I'm not sure she . . . It's just that, next week, she is frantically busy with . . . Well, I could ask her, but—"

"No."

"Actually though, she and I have been talking about a cruise, so we don't want to tie ourselves down. Oh, you mean now? I don't think so. Because she's sleeping right now. Well, you can talk to me about it. I'm handling all her—I beg your pardon? None of *my* business? Listen, pal— *Prejudiced?* It has nothing to do with that, Xylo, and you know it! Frankly, I'm insulted that you'd even— Oh. Prejudiced against musicians? Well okay, in that case, I am. What mother wouldn't be?" Vivica sighed and pressed her temple. "I understand, but I told you, sweetie, she's sleeping. She is so! I'm not . . . Oh, for pity's sake—" She covered the receiver with her palm. "Kiki, I really don't have the energy for this. Kiki? Please. He's just going to keep calling."

Kiki shook her head without any particular emotion.

"*Kalene,*" Vivica reprimanded in a hush. "I am not your personal secretary. Kalene?" She sighed and took her hand away from the mouthpiece. "I'm sorry, Xylo, but she really isn't up to it right now. As for the rest of it, I'll get Estelle to set up some auditions. She'll be in touch. I know. I'll tell her." Vivica clicked the phone off and pushed in the thin antenna with her antenna-thin index finger. "Musicians. What did I tell you girls?"

"Mama! Grandma! Watch my back dive!"

Chloe cantered around to the deep end of the pool and ceremoniously took her position.

"I'm watching, Twinkie!" Vivica called. "We're watching!"

Kiki turned away. It made her feel sick watching Chloe arch back, flying through the air in such an unnatural posture, her head so dangerously close to the cement wall.

"You're okay, sweetie," Vivica said. "You're fine."

Kiki didn't know to whom Vivica was speaking, so she didn't bother to answer.

"Yup. We're okay. Survivors by definition have God on their side. I think if you manage to lose ten pounds and I manage to find them, we'll both be good as new."

Kiki didn't say anything. Vivica kept stroking the bangs from her eyes.

"What is it, Moon Pie?"

"What is it?" Kiki laughed out loud. "Let's see. What is it? My baby's dead, my children and I are homeless, my late husband went and slept with—geez, Mama! *What is it?* What do you *think* it is? My life is a piece of *shit!* But I'm sure if I just lose a few pounds, well, that'll just make everything peachy-keen, won't it."

Vivica didn't say anything else for a while. The hammock drifted in the slow wind. Oscar and Chloe played by the pool.

"You know what we should do?" Vivica tapped Kiki's shoulder. "We should do some Richard Simmons. Feel like *Sweatin' to the Oldies?*"

Kiki rolled her eyes. Her mother worshipped Richard Simmons as the savior of the fucking universe. They were made for each other: the Two Marketeers—relentless, fucking, cheerful sadists to the heart and bone, both of them.

"Why don't you two go ahead without me?" she barbed.

"Moon Pie, maybe—"

"What time is it?" Kiki pulled Vivica's wrist up and turned it over so she could look at her watch. "I need my Valium."

"No, you don't."

"Mama, don't start with that again."

"What you need—what we both need—is to get back to work." Vivica nodded, straight ahead and then toward Kiki. "We've been sitting around for a month. I'm bored stiff. I'm going in to the office in the morning, and I want you to come with me."

"I don't feel like it." Kiki reached across her mother for a can of Sprite.

"I'm going in to the office," Vivica repeated. "And you're coming with me."

"I don't feel like it." Kiki swallowed two capsules with a swig of soda.

"Tough. You're going."

"*Mama!*"

Vivica laughed at that, because it sounded just like when she used to tell them it was bedtime. She let Kiki sulk while she shook the folds out of two large towels, wrapped her grandchildren in them, and sent them in to watch cartoons, then went back to the hammock.

"C'mon, honey. How much longer are you planning to sit around like this?"

"I have no plans at present, Mama."

"Well, let's take a look at your options."

Vivica set the empty Sprite aside and picked up a notepad. Her answer to everything was to make a list, and there was no problem on it that couldn't be solved with a princess waistline, a slipcover, or a can of mushroom soup.

"One," she bulleted the first line. "You can start singing again. Xylo's begging for you. He's gone through three girls since Ramonica left."

"No."

"Two. The Dave Rossy Combo is losing their vocalist next month. Rossy would kill for you."

"No."

Kiki wrestled onto her side, folding the pillow against her face. It always took too long for the Valium to push down on her eyes.

"Three," Vivica prodded. "Estelle and I would love to have you full-time at the agency. Who knows the business better than you do? Or part-time, even. How would that be? A few days a week to start?"

Kiki waited for the dulling to seep up over her forehead.

"Four. Have you given any more thought to my idea? About recording a children's album?"

"I don't need to give it any more thought. It's stupid. It's worse than that stupid river medley."

"You liked the concept before," Vivica reminded her.

"That was before."

"It's marketable, Kiki. That's a very hot demographic right now. And it's the perfect project for you."

"Well, maybe I'll think about it someday, Mama, but right now—"

"I already booked the studio."

"What?"

"And hired backup."

"Who?" Kiki demanded, "Who did you get?"

"Not him," Vivica assured her. "Rossy and his bass player. I thought we'd keep it simple. Just piano, bass, and the fabulous vocal stylings of Miss Kiki Smithers."

"When? How much is all this going to cost?"

"The studio is booked next month, the week of the eighteenth. And never mind the rest," she said. "I'm making an investment. So," Vivica flipped a few pages on her notepad, "the package design is already done. Estelle's seen a pasteup, and she's pleased, and I trust her. So, according to Discmakers in Philadelphia, we should be able to release in time for Christmas buying if we have negatives to their art department and a digital master to them by the twenty-ninth. I'm going with the same distributor we used on Xylo's first CD. They did a reasonable job, plus I'm planning to market through several catalogues directed toward educational products, specialty items, yuppie parents, baby boomers, etcetera. *Oo!* Bookstores. Borders, Barnes & Noble, that sort of thing. Now, I've made a list of possibilities, but we need to settle on a playlist and meet with Rossy ASAP so he can start on arrangements. Ah!"

She held her pencil up in the air as another lightbulb blinked on.

"Headshots. Call photographer," Vivica wrote aloud, then scrutinized Kiki's head. "Call Giovanni. We'll have him do something about those roots."

Kiki flopped back on the pillows. "I can't believe you're doing this."

"Correction. *You're* doing this."

"I really don't want to do this, Mama," Kiki said.

"Tough!" Vivica stood up, not caring that it rocked Kiki right out of the hammock. "You need to. You need to do it, Kalene."

"I told you before—"

"And I told you—*tough!*" Vivica countered, but then cajoled, "C'mon, now. Where's that girl who never gives up, huh? Where's my little trooper?"

"Oh, *God,* I hate that!" Kiki clapped her hands over her ears. "You've been laying that trooper thing on me all my life, and all it means is *shut up.* Shut up and take it, little girl! Be a *trooper!*"

"All right. I'm sorry. I apologize," Vivica said. "I know the last year has been tough on you. But you know what Thelma Wells said. 'Tough times don't last. Tough people do!'"

"Would you please *stop it* with all that crap! You're driving me fucking crazy!" Kiki took off her sunglasses and threw them across the terra-cotta tile, and Vivica followed their skippering trail with her eyes. "Why can't you ever stop, Mama? Why can't you see that what I need—I need— Why can't you just be somebody's *mother?*"

"Because," Vivica took her daughter's face between her hands and not very gently, "it's *your* turn to be somebody's mother, Kalene. *You* are the mommy now. And that means you don't have the luxury of laying around here licking your wounds."

"I can't do it, Mama. I tried!"

"All your life, you've had people babying you," Vivica went on without flinching. "Well, it's about time you started doing things for yourself. Kiki, you owe it to yourself and you owe it to your children to get back on your feet, and that's exactly what you're going to do. You can't continue to depend on me. I won't always be here to—"

"Don't say that!"

"*I won't be here, Kalene!* Look at me, for Christ sake! Look what's *happening* to me!"

"But you're okay now! It's okay!"

"I am not *okay!*" Now they were both crying. "I finished chemo, and everybody looked at me and said, 'Well, thank God that's over.' Only it isn't over for me! I'm sick, Kalene. I'm ugly and sick and so goddamn *tired.* I feel like I've been hit by a damn bus. And I don't know when that bus is going to turn around and hit me again, and if it does hit me again, I can't imagine how I'll survive it. I don't think I have the strength. I have to know that you're going to be all right on your own. You and Kit. To have any peace, I need to know that."

"Mama . . . ," Kiki took hold of both Vivica's hands, trying to stop their trembling, and she almost laughed. "Mama, you're *scared*."

"Oh, damn," Vivica tried to speak around her broken up breathing. "I can't explain why this is suddenly starting to hit me. It's so damn *stupid!*"

"No, Mama, it isn't."

"You know, I was never quite happy with the way they looked. My breasts. I was going to have them done. Maybe for my birthday. And then I felt it. And I knew I should go, but when I thought about chemo and that they would . . . they would— Oh, God, Kalene, they *cut them off!*" She pressed her hands to her chest as if she still couldn't believe it. "I know I was an idiot to put it off so long, but I wasn't done with them! I wasn't done being beautiful and sexual. And I sure as hell wasn't done being alive!"

When Kiki pulled her little mother into her arms, she could feel her heart beating fast as a bird's.

"Kiki, I wish I could be here for you now. But I just—I can't . . ."

"Shhhh," Kiki rocked and whispered. "You're still here, Mama. And you're still beautiful, and you're still alive. It's all right." And after stroking Vivica's temple for a while, she forgot herself and cooed softly, "Mama's here."

They settled back into the hammock again, and after some time, Vivica's breathing slowed to the rhythm of the rocking.

you took the part that once was my heart, Kiki hummed softly.

Oscar and Chloe were still inside watching television. The heat of the day was just coming on. Kiki left her mother sleeping in the shaded hammock and moved to a patio chair. She drew her finger under her blurred eyeliner and took up Vivica's pencil and pad.

"Five."

Mel hadn't worn his suit since the day of his mother's funeral, and as Mitzi and Sarah ran out to meet him in the yard, Kit noticed it was hanging sort of loosely on him.

"Wow," he walked into the living room and pointed to the side of the rifle case Kit was refinishing for Pep Seward's den. "Looks great."

"Thanks."

Kit was proud of the piece, even though it had taken her forever to get the English setter's head shaped right, and even after all that, he looked like he shared a barber with Buster Poindexter, which compelled Kit to place Buster off in the reeds, disguised in a plaid shirt and Elmer Fudd hat, raising the neck of his electric guitar at a flock of indifferent geese overhead.

"Thanks for keeping the kids," Mel said. "Carmen said to say thanks."

"How is she doing?" Kit asked.

"Oh, you know. Funerals. This was a tough day on her. And then they went ahead and read the will and everything because people were needing to leave town." Mel shuffled his foot at the corner of the drop cloth. "Carmen's taking off for Albuquerque."

"Yeah, she told me on the phone."

There is only one great adventure, she'd added Confuciously, *and that is inward toward the self,* and Kit had to smile.

Carmen sense.

"She's leaving Wednesday," Mel said.

Kit braced her brush hand on her left arm to keep it steady.

"Are you invited?" she asked him.

"Yeah, I am."

Kit nodded but didn't say anything.

"I'm not going."

"You can go if you want to, Mel."

"I wasn't waiting for your permission," he sounded annoyed. "My kids are here. My friends are here. I've got eleven years seniority built up at the hangar. I *live* here. I do still have a life, you know. With or without you."

"You're right. I'm sorry." She went back to painting, and he went back to looking forlorn. "I guess you'll miss her."

"I guess," Mel said.

"Do you love her?"

"Is that allowed?"

Kit crossed behind him to pick up a fan brush and squeezed his shoulder on her way back to the Poindexter setter.

"Yeah," she said. "Love's allowed."

Mel pulled a chair over from the kitchen and sat with his head back against the wall.

"We're going to have to make some decisions," he sighed.

"About . . ."

"I told Carmen I'd stay at the house until it's sold, but the price they're asking, it won't take long. I don't know how we're going to afford an apartment in addition to everything else. And then there's going to be lawyers and all that. I think we need to talk about selling the house."

"No."

"I was thinking, maybe we could get two apartments in the same complex, so the kids could go back and forth."

"The kids are staying right here. With me."

"Kit, I know how hard you're working, but I don't think you're ready to take responsibility for—"

"Yes, I am," she said, trying not to let the edge out of her voice, trying to make it sound like determination instead of fear, like Carmen taking flight for Albuquerque and points unknown. "I can. I will."

"Well, that's easier said than done."

"The kids are happy in school. It's a good neighborhood."

"If I could do it, I would, Kit. I don't want them to have to move any more than you do, but dammit— Why do you have to make this be so hard?"

"Mel, look around you! I can't sell this house now!"

"I'm not sure we have a choice, Kit!"

Kit knelt by the mixing pots on the other side of the room, her back to him.

"I didn't know it was decided." She stirred carefully at one of the pots. "That you weren't coming back, I mean."

"I didn't get the impression I was invited."

"Mama," Mitzi came in the back door.

"Am I invited, Kit?"

"Mama, I'm itchy."

"Sweetie," Kit sighed, "run and play now. Daddy and I are talking."

"And my head hurts. And I'm hot."

"Well then, why don't you loan Sarah one of your swim-suits, and you two can run in the sprinkler."

"C'mere, Noodle." Mel put his hand on Mitzi's forehead. "Feels like she's running a fever."

"And look at all my 'squito bites," Mitzi complained, lifting her shirt to show them.

"Oh, terrific!" Mel groaned.

Kit counted sixteen chicken pox on her tummy alone.

❧

please not another one please please please

Kit had to pee so bad she was praying.

Standing in line at the grocery store, somebody's little knee bearing down on her bladder, she knew she couldn't hold it much longer, no matter how hard she thigh-mastered her legs together.

no more price checks please please please

She and Kiki used to shut their eyes tight and mantra that same way when they turned the doorknob at the center of the Mystery Date game board.

"Please, don't let it be the dud or the bowling geek," they prayed, "please, oh, please, let it be the Dream, not the Dud!"

But Kit's heart had always betrayed her. There was no use praying around it; God saw past her fervent petition, into a secret compartment of herself that wanted what she shouldn't. You were supposed to want the beachboy or the preppie prom guy, so clean and good and wholesome. But Kit thought bowling might be kind of fun, and in the truth of truth, the dark of dark, under her covers and behind the privacy of the Mystery Door, Kit felt something for that dud. He was rumpled and rowdy looking, like someone she could talk to and tug on and lie down with. There was a lovably lazy sexuality about him, and the tickle of desire at the tip of Kit's tailbone spoke a higher, deeper prayer than any lip service she paid to the instructions on the underside of the box lid. Kit knew, every time she twisted that knob, there must be something really wrong with her.

A man stepped in line behind her, his face obscured by two gigantic plastic packages of Luvs disposable diapers.

Kit tried to ignore the idea of him as long as she could, guiltily rearranging her cereal and jelly. But she could hear the wet baby crying somewhere in the city. The little diapers were blue. One size up from newborn. The waistband festooned with those cute little itty-bitty . . . oh, *hell!*

"Why don't you go on ahead?" Kit offered.

"Oh, really? Are you sure?"

"Sure. You've just got the diapers there and . . ."

She indicated her own heaping cart.

To the trained eye, Kit's cart told the story of a sick child: ginger ale, Jell-O, liquid Tylenol, and Resolve carpet cleaner. And a weary mother: half-pound bag of M&M's, six-pack of Sharps nonalcoholic beer, and one of those truly nasty seventy-nine-cent pies with graham cracker dust on the bottom, a gluey layer of nondairy whipped topping above, and enough artificial flavoring frozen in between to mutate a pack of laboratory rats. Banana cream. Or maybe it was coconut. Same difference.

"Thanks," the diaper man said and stepped past her. "That's very sweet of you."

Kit stepped back, shifting her weight, leafing through the aisle-side tabloids to distract herself from any thought of water.

"WORLD AS WE KNOW IT IS ENDING: TEXAS HOUSE-WIFE RECEIVES SIGN FROM GOD"

"Price check on Dinty Moore beef stew," the checkout girl enunciated into a handheld microphone.

Dang! A sign from God!

"Kit! Hi there!" It was Missy Priestly. PTO fund-raiser cochair. Amway distributor.

There is no God. Kit scrunched her thighs together.

"Missy, hi. How are you?" she mumbled, searching between the folds of her brain for excuses. Why hadn't she returned Missy's last seventeen phone calls? Why was she wearing Mel's old cutoffs and a pair of terry cloth bedroom slippers? Kit figured she could plead pregnant on both counts.

"Well, I didn't know you were expecting!" Missy cried. "I'm so excited for you!"

Missy's stomach was very flat, and her hair was very large. Her groceries were in a small red basket: styling spritz, a wedge of Brie, a bottle of wine, and a skinny, square package of that tiny dark bread Kit had always wondered about. Who bought that tiny little bread? What did they do with it? Now she knew. Hapless dupes are forced to choke it down during multilevel marketing brainwashing sessions. It was probably infused with some kind of hallucinogenic drug that interacted with the low-budget, computer-animated videos. Kit tried to take her eyes off it. Tried to think of something to say.

"How's Heather?" was what she finally came up with.

"Oh, fine. She's doing great. How's Mitzi?"

"Actually, she's covered with chicken pox right now."

"Oh, poor baby! How about Cooper?"

"All clear so far."

"Whew!" Missy made a broad comic gesture across her brow. "One crisis at a time, please!"

Kit managed a polite laugh.

"And how's umm . . . how's Mel?"

"Fine. He's fine."

Kit could tell from the way Missy's eyes dropped away. She knew.

There was a long, dry moment.

"Price check on Dinty Moore," the girl repeated.

For some reason, she was standing there with the can in her hand instead of proceeding with the mountain of produce and dry goods still on the conveyor belt. It made Kit want to step up there and shake her.

"Honestly," Missy whispered, eyeing the elderly lady at the head of the line, "why don't we just stand here all night and quibble over every cent."

The diaper man cleared his throat.

"Say, Kit," Missy said in her sweetest tone, "I've got company coming in an hour . . ."

Poor suckers, Kit thought, missing the point.

"Do you s'pose—I mean, I just have these couple three items."

Her softly pencilled eyebrows inflected upward.

"Oh . . . um . . ."

Kit thought about mentioning that she had to go to the bathroom in the worst way, but Missy's hair was so perfect, her basket so dainty.

"Why don't you go ahead?" Kit backed away.

"*Thank* you *so* much!" Missy was already setting the divider in place, a plastic line of demarcation between her tiny square bread and the elderly lady's plain lumpy loaves, leaving no room for the young daddy's Luvs. "I owe you my life!"

"Sure," Kit said. "No problem."

Missy exclaimed something about the recipes in *Woman's*

Day this month, pulled an issue from the rack, and engrossed herself in it.

Last in line again, Kit tried to refocus on the tabloids.

"MENOPAUSE MIRACLE HERB DISCOVERED IN RAIN-FOREST"

So what if she had a sick kid and a bladder that was about to explode? Missy had company coming. What's more important—Brie or barf supplies? Missy deserved to go first. There was no garbage in the back of Missy's car, no soap scum in her tub, no bloodstains on her panties from the time she realized too late it really *was* her period, not just that spicy pizza burger, and the *dang* Walgreen's store closed fifteen minutes ago. Missy's hair was perfect. Missy's children were healthy and quiet. Missy's husband was probably at home right now. Probably because Missy never screwed around on him.

"BAT BOY DISCOVERED IN PENNSYLVANIA"

Missy prayed sincerely for a Dream Date life and got it, while Kit raged out of control, a magnet for duds and bowling geeks.

"NOSTRADAMUS PREDICTED DEATH OF ELVIS"

But maybe—and pregnancy is full of such epiphanies—maybe that didn't mean God had forsaken her. Maybe that just meant God wanted her to learn to bowl. Maybe God wanted her to discover she had balls of her own.

"SCIENTISTS PROVE FORGIVENESS CURES CANCER"

Kit laughed out loud. Was that the cancer that mutates your cells or the one that consumes your spirit? And were they talking about the forgiver or the forgiven? Kit had given up any hope of being the latter. The former, she'd never really thought about. To be the forgiver, one would have to feel wronged, and to be wronged, one would have to be something other than nothing, and Kit hadn't seen herself as that for quite some time.

Forgive me, she experimented, starting with herself. *I forgive you.*

It felt like opening the warm kitchen door on the dark back-yard.

Forgive me . . . forgive me . . . I forgive you . . .

God and the world and the dud at the door; her mother and Missy and Neeva and Mel.

"Ma'am?" A girl in a blue checker's smock touched the back of Kit's elbow. "I can take you on express."

Missy turned with a pained expression. The diaper man was just telling the other girl that no, he didn't mind waiting while she changed her register tape.

"I have more than ten items," Kit confessed.

"It's not like we use a calculator," the girl shrugged and tugged the cart over to a neighboring aisle.

Absolution lifted Kit's shoulder blades, strengthened her legs, stung her eyes wet like a nun's kindness. There even seemed to be a little less pressure on her bladder.

"Any coupons?" asked the priestess, skimming the final item across the scanner.

She was brown-skinned and small with a billion beautiful braids. She looked to be about half as old as Kit and a month or so further along. Probably about to deliver any day. And even though she offered the box of Kleenex with a shy smile, she must have thought it was pretty pathetic, how Kit was crying right there in the middle of the store.

࿘

Mel and Mitzi were both asleep on the couch in the corner of the dining room when Kit got home. He was holding *The Paper Bag Princess* open in his lap, and she was slumped over the crook of his arm.

Within three days of the first fever, the chicken pox were everywhere on her, including the insides of her mouth, nose, ears, and vagina. Even with the Tylenol-Codeine Kit had gotten from the pediatrician, Mitzi was miserable, and between her needs and the throw-up laundry and Mrs. Lu's neighbor's sister's guest bedroom ensemble that still had to be finished, Kit had hardly been able to lie down in the last seventy-two hours. She bent to kiss Mitzi's hot forehead and smelled the faint aroma of oatmeal bath.

"Mel?" Kit touched his shoulder.

"Huh . . . mmm . . . Guess we dozed off."

"Try not to wake her," Kit whispered, but Mitzi was already stirring.

"Mama, I don't feel good," she whimpered. "My throat hurts."

"I know, Sesame Seed. Do you think a Popsicle would help?"

Mitzi didn't look like she had a great deal of confidence in the healing power of Popsicles, but Mel went and got it, and she accepted it, propped up with pillows on the cool sheet Kit spread over the couch cushions. Kit turned on the radio for her and went back to the kitchen to put away the rest of the groceries. She heard Mel at the door behind her and was just about to say thanks for stopping by when he stepped over and put his arms around her, and that made her realize how bone-weary tired and lonely she was, and that made her throat close up so she couldn't say anything at all.

She was grateful when he didn't talk either, but simply stayed there, letting her rest heavily against him.

"Well," he finally said. "I'm gonna be late."

"Maybe you could tell them you had to take three hitch-hiking nuns back to their convent on the San Jacinto."

"Yeah," Mel laughed. "Something tells me they wouldn't buy that one any better than your mother did. Seems to me, she busted my balls pretty good that time."

"I remember. But you came back."

"Yeah."

"Mel," Kit took his hand, "would you be insulted if—if I said I forgive you?"

"No," he said after a moment.

"Do you think you'll ever be able to forgive me?"

"I don't know. I mean, I've been trying to—to think about things and . . ." He looked at the floor for another long moment, but then he nodded slightly. "Yeah, Kit. I forgive you."

She turned back to the counter where she'd started packing a lunch for him to take to the hangar, but he took the knife out of her hands and sliced the sandwiches himself while she poured coffee into his thermos. He packed it all into his cooler, and then he opened the door, shedding warm kitchen light onto the dark of the backyard.

"So . . ." Mel stared toward the swing set until Kit touched his hand.

"'Night, Mel."

"'Night, Kit."

He leaned over and kissed the top of her head, then pushed past the screen door.

Just as he opened the door of his truck, Kit thought she heard him whistling.

⁂

Mitzi was asleep, the Popsicle melting on the front of her nightshirt like an ice cube on the sidewalk.

Kit tossed the wooden stick in the bedside bucket and pulled Mitzi's shirt off over her head, gathering her in the sheet. She pulled the chain to drop the ceiling fan to low speed and settled in the rocking chair. Mitzi whimpered again and tucked her flushed cheek against Kit's neck, her forehead hot and damp, her breathing hoarse and congested. Kit drew the digital thermometer from her pocket and eased it under Mitzi's arm. It finally peeped and flashed a digital 102.7.

Opening the sheet, Kit used one corner to wipe the sweat away from Mitzi's temple and from her own chest, and then she held her baby, draped across her lap like the Pieta.

Even dotted with chicken pox, Mitzi's body was pale and beautiful in the moonlight, a reflection of Kit's own long legs

and square shoulders. But she had Mel's temple, his jaw, and—
heaven help her—his nose. She was the marriage, the joining of
them, the undivorcible bond between Kit and this man she
would always love, if for no other reason than the fact that only
he could have given her this gift, this particular projection of
her self and his that tickled Kit's curiosity and enticed her
toward the future every morning like a giggling, grimy-faced
Pied Piper.

"*Nnn . . . ,*" Mitzi stirred.

"Mama's here."

"My chicken pops are itchy."

"I know, Peppermint. Try not to scratch, though. Try not to
think about it. Shhhh . . ." she blew across Mitzi's chest and
drew the sheet around her. "Close your eyes."

"Will you finish telling me the story?"

"You've heard it six hundred times," Kit sighed. "What if I
put on a tape? What about 'Baby Beluga'?"

"You left out the part with the powerful sleep."

"I think you need a powerful sleep," Kit nuzzled her scaly
cheek.

"And she was sleeping, and she couldn't wake up . . ."

"And Eros came," Kit relented, "and he took her in his
arms and kissed her."

"Was it a magic kiss?"

"All kisses are magic."

"And she woke up?"

"Mm-hmm."

"And he gave her a cup of androja?"

"Ambrosia. And she drank it, and she became immortal."

"Which means she was a goddess instead of a plain old
human being."

"That's right," Kit smiled.

"But where was he all that time, Mama?"

"I don't know. His mother's house, I guess."

"But he came back."

"Yes." Kit closed her eyes and leaned her head against the back of the rocking chair. "He forgave her. And she forgave him."

"And they lived happily ever after."

"Sure," Kit said out loud, and to herself, *Why not?*

"Did she have the baby?"

"I guess so."

"Did she have a boy or a girl?"

"I don't know, Puddin' Pop, I don't remember." She carried Mitzi over and settled her on the couch. "Now. How 'bout that 'Baby Beluga'?"

"No," Mitzi stretched out and curled in like a baby bird. "Let's hear Aunt Kiki again."

Kit dropped a rough copy of Kiki's project into the tape deck and sank back on the couch with Mitzi's feet in her lap. She felt herself drowsing before the music came on.

At first, there was only Kiki, standing alone on the dark empty stage.

"Hushabye, don't you cry, go to sleep my little baby . . .

When you wake, you shall have all the pretty little ponies."

It wasn't the voice that had combined with Kit's to blow the grandstands back. The strength hadn't diminished, but the innocence of Kiki's bright pink mouth was gone and all of the stridency with it, replaced by a richer inflection, a caressing of each phrase that brought a woman's face forward from the painted expressions, a woman's body from beneath the armor of snapping sequins. And when the music came up from behind and put its arms around her, she opened like a magnolia.

"Blacks and bays, dapples and grays . . ."

Kit closed her eyes and rocked as Kiki's invisible world went gliding by on a carousel of wondering why, trying too hard, falling in love. Yellow tub toys, a bright red knock-knock joke, the deep purple mysteries of Bubble Man, and high green ideals of the tree fort.

And just at the periphery of it all flashed the faintest glow of gold lamé.

*H*eart that has become my heart,
My abuela would have said, "No puedo ver las cosas que están detrás de mi." I cannot see that which is behind me.

All that matters now is your voice on the phone, your heart with my heart. All I remember is the way we shared the work of our hands, the gentleness of you in the face of so much that was so ungentle.

Some women are not made to be married, and I knew early on that I was one of these. To fall in love with you—that is the thing I never expected. And you to fall in love with me—that is the thing I dared not hope for. I vowed I would not open my heart again. But nothing that has hurt me in my life is of the slightest consequence now. It's less than a heartbeat, less than a drop in a great winding river. Because I know it's only a little longer, and you'll be with me again. And this time, mi corazon, I will keep you for my own. I intend to spend each night for the rest of my life, dressing your wounds with the kindest kisses, healing you with gentlest touch, making you whole again with the giving of my love, toda una vida.

When you come to where I live now, you will find that the heat here is a beast that makes you want to lie down late in the day. But the nights are cool. The darkness brings a fresh wind and a sky full of stories. Orion and Cassiopeia, Castor and Pollux, Signus the Swan. I know because since I spoke to you on the phone, mi corazon, I've hardly slept. You and I will lie together, and we will leave the windows wide open for the scent of jasmine.

Kiki didn't mean to read over Mother Daubert's shoulder, but Mother Daubert had taken the letter out to read six or seven times since they arrived at the airport, and Kiki's willpower was simply not that strong. Mother Daubert folded the fine white paper and held it up to her nose for a moment before tucking it into the side pocket of her purse.

To an attractive young gate agent, one blue hair probably looked pretty much like another, the three of them had figured, and sure enough, Mother Daubert sailed right through with Vivica's passport in one hand and a ticket to Huatulco in the other.

"It's a beautiful day for flying," she told Kiki at the entrance to the jetway.

Through the window, they could see the caterers loading food trays onto one side of the plane while passengers tunneled in through the other. The 737 gleamed silver in the sunlight, nose like a sugar bowl, wings just ready.

"You know how to reach me, Mother Daubert, if there's anything you need," Kiki told her for the hundredth time.

"Oh, my goodness, dear," she patted away the suggestion with her soft hand, "you've done so much already. And your mother, please tell her again how much I appreciated her hospitality these last few weeks."

And Kiki said she would, though she knew Mother Daubert would send an impeccably written thank you note when she returned the passport.

"Are you sure this is what you want, Mother Daubert?"

"Well, you know, it's so funny. When Lorenza went home, I said, 'Someday, Lorenza, I'll come and keep house for you in Brazil,' I said. And we laughed, of course, but we were such good friends. We often dreamed we'd be two little old widow ladies together."

"Now, you understand you mustn't write to any of the bridge club ladies or anyone else until I tell you it's okay, and you mustn't send me a letter. You have to let Lorenza's daughter do it when she goes into the city. I promise I'll do everything I can to get this all straightened out. My mother has a friend, and he's a very good attorney. It won't be long."

Kiki looked at Mother Daubert's eyes, trying to determine if she was comprehending any of this, but all that was reflected was that invincibly well-bred finish.

"Do you understand, Mother Daubert?"

She gazed out the window, one hand on the glass, the other holding her purse to her bosom.

"We took him camping," she said. "Lorenza and I. The first night, I was afraid of the night sounds, so Lorenza came over and lay beside me. And I had to cry because I'd all but forgotten how to feel . . . how to feel . . . touching. I was afraid of feeling that. But the second night, she opened the tent and let all that jasmine in. And I was so happy. And I was so afraid.

"The next day, we went canoeing to a place called Devil's Elbow. And as we were paddling along, I realized I'd lost my ring. My diamond engagement ring with my wedding ring bonded to it. Lorenza was a good swimmer. She told me to stay in the canoe with the baby between my knees, and she dove down, trying to find it. Of course, it was impossible, but she knew what was going to happen to me if I lost that ring. She disappeared into the water for—oh, it seemed like forever. And every time she came up to take a breath, I begged her not to go down again. But she kept on until it was almost dark, and we had to go back.

"That night, I stayed in her room, and she told me how the

bougainvillea in Brazil grows seven feet high with blossoms as wide open as your hand. She said we should go there before he came home, and he could no more find us than we could find that diamond ring in all of a whole wide river. But the next day, he came home. And when he started to beat me, I thought it must be God punishing me. I knew what we did together was a shame and a sin, and this must be the wrath of God. But Lorenza made him stop. She told him she'd stolen the ring to pay for her mother's medicine. He told her to go into his study, and when he closed the door, it was like seeing her disappear into the water again."

"What did you do?"

"Nothing. I did nothing. I took the baby, and I went outside. I wanted the sun to burn me, I wanted to drown in the pool. If I hadn't had Wayne, I would have slashed my wrists." She hugged her handbag to her chest, and her hands were trembling. "When she was well enough, he had her deported."

"But Lorenza kept writing to you all these years?"

"I couldn't bear to read her letters. I couldn't stand to think about . . . How she could forgive me, I don't understand." She closed her eyes against the stinging. "We should have never come back. We should have kept floating on down the river until . . . It was all my fault. I was so . . . I was afraid for my mother to find out. My parents' friends. People. He found the letters. He said he would tell everyone about . . . about everything. I tried to tell myself that I was protecting my family, that I couldn't disgrace them. But in my own heart, I know. It was my own . . . it was . . . There are certain things that simply are not done."

"Oh, Mother Daubert."

"I don't understand anything anymore. Everything I thought was sure and solid turned into dust, and something I was brought up to believe an abomination—I don't know what my life is anymore. I don't know what's going to happen. I only know—" She took the letter from the side pocket of her handbag and held it in both hands. "I only *hope* that maybe, sometimes you get one more chance."

Kiki put her arms around her mother-in-law, and for the first time in Kiki's memory, it felt like Mother Daubert was hugging back.

It would have been easy, in light of that, to try to comfort her. But Kiki purposely pushed that impulse aside. They both knew what it was to marry an angry husband and bear a tragically flawed son, to survive losing what they loved, like lifeboats off the Titanic or someone crawling out from under the wreckage of chemotherapy, skinny and bald, but *still-here-sweetie*. Survivors, by definition, have God on their side. But to tell her that now—about how that which had not killed them made them stronger—it would have been as trite and comfortless as some Precious Sentiment about Wayne and Luke being together now, just to the other side of heaven. If there was any truth to it at all, then truth was a hard, ironic thing.

"Mother Daubert," Kiki whispered, not wanting to let go.

"Oh, please," she pulled away, but kept Kiki's hand. "Won't you call me Beatrice?"

⁂

Kit was painting ponies on a half-wall when she heard Kiki's name on the radio. She reached and put another check by that station's call letters on the list Vivica had sent her.

"—on KTSU, Houston's choice for great jazz music, and I've had another request for something off a brand new CD from local girlfriend Kiki Smithers, *Sugar Land: Lullabies and Other Love Songs*. Look for it in stores on the Blues Mommies label, featuring killer renditions of some great jazz standards along with too-cool interpretations of classic children's songs, so you can get into Kiki's vocal stylings and simultaneously expose the rug rats to some amazing instrumentals by the Dave

Rossy Trio and special guest Xylo Haines. Let's set the last track and let Miss Kiki do her thang."

And Kiki did.

"Come to me, my melancholy baby . . . cuddle up and don't be blue . . ."

A wry smile was audible in her voice; a willingness to patronize the simple sentiment, to be fond of it without fully buying in.

Kit smiled, returning to the half-wall that portioned off part of Mitzi's room for a nursery. She tipped tiny bird-wing V's up from the corner where the mother was nesting and gave one last dash to the flying tails of all the pretty little ponies.

Mel had brought the old crib down from the attic when he came to pick up Mitzi and Coo a couple of weekends earlier, and while they were gone, Kit had spent two days assembling it and scavenging for sleepers and onesies on the clearance rack at Walmart. She'd combined the proceeds from Carse and Debbie Munda's kitchen chairs with her cache of diaper coupons and stacked the first month's supply of Huggies and Luvs in the corner of the closet, along with wipes, powder, Q-tips, and newborn-size Binkies.

She was nesting, Mel teased, and she laughed and let herself enjoy it.

The half-wall was his idea, and Kit was grateful when he offered to get the materials and build it one Sunday. Now Mitzi's side jumped with a cartooned jukebox and bobby soxers, while tranquil watercolor lullabies stretched across the prairie side in view of the crib and rocker. A silo of grain, a boy with a horn, sheep in the meadow, cows in the corn; all lay still now, even the motion of the ponies seemed sleepy.

The luxurious ache in Kit's back acknowledged the work of her hands. She hadn't allowed herself the solace of this sweet anticipation until now. But now, she spanned her hands over her stomach and let herself be happy. She let herself want this baby, love her, make promises to her. As she rinsed her brushes and laid them out to dry, she even allowed herself a few hopes and dreams.

Kit lay back, resting her head in the lap of an enormously plush pink bear from Vivica. Within the two minutes it took for Xylo to tumble and touch a wandering solo across the bridge of the song, Kit was sleeping, and Kiki was singing right into her dream.

"Come on and smile, my honey dear, while I kiss away each tear . . . or else I shall be melancholy too . . ."

It was easier in the dream to find Frank Dupuis' grave. Not like in real life, when Kit spent the whole weekend driving to Corpus Christi, scouting and map searching for the cemetery, then hefting her heavy front over hill and dale, determined to find the exact weather-whitened stone.

In the dream, Neeva walked right to it, and Kit simply followed her over the hill and between two crepe myrtles to the slope just beyond the big stone angel. The paper was so brittle it sighed dryly as Kit tore it into small even pieces. She made a neat pile of them along with someone else's wilted rose petals on the face of the low, slanted stone, but the wind quickly fluttered them across the cemetery like dandelion tatters.

"As if there isn't enough smut in the world," Neeva complained, as she turned and walked away.

"Neeva, wait!" Kit called and caught up to her. "Do you remember—did they have the baby? Was it a boy or a girl?"

Neeva leaned back against the open stance of the grave marker angel, looking like a four-armed, stone-winged Vishnu. She might have been smiling. Kit couldn't tell around the cigarette in her mouth.

"According to Bulfinch," she said, "they named her Pleasure."

please please please please

Kit was doing the Mystery Date mantra when Dr. Poplin came in.

"Hi there, Kit." She attached her chart to a clipboard. "How's Mitzi doing?"

"Great," Kit said, trying to sound cheerful and chatty. "Back to school last week. Thank the Lord. Maybe I can get some work done now."

"How about Cooper?"

"All clear so far. He had a very light case when he was three, so I'm hoping that'll hold him."

"It should, as long as he had at least a dozen visible pox," she said, noting Kit's steadily advancing weight gain on the chart. "And how are you feeling?"

"Great. Fine," Kit said, though her pulse was practically bruising *please don't let it be Wayne please don't let it be Wayne.* "I'm ok."

"How are the headaches?" Dr. Poplin looked into her eyes with a little light.

"Better."

"Have you been sleeping?"

"All the time," Kit said. "I dozed off on the floor one day last week and haven't seen midnight since."

"Good," Dr. Poplin said and pressed a stethoscope to Kit's back.

"Less than two weeks to go," the nurse encouraged before taking Kit's urine sample and bustling out the door.

"I think you're going to make it," Dr. Poplin smiled.

Kit tried to look heartened so she would just get on with it.

Ander Ander Ander Ander please please please god sir

"Of course, those due dates are iffy. The baby's head-down now. All set to go. So, you never know."

"I'd bet money on the due date," Kit said as the obstetrician supported her back and guided her feet into the stirrups. "Both Mitzi and Coo were born smack dab on their due dates."

"Really?" Dr. Poplin raised her eyebrows but didn't pause from palpating Kit's abdomen. "Do you know the statistical improbability of that?"

"Stranger things have happened," Kit prophesied.

"That's for sure. Deep breath. You're probably in the ball park with another ten days or so. You don't seem to be effaced or dilated at all yet. Anyway, I make it a point never to argue with a woman's intuition. One more deep breath."

She moved her stethoscope over Kit's belly and then gave her a turn at listening.

"Chugging like a little choo-choo."

She finished the exam and helped Kit sit up sideways on the table.

"Okay, Kit. Let's talk about the amnio."

"Okay," Kit nodded obediently.

Ander Ander Ander please please not that skinny little inbred weasel

"It's a girl, and she's perfectly healthy as far as we can determine." Dr. Poplin smiled, and Kit smiled too. "But, Kit," she continued, "the tests ruled out both subjects in terms of paternity."

"What?"

"Neither of these subjects is the father, Kit."

"But . . . they're not? Are you sure?"

"It's a virtual certainty. These tests are extremely accurate." Dr. Poplin scootched closer on the wheelie stool. "Is there another possibility?" she asked delicately.

Kit sat on the examining table with her mouth open.

There was only one other possibility.

The impossible.

"Kit, I've known you for several years, and I know it's not like you to play some kind of dangerous game, but we discussed high-risk behaviors, and the need for you to be honest with me about what's going on." She referred back to the chart. "Now, your HIV and STD tests came back negative, and I'm not making any value judgements. I just want you to feel that you can tell me if we need to take further precautions for . . . Kit?"

But Kit had gone off laughing so hard she was afraid she might lose the contents of her microscopic bladder. Laughing because she'd almost forgotten that babies don't understand anything except miracles. And because she should have known that neither thunder nor hail nor all the prolific blonde sperm of Scandinavia could reach her.

Only Melvin Thadeus Prizer could swim upstream, against all odds, swim despite everything in his path, swim to her, despite her own best efforts to see that path taken away altogether.

Of course, she laughed.

Only Mel could have given her a gift like this.

"But that's the thing about love," Xylo explained, stroking the damp hair away from Kiki's face like she was a fevered child and he the mommy. "Love tends to juxtapose the laws of physics. You give of your deepest self, and instead of depleting your soul, it causes you to manifest and unfold, to become increased exponentially."

He described the phenomenon with his ivory-tickling hands and his blues-man lips, the Tao Te Ching, and the calm that came to him after fourteen angry years in the joint.

"The Tao gives birth to One.

One gives birth to Two.

Two gives birth to Three.

Three gives birth to all things."

He illustrated the koan with his body over hers, defining his words, allowing her questions, saying her name, singing soft phrases to her soft inside, sounding her out with vibrations and vibes, multiplying and quantifying on the clean carpet floor of Kiki's new home.

"When the male and female combine,
all things achieve harmony."

✥

"It's a girl," Kit said, and Vivica laughed with pure joy.

"Oh, Kitty, I'm so excited for you. Does Mel know yet?"

"I haven't found the right opportunity. But I've still got a week or so to go. Mitzi and Coo are helping him move over to his new apartment today, and he's bringing them back here tomorrow night. I'll probably tell him then."

"Do you think you two are any closer to working things out?"

"Things are working out fine." Kit tucked the phone into her shoulder and started rattling plates into the dishwasher. "Not exactly what we had planned, but it's okay. We decided to use a mediator instead of getting lawyers and all that. That simplifies things a little. And it's a lot less expensive."

They both knew she wasn't talking about money.

"Oh, Kitty."

"It's okay, Mama. Really. I know everybody thinks I should be falling apart, but I actually feel pretty solid on my own."

"That's the first step to building a solid marriage," Vivica said. "First you have to be strong enough to not need a man. Then you have to be brave enough to go on and need him anyhow."

"Well, anyway," Kit maintained a tone that deliberately changed the subject, "that's all about my doctor's appointment. Now let's hear about yours."

"Oh, let's not," Vivica sighed.

"Did you go to your CAT scans?"

"Honestly, you sound just like your sister. She's practically taken over the agency. Now you think you can boss me around, too?"

Kit could hear Vivica tapping something on her desk.

"Mama?"

"I'm still here, Kitten."

"What did they say?"

"They said there's a spot on my lung now."

"Oh . . . no." Kit had to stop loading the dishwasher and sit down on a chair. "So what do they want to do about it?"

"Oh, you know those philistines. They're just full of ideas. But it's not a matter of what *they* want to do."

"When do you start chemo again?"

"I don't, Kit. This is enough."

"What? Mama, you don't mean that!"

"Yes, I do, Kitty," Vivica assured her. "I know it's hard for you and Kiki to understand, and I've already heard the whole lecture from her—"

"Well, you're going to hear it again! We're not going to let you give up that easy."

"*Easy?*" Vivica's voice wrinkled with irritation. "Kit, you know damn well it's been anything but easy. I've already taken so much chemo and radiation that, when I do die, you'll have to scatter my ashes over a toxic waste dump! I did what they told me. I fought a good fight. And it was always a positive direction, it always felt like the right thing. Until now. Now it feels like . . . like swimming against the tide. I think I'm ready to float for a while. Let that tide take me out a ways. I think I'm ready to see what's out there."

"No, Mama! Not you! You're the last person who would ever—"

"What? Give up the great battle? I don't see it that way, Kitten. I'm not talking about dying. For one thing, every day I stay alive, I'm *surviving,* not dying. And for another, chemotherapy isn't the be all and end all of cancer treatment. I've already made an appointment with a naturopath, and I've been reading all these wonderful books. 'The bald doctor book club,' Kiki calls them: Andrew Weil and Bernie Seigel and O. T.

Bonnet. Healing doesn't happen from bombarding your body with poison, Kit, it happens when something changes inside your soul. And it doesn't always mean a continuation of the status quo. In fact, I suspect it never means that."

She paused, giving Kit an opportunity to respond, but Kit couldn't speak.

"You know what? I've decided to become a vegetarian," Vivica sounded more like her take-charge self again. "It's a very *wellness* kind of thing to do. And a great excuse to order lobster."

"Don't joke."

"Who's joking? At thirty-two dollars a tail, it better be a matter of life and death."

Vivica laughed for both of them, waiting another long moment for Kit to say something.

"All that alternative stuff, Mama—What if it doesn't work?"

"Then I'll die, Kit. And I hope I raised you girls with enough faith in God to know that isn't a terrible thing. It's a peaceful thing. A natural thing. 'No cruelty, but a cup of ambrosia.' That's what Alexandra Firestein said."

"She also said 'Traditional marriage is the daily rape of womankind.'"

"Did she?" Vivica *tsked*. "Sometimes I think she should have used a little more fiber in her diet. A bowl of raisin bran, a prune or two. It might have changed history."

Kit did laugh a little this time, but the sound of it was broken enough to make her mother hush softly, "Shh, Bitty Kitty. No more crying."

"I can't help it."

"Now, don't start feeling sorry for me," Vivica reprimanded. "You know I hate that."

"I'm not feeling sorry for you, Mama. I'm feeling sorry for *myself*. And Kiki. We need you."

"Oh, I think you and Kiki are going to be just fine."

"And what about this baby? She needs you, too, Mama. And Mitzi and Chloe and Coo and Oscar—"

"Well, I'm here, aren't I? I'm here now. And I have no immediate plans to go anywhere. Except Mervyn's. They're having an amazing sale right now."

"Oh, Mama. I just . . . I just wanted everything to be okay."

"It is, Bitty Kitty. It's fine. Not exactly what I had planned, but it's okay."

*M*itzi and Coo burst in the door, hot on the scent of the vanilla ice cream Kit was scooping out for root beer floats.

"Hey, guys," she called.

"Hey," said Mel, and he leaned on the inside of the door frame.

"How's the new place?"

Mel shrugged, but Mitzi was overflowing with enthusiasm.

"Daddy has a pool! With a slide! And there's a dumpster!"

"And we went and bought bunk beds," Cooper added, "and I get the top."

"Sounds great," Kit said, but Mel shrugged again.

"Thanks for the pillows and blankets and all that," he said.

"Sure. No problem."

"So, I'll see y'all on Friday, I guess."

"Can Daddy stay for the bedtime treat?" Mitzi tugged on the expansive fabric of her mother's maternity dress.

"If he wants to." Kit caught Mel's hand on the doorknob. "Feel like hanging out for a while?"

"Stay, Dad?" Cooper pleaded. "We could do some more on my airplane model."

"Sure," he nodded. "I'll skip the ice cream, though," he added toward Kit. "I'm trying to take off a few pounds."

"Me too!" Kit said, and he laughed and touched the side of her face.

"You look tired. Are you feeling okay?"

"Oh yeah. I'm into that last couple weeks, though. So my feet are like pontoons." She went back to scooping. "And my back is killing me today. Ever since I got back from the grocery store, I keep getting these incredible muscle spasms."

"What can I do to help?"

"Well, you could put these on the table." She handed him the floats for Mitzi and Coo. "And then you could stick around and help me get these wild bandicoots into bed, if you're not otherwise—you know—busy or whatever."

"I'm not busy." He fizzed a root beer open over the sink.

After the floats, a couple games of Go Fish, a story, prayers, and the tuck-in ritual, Mel came back down to the kitchen, opened the last two bottles of root beer, and handed one to Kit.

"Thanks," she said. "Would you believe this is my fourth bottle today? I started craving it last night. Had to go to the store at eleven-thirty. And it can't be the canned stuff. This craving is very specific. IBC Root Beer, in the bottle."

"How's your back?" he asked, pushing his hand against the small of it.

"It's okay," Kit said, but it felt better when she leaned into his hand.

Mel sat at the table, folding towels and T-shirts, and she stood at the counter, matching little socks that all looked the same to him but combined in subtly different pairs for her. She asked him about the new airplanes at the hangar, he asked her about the contract she'd gotten on a window for an Italian restaurant in the mall, and they went on like that for a while.

"So . . ." He finally leaned his elbows on the table and rolled the root beer bottle between his palms. "You never did say. How'd it go with Poplin last week?"

"Fine."

"Yeah?"

"Mm-hmm."

"What was the um . . . the news?"

"It's a girl," Kit loved saying it, "and she's perfect."

"I meant—" But then he stopped and peered down the neck of the brown bottle. She knew what he meant, and he knew that she knew.

"Well. Congratulations." He tipped the bottle up to his mouth, and just as it reached his lips, he added acerbically, "Tell Ander I said congratulations."

"Please, don't pick a fight with me right now, Mel."

"I'm not picking a fight. I just—"

"Mel, *please*. I'm telling you, I don't have the energy for it."

Kit piled the clean, folded towels back in the basket and handed it to him, but when he took hold of the rim, she kept her hands there, touching his.

"Please," she said.

Mel nodded and took the basket from her, but he stopped at the bottom of the stairs.

"I need to know, Kit," he said without looking back. "Is it him?"

"Would you believe me if I said it's you?"

He shrugged and took the towels upstairs to the linen closet. Kit heard his footsteps creak down the hallway, pausing to look in on Mitzi and Coo before making his way back down.

"I was thinking," he said as he meandered back to the kitchen, "if you want—I mean just so it would be the same as Mitzi and Cooper—you could give her the last name Prizer. If you like."

"I would like that, Mel. Thank you."

He shrugged again, thumbing through a stack of bills from the basket on the hall desk.

"What's the extra charge on the cable?"

"Disney Channel."

"I thought you said no premium channels."

"Some compromises had to be made," she said.

"Is it really worth it on that dinky little black-and-white thing? I mean, I thought they couldn't even watch TV on school days, and they're with me all weekend."

"Mel, it's the only way I can get any work done in the evenings. Ander's going to Sweden for six weeks, and he's subcontracting all his work to me. Plus I'm going to teach his tole painting classes, plus Christmas coming on—I'm swamped. Which is great. I'm not complaining. I'm trying to earn as much as I can before the baby comes."

"I told you," he bristled, "I'm working all the overtime I can get."

"I know. But the answer isn't for you to work enough overtime to support two households. The answer is for you to support your household, and I support mine. Then the kids, we support together. You can't keep working like this, Mel. You need some time to yourself. You need some joy in your life."

"How can you say that to me?" he asked in amazement.

"I care about you. I want you to be happy."

"I was happy. I had joy. Until you yanked it all out from under me."

"You didn't have joy, Mel. You had comfort. You were in a nice comfy place where you didn't have to make any extraordinary effort for me, and you didn't expect me to make any extraordinary effort for you, and it just got easier and easier to let things slide."

"So that's your excuse now."

"I'm not offering any excuses. But I can't live the rest of my life feeling like a terrible person and trying to make it up to everybody. I can't be any kind of mother if I sit around wallowing in the past. All I can do is take what I have left and go forward."

"Well, it's great that you can shrug off our family so easily."

"We're still a family."

"I'm not talking about that politically correct Mr. Rogers bullshit you dish up for Mitzi and Coo. I'm talking about our *family*, Kit—you and me together with our kids in one house."

"I just don't think that's a realistic—"

"I told you, I forgive you. Why can't you believe that?"

"Do you believe it, Mel?"

"Yes! I forgive you! It's forgotten!"

"But I don't want to forget! I don't ever want to forget again. And I don't want you to forget, either. I want you to hold me to my promises, because I need to know that I can hold you to yours."

"What do you want me to do here, Kit? What do you want me to say? I keep trying to shovel through all this crap so we can get on with our lives, but nothing I say seems to make you happy."

"It's not your job to make me happy."

"Then *what*? What the hell do you want from me?"

"*You*, Mel. Just you. Not some half-assed, sloppy version of you. I want the man Carmen fell in love with, the man *I* fell in love with. But that's not the man I was living with those last three years."

"I can't believe you're trying to turn this around so it's my fault."

"I'm not. But we've come too far to go back to the way things were. Especially now, with the added element of this baby between us."

"I told you, I'm ready to accept the baby—"

"*Accept* her? Not love her, like you do Mitzi? It doesn't matter who her father is, Mel. She needs a *daddy*."

"Ah, Christ, I can't argue with you." He pushed his chair back and got up from the table. "I don't know what you want me to say. I'm sorry, Kit, but I can't quote any philosophers for you or spout a bunch of sensitive buzzword marriage counselor crap. I can only—all I can do is just—I *fix* things, Kit. That's who I am. When stuff gets broke, I *fix* it, and then I move on."

"But that's not who I am, Mel. When I make a mistake, I can't just fix it. I have to incorporate it into the design. Or start all over again. And sometimes that makes for a more beautiful—"

"Oh, spare me the allegory."

"I'm just saying—"

"I know what you're saying! And I'm saying, I want my family back. I want my *home*. I don't want to drag my ass to work every night, feeling like crap because I didn't get any sleep, and then drag my ass back to a strange, empty apartment every morning, feeling worse and knowing I still won't get any sleep because I'm . . . I'm just . . . too damn *sad*."

Mel leaned against the counter, and Kit came over to stroke his hand, soft as the waters at Matagorda.

"Don't be sad," she whispered.

She placed his palm on her stomach and let him feel the turbulence inside. Despite everything, he had to smile when he felt the globe, oceans, continents, thunderstorms and all, turning beneath his fingertips.

"C'mon. You can't be sad," Kit laughed like Mitzi on the high side of the swing. "We're gonna have a baby."

"Just what the world needs," Mel gruffed. "Another Kitty Smithers."

He sat down and used his foot to push a chair back for Kit, and then they both sat, taking turns sipping on his root beer.

"The problem is," he said after a while, "I can't picture myself building a life with anybody else."

"Then maybe coming home isn't what you really want, Mel. Maybe you're just scared."

"Maybe." He studied his thumbs and then asked. "What do *you* really want?"

"I want the rest of your root beer."

He pushed it across the table toward her.

"Ah," she relished, "nectar of the gods."

"Seriously, Kit."

"I want . . . ," she pondered. "I guess I want things like they are now, only . . . with sex."

"Okay!" Mel responded instantly, rubbing his hands together for comic effect. "Finally, we agree on something!"

"But right now," Kit laughed, "I'd settle for somebody to rub my swollen ankles."

He brought her feet up onto his lap and pulled off her worn-out huarache sandals, and Kit leaned her head back against the wall as he worked her ankles and insteps for a long while.

"Look at you," he said just as she was beginning to drift off. "Barefoot and pregnant."

"Look at *you* . . ."

She wriggled her foot down between his legs where it warmed and conformed to the natural configuration of him.

They sat that way, wooden clock ticking on the dining room wall, roses growing outside the bay window. A gecko had come out onto the screen, its tail curving like a crescent moon, its pale green belly pulsing with life. Beyond the window box, the swing set creaked in the late evening breeze, waiting, resting itself in preparation for morning.

"I'm not scared," he said quietly. "I want to have a life with you."

"Mel, I don't think—"

"How do I fix this, Kit? Tell me. What do I have to do?"

Kit made a conscious decision to let the tide take her, to feel herself float awhile, and see what was out there. She gathered her courage in a space just behind her heart and let herself go, like stepping off a ledge.

"You have to kiss me," she told him. "Fifteen seconds a day. And you have to let me do the rest myself."

Mel leaned forward, fulfilled his promise for that day, and then started stockpiling for the next several months. He kissed her cheeks and chin and mouth and neck, and she kissed him back without waiting for script or stage directions.

They tried to hold each other sideways on their chairs, but after a while, that wasn't working, so they stood up and tried to come together that way, which was still not ideal, what with the difference in height and both their big stomachs in the way, but they both did what they had to in order to adjust.

Mel lifted her onto the kitchen table, and Kit leaned back, resting her head on the quilted toaster cozy, wrangling her dress up so he could stroke and suckle and taste the colostrum at her breast. He rubbed his rough cheek against her enormous midsection and dragged her plain cotton panties out from under her. When he saw that Dr. Poplin's nurse had shaven her clean in preparation for the delivery, he groaned and kissed her there as if it were her open mouth. He kissed her thighs and fingers and the inside of her knees, kissed her ankles and calves and her wrists and ribs.

He stood and pulled her hips to the edge of the table, cuddling and nudging his way inside her, moaning, "Oh, Kit...," and "I love you, Kit . . . ," and "God, I've missed you so bad . . ."

Kit watched his reflection in the patio door, pants dropped down around his ankles, shirttail not quite covering his pale backside. He was moving his hands in circles over her stomach, rocking back and forth, bumping into her, swaying her swollen breasts up and down on her chest like tub toys bobbing on water. Mel caught her eye in the glass, and the way she squeezed him inside when she laughed made him moan and rock faster.

Kit's fingers found the edge of the table, and she anchored

herself, pulling forward to meet him, disbelieving, desperately grateful, for traveling her changed inner landscape, he'd found the exact place she couldn't quite reach with her middle finger anymore, and every time he drew back with his thick, solid shaft, that rounded ridge part of him worked across the altered underside of her pelvis, drawing her closer and closer to a feeling she'd been fighting to remember.

"*Oh, Kit,*" he moaned, stirruping her feet with his hands. "*Oh, God, Kit! I'm almost there . . .*"

"*Don't lose me, Mel Prizer,*" she threatened. "*Don't you go on and lose me!*"

"*never . . . never . . . never . . . ,*" he rhythmed with the commitment, rocking and promising, promising, rocking.

She reached for the wall above her head. Her wrist tangled in something, and the toaster clanged onto the floor. She felt herself searching, finding, approaching, arriving.

"*Aaaaaaaaaaaaaaahhhnnnnnnnng,*" Kit luxuriated.

Her back surged up. Ivory droplets tickled back from her nipples. She breached like a whale, the ocean of release rolling over her, and then—

"*Oh!*"

She'd felt a distinct internal—

((pobb))

"Jesus Christ, Kit!" Mel stared in horror at the amniotic fluid gushing down the front of his legs. "I think your water broke!"

He choked on the words, not knowing if he should pull out of her or stand there like a pornographic version of the little Dutch boy. When that image came to Kit's mind, her first impulse was to laugh, and Mel nervously joined her, but then he began to notice she couldn't seem to pull any air back into her lungs.

"Kit?" Mel's laughter dwindled. "Kit, what . . . what are you doing . . ."

She tried to answer, but the contraction was on her, surrounding her, sudden and profound.

"*Agh, geez!*" Mel winced in reaction to the clench of her hands on his forearms. "No. No, you can't do this right now, honey. Please, Kit, don't do this! Kit! What should I do?"

"*Don't leave me!*"

"Okay . . . okay, I'm here."

He stretched and groped for the phone on the wall, still holding her pelvis against his own. He tucked the receiver under his chin, punched in 911.

"Oh God . . . oh my God . . . *come on come on come on! Yes!* Yes, it is an emergency! Don't put me on hold! I need—my wife—we need an ambulance. She's having a baby, and she always has 'em fast. Really fast!"

Kit groaned and gripped Mel with another contraction.

"Ah, God . . . oh, geez . . . No, it's her third. Poplin. Dr. Jane Poplin. I'm not sure. I—I don't know. Nine months, I guess. I think it was supposed to be next week, but her water broke and . . . No, I can't see anything, but—but I'm sort of—I'm not in—in position to—to . . . Well, yeah, she is laying down but . . . on the kitchen table and . . . I AM CALM, FOR CHRIST'S SAKE! Just tell me what I'm supposed to— Yeah? Okay. Right. Okay. Kit?"

"*Oh, God!*"

"Kit, honey? Whatever you do, don't push, honey. Just relax. The paramedics will be here in just a few minutes."

"*Oh, God!*"

"Just hang on, honey. You're okay. Everything's gonna be— Kit! Kit, don't do that! Honey, she said not to push! *Kit, stop it!*"

She could have sooner stopped a freight train.

"Ma'am? Ma'am? She's pushing! Yes, I told her! But she's—"

"*Mel* . . ." Kit groaned and slapped her palms flat against the tabletop, "*Don't leave me, Mel. I need you.*"

"I'm here, Kit. I'm right here."

"Oh . . . *ooohhh!* God . . . God, help me. *Ooooh Gaaaaaaaaaaahhhd!*"

"Ma'am, please! For Christ's sake, tell 'em they have to hurry! She's really—Oh . . . oh, shit," Mel's urgent tone turned to cold horror. "I can feel it. I think it's— *Oh, Jesus God! IT'S COMING OUT!*"

That was the last Kit heard.

The overwhelming force closed over her head and constricted around her body like a hungry boa, tensing, tightening, compressing. It swallowed her, squeezed her through a funneling rib cage of panic and pain, transporting her to a plane of agony inconceivable except to a woman in her time of travail. She strained her head back—screaming, expanding, spreading open to an impossible extent. On pure, biological instinct, she inhaled, clenched, and bore down with a power that companioned the overpowering contraction.

Kit ceased spinning on the axis of the earth. Mel, the house, and Houston all orbited out away from her, disappearing down into the blue surface of the distant planet. She transcended, alone, pedestaled on the towering kitchen table, splayed open on the Formica as the female forces of the universe gathered beneath her wings, benevolent, omnipotent, and raging with love.

She inhaled again and again bore down. Searing pain knifed through the astounding pressure, but Kit took hold of the energy that would have been her screaming and deflected it inward, downward, outward.

She surfaced for only a moment, struggling for enough breath to bear down once more. She held her knees to her chest and roared, sounding with orca, nova, Eve, and aboriginal woman. An indescribable rending tore into an even deeper agony, which transmuted to an eternity of unbearable bringing, then a slick, sliding moment of something almost akin to pleasure, followed by a rush of viscosity, and then, at last—by the grace of God our Mother who art in Heaven—relief. Respiration. Resolution.

Euphoria.

She fell back into the areola of the galaxy where nebulae swirled as blue as smoke over sky, past gold lamé clusters and sequin stars, through the silken underbelly of a thunderhead, and home.

Mel was there, whooping and crying, and there were sirens outside.

Kit opened her arms, and her daughter descended into them; slippery and singing and still tethered to her, graceful as the Gulf of Mexico, joyful as the day.

Other Novels from Spinsters Ink

Spinsters Ink was founded in 1978 to produce vital books for diverse women's communities. In 1986, we merged with Aunt Lute Books to become Spinsters/Aunt Lute. In 1990, the Aunt Lute Foundation became an independent nonprofit publishing program. In 1992, Spinsters moved to Minnesota.

Spinsters Ink publishes novels and nonfiction works that deal with significant issues in women's lives from a feminist perspective: books that not only name these crucial issues, but—more important—encourage change and growth. We are committed to publishing works by women writing from the periphery: fat women, Jewish women, lesbians, old women, poor women, rural women, women examining classism, women of color, women with disabilities, women who are writing books that help make the best in our lives more possible.

Spinsters titles are available at your local booksellers or by mail order through Spinsters Ink. A free catalog is available upon request. Please include $2.00 for the first title ordered and 50¢ for every title thereafter. Visa and Mastercard accepted.

Spinsters Ink
32 E. First St., #330
Duluth, MN 55802-2002
USA

218-727-3222 (phone)   (fax) 218-727-3119
(e-mail) spinster@spinsters-ink.com
(website) http://www.spinsters-ink.com

Photo by Allen Milner

Joni Rodgers was born into a family of bluegrass/gospel music performers and grew up on stage, opening for Ernest Tubb, Grampa Jones, Patsy Montana, and other country legends. Her debut novel, *Crazy for Trying,* was a Fall 1996 Barnes & Noble Discover Great New Writers selection and a finalist for the 1996 Discover Award. Ms. Rodgers lives in Houston, Texas.